The Farm

Other books by Louis Bromfield:

Pleasant Valley

Malabar Farm

From My Experience

The Farm

LOUIS BROMFIELD

*with an Introduction by James M. Hughes
and Drawings by Kate Lord*

The Wooster Book Company
Wooster • Ohio
1999

The Wooster Book Company • Wooster Ohio • 44691

Copyright © 1933 Louis Bromfield
Copyright renewed © 1960 Hope Bromfield Stevens
Introduction © 1999 James M. Hughes
Cover Quotation © 1998 WOSU-TV The Ohio State University
Printed in the United States of America.
ISBN 1-888683-33-3

Library of Congress Cataloging-In-Publication Data
Bromfield, Louis, 1896 – 1956.
The farm / Louis Bromfield ; with an introduction by James M. Hughes
    and drawings by Kate Lord.
            p.   cm.
ISBN 1-888683-33-3 (trade pbk : alk. paper)
    I. Title.
PS3503.R66F37 1999   99-35559
813'.52—dc21   CIP

∞ This book is printed on acid-free paper.

The Farm

CONTENTS

INTRODUCTION

A S I RE-READ *THE FARM* IN ORDER TO WRITE THIS INTRODUCTION, one word came into my mind repeatedly—*integrity*. Of course I checked the dictionary, and of course the dictionary I consulted was the *American Heritage*. The third meaning of the word is the one that Bromfield's book illustrates so profoundly: "the quality or condition of being whole or undivided; completeness." *The Farm* is a complete blueprint and grab-bag, a blueprint for Bromfield's later creation of Malabar Farm in Ohio and a grab-bag of family and regional history for America's later benefit. As we approach the twenty-first century, we Americans need Bromfield's, at once conservative and liberal, at once high-minded and earthy, at once Jeffersonian and Thoreauvian, concept of completeness, of personal and societal integrity.

In the 1990s the memoir has become an important literary genre and psychological instrument. Bromfield, in *The Farm*, fictionalizes and socializes that form. Its complex point of view combines, completes, if you will, the multiple perspectives of the fictional Johnny Willingdon and Bromfield-as-Willingdon and Bromfield himself as the authorial observer of the other two. All three divisions of Bromfield himself are so integrated that there is a rich confusion of confession, narrative, and essay. Personal and regional histories merge. Complexities and contradictions of self are not ignored and not even transcended; they are, instead, weighed, respected, accepted, and balanced as parts of the whole, complete, integrated, and unflinchingly honest.

No where is the grab-bag quality of *The Farm* more obvious than in its richness of character. The remembering and creative authorial self peoples his real and fictional world with marvelous persons who have appeared in fuller form in Bromfield's earlier novels and will appear again in his writings after *The Farm*. Here these family members and friends, these townspeople and farmers come together in a context that is as political as it is historical. What kinds of people must a successful democracy produce and need? The answer is, undoubtedly, strong individuals. That among these strong individuals are many wonderfully strong women gives *The Farm* even more relevance to our own time. Such women take life seriously and magnificently; they are above conventional gender distinctions; they may even elevate stereotypes into artistry and power. In a world of the increasingly conventional, they may relish eccentricity. Many share Louis Bromfield's only permissible aristocracy—an elite society of talent, of whatever integrity is most natural.

Bromfield's Ohio is the perfect place to find his special challenge to our own time. Bromfield celebrated Ohio's distinctive lack of and embodiment of all American geographical variations. *The Farm* and Bromfield's œuvre all illustrate Ohio as at once North and South, East and West. Thus Ohio as a place represents an integrity of divisions. It is open enough to allow the self complete expression of its inner contradictions. Though described as fiction, *The Farm* plays down the conflicts it so variously contains. But these conflicts are basic to America and beg the question which the looming new century asks us all. Will Town or Farm values prevail? Has Hamilton's legacy already triumphed over Jefferson's? What will be the fate of eccentricity and individuality in an increasingly conformist world? Will both women and men be able to realize their individual strengths? What will become of the natural world? Will farms and good family husbandry go the way of the American wilderness? Bromfield returned to Ohio to achieve the family legacy of a farm that could restore the natural landscape. But his wanderlust was also a family inheritance, a carryover from pioneer forebearers. Bromfield's integrity can be seen in his balance between the expository writings of his return-to-home experiences at Malabar Farm and his fictional forays into the farthest South of New Orleans, the farthest East of India and New York, the farthest North of New England and the farthest West of the Rockies. *The Farm* is integral to this complete resolution of opposing inheritances and personal tendencies.

In *The Farm*, Bromfield fictionalizes names and places. Ohio's Richland County becomes the book's Midland County. But the middle *is* rich. The city of Mansfield becomes the town of Pentland. Bromfield's kind of man will feel pent up in towns, needing fields in which to commune and work with plenty. Only then may Bromfield's hero realize the heroism of what he, in the 1955 memoir, *From My Experience*, defined: "The *complete* man is a happy man, even in misery and tragedy, because he has always an inner awareness that he has lived a *complete* existence." As we move ahead of or behind Louis Bromfield into the twenty-first century, we dare not forget the rich contradictions that such completeness embraces, the dangerous single-mindedness it challenges so prophetically.

—JAMES M. HUGHES
Emeritus Professor of English
Wright State University

Dear Anne and Hope and Ellen;

                           "The Farm" is written for you,
who were all born long after the war ended, so that you may know a
little what it was like to have lived before 1914. Something came to an
end about that year and I fancy it was the nineteenth century. You
will never know what it was like at firsthand, and you will never
know the country from which your father came, because even if you
ever went to visit it, you would fail to find it. You might discover a
stream or hill which you would recognize from hearsay and legend,
but that is all. The rest has vanished. One thing you would never find,
and that is the feel of the country as it was thirty years before you were
born, and certainly you would never find people like Great-aunt Jane
and Old Jamie and Zenobia van Essen. There is no longer either space
or time for them.. And you will find nothing of the eighteenth centu-
ry. You would never hear Great-aunt Jane say of someone she detest-
ed, "That woman is a Hessian!" nor hear words like "buttery" and
"still-room" and "wench", nor witness a respectable old lady dressed
in black taffeta using the word "bastard" as if she were saying "cat" or
"dog." In your father's childhood, the eighteenth century was just
round the corner. For you, born after 1914, it has become as remote as
the tenth century.
        "The Farm" is the story of a way of living which has largely gone out
of fashion, save in a few half-forgotten corners and in a few families

which have stuck to it with admirable stubbornness in spite of everything. It was and is a good way of life, and although you live to be as old as the Colonel, I doubt that you will find a better way. I counsel you to cherish it as most of the descendants of the Colonel and the stalwart Elvira van Essen have done. It has in it two fundamentals which were once and may be again intensely American characteristics. These are integrity and idealism. Jefferson has been dead more than a hundred years and there is no longer any frontier, but the things which both represented are immortal. They are tough qualities needed in times of crisis.

"The Farm" was written for the three of you and for your children and grandchildren. If anyone else likes it, so much the better.

LOUIS BROMFIELD
Gstaad, Switzerland
December 23, 1932

The Farm

THE COLONEL

JOHNNY'S EARLIEST MEMORY OF THE FARM WAS FILLED WITH SNOW and the sound of sleigh bells. Riding through the soft-falling drift of white, he could see the fat rumps of the horses which drew the sleigh and the steam which rose from their wet coats as they plunged forward to drag it up the steep rise in the lane beyond the bridge over the brook. He sat on his mother's lap, and in his nostrils was the odd musty odor which the worn old buffalo robe gave off when it was wet.

Then the sleigh came to a halt beside a white picket gate beneath the drooping black branches of the Norway spruce, and the flakes ceased to fly past to the accompaniment of a wild gay jangling, and only came down softly like feathers, and the bells gave out only an occasional tinkle when one of the horses shook himself.

A door opened and there was the sound of music, and out of the house came a tiny old lady and three or four enormous people, and Johnny was swept in through a hubbub of greetings and noisy kissing into a room which was warm and had a delicious smell compounded of coffee and sausages, roast turkey and mince pie. It was a big room and the people in it all seemed giants. The music came out of a little machine on the big table. One of the giantesses said, "Rex brought it home for Pa and Ma. It's a Christmas present.

It's playing a song from the Rogers Brothers in Panama." Two of the giants were smoking and shouting at each other across the table about "free silver" and "the Philippines."

And the little old lady said, "Put Johnny in the Colonel's chair till I take off his things." And they put him in a big wooden chair with a slatted back, and the old lady, who was his grandmother, Maria Ferguson, took off his muffler and reefer and leggings and then kissed him. She smelled of lavender, and when she had kissed him she stood back a little and said, "He looks a lot stronger, Esther," and one of the giantesses said, "You'd never know him for the same child. When he was a baby I used to tell Jim that Ellen would never raise him. Of course I never said anything to Ellen about it then."

Johnny felt dazed and stayed there, a little terrified by all the big people, until the grandmother brought him a sugar cookie from the buttery. He was a thin child with a big head, and ears which stuck out. He leaned back in the Colonel's chair, and one of his thin hands grasped the arm. It was of walnut and the wood was worn dark and smooth by the hands of six generations. It had come from Scotland long ago with the Jacobites.

The Colonel came to Midland County in the spring of the year 1815, arriving in sight of the blockhouse just at twilight. He rode a mare called Belle, and with him there rode a guide called Hallie Chambers, who had a thin tough horse and wore buckskin pants, a jacket of bottle green woolen stuff, fastened with brass buttons, and a beaver cap. Hallie Chambers could not read or write and a great many people thought him half-witted, but he had the sense of an animal and could find his way anywhere in the Western Reserve and he knew how to get on with the Shawnees, the Wyandots, and the Delawares. He had a way of telling long stories from which he always drew a moral, and he carried a Bible with him, though he could not read a word of it, and prayed every evening, kneeling down unashamed in the mud or the dust or the snow. For fifteen days they had been on the way north from Marietta and the Colonel was bored with Hallie Chambers. In the beginning Hallie had seemed a strange and interesting character, and the Colonel thought that at last he had discovered Jean

Jacques' "natural man," for had not Hallie been born and brought up in the wilderness, simple and pure and uncorrupted by the civilization which lay east of the mountains? The Colonel had wanted to like him. He had felt a desire to attach Hallie to him so that he might study a simple man who knew nothing of Hamilton or politics or banks and bargaining or New England business men. But after a week, while the Colonel lay on his back, sleepless, under one of the oxcarts, he admitted to himself that Hallie Chambers was all surface and had no more depth than a friendly dog. Being a child of nature had given him nothing but simplicity, and the Colonel saw that simplicity unadorned might have a deadly lack of interest. Hallie Chambers had not even a natural sense of God, for somewhere corruption had been carried over the mountains, perhaps by Hallie's mother, and his God was simply the commonplace, somewhat crude God of the Methodists who kept shops, and bartered horses back in Maryland.

The Colonel's mare, Belle, was a thoroughbred chestnut with a white star on her forehead, and as they halted in sight of the Pentland settlement, until the oxcarts caught up with them, her pretty head drooped a little after the long ride. It was not the Colonel's weight which wearied her, but the long, heavy going. He was a spare man, with a small bony head and a hawklike nose. But for his eyes and the gentleness of his mouth, which drew in at the corners into small, humorous wrinkles, he would have been a man of fierce appearance. His brow was square and his jaw set at a sharp angle. The Colonel was fifty-two, but he had the appearance of a man ten years younger, for he had always lived well and sensibly, neither crucifying the flesh nor plunging it into debauchery and excess. He had eaten good food and drunk fine wines and loved now and then when love had offered itself pleasantly. Behind him lay an easy life, a big house, and broad rich fields, but as he sat on the weary Belle, looking across the marshes toward Pentland he knew there was small chance of his ever seeing Maryland and those fields again. At fifty-two he was beginning life over again, with a young wife left behind in Maryland in her first pregnancy, to join him when the baby was born and a decent house built to shelter her in the wilderness. In spite of the youth in the blue eyes, something inside the Colonel was dead. He was sick of the old life and the politicians and the bankers. He was sick of dishonesty and corruption and intolerance and all the meanness of civilization and of man himself. Because something deep inside him was dead, he had begun to seek peace in a dream. It was the dream of his time, for he belonged to the Eighteenth Century and in it he remained until he died, when the Nineteenth Century was halfway to its end.

While they waited for the carts, he asked Hallie Chambers about the two low mounds which rose out of the flat marshes. They were not large and irregular like the hills through which they had been riding all day, but small and perfectly symmetrical and so beautifully molded beneath their blanket of dogwood and sassafras that they aroused his curiosity.

"Indian mounds," said Hallie. "Some say they're tombs of Indian kings, but the Wyandots and Delawares won't go near them. They won't shoot deer or pigeons when they're on those mounds. The pigeons know it, too." And while he spoke a great flock of wood pigeons rose and circled about them, to settle once more on the mounds.

"I've seen flocks that hid the sun," said Hallie.

But the Colonel wasn't listening to any more of Hallie's fabulous stories of the game in this new country. He was tired and he was listening to the shouts which came distantly toward them, "Heigh, Buck! Ho, Berry!" as his men encouraged the oxen dragging the heavy carts through the mud of the marshes. Before him against the sunset he saw the settlement, a long blockhouse and a stockade surrounded by a cluster of cabins. From the chimneys the smoke curled upward and lost itself in the mist of the spring evening. A golden light fell on the surface of the little sluggish stream which meandered through the marshes.

"What's it called—the brook?" asked the Colonel.

"Toby's Run. It's called for an old Delaware chief who got drunk one night in the blockhouse and fell into the branch on his way home to his camp. He was so drunk he couldn't get up. The water ain't deep, but he drownded."

The oxcarts creaked up through the dusk and the Colonel

pulled up Belle's head and set on his way again. After a hundred yards, the little procession reached the ford over the creek and the oxen moved reluctantly, belly deep, through the muddy stream. On the other side, just beyond a thicket of sassafras, there was a clearing, and in the clearing stood the settlement. Already there were lights in the windows of the cabins. The carts drew up under the shadow of the blockhouse and the Colonel swung down from his mare and tossed the reins to one of his men. He was at the end of his journey. This was the wilderness where he was to live the rest of his life and to die, where one could begin life over again and find a new and decent world. As the night fell, it grew colder and the wind rose, and, listening to it, the Colonel felt weary and a little afraid. He might never see Maryland again and never again would he see London and Scotland, nor talk with the men and women he had known in Paris in his youth when there was no Bonaparte and Voltaire had come home from Ferney to die.

In the little cluster of houses, the first citizens of Pentland had been awaiting the Colonel's party, for he was a man of importance and news of his coming had preceded him. They knew that he was the last man out of Washington the day the British burned the White House, and that he had a ball in his thigh, and that Congress had awarded him a sword and the rank of Colonel and a grant of land in the Western Reserve. And they had heard that before he set out for the West he had given all his slaves their freedom and sent them into the world with new clothes and money in their pockets.

That night when the oxen had been turned loose and the Colonel had eaten and drunk the wine he brought with him in one of the carts, the "citizens" gathered round the big fire in the ground floor of the blockhouse. There were seven of them in all, not counting the lieutenant and the four soldiers who garrisoned the blockhouse. There were the two traders, one like Hallie Chambers, born on the Kentucky frontier, and the other a Canuck, half-Indian, half-French, who came from the Lakes; and there were the two surveyors who were blocking out the county, and a young Swiss, named Weiler, who was big and blond. He had come to make his fortune as a tavern-keeper in the new country and brought his wife with him. As yet there was no need for a real tavern, but Weiler and his wife Marie were young and strong and they thought about the future. They had a piece of land along the creek and the biggest log house in the settlement. In front of it hung a sign with the legend "Weiler's Tavern." There were only two rooms, but it served as a tavern for guides and surveyors and an occasional wanderer. It was in Weiler's Tavern that the Colonel and his men and Hallie Chambers were lodged for the night.

Just inside the door, seated on the earthen floor of the blockhouse, was the Indian woman, called Mary, who lived with the furtraders and followed them wherever they went. She was fat and untidy, with long greasy black hair half-hidden by a cap made of skins. She wore a calico dress and over it a man's torn threadbare jacket. While the men talked in the firelight she kept dozing and waking, starting up suddenly to mumble to herself. She was drunk and now and then when she mumbled too loudly the lieutenant swore at her in crude French and she became silent once more.

The other man in the room was neither a settler nor a surveyor, a trapper or a soldier. He wore the dress of a Jesuit, and the Colonel addressed him as Father Duchesne. He had a lean, hard body and a lean, gentle face, cut with deep lines on each side of the big mouth. His hair was cut short and was grizzled. The Colonel and the priest knew each other. A dozen times they had met in Washington, and once the priest had come to pass ten days with the Colonel at his place on the shores of Chesapeake Bay. It was a miracle now that they should meet here by chance in the wilderness.

"Not altogether a miracle," Father Duchesne had said, "because I heard you were coming here and I've been waiting four days for you to arrive. I was on my way to Sandusky."

"Alone?" the Colonel had asked.

"Alone. It's a journey I've made many times."

"Some day you'll meet a drunken Indian."

"That is in the hands of God."

While they sat by the fire, the men asked the Colonel and Hallie Chambers for news, but they had little which the Jesuit had not already given them. There was only the tragedy of a family near

Chillicothe who had been tomahawked in their lone cabin by some
wandering Indians. One of the soldiers cursed at the news and said
the sooner the Indians were all wiped out the better, because they
were a drunken lot of animals, and the Jesuit said: "There aren't
many left. It won't be long until they're all gone."

And then Weiler said he had seen the Dauphin. And all of them
listened while he told of the young man called Lazare who lived
with the Indians but was white and remembered mobs and torches and the Revolution, and then for a long time they argued about
him and whether the Dauphin had really died in the Temple or
been carried off to Canada. Father Duchesne had seen him twice,
but did not believe he was the Dauphin. "Nobody knows who he
is. The Indians tell one story and then another."

The lieutenant said that all Indians were liars, and Father
Duchesne looked at him but said nothing, perhaps because he
knew that his time was at an end in this part of the wilderness.

Then the Indian woman, Mary, was sick and the Canuck trapper rose and crossed the room and pushed her out of the door, and
Weiler rose, yawning, and said he must go to bed, and the little
party broke up and one by one climbed the ladder into the loft
above or went toward Weiler's Tavern until only the Colonel and
the Jesuit were left sitting before the fire, and in the shadows the
soldier who was on guard.

When all the others had gone save the sleepy soldier the Colonel
and the Jesuit looked at each other and smiled. It was a smile of
understanding which came from the secret parts of their souls. By
the smile they told each other that they had been waiting all the
evening for this moment when, alone, they might relax and reveal
themselves. For the Jesuit the moment was one of luxury and it was
a luxury which the Colonel had come to understand after the long
journey into the wilderness. The smile, so subtle and quiet,
betrayed the two men—that the Jesuit was less a man of God than
an intellectual, and the Colonel less of a Democrat and philosopher than he had believed himself, and much more of an aristo-
crat. In his soul the Colonel was weary of the constraint of those
long weeks spent in journeying through forest and by river, always
in the company of his two men and Hallie Chambers, when he

found himself forced always to speak with simplicity and even to think with childishness that he might not puzzle his companions or disturb their simple beliefs. For more than six long weeks he had not been alive at all, save for those brief interludes when a strange tree or a new kind of rock or the call of an unknown bird roused his curiosity for a moment. He was weary and a little homesick, and the disillusionment he found in that child of nature, Hallie Chambers, troubled him, because it concerned not only Hallie Chambers, but all the future of the Colonel and the dream which had caused him to sell everything he had and go into the West.

But now, sitting opposite the lean Jesuit, life seemed to flow back into his veins. The gray look went out of his face and fire returned to the blue eyes. He lighted his pipe and refilled the glasses of himself and his friend, and then he asked Father Duchesne his plans.

The priest sighed and told him that this was probably the last time they would ever meet. He was going to Mexico. The mission at Sandusky was finished. Times had changed. The wilderness was vanishing. The government was unsympathetic to Jesuit missions, and fanatics accused them of being centers of intrigue and Indian plots.

"That is not true," said the priest, gravely. "The Indians have been friendly to us because we have been friendly."

And there were the settlers. They were fiercely Protestant. They came, nearly all of them, from Massachusetts and Connecticut. They were Puritan and New England. They suspected and hated Jesuits.

At the mention of New England, the Colonel gave a grunt of disapproval. He cherished New Englanders less than Father Duchesne himself. They were tradespeople and shopkeepers, interested only in making money and swindling one another and the rest of the country. Was it not the Essex Junto and the noble New Englanders who, aided by that scoundrel Hamilton, had swindled the old soldiers and speculated on the rewards of the men who had fought to free their country and establish a democratic republic?

At the word "democratic" the priest smiled but said nothing. After a little silence he put down his glass and said, thoughtfully,

"I'm not going to Mexico because new settlers hate me nor because the government is determined to force me out. Those things are nothing to a Jesuit. It is because I am left in a barren spot, like a seed lodged in a rock from which the hurricane has torn all the soil. Who am I to defeat a whole race, a whole civilization? I am a Latin. This new country is lost to us. In a little while there will be no more redskins, no Delawares, no Wyandots—only shopkeepers where God is a tradesman's god. In Mexico, it is different."

The Colonel did not answer him and presently the priest, smiling, asked: "And what of your wilderness? What do you think of it?"

"It is a fine country. It is fresh and new."

The gray eyes of the priest twinkled, "And the children of nature—Hallie Chambers and Mary?"

"Mary?"

"The Indian woman who was squatting by the door."

"She has been corrupted."

"The soldiers and the lieutenant?"

The Colonel gave a scornful snort, "They are merely soldiers. One doesn't count them."

"And the trappers? *Voilà!*—children of nature."

"They seem not a bad sort."

"It is they who corrupted Mary. They carry her about with them. She lives with both of them."

The Colonel did not answer him.

"And the innkeeper, Weiler?"

"He seems an honest, wholesome fellow."

"Shrewd and thrifty. He will succeed in your Utopia."

The Colonel put down his pipe. "It is easy to mock."

"No, my friend, your 'children of nature' are too much like the noble savages in the plays of Voltaire who never saw a redskin and could not himself live without an excellent cook and a house filled with civilized people."

Again the Colonel was silent, and the Jesuit said, "There is the Kingdom of God and the kingdom of man. The kingdoms of men are alike, whether they be republics or tyrannies."

Without thinking of it they had fallen into speaking French.

The sleepy soldier could understand them now even less than he had understood them before when they talked of nature and civilization and God. It was a tongue which the Colonel spoke easily, for in his youth there had always been a French Jesuit in the big house on the shores of the Chesapeake. The first MacDougal in the Colonies was a Jacobite, and the Colonel was brought up as a Roman Catholic, but since his childhood he had wandered a long way. At twenty he had been a Deist, and now, if he believed in God at all, it was in the vague romantic God of Jean Jacques.

While they talked there grew up about the two of them a strange atmosphere of elegance, as if, instead of sitting in the log blockhouse with only good earth beneath them for a floor, their chairs rested upon a floor of nutwood and the crude mugs which held their wine were of delicate crystal. Presently in his corner the guard began to snore, for he, like the priest, knew that there were really no dangers against which a sentinel was needed. Since the Battle of Fallen Timbers the menace of Indians was over and their power gone.

The candles burned out and at last there was only the firelight, but the two men stayed, sometimes talking, sometimes silent. When one of them made a speech which failed to take fire, kindling the mind of the other, there were no dull phrases uttered, without meaning, for both men were of mature years and long ago they had learned to scorn the talk which begins and ends in nothing. But even in their silence there was a kind of melancholy communication as if the two minds were aware of a common sadness. The Jesuit knew what it was that troubled him, but of the two he was the happier because beneath the shining surface of his intellect he really believed in a God who could serve as a refuge from his disillusionment. The mind of the Colonel, less clear and realistic than that of the Frenchman, neither accepted his disillusionment nor found a refuge in God.

At last the fire, too, began to die away and shyly, as if he did it as a suggestion, the Colonel rose and threw more logs into the cavernous fireplace and as he turned away he stopped abruptly, listening.

"A man calling. Did you hear him?"

The priest listened, "No, but my ears are no longer good."

Again the call was repeated, and this time Father Duchesne heard the distant "Halloo" and, rising, went to the door, where he took down the lantern meant for the sleeping sentinel. Opening the door, he stepped outside and held the lantern high above his head. The Colonel followed him and stood at his side, peering across the clearing.

It was a chill night with a bright clear moon, and underfoot the mud was frozen now, so that when the Colonel stepped out of the door the crust broke beneath his square-toed riding-boots. They waited, listening, but for a long time the cry was not repeated and they heard only the hooting of an owl somewhere in the forest nearby. Then quite suddenly, near at hand, the "Halloo" rose again and out of the forest into the moonlit clearing they saw the figure of a tall, lean man approaching. He was leading a mule so heavily laden that there was no place left for the man to ride. He saw the lantern and came toward them. When he reached the light they saw that he was dressed in homespun, with a leather jacket and a top hat. Over his shoulders he wore a shabby bearskin. Coming out of the wall of forest into the wilderness clearing, he was a moonlit scarecrow. Even the Jesuit seemed less strange. As the priest held the lantern high, the two friends saw that the newcomer was a youngish man. His face was long, with a long nose and a lantern jaw and a hard mouth.

He said, "Good evening, gentlemen. I take it this is Pentland blockhouse. My name is Silas Bentham. I'm from Massachusetts. From Worcester, to be exact."

The man held out his hand and the Colonel took it, but the faintest shadow of a frown crossed his face as if he had said again, "shopkeepers and tradesmen, intended only to swindle one another." It was as if he had encountered a ghost in paradise.

The stranger asked for shelter for his mule, and the Colonel showed him the shed where his mare and the four oxen were stabled, going with the man while he swung the pack down from the back of the tired animal.

"I'd 'a' been lost but for the bright moon," he said. "I calculated to reach here before dark." He had a dry voice, not unpleasant, but curiously flat and empty of feeling.

"I suppose you know the trail," said the Colonel.

"Never been in these parts before," said the man.

"It's dangerous without a guide."

The man grunted as he swung down the second pack. "Guides cost money. A man setting up a business can't spend good money on a guide. Anyway, I been lost a couple of times, but I just turned in an' slept against the mule. He's right well trained for that."

Something in the tough indifference of the man roused a flicker of amusement in the Colonel. There was something comical about the lean, weatherbeaten fellow in his shopkeeper's clothes which made mock of the big stories of frontiermen like Hallie Chambers. The man was not boasting. He made the statement flatly, like a man who was the prey of a fixed idea so strong that hardships and perils were a matter of indifference.

The Jesuit never spoke at all, but stood silently in his rusty black, like a grave bird, yet in his silence and concentration there was a curious air of hostility and contempt.

When the mule had been bedded down with oak leaves, the three of them turned and in silence crossed the frozen, trampled mud and entered the blockhouse. The fire was blazing now, and in his corner the sentinel still snored. The stranger put down the pack he had brought with him and turned to fetch the second.

"It's safe in the shed," said the priest, but the man opened the door and went out, and when he returned he said: "You never can tell. Things disappear sometimes like as if there was magic about it."

He shivered and went over to the fire, standing with his lank figure silhouetted against the flames.

"Have you supped?" asked the Colonel.

"Yes. I always calculate to be independent."

The Colonel picked up the jug of wine. "A drink will warm you."

"No. Thanks just the same."

"It's good wine. ... Maybe some brandy." The Colonel spoke graciously, as if the blockhouse were his own dwelling and he were entertaining a chance guest.

But the man refused: "No, thanks. I'm a teetotaler. A man can spend a pretty penny on drink once he gets started. I never got started yet. But if there's some good spring water."

The manner of the Colonel chilled a little. He pointed to the iron pail with the handle of a gourd visible in it. The man called Bentham refreshed himself, and then, as if the water had been something stronger, he began to talk and the small blue eyes set a little too close together in the long face lighted up.

He told them that he had come into the West because it was a new country where a man had a chance to begin life over again and make a fortune. Times were hard back East. A fellow couldn't make a living as a peddler in New England. Farmers and village people hadn't any money. People in this new country hadn't any money, either, but it was different here. People *had* to buy things, because they needed them—thread, and buttons and pewterware and calico, and the market was growing all the time instead of getting smaller. By the time the country was pretty well settled he'd have enough to set up a good business. Did they know how much could be made on twelve dozen bone buttons in a country where buttons were a necessity?

He went on talking like one hypnotized by visions of profits, but the Colonel and the priest scarcely heard him. Now and then the Colonel pulled himself up with a start and feigned a semblance of interest, as if he still had the illusion that this was his house and this man his guest, but he really heard nothing the man said. Father Duchesne made no pretense of interest, but simply stared into the fire, never troubling to look at the man.

"I calculate that if things go right I ought to be a rich man by the time I'm fifty. It's a wonderful new country."

The Jesuit rose slowly and said, "I'll be moving soon," and at the sound of his voice the stranger said, "French, ain't you?"

"Yes."

"Catholic?"

"Yes."

"I reckoned so. It's hard luck for you, losing a fine country like this."

The Jesuit did not answer him, and as the Colonel rose the peddler stepped forward quickly, moving in front of them, "Wait a minute, gentlemen. I've some things to show you. Silver buttons for your waistcoat. Fine silk for your neckerchief. Handkerchiefs ... fine things such as befits gentlemen like you."

With miraculous speed he had one of the packs open and was ready to spread his wares.

"Don't trouble," said the Colonel. "There's nothing I need."

The priest passed him on his way to the door, and Bentham, looking up from his pack, said: "You'll regret it, gentlemen, if you miss this chance. See this fine bit of silk—just the thing for a gentleman like you."

The Colonel turned, "If you're going to the tavern we'll show you the way."

"You'll regret it, gentlemen." Then suddenly his instinct told him that there was no business to be done, and he stood up once more, his great length unfolding joint by joint like a carpenter's rule. "I don't count on sleeping in a tavern. I've got my jacket and packs. I'll make up a bed right here. Many a time I've slept that way without a roof over my head. Thank you, gentlemen." He moved toward the door, "Good night to you."

"Good night," said the Colonel.

The door closed behind them and in silence they set out over the frozen mud to the log house with the crude little sign, "Weiler's Tavern." In the brilliant moonlight they walked in silence to the door. The magic of the evening was gone now and suddenly they were both tired.

The Colonel pushed open the door of the tavern and stepped into the common room, where his two men, the surveyor, the trappers, and Hallie Chambers were snoring. There was no light, but the dying fire cast a glow over the room. When the priest had closed the heavy door, they stood looking at each other in silence and presently the Colonel said, "You'll be off early, no doubt."

"Soon after sunup. I want to ride to Frémont by sundown."

"I'll ride with you a part of the way." He began unbuttoning the tobacco-colored jacket, and presently he said, "I wish I was a young man again."

"All of us wish that."

"I'd go with you to Mexico."

‹∂

At dawn they rose and ate the smoking breakfast which Weiler's wife cooked for them. The priest saddled his old horse, and one of the Colonel's men brought up Belle, freshened by rest and corn and water, and the two set out through the opening in the clearing where the trail led to the north.

It was a brilliant spring morning, with the nip of the frost still in the air, and as they rode the vague sense of depression flowed away from the Colonel. It was beautiful, mellow country, all low hills and pleasant wooded valleys, and the little swollen streams flowed between banks where the pussywillows were in flower and the tropical green of the skunk cabbages pushed through the brown of last year's leaves. They did not talk much, but the Colonel saw that his companion was sad and he fancied he knew the reason.

" 'Tis true it's a fine brave country," he said. "But I've read that the Mexican country is all red and gold and purple." And when the Jesuit did not answer he said, again, "I wish that I was young again, that I might go with you." But now in the brilliance of the fine morning the words were insincere and he was troubled lest his friend should sense their falseness. And in his heart he knew that for all its newness, this was the kind of country to which he belonged—a country, gentle, smiling, well-watered and fertile, out of which man might make a new paradise if he were good and wise enough. In that other country, for all its purple and golden deserts, he would be forever lost and uneasy.

Thrushes ran across the trampled path and twice they started rabbits from beneath the very hoofs of the horses. The squirrels chattered in the sunlight and once a deer crossed the trail, and then presently they came to the top of a low hill, and then the Colonel drew up his mare and the Jesuit reined in his old horse so that the two animals stood close together. The Colonel held out his hand and the priest took it, and then suddenly, as if the thought had come to them at the same instant, the two men put their arms about each other and embraced in the French fashion.

"*Bon voyage*," said the Colonel, "*Écris moi de temps en temps.*"

"*Bonne chance*," said Father Duchesne, and for a moment a shadow of irony crossed his lean face. "Good luck with your new paradise."

Then without looking back the two men parted, aware that they would never meet again. They knew too that this parting was far more than a farewell between two friends. Each of them had said farewell to a life which in their hearts they loved.

On the way back to the settlement, the Colonel gave the mare her head, and when they arrived Belle was wet and flecked with foam.

The Colonel's piece of land stood on the very watershed, whence the waters flowed on one side into the Ohio and on the other into Lake Erie. It was gently rolling land like that through which he had been riding, half the morning, with the priest, and save for a narrow strip of damp ground which bordered the tiny brook it was covered with great oaks and maples and hickory trees. When the surveyor had shown him roughly where its boundaries lay, he turned the mare loose and set out on foot to examine all the land given him by the Act of Congress. He followed the little brook through the forest, hoping that its source lay in his land so that he might build his house near a spring, and as he followed the stream it struck him as odd that there should be such a brook on land which lay on a watershed; but after a mile he came to its source and the mystery was explained. The source was not simply a spring. From among the rocks a whole brook gushed, full-born, one of the miracles of this new country where brooks and even small rivers disappeared suddenly in the earth, to journey for miles underground through cold caverns of limestone, and emerge at last with equal suddenness at some point miles away.

The source, alas! was not on his land, and as he trudged back through the forest he fixed the site of his house in his mind. It would be the top of the low hill which sloped down to the brook and dominated all the other land. It was always a fine thing to plant a house on a hill, for it gave a man a sense of power and freedom and repose, and in the easy largeness of his nature there was nothing which disturbed the Colonel so much as feeling cramped for space. And as he walked he began to plan his house—not that first log hut which must shelter him and his men until the forest was cut down and a road built, but the house as it would be when the wilderness was conquered and he was living once more as a gentleman should live. It was a big white rambling house set under trees with a garden filled with blooming plants, rare and beautiful, which he would have sent to him from the East and from Europe; and presently he saw that the house was born more of homesickness than of ideas which were original, for it was, for all the world, like the big house which stood on the shore of Chesapeake Bay in the Maryland Free State.

It was growing dark and the chill of frost was again in the air when he saw the gleam of fire through the trees and came upon his two men. One of them, Jed Wilkes, was cooking bacon over the fire, and the other, Henry Sloane, was busy constructing a shelter against the side of one of the oxcarts. They were both youngish men, the one stalwart, short, and rosy, and the other dark, lean, and sallow. For Jed, the stocky one, he had an affection born of long association, since Jed was born in his house and had never lived elsewhere. The other he had picked up in Hagerstown, where he worked as bailiff with the family of the Colonel's cousin. He had wanted to leave Hagerstown, where there were small opportunities for a man, to come into the new country.

That night they slept beneath the wagons, and in the morning, on the top of the low hill, they began cutting down the trees. With the aid of his silver compass the Colonel traced in the thick rotting leaves the outline of a cabin which was to be built east and west, so that one side of it should always catch the morning sun.

Day after day it grew warmer, and all about the cabin the woods broke into a glory of wild flowers—hepaticas and spring beauties, violets purple and yellow, the white stars of trilliums, bloodroot; and last of all, beneath the forest trees came the white of the dogwood, like the beauty of thick white clouds caught and entangled in the lower branches of the great oaks and beeches. Surely a land so full of beauty was a blessed land.

When it was finished the cabin had a single room, longer and

higher than any of the cabins in the settlement, with a big fireplace
built of mud and stones at one side opposite the door. At one end,
in crude bunks, slept Jed and Henry, and in the other, behind a
curtain of calico, the big cherrywood bed which the oxen had
dragged all the way from Maryland was set up. The floor was of
earth and had an odd, incongruous look so near to the chairs and
the decanters of wine and the walnut table covered with books and
the big chest of drawers filled with the linen and stockings and
small clothes of the Colonel.

By day they worked hard, the Colonel swinging his ax as stur-
dily as Jed or Henry. They cut down trees and cleared away the
brush, and with the oxen they dragged out the stumps and heaped
them in great piles to burn when the fierce sun of August had dried
the sap in them. It was Jed who did the cooking, and they ate beans
and bacon and the game they shot, and now and then they got
cornmeal from Weiler, from which Jed made hoecake and corn-
pone in the hot ashes of the fireplace.

And in the evening, when the two men had gone to bed, the
Colonel, sitting elegantly in peignoir and slippers in the ladder-
backed walnut chair behind the calico curtains, read and wrote in
his diary and contrived affectionate, rather pompous letters, written in the pure style of his century, to his wife Susan back in
Maryland, awaiting her baby.

"*My beloved wife,*" he would write, "*owing to the inclemency of
the weather we have this day made little progress toward the contriv-
ing of a proper dwelling place.*"

Or, "*My dear Susan; I would be grateful if you could send me by
the next carrier two new linen shirts and some plain black hose.*"

Always he signed the letters, "*Your affectionate husband.*" In his
dignity and honesty, he did not pretend any overwhelming or
romantic passion for the young woman whom he had married late
in life when passion had long since burned out of him. She was his
Susan, pretty, virtuous, a little stupid and sometimes vain and frivolous and too fond of a ribbon or a bit of sprigged satin. In his attitude there was something dignified and decorous and almost
fatherly.

"*My honored wife*"; he wrote again, "*I am somewhat uneasy regarding your happiness in this new country, owing to the hardships of the life and the scarcity of womenfolk. It is true that there are already several females well established in this county, but they are hardly, for all their other good qualities, females either of high station or of breeding, and their virtues are less those of fine ladies, than those of good solid housewives. I fear you will be forced a great deal into the company of your adoring husband, and for that reason I hope that you are persevering in the perusal of those books with which I presented you before parting. It is a handsome country and full of natural phenomena and material for the study of botany. You will be able to add many new pages to your collection of pressed specimens. I fear that too many newcomers in this region are men who have fared badly in the East and are seeking the descent of a miraculous fortune."*

When he had finished his letters to his wife, he would open the big book and in its brown-paper pages write down in an orderly way an account of what he spent that day, the temperature at six in the morning and at midday, and note whatever he had observed that was new or interesting about the plants or the animals on the place. Then he would note the progress made in the clearing of the forest and finish with a few philosophical observations regarding the new settlers he had encountered and the behavior of Jed and Henry.

"Spent yesterday and the day before journeying to Frémont, where I bought two good heifers (bred) for which I paid seventeen dollars each, and three sows and a boar (sows seven dollars each. Boar nine dollars.) By this time twelvemonth we shall be well established."

But Jed and Henry interested him most, for they served him as specimens in a philosophical laboratory. While he worked side by side with them, he was always watching them, trying to discover what changes this new country and this new life were working upon their souls. In the brown-paper diary he wrote his observations, noting that they had grown less secretive and more frank, and that the sense of class appeared to be fading from their consciousness and that as they came to feel less strongly the difference in manners and education between themselves and their employer, they became more useful and less dependent upon him for orders. But he was forced to notice that they grew dull and irritable through lack of amusement, and that Henry, who had had a talent for intrigue in the servants' hall, grew restive for lack of material to work upon, since his only material was Jed, who was phlegmatic and solid. And he noted, too, that Henry and Jed sometimes grew quick-tempered, and Henry told him that it was because he had need of a woman.

Long afterward, Johnny, reading the old brown-paper diary, found the entry *"Have spoken to Henry sharply this day about making sheep's eyes at Mistress Weiler, who is a good woman in love with her Switzer husband and not to be debauched by one of my men."*

When he had finished his writing the Colonel read for a time, and then after a pipe and a glass of port put out his candle and went to bed.

⊷

In late May they planted corn in the red-black soil about the cabin, and by September ten acres were cleared of trees and underbrush and a road built from the cabin to the rough trail which the settlement called grandiosely "the Onara Turnpike." On each side of the long lane the Colonel planted a row of locust trees, which when grown would form a dignified avenue, fragrant in May with flowers, which would serve to feed the bees. And then they built two more rooms to the cabin, one for a kitchen, with a loft over it for Henry and Jed, and the other a sleeping-chamber for himself and Susan and the baby.

In November the carrier brought a letter telling him that Susan had had a stillborn girl and that Susan herself was ill, and Doctor Brandon said she ought not start for Ohio with the winter coming on.

All of that summer and far into the winter new settlers came into the county, families, young married couples, young men, and even two young women to work as hired girls, one at Weiler's Tavern, and presently the population of the county was reported at the blockhouse as two hundred and eighty-seven souls. In March Jed set out with the two brown oxen, Buck and Berry, for Maryland to fetch Susan and a hired girl and the rest of the furniture and the Colonel's library and two more blood mares and a stallion to join

Belle in the log stables set on the opposite side of the quadrangle laid out crudely before the house by the Colonel.

In April the Colonel wrote, "*Henry has seduced the girl at Weiler's Tavern, who is a buxom wench, and he visits her each Saturday night. His temper is much softened. Women are as necessary in a wilderness as fire and shelter. 'Twill be good to have Susan again. With luck she should arrive before Whitsuntide.*"

Susan arrived before Whitsuntide with the mares and stallion, books and wines.

She was twenty-four and plump and pretty, with small soft hands and small feet of which she was vain, and when she saw that her *salon* still had an earthen floor because there was still no sawn timber to be had in the county, the tears came into her eyes; but if she was a frivolous woman, she was also a good-natured one, and by evening, when the spinet was set up (near the fire where the damp could not harm it) she sat down and played and sang very prettily, "Let us fly to the West, to the eagle's nest," and the sight of her made the Colonel feel more than ever a man of half his years. All through the evening she sparkled and bubbled, talking about her trip over the rough trail and down the river. In her youth and frivolity and good humor, she had been unaware of the hardships and looked upon the journey as a lark and an adventure. Jed, she thought, would end by marrying Maria Savage, the hired girl who came with her, and then they'd have no servants at all but Henry, because if a man married in this new country he'd want to set out on his own. She poured out news of their old countryside and described the family which had joined up with them at Cambridge on the way north and were settling in the same county—a man and wife and twelve children, the youngest only six months old. They, too, came from Maryland and they had been six weeks on the way.

It was long after nine o'clock when the Colonel put an end to her chatter and led her off to the bedroom.

In August the Colonel wrote in his diary: "*Rose last night to have me some cold water from the pail in the kitchen, and discovered Jed in Maria Savage's bed. Counseled them to marry. Henry has got the Tavern wench with child. Sure this is a fertile county. Alas, no signs in Susan.*"

And day by day and week by week and month by month the entries in the brown-paper diary grew longer and more complicated. The three sows multiplied, the heifers had calves. Belle had a fine colt. The Tavern wench had a miscarriage and so Henry escaped marrying her. Jed and Maria Savage married. Neighbors settled in the section to the north and the west. The settlement became incorporated as a village. Every few months a letter came from Father Duchesne. They were letters filled with descriptions of the Indians and the Spanish families, of the rocks and deserts and fantastic unearthly flora of that country to which the Jesuit had gone. And the Colonel wrote news of the war and the peace, of the way the wilderness was ceasing to be a wilderness, of how he had built two wings of sawn timber painted white to join the cabin, of politics and philosophy, of botany and biology, but he never wrote of his dream. And one day he noted with disgust in his diary that the peddler, Silas Bentham, had appeared in the village to open a shop.

The years passed, ten of them, one by one, and still Susan gave no sign, and then in the eleventh year she presented him with a son. The Colonel was sixty-three years old when he was born, but he had not yet finished, for in the next eight years Susan bore him four more children, and to his disgust they were all girls, named Susan, Esther, Maria and Jane. The Colonel was seventy when the last of them was born. It was Susan, immensely fat and short of breath and still vain, who had grown too old to go on producing.

THE PATRIARCH AND MATRIARCH

THE LITTLE CARAVAN WHICH SUSAN ENCOUNTERED ON HER WAY came from Anderstown in the Free State of Maryland, and at the head of it walked a man named Jorge van Essen. In the two wagons which followed rode his wife and those of his twelve children who were too small to walk. Now and then along the way the smaller children were allowed to climb down and run behind the wagons as they moved along the trail. They played and frisked along the way, gathering the blossoms of bloodroot and spring beauties, poking about among the rotting leaves and uncovering snails and beetles and now and then a sluggish garter snake.

The twins, Sapphira and Marianna, who were eight years old, ran along by the trail until they grew tired and were lifted back into the wagon with their mother. Sapphira was a small, thin, wiry child with brilliant black eyes and a mop of black hair. She carried a little cloth bag in which she collected, like a magpie, treasures she found along the way. In it were the feathers of the hawk and the blue jay, the crow and the cardinal, three or four quartz pebbles, the tail of a chipmunk, some of last year's acorns and the shell of a tiny mud turtle. Marianna was very unlike her and looked like their father. She was plump and pretty, with blue eyes and redgold hair. She had an affectionate nature which knew sudden wild outbursts of love and anger. She was the favorite of her father among all his twelve children, perhaps because there was something in her nature which he understood as coming down to her from himself.

He was a man of middle height, vigorous, muscular, and broad of shoulder, and handsome save for the weakness of a mouth which was too pretty, and the dark-blue eyes which had about them the shifty, tormented look of a man to whom the peace which comes of self-respect is unknown. For Jorge van Essen had no great reverence for himself, not because he had ever been guilty of any act that was either criminal or malicious, but because he was forever wavering between extreme virtue and the wildness of a libertine endowed with enormous vigor and a relentless animal energy. He was a converted Methodist with a terror of hell, but what he loved

best in life was women, horses, and gambling. Just turned forty, he knew that the struggle for saintliness was more difficult upon the borders of middle age than it had been at twenty-five. He was a man born to unhappiness, with no peace in his nature. Besides the twelve children who traveled with him there were three bastards left behind in Maryland. For these, during various recurrent attacks of conscience and remorse, he had made provision, taking the bread from the mouths of his twelve legitimate children and his wife Elvira, who he knew was as stalwart and virtuous and dependable as he was wild and vacillating. In Jorge van Essen, one saw the spectacle of a man made the battleground between nature and revealed religion. Nature had created him fertile, vigorous, intelligent, concupiscent, to beget indiscriminately after nature's own ruthless plan, but man had invented Methodism to hold him in restraint, and thereby rose the problem of his tormented existence. It was a battle in which nature, as usual, always won.

He was the great-grandson of a German of Netherlandish extraction who came to Pennsylvania after the Palatinate had been reduced to a wilderness by the Thirty Years' War. The first van Essen, likewise Jorge by name, had prospered, and in turn his sons had prospered, and in the third generation there were twelve male descendants, good thriving citizens in Maryland and Delaware and Pennsylvania. Of these, the man who walked at the head of the caravan was the son of one called Peter, who died at Valley Forge, leaving his widow and a son prosperous and well-off with three hundred acres of good Maryland earth, a big house, a fine library, a tavern, slaves, and some fine horses. But all these things were gone now. The tavern, the horses, and the library, due to Elvira, had been the last to go. They were a part of the price for the struggle which went on in Jorge van Essen's tormented nature. They were gone and there was nothing left for Jorge to do but to begin his life all over again in the wilderness where one would be close to God and the temptations of horses and gaming and fighting-cocks and even of women were remote.

In the little iron box containing the papers left from the wreckage of the estate there was a handbill announcing the final sale. It read:

Public Sale

The subscriber intending to remove to the Western Country, will
   expose to Public Sale, on Thursday, the 12th day of March next:
That well-known Tavern Stand—Sign of the Cross Keys, in the Town
   of Anderstown, Baltimore County, Maryland, with about five acres
   of land. The place being *so well-known*, a further description is
   thought unnecessary. Possession may be had on the first day of
   April next.
At the same time and place there will also be sold: *A valuable running
   mare, a quantity of valuable books*, and a variety of household and
   kitchen furniture and farming utensils, *too tedious to mention*.
The sale to commence at 10 o'clock on said day & continue until all is
   sold.
Terms will be made known on day of sale & due attendance given by
   Jorge van Essen.
N.B. All persons indebted to the said Jorge van Essen are hereby
   requested to make immediate payment; and those having any
   claims, will please present their accounts on the day of sale.

Jorge van Essen
Baltimore County
(Hanover, Printed by Starch & Lange)

Alas, neither Jorge's creditors nor the purchasers at the sale had been "forward in paying their just debts." Thus Jorge had written to his hard and prosperous Uncle William—and Jorge's pockets were nearly empty as he trudged along with his eldest son, a big lad of eighteen, at the head of the little procession. But times were hard in the east and few men could pay any debt in full.

Mistress van Essen herself drove the second wagon, perched high on the crude seat with the six-months-old Annette in her arms. Luckily the horses were old and steady so that when Annette set up a wail her mother could drive with one hand while she held the child to suck with the other. She was a big, handsome woman upon whom had fallen the doubtful lot of being Jorge van Essen's wife, but in moments of depression she wrote to her cousin Mary back in Virginia that *"I have no one to blame but myself, for God knows nobody forced me into marrying him. Everyone in the family was against it."* She was a cousin of John Randolph of Roanoke, and in her there was some of that great man's poise and judgment, for in all things save Jorge she was a realist, and even in the case of Jorge there were moments when she saw him in the same clear, cold light which the great Anti-Federalist might have shed upon the handsome rake. Like John Randolph, she was a great letter writer.

"When I reflect upon all the circumstances together," she wrote to her cousin Mary, *"I cannot bemoan those into which God and my own headstrong will have delivered me. For Jorge, with all his faults—and God knows they are many—is a fine strapping man who seems not a day older than on that Saturday when we were married in Richmond against the wishes of everyone. I know that many say I married beneath me but it is better to have a man of vigor, even if his family did own a tavern and made money in the wool trade than a weakling and a fop of high station. All my twelve children are healthy and strong or God knows I would never have dared to set out upon this perilous journey. Sometimes Jorge is a great trial to me but I have never seen another for whom I would change him as a bed fellow. I think his wildness and extravagances and his taste for wenching cause me hardly as much annoyance as his remorse after. You may thank God that your own Eben is a straight home-loving creature not*

because wrongdoing in itself is so terrible as because the remorse afterward is so boresome. Sometimes I think Jorge's worst fault is in being a Methodist. His wenches never have to endure his remorse when he thinks his soul will boil in Hell, but after a bout of wrongdoing I have to treat him like he was the smallest of children. But for all that, I still love him after seventeen years of matrimony and twelve offspring.

"The new country is very handsome and according to reports is rich and fertile. I have not yet suffered from homesickness and do not expect to as it seems there will be little time for such nostalgias. Two days back we met up with the lady of Colonel MacDougal, of whom you have no doubt heard tell on acc't his gallantry in the defense of the capital. She is a young creature, amiable and agreeable, who lost her first child in September last year by the cord getting round its neck and strangling it before it was born. She is a vain thing and not much suited for life in this heathen country. The Colonel, it seems, is a generation older than her. Jorge thinks her a beauty but to my mind she is changeable, sometimes pretty and sometimes plain as Punch. Jorge is getting to the age when he looks at young ones.

"Write me news. I calculate to need excitement.

"Y'r loving cousin,

"Elvira"

At the settlement the two caravans separated, the Colonel's and Jorge van Essen's, the one going to the Colonel's "estate" and the other south to the land along the edge of Toby's Run, four miles beyond the point where it left the marshes and ran, tinged with tawny yellow for most of the year, between low flat stretches of black soil. It was rich land, better than the Colonel's, but less pretty in the way it lay. It was Jorge's uncle William who had chosen it when he saw the new country as a means of getting his rakish nephew and all his children out of the way, and he had chosen well, so that Jorge could have no excuse about the land being poor.

Here, with the help of his two half-grown sons, Jorge built a cabin and cleared away the reeds and underbrush. Elvira had no more children and Jorge began a life of saintly chastity. Elvira wrote to her cousin Mary that although "*it was hard to believe, the wilderness had like to have changed Jorge's whole character."* For more than two years, she wrote, he had not had any attacks of remorse. *"He has either reformed or he is no longer a good Methodist, and however it is, the life has been more agreeable. There is as yet no church nor any parson here although there is talk of a circuit preacher, which I hope is not true as I do not want to see Jorge stirred up again. It seems like wenching and religion go together with him—that wenching brings on religion and religion brings on wenching. As there is not much of the one or the other things go along in peace.*

"There is talk of Jorge's cousin Henry coming into these parts to start a sawing mill and tannery business with Jorge. There is great need of both things and it may be that your cousin Elvira will end her old age in affluence and plenty."

Only once did she write again of the Colonel, when she said, *"We have not seen much of the Colonel or his wife. Jorge and the Colonel do not get on. Jorge thinks him old-fogey and thinks a man ought not to put on airs in this new country as the Colonel does with fine horses and servants. And Mrs. MacDougal continues vain and giddy and wanting in common sense."*

It was Elvira who taught her younger children to read and write, to sew and cook. It was Elvira who taught them religion— not the emotional faith of their father, but the more decorous teachings of the Episcopal Church. Of them all only Marianna, the twin of the shock-headed Sapphira (with her magpie's bag of sticks and stones), found the faith of her mother too cold for her nature. Cousin Henry came from Maryland with money, and with Jorge built a mill and a tannery which prospered. When at last the Methodist church was built in the village, wenching and religion overtook Jorge once more, but Elvira no longer listened to his remorse. After Cousin Henry died by a fall from the mill loft she had enough to do with running the mill and tannery business and caring for the grandchildren who came into the world at an astonishing rate. One by one the children married, and the sons begot and the daughters bore until at seventy she had one hundred and three grandchildren, and she knew that Jorge had all those, too, and no doubt many more—how many he did not himself know. Of her own brood, Marianna, the Methodist, who took after her

father, married a New Englander named Willingdon. who came
into the new country as a schoolmaster and abandoned the profession to enter the more profitable mill and tannery business. He
was a cold Congregationalist with no hell-fire nonsense. "*Just the
proper sort,*" wrote Elvira to her cousin Mary, whom she had not
seen in twelve years, "*to deal with the carryings-on of people like
Marianna and her Pa. He will keep her in order.*"

One of her sons, Jacob, who was seventeen when he came over
the mountains, married the child of a marriage between a trapper
and the daughter of a Wyandot chief.

THE CONGREGATIONALIST AND THE METHODIST

IN THE DAGUERREOTYPE WHICH JOHNNY SAW FOR THE FIRST TIME when he was twelve years old, the two faces looked out at him, yellow and ancient and bitter. It was taken on their golden wedding anniversary when he, Thomas Willingdon, was eighty-nine and she, Marianna Willingdon, was seventy-two. When Johnny thought of it, it seemed to him that they were really much older than eighty-nine and seventy-two, for they had the look of a pair of immensely aged eagles, so old that only God knew how many years had passed since they came into the world. The two faces were ugly, yet behind the ugliness you were aware that once there had been comeliness, if not beauty. The mouths of both had a collapsed sunken look; the sharp noses were those of carnivorous birds and the chins were sharp tilted and pointed. Surely these yellowed faces were those of a witch and a warlock. In their old age the Congregationalist and the Methodist had come to look alike, as if in the end their one obsession had slowly remolded their faces, so different in the beginning, into the sharp, hard, bitter lines.

In the beginning, when Marianna was still unmarried, she looked like her father, Jorge van Essen. She had the same vigorous, handsome features, the lips a little too red and too ripe, the skin a trifle too high-colored. Passionate women looking upon her father in his youth, in his prime, and even in his old age, had felt a sudden quickening of the senses. The color came into their cheeks; their blood ran more swiftly. Without consciousness of it, they tossed their heads a little and their eyes grew brighter. It was as if the very sight of him, even when he was unconscious of their presence, aroused intimations of breathless delights and promises of inexhaustible vigor. For strong men his daughter Marianna gave off the same disturbing and delightful sense of excitement. When Thomas Willingdon first appeared to help her father with the mill and tannery business, her face was not old and shrunken and bitter. When one looked at her one felt that she was not meant for stuffy bodices and thick, cluttering skirts. She should have gone naked for the delight of everyone who saw her. Her father, too, had been like that in his youth. Only her mother, the wise Elvira, ever saw into the depths of her nature. To the others, her brothers and sisters, her father, the rakish Jorge, who was not a clever man, and the neighbors, Marianna was merely an hysterical, unbalanced woman who fainted and had visions. When she was eighteen, the Prophet, Elias Dunker, came to the village to preach his immoral and pernicious doctrines. He was a big muscular man with black hair and black beard and red lips, and when he left the village to preach at the next place, Marianna ran away from home to follow him. Only Elvira guessed whither she had gone, and Elvira it was who saddled a horse and rode after the Prophet to fetch her daughter home, and for a month never allowed her out of her sight.

At the end of that month Thomas Willingdon came to live in the house at van Essen's Mills, and Marianna fell in love with his cameo profile. The Prophet was forgotten.

The newcomer was as little like the leader of the Dunkerites as it was possible to be. They were both tall men, but the Prophet had immense muscular shoulders and Thomas Willingdon was long, lean, and wiry. The New Englander's head was finely chiseled, with a high narrow nose and thin but beautiful lips. He was blond and had side whiskers and wore his hair long, falling just below the lobes of his fine ears. There was about him something fine and nervous and overbred, yet he was not a weakling. He had force, but one felt a sense of coldness and decision, as if with him passion did not exist and desire was a matter of calculation. No one had ever seen him either gay or angry. He always carried with him an air of ominous calm.

Like the Colonel, he belonged to a tradition. The Colonel, philosophically, was a Democrat, and Thomas Willingdon never pretended to be one, but in their hearts both men cherished a sense of being more intelligent, more cultivated, more discerning, and more sensitive than the other citizens of the county. Yet they were never friends and never exchanged more than a civil word or two when they met. The one was the offspring of New England shipping merchants, the other of Maryland landed people.

Thomas Willingdon might have come straight from England, for in his family the tradition had been kept pure. In the beginning his people had not been Puritans and small shopkeepers like so many of the settlers in New England. His great-grandfather was a soldier who came from Shropshire to Boston with Governor Andros; but by temperament he had been a poor soldier, caring nothing for the life or its gawdy honors, and when Governor Andros returned to England he stayed behind in the Colonies to found a family. He was an eccentric man, shrewd on the one hand and temperamental on the other. He was a musician and had built from his own designs the first pipe organ in America. When he died he left two sons and a widow who lived in a country house near Boston, where they went to the Church of England and occupied the Squire's pew just beneath the pulpit. The sons were painted by Copley and carried on the tradition of Shropshire County life, which was broken for the first time in the third generation when two Willingdons (perhaps with their blood corrupted by two generations of Colonial marriages) became Congregationalists. Of one of these Thomas Willingdon was the third son. His parents had meant him to be a preacher, but he was never ordained, and when he was nearly thirty he went to the Western Reserve to try his fortune as a schoolmaster.

But Thomas Willingdon was an ambitious man, and he saw that being a schoolteacher in that new country was a dreary business without great prospects, and when he was thirty-three he married Marianna, the daughter of Jorge van Essen, who owned the only sawmill and tannery in the county. For his wife he felt as much love as his cold nature ever allowed him to feel for any woman. She excited the desire of his imagination, for he was a man whose passions were always of the mind rather than of the body. His soul was as cold as his own chiseled beauty.

There was no honeymoon, for travel was still difficult and there was no place to go nearer than Philadelphia, and in those days one needed more than two weeks to make such a journey. It was easier than when the Colonel and Jorge van Essen came over the mountains, but it was not yet simple and Thomas Willingdon had no desire to leave the business for six weeks to a father-in-law who had begun again to philander and have fits of remorse. Whether Jorge van Essen went wenching or was remorseful, he abandoned himself so completely to the debauch that for the whole period of the undertaking he allowed his business to fall into ruin. Once the stout-hearted Elvira managed it, but Elvira was growing old and a little tired, and now she had not only her own twelve children, but a half-dozen daughters and sons-in-law and dozens of grandchildren whose lives she felt it her duty to oversee and arrange. They were scattering, her children, one by one over the whole state, and she began to "visit," making a kind of stately circuit which took the better part of six months. Always she went on horseback accompanied by a hired girl, for she refused to "be a burden" upon anyone.

From the first it was Elvira who saw that it was her daughter Marianna and her husband who would need the most managing. From the beginning the marriage went badly. Thomas, the cold and calculating, could not endure his young wife's gusts of passion and hysterics. No matter how much he loved her or simulated to love her, it was not enough. She was a woman capable of devouring ten men, and Thomas really cared nothing whatever about women save as they suited his convenience and his appetite. He "loved" as he ate a beefsteak or drank a glass of whisky, and when Marianna satiated him with love he vomited sarcasm, bitterness, and contempt. But he never grew angry, which was all the worse for Marianna, who in her deepest nature had need of scenes and violence. Rich blood flowed in her veins.

And then it went from bad to worse. They had three children, a boy and two girls. The son was called Thomas after his father, and the two girls received the names of Clementine and Georgina, in accordance with the romantic nature of their mother. Times were changing and fashionable names changed with the times. Thomas and Marianna quarreled and had reconciliations when Thomas felt the need of them, and at such times Marianna suffocated him with love. But there was never any question of divorce or separation. God had joined them together and no man could put them asunder. And for Marianna there was no such thing as infidelity. If ever she considered it, she stifled the temptation, for she had in her a strength, perhaps come down from Elvira, which her father did not have, and she looked upon adultery as the deadliest of sins. And in that welter of hatred and passion they slept side by side for fifty-seven years.

Old Elvira, who saw things with the directness and honesty of the eighteenth century, understood that her daughter Marianna would have been happy married to a man like her own father or the Prophet Elias Dunker, and that Thomas Willingdon should have married not her daughter Marianna, but Marianna's sister Sapphira, the black-eyed girl who had collected quartz pebbles and blue jay feathers in a cloth bag on the long trip from Maryland. Sapphira was married, too, to a young farmer who lived two counties away. Already she had three children, and she had eleven more before her family was complete. But Sapphira cared more for affairs than for love. She bore her children in a practical fashion with as little fuss as possible, and managed the big farm herself so that her husband might give all his time to buying and selling land and houses and cattle. Most of the time he was away from home, a circumstance which seemed to trouble Sapphira not at all. He returned often enough to give them fourteen children, and when he was not there she educated the children, managed the farm, and acquired more and more land, played the spinet and sang and smoked cigars. She was a tiny, sprightly woman who never weighed more than ninety-eight pounds.

As young Thomas began to grow up, a little of the love in Marianna's overflowing nature turned toward him and she began to take possession of him and devour him. The girls, Clementine and Georgina, did not matter, and if old Elvira had not taken a hand in their upbringing they would have grown to womanhood rude and untutored. Marianna cared only for the son who looked like his father but had, too, a rich share of his mother's nature. He was a moody, unhappy, hysterical boy who was as soft wax in the hands of his mother. She it was who taught him to hate his father. She it was who determined that there were to be no women in his life, and she it was who saw him as a great preacher, powerful and magnetic like the Prophet, but with the impossible chastity of a saint. He was hers to do with as she liked.

As they grew older, the hatred between Thomas Willingdon and his wife grew more cold and bitter and profound, and when Thomas climbed into bed beside his wife each night, he arranged the bedclothes so that their bodies should not touch. The hatred became a dreadful thing, consuming them both, so that in a way he came to live for it, spending hours in devising ways to torment her, and she, through his son, found her revenge, until toward the end the hatred nourished them both and kept them alive, since each sought to spite the other by living the longer.

"Whom God has joined, let no man seek to put asunder."

When they had been married for fifty years they were photographed together. Thomas Willingdon seated, with his wife, Marianna, standing with one hand on his shoulder. In the end, the two faces, so unlike in the beginning, were the faces of a brother and sister bred and born of hatred and contempt.

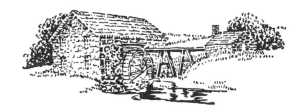

THE FORTY NINER

I N THE SPRING OF THE YEAR 1850 A BIG BOY OF TWENTY WENT DOWN
the lane of a pleasant Pennsylvania farm. He led a mule and carried over his shoulders a pack containing everything he possessed
in the world. He was a big fellow, four inches over six feet, with fair
skin and red hair and dark-blue eyes, and as he trudged along his
throat contracted with sobs and the tears poured down his face. He
was a manly fellow and did not weep easily, but what had happened to him was no simple thing. He had been forced to strike his
own father, not once but many times, until the older man, bloody
and beaten, gave way in defeat before a son who he found was no
longer a little boy.

The father was a Scot named Ferguson who came into the
country in 1798 as a boy straight from the Highlands, bringing with
him his bagpipes and kilts. He was a giant and a Red Scot and a
Presbyterian, and he spoke Gaelic as well as a strongly burred
English, and beneath the surface of the handsome physique lay
hidden a Gael who had never been tamed or civilized. He had two
sons and a daughter, all younger than Jamie who set out into the
world with his mule and eighteen dollars he had saved on the sly.
Ferguson believed in God and the Bible and the divine right of
parents. Neither his wife nor his children had any pleasures save
those which he chose to allow them, doling them out meanly at

great intervals, for to Ferguson earthly pleasures were to be feared as the devil himself. He loved work and a good fire-and-brimstone sermon and he had a strange wild love for hymns and the music of his own pipes. Sometimes in the long summer evenings his neighbors would hear the shrill half-savage sound of the pipes far into the night. He loved his children as the jealous God Jehovah and believed that hardness was chastening and mortification good for the soul.

And thus he had treated them, refusing to believe that they were growing into men and women with lives of their own, and so he had sought to chasten his son Jamie when Jamie ran off secretly one Saturday night to the town of Chester. But when he sought to chastise the boy, something in Jamie, some hidden sense of dignity, rebelled, and he called out wildly to his father not to lay his hands upon him. But the fierce old Ferguson had never yielded to any man, and the sight of his own son defying him was too much to be borne. The boy resisted as gently as he could, but in Ferguson there was no gentleness and the chastisement turned into a fight in which fists brought blood and which did not finish until the older man could fight no longer. When he lay in a corner of the mow, beaten and bloody and whipped, his son, sobbing, ran into the farmhouse, took his clothes and money, kissed his mother good-by and set off down the lane. He never saw either his mother or his father again.

While he walked along the muddy roads he pondered where he should go, and at last he decided that he could no longer live in a country where he might see his father, and so set out to ride his mule to Philadelphia.

He did not like the city, but he liked it as well as he would have liked any other, for it was in his nature to distrust and even to hate cities, and until the end of his life they always made him uneasy and restless and filled him with an odd sense of contamination. It was a time when every port was filled with men seeking passage for California to find some of Sutter's gold, and in the taverns, on the wharves, and in the streets Jamie met them and talked with them, and at last he sold his mule for twenty dollars, and with that as capital sailed on a ship called the *Amasa B. Weeks* for Panama.

It was a long journey of more than three weeks, on which he worked at odd jobs in order to make up for his lack of passage money. He was a bad sailor and the *Amasa B. Weeks* passed through storm after storm. When he reached Panama his great muscular frame had lost eighteen pounds and the journey was only begun. The worst of it lay ahead.

But he was young and had a confidence, come down, perhaps, from his tough, hard father, which never left him until he died at last, an old man of eighty-seven. With a party of twenty-three men he set out over the jungle trail which led from Colon to Panama. They became lost and had to cut their way for miles with the long knives they had bought in Colon, and when they arrived in Panama City they were only nineteen, for four had died on the way of yellow fever. And in Panama City the yellow fever was everywhere and there were no boats by which they might escape. The town was crowded with soft, white-skinned men who kept dying, sometimes as many as twenty in a day. Death held the city and there was no escape, but somehow Jamie Ferguson, despite the liking of mosquitoes for fair-skinned, red-haired people, managed to survive. He tended the sick and buried the dead until at the end there remained of his party, besides himself, only a German and a man from Virginia named Crosby. When at last a boat appeared in the harbor there was no rush for it, because in all the city there remained only a handful of men seeking passage for San Francisco. Jamie had no money, so at night he swam to the ship and hid himself in the hold.

It was a small, dirty sailing-ship owned by a Mexican with a Mexican crew. Its ropes were rotten and it leaked so badly that half of the time the pumps were used. But when they left the harbor the yellow fever did not follow them. Not one man on the ship sickened and at last the terror was gone. Knowing nothing of mosquitoes, the passengers regarded the change as a miracle.

For two weeks they sloughed through the waves of the Pacific. It was June and the sun scorched the decks, and for a part of each day the water had to be pumped from the hold. And then off Los Angeles a storm came up and for three days the ship was knocked about by great waves. Water filled the hold and the captain and his

Mexican crew abandoned themselves to the care of the Holy
Virgin, and to the Holy Virgin they would have gone save for Jamie
Ferguson and the man named Crosby from Virginia, who left the
Mexicans to wailing and prayer and manned the pumps and took
command of the ship. All one night and part of a day they pumped
desperately, and at last they found themselves in waters more quiet
between the island of Santa Cruz and the mainland where the
dying mission of Santa Barbara rose white against the line of
brown mountains. There the ship quietly sank and Jamie Ferguson
and the man called Crosby and forty-eight others swam to the
white beach. When Jamie walked into the mission he had only the
dripping clothes on his back and not a penny in his pockets, but he
was at last in California.

From Santa Barbara Jamie walked to San Francisco, and there
he found work as a carpenter. In that new city there were never
enough carpenters. There were houses to be built and dance halls
and saloons and brothels and gambling establishments, for newcomers arrived each day by land and by sea. Ships come to anchor
in the beautiful bay found themselves suddenly without crews. At
the moment Jamie arrived nearly five hundred lay anchored thus,
empty and deserted, in sight of the new city built of clapboards
and cheap brick. It was a city made of Russians and Negroes,
Italians and Chinese, Americans and Scotch, Scandinavians and
Indians, French and Germans. They slept in tents and in the open
fields and on the floors of saloons and gambling halls. Carpenters
were paid enormous wages, sometimes in the gold dust brought
straight from California rivers and mountains. Jamie made money,
which he put away with Scottish thrift in a belt about his waist.
And when the building began to overtake the populace and wages
began to fall, the carpenters set fire to the city and the building had
to begin all over again. Twice the whole town was burned and had
to be rebuilt. It was a raw and lawless country in which gold alone
was ruler.

But Jamie made no fortune in that new country. He went, like
all the others, to dig for gold in the mountains and pan for it in the
flooding streams, but his heart was not in it. If his heart was moved
by anything it was by the wide fertile fields and the great herds of

cattle guarded by the Mexican *vaqueros*. And the sight of so much greed and so much lawlessness distressed his Scottish Presbyterian soul. At twenty he was already a good citizen. At twenty he was already filled with a passion for order and cleanliness, for justice and a decent prosperity, and for making others see the light as he saw it, even though one had to take them by the scruff of the neck and beat them into it. When others dug for gold Jamie, with two guns strapped about his muscular middle, enforced the laws of Vigilance Committees, suppressed brawls in brothels and gambling houses, and helped to devise laws which made it possible for men to live together in wild valleys in the high Sierras. There was in him a blunt, philosophical strain, far more practical and far less gentlemanly than the old-fashioned aristocratic beliefs of the Colonel. The sight of men quarreling over gold disgusted him. It was not in gold that one found satisfaction, but in building. At twenty he already knew whither he was bound and his goal never changed until he died. Older men were impressed by his gravity and perhaps by the great red-gold beard which helped to conceal his boyishness.

At the end of two years nostalgia overtook him and a disgust for a life so restless and disordered. He wanted land of his own and a house and a wife and a family. So at last he sold what belongings he had, purchased a pony, and set out for the east once more. The California country was not to his taste. He did not have the feel of it. It was too vast and wild. Perhaps, also, it was too grandly beautiful, for in his blood he had no feeling for pastures of a thousand acres nor orchards and vineyards which extended as far as the eye could see. He wanted well-ordered fields with brooks which ran clear and cool unmuddied by torrents in spring. He wanted gardens and a fine dairy and a half-dozen good horses. His dream was of a farm which could survive, cut off from all the rest of the earth, which was in itself a small world complete and above all else independent.

So one fine morning in June he set out from Sacramento to find the country of which he dreamed. He had his pony and one hundred and forty dollars in his pocket. He was young and powerful, with a colossal strength and vitality, and he was free—free as few men had ever been before and as fewer men will ever be again. Before him lay a vast country, rich with minerals and fertile prairies, crossed by great rivers, filled with virgin forests. It was his for the taking. Whenever he chose to stop he might claim for himself an expanse of land bigger than many a kingdom. For days he rode, and for weeks and for months, across Nevada and Utah, where the Mormons had settled by the Great Salt Lake, across a corner of Nevada over the endless fertile flatness of Nebraska, over the rich prairies of Iowa and Indiana, always east. It was a calm and beautiful journey. He had no troubles with Indians. He saw bison cover the prairies in thousands, and flocks of wood pigeons which darkened the sky. Sometimes he met wagon trains bound for the Far West with men and women who wondered at him for returning from the Promised Land. He rode for three thousand miles, and he was not tempted until he reached a corner of Iowa where the low wooded hills and the streams pleased him. There he lingered for three days, riding this way and that over Indian trails and the beds of streams, but in the end he found that this was not quite what he sought, and he went on his way again across the flatness of southern Indiana and Illinois, and presently one evening in late October he came at dusk to a town which lay in the midst of a smiling fertile country where already the forest had been cleared away and the corn stood in shocks in the fields where once the oaks and maples had grown so close that in summer the sun never reached the earth. He had still a few dollars left, and one of them he spent for supper and bed in a hotel called the Weiler House. It was a building of brick which stood near the hay scales in a little square filled with trees, and the proprietor was a big plump man past middle age who spoke with a Swiss accent. The supper was excellent and the bed soft and big enough for him to stretch his full six feet four.

In the morning when he wakened he knew that he had come home. This was the land for which he had been searching and here he would stay.

Looking out of the window of his bedchamber, he saw a small square, for all the world like the squares of a New England town. In the center there was a little park filled with trees left standing from the virgin forest, beeches and oak and maples all growing together amiably and pruned into the decent order which the soul of Jamie demanded. On the street which surrounded the square were shops and houses built of a great variety of materials, but possessing a unity in the thrift and neatness of their appearance. At one end stood the courthouse, a building of brick with a dignified portico of white columns, and at the other the Methodist church, also of brick, flat, even, and simple, more like a New England meeting house than an edifice dedicated to the worship of a highly emotional sect. Between the two there were houses built in of clapboard in the New England manner with bow windows on the second story, where housewives could sit while darning and witness the traffic in the square; and there were houses of brick, flat, retiring, and discreet, with shallow steps of white scoured stone in the manner of Jamie's own Pennsylvania country; and there were even two log houses, one of them partly covered by clapboards, which were left from the days when the Town was only the Village. Of the settlement where the Colonel and the Jesuit walked in the frosty moonlight, nothing remained but the trees. But of that other newcomer, Silas Bentham, the peddler, there was rich evidence. On the opposite side of the square from the Weiler House the ground floors of three adjoining houses had been made over into a single shop. The whole front had been painted red, and in gold letters one read *Bentham's Great Bazaar. Household Goods, Hardware and Miscellany.* For Jamie, looking out of the window of the Weiler House, it was the only discordant note. Something about it looked wrong.

It was only seven o'clock, but in the little square people were already stirring, and as he stood watching, the sight of them gave him comfort because they were so different from the wild people he had been accustomed to seeing in Sacramento and San Francisco. They seemed rosy and plump and prosperous. A farmer drove his load of hay onto the weighing scales before the courthouse and Jamie saw that the hay was of a good green color and the horses were sleek and shining.

When he had eaten a big breakfast in the taproom of the Weiler House, with the fat Mrs. Weiler standing by his side to see that he approved, he set out to explore the little town.

It was compact and neat, spreading itself over the low hills and shallow valleys. It was only forty years old, yet it had a settled look. That the New Englanders had given it with their solid, modest houses set back from the street in gardens planted with lilacs and syringas and candleberry bushes. The elms and maples planted on the borders of the principal streets already arched them over. Their leaves, yellow and red and purple, strewed the gutters and the wooden sidewalks. The people he encountered looked solid, contented, prosperous, and neat, as citizens of a solid community should look. On Elm Street he discovered a church, handsome and new, and large out of all proportion to the rest of the buildings in the Town. It stood back from the street in a kind of park surrounded by lawn and trees, with two wide flights of stone steps leading down to the level of the street. It was built of red brick, with Gothic windows and a spire which was the highest Jamie had ever seen. It belonged to the New Englanders, the Congregationalists. It was a church built for the future, for no matter how large the Town became, there would never be need of a larger church. It was as if the New Englanders said, "This is the Western Reserve which belonged to New Englanders and will forever belong to them." Jamie walked round it twice in admiration and awe.

When at last he returned to Main Street, which led down the gentle hill toward the marshes, he discovered another building as fantastic as the church. It stood on one of the low hills which rose from the swamps made by Toby's Run where it appeared to grow undecided as to its course and took to wandering here and there among reeds and willows. It was a huge house of an architecture the like of which Jamie had never encountered in all his wanderings. It was built of red brick and had Gothic windows and doors pointed at the top, with small colored panes of glass set in about the edges. It had a great piazza along one side, with a balustrade of iron cast in a design of grapes and leaves (for Jamie, overcome by curiosity, boldly crossed the artificial causeway which had been built across the marsh to connect the property with the highroad leading to the north and took to examining the place at a close range). There were workmen about, some planting trees and some engaged in whitewashing cast iron copies of ancient Greek statues which had been set up here and there in the park surrounding the house. At the door there was already a mounting block, and a hitching ring held in the outstretched hand of an Eros made of cast iron and whitewashed.

As Jamie wandered farther he came upon the stables and quarters for the servants attached to the house by a wooden trellis painted white. Wandering inside, he saw the five boxes built to stable horses which must have been of royal blood, and when he had finished he returned again to gape at the splendid house with its Strawberry Hill Gothic windows and gables.

When he approached one of the workmen and asked who owned the house, he learned that it was a man called Dr. Trefusis, about whom he could learn nothing whatever. He was a newcomer. No one knew whence he came or who he was. The house, said the workmen, was already called by some "Trefusis' Folly" and by others "Trefusis' Castle," but no one knew why the builder had chosen so bizarre a site for so splendid a house.

And Jamie himself never discovered why until years afterward when Dr. Trefusis became his brother-in-law and his great friend, and he found that the big strange house was no more curious than the character of the doctor himself.

When he returned to the hotel Jamie asked where he might find work. He was no longer a boy; he felt himself already middle-aged and experienced, and he had always known his own mind. He knew it now, and set himself at once to thrusting down roots in this country which he had chosen for his own.

Weiler, the innkeeper, said that old Colonel MacDougal was looking for men. He was, he said, the first gentleman in the county and he never had enough men to run his place, not because he was a hard master, but because the men were forever getting married and going on land for themselves or leaving for the West where there was more room. He could not, said the Swiss Weiler, find a better place than that of the old Colonel. He had known him since the day he came into the county. The Colonel had spent his

first night in the new county in Weiler's own tavern. And then he winked and added that the Colonel still had left two marriageable daughters. They were, he implied, choosy and had already turned down many offers.

So Jamie thanked him and, taking his pony and his pack, set out for the MacDougal place, three miles to the west of the town. He rode through one little valley and then through another, and as he came on to higher ground he caught sight of a white rambling house and a big gray barn set among trees on the top of a low hill half a mile from the highroad, and when he came to the lane he turned in riding all the way to the house in admiration of the fine avenue of trees, of the corn which stood in shock, and of the fine cattle which raised their heads to stare at him as he passed. This was the sort of farm of which he had dreamed, but as he rode over the brook and the steep part of the lane to the white house, he dared not to hope that one day this land and house and brook would be his forever.

The Colonel, he discovered, was a spry, lean old man of eighty-six, dressed in old-fashioned, snuff-colored clothes with silver buttons, and he wore his thin gray hair long and neatly dressed, with a bow at the back of his head like one or two old men Jamie remembered having seen on the streets of Chester when he was a boy. His eyes twinkled when he talked to Jamie, and before ten minutes had passed they had made their bargain, and Jamie, wondering, put up his pony in the vast gray barn and came in to sit down at noon dinner with the Colonel and his family.

The family consisted of two unmarried daughters, Maria and Jane, and one of the married daughters, Esther, Mrs. Widcome by name, who was on a visit. The Colonel's wife, Susan—the plump, vain, good-natured Susan—was not there, for she had been dead these ten years, having fallen down the stairs and died in a fit brought on by her vast obesity. Mrs. Widcome was a plump young woman of twenty-five or six, with a humorous mocking manner. Jane was the youngest, and just eighteen, having been born when her father was seventy years old. She resembled the Colonel, having the same fine small head and splendid Roman nose. It was her nose which gave her a dominating expression and spoiled her looks. Jamie looked upon them all, perhaps with the advice of the tavern-keeper in his mind, and his choice fell upon the third sister, Maria. She was as small as he was large, as delicately made as he was herculean, as feminine as he was virile. By the middle of dinner he saw that Mrs. Widcome was not the sort of woman to please him, even if she had been unmarried, for she mocked and made a joke of everything and even bated the dignified old gentleman at the head of the table on his old-fashioned manners and clothes. She was too smartly dressed and clearly she was vain and extravagant. Indeed she was a little like her mother, Susan, save that she had wits and a brain where poor Susan had had neither the one nor the other. And the younger sister, Jane, was clearly not for him. He could not stomach arrogance in a female, and one had only to glance at Jane to see her pride and independence. But Maria had a sweetness and a gentleness about her, and as she looked at him shyly and with so much earnestness in her blue eyes, he began to fall in love with her. Here was a woman who found life as tremendous and serious a thing as he himself found it. There was no mockery in her, nor any pride. He knew that he would have fallen in love with her no matter where he saw her, whether she had been the Colonel's daughter or the chambermaid in Weiler's Tavern. She was, he thought, like a violet, and having in him a rich strain of religion he began to wonder at the Providence which had brought him through the perils of yellow fever and shipwreck, of hunger and thirst and fire, to find her at last sitting opposite him.

And as he ate he was overcome with shyness, not only at the mocking gaze of Mrs. Widcome, but also by the fineness of the silver and the linen that bedecked the big table. In his father's house there had been no money wasted on what the elder Ferguson called "fripperies," and in his wanderings he had eaten with whatever implements he found at hand, sometimes with his fingers. The young giant sitting there at the fine table felt twice his great size. All his fingers were thumbs. When he spoke he blushed and mumbled his words and Mrs. Widcome chuckled and continued to make mock of him.

There was nothing remarkable in the fact that the Colonel asked the young man he had just engaged as a hired man to sit at the same table with him and his daughters. There was also present a big plain girl called Sally Blaine, who carried in the food and then sat at the table with the others to consume it. It was the custom of the county, and the young men who came to work for the Colonel were no fly-by-night laborers, wastrels, here today and gone tomorrow. Most of them had come into the new country to make their fortunes. Most of them would settle there and help to populate it and mold its history. Certainly there were wasters among the newcomers, and knaves and vagabonds, but the old Colonel had lived long and shrewdly and considered himself a judge of men, and it was seldom that he made a mistake. It was a custom to the liking of the Colonel. It was part of his philosophy that work was honorable and that a good worker should know equality with his master. It was part of his dream of this new country that it should be like this—simple and direct, in which good citizens, no matter what their station under any other scheme of things, should respect one another and live in a state of absolute democracy. There had been for him disappointments enough in the new country. There were cases enough of greed and dishonesty and inhumanity, infections which somehow had been transported by the emigrants into his paradisical wilderness, but on his own domain he could at least create and practice the ideals of a genuine pastoral democracy. There were those in the county who mocked him, but mockery did not much annoy the Colonel. He had been the friend of men like Thomas Jefferson and John Randolph of Roanoke. Behind him lay the solid charm and civilization of the eighteenth century, and before him forever hovered the dream of a new world carved out of the wilderness which should be Utopia. Between the two he sat secure, armored as well by a gentle contempt for those who stooped to greed and trickery and mischief. Wealth helped to preserve his illusions, for there still remained enough of the fortune brought from Maryland to permit him, when his dream was threatened by reality, to reinforce and prop up the corners of the creaking edifice.

In his heart he must have been aware that already the false security of a century which was gone lay gravely threatened. He must have known that the day would surely come when it was no longer

possible to live thus lavishly as a gentleman landowner in a tradition which was becoming rapidly as remote as the shepherds in
"The Faerie Queene." He did suspect, for again and again in the
brown-paper diary which he still kept in the good eighteenth-century manner, he recorded his doubts, as well as his anxiety for
someone to carry on when he was dead the pastoral, faintly idyllic
world which he had created out of the forest.

At first he had believed in his only son, but as the son Jacob
grew through adolescence into boyhood, the old man saw that
surely his hope was barren. Jacob would never be the one to carry
on the Farm. He had no love for the land, nor any feeling for it. He
was airy and erratic and loved a good prank better than his supper.
Ruefully the Colonel saw that, although the giddy Susan had been
fine breeding stock in the way of vigor and health, she had trans-
mitted her levity and vanity as well as her vitality and high spirits.
Jacob had all the tastes of a dandy. It was a pity, for his wits were
good enough even though they went off like fireworks in fantastic
dreams and enthusiasms and a passion for devising all manner of
useless mechanical contrivances—rocking chairs which rocked
themselves when you sat in them, and churns for the dairy which
operated by a windmill fan set in the roof. And he had fantastic
dreams about discovering the secret of perpetual motion. "*No*," the
Colonel recorded, wearily, "*Jacob is flighty and irresponsible and gay
and in many ways more like another daughter than a son, and God
knows I have had enough daughters.*" And then when Jacob married
an heiress, the daughter of the banker Hastings, the old man knew
that he was lost, and in the worst way, for Jacob went to work airi-
ly in the bank and joined the forces of "that confounded upstart,
Hamilton."

And then one day he noted in his diary the one consolation of
his sad state. It was a line written him from New Mexico by his old
friend the Jesuit—a saying which he found in that new country, so
different from the Middle Western Utopia of the Colonel's. "The
Spanish," wrote Father Duchesne, "have a saying, 'The children of
great lovers are always girls.'" and after noting it down, the Colonel,
clearly pleased by the consoling adage, sought to prove its truth by
the experiments he himself had conducted with his own pigs and

rabbits. "*A great lover*," he wrote clearly with satisfaction at eighty-three, "*must by the nature of things be sensual, and a man who is sensual must have a taste for good food and good drink as well as pretty women. In my experiments I have observed in every case that the offspring of overfed males and females are in a high proportion females, and in the converse sense, the offspring of undernourished mates has a likelihood to be of the male sex. N.B. Herein perhaps lies the truth of the superstition that in time of war only male children are born.*"

Whatever he observed, whatever legend was told him, whatever old wives' tale was repeated in his presence, had to be turned over and over in his mind in the light of reason. In the beginning of that new century, when religion and sentimentality were in fashion, when Huxley and Darwin were still little boys with prominent foreheads, the Colonel had clung to the eighteenth-century habit of mind as he clung to his old-fashioned snuff-colored clothes with silver buttons. And now when he was old, a new light had risen on the horizon. He had been a child of Voltaire and Rousseau but he lived long enough to witness the first faint stirrings of the twentieth century. In his diary he wrote, "*I have received this day from London 'The Voyage of the Beagle' and the 'Journal of a Naturalist' by Charles Robert Darwin.*" The books went to join the library which he kept in the "dark room" with his collection of flint arrowheads
and dried botanical specimens and glacial fossils and polished stones which existed in such abundance on his farm.

⤙⤚

It may have been that as the Colonel sat, that fine October day, looking across his well-laden table at the young man opposite, he regarded him with his sharp blue eyes in the light of science and reason, mingled a little with a dubious sense of Providence. Here was the kind of young man he had been hoping for—big, virile, healthy, with honesty and naiveté in his glowing blue eyes. Here was a young man who could carry on what he had created. He would breed strapping grandchildren like himself who could take over the Farm when he had gone the way the Colonel himself must go before long. And miraculously he was a Scotchman.

Jamie Ferguson stayed on. He never again left the Farm save for three restless years, and in the end he returned to it to die.

In June of the next year he married the modest, quiet young woman who sat opposite him between the proud sister and the mocking one.

The daguerreotypes taken the day before their wedding, Johnny saw long afterward. They were individual portraits, touching to look upon and a little awesome. In them Jamie Ferguson sits bolt upright in all his enormous vigor, his big hands placed awkwardly on his bony knees as if the fine clothes in which he found himself on that occasion were unnatural and suffocating. He fills the whole oval inside the tiny tinselly frame as if he longed to burst from it and breathe freely. His heavy coat strains across the muscles of his great chest, revealing a waistcoat sprigged with comically feminine flowers, and his red hair is worn long, covering his ears and combed into a great "roach" on the top of his head. His red beard, of which he was clearly proud, is magnificent. The nose is rather snub, the eyes fierce, and the mouth full and sensual but subdued as if by an heroic effort. From the discolored old picture he stares out, fiercely challenging the world with all the fire and conviction of a youth supremely confident. It is the portrait of one who expected constantly to be contradicted, who was born seeking an argument, who enjoyed a battle, and who without constant struggles would have pined away from boredom.

Far better the little gilt frame suits the portrait of the Colonel's daughter, Maria. Primly she sits within its oval, her terribly capable little hands folded on the sprigged satin of her lap. Her dress is full and plain save for the lace at the wrists and throat and she wears a little bonnet trimmed with ostrich tips and tied under her chin. The bonnet gives her a rather ridiculous dressed-up appearance, because there is so little of coquetry in the serious, sensitive young face. It would have suited better her mother, Susan. She is neither plain nor beautiful, yet in the face there is the beauty which Providence so rarely gives to women of perfect features—a beauty of the spirit which has abandoned vanity if it ever knew it, and which at nineteen understood that life was a tremendous business. For this was no fly-by-night marriage. It was sober and serious—the founding of a dynasty.

The cabin built on the hill during the first summer by the Colonel and Jed and Henry had long since grown two wings, so that the Colonel's wife and children might have the privacy of a gentleman's family. The cabin now had a floor of wood, sawn at van Essen's Mills and its walls were plastered, and because it was a big room it was used as the common room where the family and the hired men and Sally Blaine sat in the evenings. Here Jamie and Maria were married by the Presbyterian minister beneath the yoke which the oxen, Buck and Berry, wore when they came West from Maryland. It was covered with spice pinks from the garden and hung suspended above the bride and bridegroom.

It was a great occasion and the farmers and their families came from all parts of the County to eat and drink and celebrate, and among them there were many Scots. At the end of the day Jamie and his bride were put to bed in the old Scottish manner and left alone by the wedding guests, who returned to their eating and drinking until daylight.

There was no honeymoon, for it was midsummer and already the hay stood ready to be cut and the wheat was turning yellow in the broad fields below the house. In midsummer the earth cannot be left untended, least of all by a bridegroom who himself wants sons. And the next day work was begun on a new wing to the old cabin which was to house the family of Jamie and Maria. It, like the other wings, joined itself to the cabin, and as it rose the last window of the old log house disappeared and it became known as "the dark room," abandoned now save as a museum for the Colonel's flints and fossils and books and as a repository for the cloaks and furs and hats on the occasions of great family gatherings.

⌐⊃

Now that he had a proper son, the Colonel left off the management of the Farm and lost himself more and more in his books and curiosities. Sometimes, dry and spare in his old-fashioned clothes, he made a round of the Farm on foot, accompanied by two or three big sheep-dogs. He began to forget the world and let it slip past him, for the time had come when it no longer mattered to him whether men were Jeffersonians or Hamiltonians, Whigs or

Federalists or Democrats. He no longer watched with mild dismay the changes in the county and the state. He found more interest in one *orchis mirabilis*, poking its mauve head through the dead leaves of the thicket, than in all the affairs of men. It was only when men began to talk hotly of the slave question that he opened his blue eyes and seemed once more to feel the old fire alight inside his soul. He had a plan, and it was simple enough. It was the plan he had himself carried out. There would be no problem if slave-owners gave their slaves the freedom which was the right of every man; but since man was a cantankerous animal, it was likely that the government would have to buy the freedom of the negroes.

But there was no man to agree with him. There were some who believed in slavery and others who held that it should be abolished by force. In the latter party the leaders were the New Englanders whom he had always held in contempt, but among them, too, was his own son-in-law, Jamie, dogmatic, hot-headed, and willful. The old man argued for a time because he had always loved argument, but he found no satisfaction in arguing with Jamie, who never troubled to invoke logic or reason, but relied wholly upon righteous emotion and "moral" law. Jamie did not understand the pleasure and the intellectual exercise to be had in a good complicated argument. He only believed in "shouting down," and because he had the strongest lungs and the most powerful voice, there was no one in the county who could hold out against him.

So in the end the Colonel forgot even slavery and abolition and turned away his head when his son-in-law began to shelter escaping slaves on their way to Canada, in defiance of all law and civilized order. He pottered about his orchard and his herb garden and had outlandish plants sent from all over the world for his garden.

He lived to see two grandsons born, the children of Jamie, as stout and healthy as their father and well able to carry on the Farm when Jamie himself had grown old and began to potter about. And he saw his daughter Jane, the proud one, married to the rich and mysterious Dr. Trefusis and go to live in Trefusis' Castle, and then one day they heard the sheepdogs barking, and Maria, leaving her babies in alarm, ran toward the sound and found the Colonel lying on his back, dead, under the trees in the far end of the orchard.

Just beyond the vegetable garden on a little knoll above the brook there was a burying-ground established long ago, when there was no graveyard in the county and the Colonel was the Squire. Here beneath a carpet of periwinkle lay his wife Susan and a dozen men, women, and children who had died when the country was still a wilderness, and here they buried the Colonel in the midst of his own land, a hundred paces from the rambling white house and on the edge of the garden he had loved. With him they buried the eighteenth century which somehow he had managed to carry on so far beyond its time. Jamie and the nineteenth century came into their own, for Jamie was as much of the nineteenth—muddled, vigorous, uncivilized, and ardent—as the Colonel had been the eighteenth.

THE GOOD CITIZEN

B Y THE TIME JAMIE FERGUSON WAS THIRTY HE WAS ONE OF THE important men in the county. He had inherited the prestige of the Colonel, which descended upon his shoulders rather than upon those of the Colonel's giddy son, Jacob, but to that prestige he brought qualities of his own, far more suited to the times and the community, than those of the old-fashioned Colonel had been. In Jamie Ferguson there was none of the old gentleman's cynicism. Jamie always believed in a thing or did not believe in it, and there was none of the weakness which accompanies a temperament given to doubt and questioning and wavering intellectual processes. Like the Colonel, he had dreams of a fine new world, but he was forever seeking to hammer them into reality by the sheer force of his own physical strength and immense vitality.

The Colonel had always been a "gentleman." He loved his land and would never have lived in any city, but he was never, like Jamie, a part of it. Jamie, in the mere necessity for physical activity, could never, like his father-in-law, have remained apart, surrounded by books and specimens, simply supervising the work. For his temperament it was a necessity that he should take part, helping with the plowing and threshing, the harvest and the milking. He had to have the feel of the earth on his big freckled hands. The Colonel had been a squire. Jamie was a farmer.

And it was good luck that brought to the Farm a farmer rather than a squire, for save in the parts of the country where there were slaves, the day of the squire was already drawing to an end when the Colonel died. When his will was read, they discovered that the old philosopher must have known that the life he had loved on the shores of Chesapeake Bay was doomed. Even in this new country it was no longer possible to live in style, leaving the Farm to the care of others. When the estate was settled, they found that for a long time he had been selling property in the East bit by bit in order that he might live until the end of his life in the old-fashioned manner. Horses and servants, even though they were "hired" young people who sat at the same table, cost money, and the Farm for a long time before his death had not made profits large enough for that.

Jamie and Maria kept the Farm as the Colonel had directed in his will, but they were forced to borrow money on mortgage in order to adjust the inheritance of the old man's other children. At thirty Jamie became a proprietor on his own with the Farm he had dreamed of, a wife whom he worshiped, and four children, the oldest of whom was nearly seven and in need of education.

Unlike the cultivated Colonel, who believed mildly that education corrupted the natural man, Jamie, who had never had much schooling, regarded learning with an exaggerated awe. (The Colonel himself, with his books and fine language and his letters in French from a priest in Mexico, had always filled him with awe.) Indeed, Jamie was, in his way, a symbol of the inflated reverence for schools and academies and universities which caused them to spring up like mushrooms everywhere in the Middle Western country during the second half of the nineteenth century. The whole inflated mass of educational institutions was born of a generation or two which, like Jamie, had had little opportunity for education and so sought exaggerated advantages for their children and grandchildren.

At twenty, Jamie had gone into the world abandoning all further hope of schooling. He could read and write and he had an elementary knowledge of mathematics, and a Calvinistic training, the results of which he jettisoned later as nonsense. Humbly he never saw that within himself lay the greatest and surest means of acquiring an education. He never saw that his own passionate curiosity about everything in the world and his own hunger for knowledge was a better means than all sorts of professors and academies.

He created his own curriculum, studying books and papers and articles dealing with biology and chemistry and botany which all had to do with the earth which he loved. In the few hours a day he had left from the stiff job of running a big farm and bringing up a large family, he read anything and everything. It would have been impossible for him to have gone uneducated, because he could not help himself. His passion for knowledge was like a disease. In his own field—the world of agriculture and horticulture and beekeeping and stock-breeding—he possessed a knowledge and experience which was intensely practical and unsurpassed by any man in the whole county. His best work was done in the days before there were government experimental farms and departments of agriculture specialists. The Colonel's farm under his guidance became a practical experimental station in itself.

Nevertheless, his social conscience, always concerning itself with his duties to the State which he idealized as much as the Colonel, but in quite a different way, was troubled unceasingly by problems of education. When his first children were reading-school age, the problem was solved by the traveling schoolmaster—an institution never very satisfactory in a social sense and very spotty as to results. A group of neighboring farmers banded together and engaged a man, sometimes young, sometimes old, usually shiftless, to undertake the instruction of their children. For a period covering most of the winter he went from house to house in the community, spending a few weeks in each and holding his classes in whatever house he was boarding at the moment. It was a bad system, good enough to teach reading, writing, and arithmetic, but beyond that of very little use. Even then it sometimes failed, for the traveling schoolmaster was of a dubious quality, and as often as not was lazy and sometimes drunken and immoral. Occasionally a good one appeared, but inevitably, in that new country so full of opportunity, a man of energy quickly abandoned schoolteaching for work more profitable. They came and went, leaving very little

impression. But what troubled Jamie most was the fact that under this system the poorer children of the county received no education whatever and grew up without learning to read or write, into that romanticized and pathetic product of American civilization known as "the poor white."

It was the farmers who led in the movement, and not the townspeople, who already had their schools. The whole thing began with a committee of which Jamie was elected chairman. Other committees were formed in other counties, and presently schoolhouses began to appear here and there in the county, and at last it became a state affair and the problem of illiteracy vanished from the rich and prosperous countryside. Jamie remained president of the county school board for two decades, and at last, when he was superseded, it was by a Town man.

At the time the first county schoolhouses came into existence there was no such thing as a high school, and to meet the needs of an education which went beyond reading and writing and arithmetic, Jamie and a dozen other farmers set about building an academy. For a time there was a long dispute whether the academy was to be placed in the Town or in the village of Onara, six miles away. Jamie and all other intelligent citizens knew that in the end it would be the railroads which would settle the relative importance of the half-dozen rival communities in the county, and they knew already that the second of the great railroads was laying its iron rails through the Town from the east to the far west. Some felt that this would be advantageous to the academy, but another party, headed by Jamie, with his old distrust of cities, believed that after the second railroad came, the Town would boom and with its growth would come all the corruption which went with cities, and that the youth of the academy would be submitted "to all manner of vice and loose living." Jamie made speeches and wrote letters on the subject and in the end his party won and the academy was built at Onara.

It was a large, square, simple building, severe and New England in style, set back from the road at the end of a long avenue of trees. It was a first fumbling effort toward higher education, and the curriculum included the Latin and Greek poets and other highfalutin elegancies which in that world and time were of little value save to those few young men who chose to be clergymen. The whole curriculum was left to the three or four schoolteachers who were imported from New England and engaged to arrange and carry on the courses, and they brought with them no new ideas nor any very practical ones, but instead the first faint germs of an academic decay that was later to spread over their corner of the country.

The academy was never very successful and its little board of overseers had a hard time keeping it out of bankruptcy, but it managed to struggle on for almost a decade. It had, however, moments and flashes of glory. Ralph Waldo Emerson was driven over muddy roads from the Town to Onara to lecture to an audience of farmers who had little need and less understanding of the doctrines of transcendentalism. Oliver Wendell Holmes discussed elegantly not upon the interesting and valuable experiments he was making in the field of medicine, but upon this and that; and Bronson Alcott talked of Utopias in a community which was as near Utopia as any county had been before or has been since that day. That solid, prosperous, pathetically idealistic world had curiosity and a touching desire, once so typical of America, to learn, to grow and expand, not in the pocketbook, but in the mind and spirit. Its men did not leave their "culture" to their wives. They too listened to lectures, not upon profits and business promotion, but upon ethics and poets and philosophers. But it was a world not yet old enough for Epictetus and Tacitus and high-flown philosophies. It was a Utopia in the making which had already failed, although none knew it save the Colonel in his grave under the tree planted by Johnny Appleseed. Whatever problems it had were intensely practical ones. There was still too much to be done.

So quietly one June day, a little more than eight years after the first country boy had entered its doors the last of the dry New England schoolmasters turned the key in the lock and scornfully set off for Massachusetts. His sojourn among the barbarians was ended and it scarcely occurred to him that one day not many years off the New England from which he came would cease to be of very much importance and that for good or bad this land of Philistines would determine the politics and the thought and even the character of America as a nation.

Thus ended the dream, conceived too soon by Jamie and his friends, that the county should one day become the seat of a great university. The building at the end of the long avenue of trees stood for nearly fifty years more, abandoned, with shattered, gaping windows. A second railroad came to the Town, and then another, and the village of Onara died like the academy, overshadowed by the city with its factories and hordes of dark foreign people.

Elsewhere in the state sectarian colleges, deeply colored by religious and emotional tendencies and very little by intellectual qualities, took root and made great progress and became firmly established. It was a religious era. Only a decade earlier there had been a colony of Mormons a few miles away. Prophets sprang up everywhere, false and sincere, but always fantastic and not a little mad. Sometimes they were sexual athletes of astounding prowess and sometimes they were ascetics with an insane passion for purity. There were within the borders of the state colonies of Shakers, Dunkards, Mennonites and a dozen other sects of diverse origins and nationalities. Religion and religious emotion took the place of theaters and cinemas.

Of the more respectable sects, the Congregationalists and the Presbyterians were the strongest. The Baptists had penetrated from the South and the Methodists, represented by several varieties, succeeded in founding a prosperous college. The Roman Catholic Church had no foothold except in one or two places like Sandusky, where churches existed as survivals of the missions established by adventurous Jesuits a century earlier. Its growth came much later with the wave of immigrant Irish who built the railroads, and the Poles and Italians who worked the mills. At that time, on the eve of the Civil War, the whole county and the whole state presented a riotous spectacle of evangelism. One could get to heaven in a hundred different ways, ranging from celibacy destined to end in the extermination of the human race, to standing on the head or rolling frantically on the ground and frothing at the mouth—rites which usually ended in an increase, legitimate or otherwise, of the race. One had a great variety of choice. Almost every temperament could find a comfortable spiritual creed, or the solace of a reasonable physical mode of life. A few of the odd doctrines were highly sexual.

But in the midst of the riotous scenes there existed here and there little groups whose lives on this earth were so pleasant and so solid and satisfactory that they were content to live respectably in the present, turning neither to religious orgies nor to a shadowy mystery which fixed the gaze upon an after-life vividly described by hysterical preachers possessing no very definite information upon the subject. There were the Unitarians, as always in a small minority, with their cold, intellectual creed, and their cousins, the Congregationalists, but there were others who remained unattached to any dogma, believing if they ever thought of God, in something very close to the Deist doctrines of Lord Herbert of Cherbury. They worked and built and begot families, and among them intelligence burned with a clear blue flame. They sought to glorify the mind, the body, and the spirit with none of the vulgar humbug which had become so much a part of the teachings of the debased Christianity surrounding them. They sought to find their reward in good works upon this earth. Among these was Jamie, who slowly abandoned his theologically complicated Presbyterian beliefs. His wife gave him no opposition. She was the Colonel's daughter and she had never known any religious training save that of the philosopher. They, like so many others about them, found life good, and they concerned themselves only over the problem of slavery, to, which already there seemed to be no way out save by violence and bitter tragedy.

Over all the prosperous county and over all the state, as over all the nation, there brooded during that decade a sense of doom and foreboding, and a horror of something which hung invisible over the heads of man, woman, and child—the worst and bitterest of all wars.

The Colonel had been aware of it, and after he was dead it troubled his son-in-law Jamie as no other question ever troubled him before or afterward. Almost always he was sure he was right. He never had doubts upon the necessity of public schools, nor suffrage for women, nor prohibition, but on the slavery question he found himself, like other men far more trained and able, although no more ardent, in a quandary. As to slavery itself he had no doubts. He admired Emerson for his moral stand and was forever quoting him, "We must give up slavery or we must give up freedom." I suspect that his doubts arose from his distrust of New Englanders and their tradesmen motives, and although he was something of a fanatic himself, from his dislike of the frantic rantings of the more cranky abolitionists. And he was a pacifist believing that wars solved nothing, but only led to fresh wars, and whenever the question of abolishing slavery by force came into discussion he grew either fiery, or perplexed and silent. But at the first whispers of secession, he found the problem still further complicated and disturbed. Secession was unthinkable. It was not possible to divide this country in which he had such a burning faith. That could never be. But when anyone suggested that if the southern states chose to secede, there was no way of stopping them save by force, he could find no answer.

But in all his perplexity there was one question on which he stood firm, and that was the right of an honest man's conscience and convictions over any law which was questionable. When it came to the problem of regarding slaves as chattels, and those who aided them to escape as comparable to receivers of stolen property, the old Calvinism rose and asserted itself.

On the next farm lived a patriarch called Job Finney. He was a Quaker and, like Jamie, a pacifist and abhorred slavery, and, like Jamie, he held in equal contempt the hysterical New England abolitionists. He was a very old man, over eighty, who, like the Colonel, had been a boy at the moment of the Revolution, but his liberalism was that of the Quaker, earnest and good and full of faith, rather than the faintly mocking liberalism descended from Voltaire and the Encyclopedists.

Slowly, step by step, old Job and young Jamie felt their way toward each other and the common idea which was stirring in their brains. It was an idea shared by other men in the state, here and there, in every town and village, but there was need for caution, since there were everywhere Copperheads and informers. But in the end, one evening in May, they made their plans and Jamie went off on a mysterious journey to the southern part of the state. When he returned, the plan was complete. The Farm became a "station" of the Underground Railroad and Jamie and Job Finney became "conductors." From then on Negroes began to arrive at the Farm, singly and in pairs and in threes, to spend a night or two and be sent on their way north to Canada and freedom.

They were a strange assortment, old and young, fat and thin, dark and light. It did not matter to Job Finney and Jamie that they were breaking the Fugitive Slave Law. They were obeying the higher laws of humanity, of liberalism, laws for which their hero, Jefferson, had always battled. If a parcel of professional windbags chose to pass laws which could not be enforced, it was no concern of theirs, nor of thousands of other citizens who were breaking the same laws.

At the Farm "station" they were aided by the women of Job's family. Maria saw to it that the escaped slaves were well fed during their sojourn, and Jamie's own sister sometimes helped them north to the next "station" at Oberlin.

Martha Ferguson was a big, handsome woman built like an Amazon and a fit sister to the big Jamie. Like him she had red hair and white skin and very bright blue eyes, and like him, she had fled from the brutal severity of her Presbyterian father. She must have been very happy at the Farm, for there she had the horses she loved and the freedom which until then she had never known. She was an active, restless woman and at the Farm she found plenty of occupation. It was inevitable that she should have become a "conductress" of the Underground Railroad. In her wild Amazonian nature there was much that was masculine. She had immense physical strength and undertook a great many tasks which by convention were reserved for men. She took entire charge of the calving and the dairy, and in her moments of leisure she broke the unruly colts to bridle, saddle, and harness, not only for her brother Jamie, but for Dr. Trefusis and some of the neighbors. In a household where a new child arrived every eighteen months she was a gift from God. She became as expert as a midwife and a nurse as she was at bringing calves into the world. She was intelligent and knew how to make a decision without fiddle-fuddle. She was nineteen when she fled from her father's farm in Pennsylvania, and she had many offers of marriage, made, I think, as much for her extraordinary virtues as a farmer's wife as for her good looks; but she chose to accept none of them, perhaps because she was unwilling to surrender the independence she knew in her brother's household.

During the days of the Underground Railroad all sorts of strange people came to the Farm, wild abolitionists who threatened by their rantings to undo the work of the Railroad, Negroes who were freedmen working for their people, other farmers who were "conductors," and often enough federal agents and privately employed slave-hunters who knew that something strange went on at the Farm and at Job Finney's place. Once Jamie had a visit from Harriet Tubman, a big Negro freedwoman who was called "General" Tubman by John Brown, and "Moses" by her own people. She was a big fat Negress with a jolly manner, but she had, too, a fanatic sense of having been called by God to lead her people out of the wilderness into Canaan. She had great intelligence and more than once outwitted slave-hunters. From time to time she went into the South alone to aid slaves until they reached the borders of Ohio and Pennsylvania and were turned over to the care of "conductors." Before the Civil War put an end to the Railroad, she helped more than three hundred Negroes to escape.

The tradition of the Colonel continued as he would have wished. All of the strange procession of visitors, sometimes even the slave-hunters, for reasons of expediency, were fed and sheltered and sent on their way.

There came a day in May when all the countryside was green and the fields were filled with new lambs and new calves. It was a Sunday, early, a little after dawn with the dew still lingering in the hedgerows. Martha had been up for an hour. The cows were milked and turned back into the pasture and she had taken breakfast and coffee to three miserable Negroes who lay hidden in the great mow, still twenty-four hours' journey from freedom and safety, and as she came through the big doors of the barn she saw moving toward her up the long lane under the locust trees the figures of two slave-hunters on horseback, accompanied by their dogs. She had just time to run to the house and tell Jamie the news. It was a sinister sign that the hunters were about so early, for usually they rose late and arrived only after warnings had been sent about and the birds they sought had flown. They must, Jamie and his sister knew, have had exact news from some Copperhead who knew of the Negroes' presence.

Martha acted with that same decision which she used with a cow in trouble in her birthing. She said to her brother: "Ask them to breakfast. Pray and pray. Keep them there and leave the rest to me. But for God's sake, pray and pray." And with that she made her way, behind hedgerows and outbuildings hidden from the sight of the slave-hunters, back to the barn.

Jamie went to the gate opening into the quadrangle and there met the two slave-hunters. They were not very unlike the slave-hunters of *Uncle Tom's Cabin*, useless scoundrels out after a bounty, and they had dogs with them. Jamie received them with as soft words as his violent nature allowed him to utter, and assuring them, with an odd combination of Calvinistic and Jesuitical conscience, that there were no negroes about, he blandly gave them permission to search every corner of his farm. Then assuring them that their search would be useless, he suggested that they have breakfast before they begin. It was, he pointed out, rather a chilly May morning. He may, too, have dropped a hint that there were chicken and waffles to be had. The slave-hunters, seduced, took their horses to the hitching ring and went into the house.

There were six others at the breakfast table—two children, two hired men, Maria and her sister Esther, who was making one of her periodical visits. Maria laid places for the two slave-hunters and Jamie seated himself opposite one of the windows which commanded a view of the barn. It was his habit to thank God for his blessings, but this morning the grace was not short. It was a whole prayer which rambled on indefinitely. He prayed for rain, for the new crops, for the souls of his neighbors, for a good harvest, for the souls of the slave-hunters, and when he had finished with the future, he thanked God for all the blessings of the past, one by one, until a good half hour had been consumed. The breakfast began, a lavish feast after Maria's heart, during which another full hour passed away. Cigars were smoked in the open air, and at last the search began. The slave-hunters examined every inch of the house and the barn, thrusting pitchforks viciously into the hay which they were too lazy to move. They searched even the hedgerows and the thickets, and never paused until they gave up at last and, cursing, set off down the lane all scented with locust blossoms. They knew from the behavior of the hounds that the frightened negroes they sought had been there and were gone.

When they were well out of sight Martha appeared suddenly from the orchard. She had turned the trick neatly and did not choose to appear until the slave-hunters, ignorant of her existence, had disappeared. While her brother made his interminable prayer, she had entered the mows, roused the Negroes from their hiding place and led them through the mud of the barnyard down the bed of the brook, whither the hounds could not track them, and through the thick woods to Job Finney's place. Here the Negroes were placed in a load of hay and driven by the venerable Job northward and into an impenetrable thicket-swamp, where they passed the rest of that day and the following night before going on their way.

Afterward Jamie learned that the unusual zeal of the two slave-hunters arose from a special reward of three hundred dollars offered by the vindictive owner of two of the escaped slaves. The Negroes escaped to Canada, and long afterward one of them returned, an old man, to live in the Town. He was called Josiah Wetherill.

A month after the escape Dr. Trefusis brought a new colt to the Farm to be broken and put in order. He was a fine chestnut gelding and Martha Ferguson took him in hand. One Sunday morning the doctor came out to see him put through his paces and stood leaning on the gate of the pasture while Martha rode him round and round the field, showing how well she had done her work. Then suddenly, at the far end of the pasture, the doctor saw the colt stumble and buck suddenly, and he saw the rider, caught unawares, thrown to the edge of the brook. He waited for a moment, but she did not rise. The colt ran wildly round and round the field. When the doctor crossed the long pasture he found her lying under the ancient willow tree. She was dead, with her neck broken by the fall. She was twenty-four when she died.

⌑

On the eve of the Civil War the county was no longer the wilderness into which the Colonel had come full of impractical hopes. The forests had vanished and the Town sat surrounded by fertile, cultivated fields. Some of the Colonel's democratic hopes were already withered or dead, but the Town still had none of the ugliness nor the corruption of a city. There were no peasants in the county; there were only farmers who lived well and sent into the world families well-nourished to carry on the battles they had begun. The Town had not yet imposed itself upon the county; it was merely a market place where things were bought and sold. If the bizarre Dr. Trefusis was excluded, there was not an absentee landlord in the county, nor any half-starved tenants settling upon land which grew poorer and poorer. The rewards, the prestige, the government, were utterly in the hands of the farmer. He knew the full dignity which is the right of the man who produces. In that part of the world the good citizen was not yet ignored. And each farm was in itself a world as nearly complete and self-sustaining as it is possible for such a small unit ever to be. As yet there were no tariffs to protect the "business man" and "infant industries" at the farmer's expense.

Even the laborer was well off. He did not receive a high wage, but everything was "found" and what was paid him was his and he had no need to spend much of it. He was housed decently and he had, too, the great privilege, incalculable in money, of living in a patriarchal pastoral world where the dignity of labor was understood and where he shared the life of his employer and his family. His food, his bed, his amusements were the same as those of the man who hired him and were largely provided by him. In that the Colonel's dream of a "natural" democracy had come true.

But the seeds of change were already present and beginning to grow. The railroads had received concessions from the government, and in return were beginning, mildly but surely, to reward the people whose government it was by extortion and thievery. Already there were three banks in the Town, and bankers who went to state conventions to arrange about the "proper influence which must be brought to bear upon the legislature." And Bentham, the son of the New England peddler with the mule who interrupted the talk of the Colonel and the Jesuit long ago in the vanished blockhouse, had bought up all the available land about the Town and was helping to organize the Republican party, both for a gain which was to come to him later on. The shops and the banks were in the hands of New Englanders, who all too often went to the Congregational Church on Sunday and watered the milk and put sand in the sugar during the week. The traditional figure of the Yankee storekeeper did not, like Topsy, "just grow." Stories of wooden nutmegs do not spring without reason any more than stories of Oakes Ames, Jim Fiske, Aldrich, and the Plumed Knight.

In the nation things ran smoothly enough save for the one great tragic problem which could be neither solved nor ignored. Congress had a few windbags, but it still retained something of the old semiaristocratic characteristics visioned by those founders of the American republic who were disciples of the eighteenth century and talked much of the "natural" man and his rights, but had not yet learned to trust the common people all the way. It had not yet attained new records in the world for bombast, demagoguery and hypocrisy. The politician of the Middle West with his chicanery, his opportunism, and his hypocrisy, born more of the times and the sketchy ethics of a people greedy for quick riches than of any individual baseness, was only beginning to show his character. Ohio had not yet produced her array of weak Presidents and corrupt, arrogant, and unscrupulous "bosses." It was still the simple country of Jefferson and Jackson. The rule of Hamiltonian ideals had not yet brought its mess of fantastic troubles and tragedy. The "big-business men" had not yet become gods with clay feet.

It was a new country, neither too new nor too old, but like good wine at exactly the proper point. The hardships of the wilderness had vanished and the hardships of banking systems and industries which attracted all available labor to the cities, stock market depressions and wheat pools, had not yet appeared on the horizon. In New England, the machine was already beginning to dominate life, but in the Middle West the machine was still a long way off. If one had listened closely he might have heard its beginning in the wheezing of the wood-burning locomotives which now passed through the Town, and in the clank of the crude stamp for work- ing iron set up in the shadow of Trefusis' Castle in the first tiny fac- tory which manufactured chains for the well pumps, logging, and the hoisting apparatus of the farmers in the county. If one had looked inside the brain of Great-uncle Jacob MacDougal, the machine would have been seen coming to life there, in one of the million small births that had begun to take place in the brains of hundreds and thousands of men throughout the world—men with a gift for experimenting and thinking up tricky contrivances, which with an uncanny intelligence performed the work of scores of living workmen, machines which took out of the hands of man the satisfaction of doing a job well, which destroyed the future of craftsmen and placed all workmanship, together with the souls of the workman, upon a single, colorless, mechanical level. It was all still far away. There were no great "industrial kings" or any "high- pressure salesmen" or bankers who were "omnipotent." There was no overproduction. There was no lack of market. There was no unemployment. There was no starvation.

Then came the War of the Secession and out of it a great figure who was born of that world in which Jamie and the children of the Colonel were so much a part. He was born of that country and of those times. He could not have come from the East nor from New England nor from the South, for already they were too old to bear children so great in their simplicity. He came from the earth and from the wilderness, and his simplicity and goodness were born of them, and so in the end the failing dream of the Colonel was justified.

THE FARM

WHEN JOHNNY WAS THREE OR FOUR YEARS OLD THE LIFE OF the Farm began to make an impression upon his consciousness. After that first moment of illumination when he was carried in out of the softly falling snow to be placed in the Colonel's chair and surrounded by giantesses, he began slowly to understand it all and to attach himself to it with a strange tenacity, as if the Farm, instead of the house in the town where his parents lived, was really his home.

It came into his consciousness in flashes isolated, and yet in their separateness curiously distinct—the sound of the primitive gramophone, the delicious smell of food when he crawled or toddled into the east wing, the barking of the old sheepdog, Beattie, the smell of the spice pinks and the red of the strawberries on a dewy Sunday morning in May. Slowly the impressions built themselves up, growing together into warm unity about the central figure of the little thin old lady who had long ago given birth to the giants and giantesses who were his mother, his uncles, and his aunts. Jamie and Maria were Johnny's grandparents, for his mother, Ellen, was one of their eight children.

In all her life the Colonel's daughter Maria never weighed more than a hundred pounds and after she had borne eight children she was always frail, so that there were times when the strength of her body gave out and she no longer had the force to stand. On these occasions she stayed in the bedroom with the picture of Pocahontas saving John Smith, lying in the great bed, small as a leaf on an autumn bank, sometimes for days and sometimes for weeks; but if the body failed in strength, the will remained alive, and even in her bed the old lady refused to cede even the smallest of her rights as head of the big household to any of her strapping daughters. Lying weak and ill, she saw to it that her menfolk were properly clothed and fed; she superintended, too, the making of pickles and jellies, and managed to spoil her grandchildren. Until the very end when she grew helpless and her wits wandered in the abyss of illness, she remained the force which kept the household and the garden and the kitchen and the dairy running as no one else could run them.

Johnny saw her for the last time when he was seven or eight years old and she asked that her grandchildren be brought in to her. A dozen times before that she had been near to dying, but on this occasion she must have sensed a difference, for she asked to see those she loved. Some of them were far off in the West and never saw her again, but of the others there were aplenty. They came and went all one day, and with all of them she was merry. She made no farewells and said nothing of death, and when Johnny's turn came he found her sitting propped up among the pillows, a little tired but very bright and with the look in her blue eyes (which were the Colonel's over again) of teasing and gentle mockery which she always had for the grandchildren. It was the sort of teasing they did not mind, since they knew that it was always the prelude to a treat. A little while after Johnny had gone, she fell asleep, and when she wakened her wits were dimmed and in her weakness she had gone back again into her childhood, and as she died she fancied that she was a girl again and that the Colonel had come to fetch her on a journey. She rose up a little in bed and cried out in a strong young voice, "It's all right, Pappy. I'm ready," and then she died.

There was something about her, as there was about her sisters— a dry quaintness, subtle and indefinable—which always set her apart from the other old ladies of the Town and county. As a small boy, Johnny was aware of it, but he did not know it then as the faint

lingering aroma of the eighteenth century. She had been born when the Colonel was nearly seventy, and upon her, as upon the other children of the old gentleman, there descended the spell of his personality, his humor which was light and dry, his wits so unlike the wits of the clumsy human century into which he survived. With his whimsies and his speech, his beliefs and even his language, she brought his century into the lives of his great-grandchildren. She called her husband, the rugged Jamie, Pa, and whenever she spoke of the Colonel it was as Pappy. She knew old songs which other women her age had never heard, and in her own household she used words which were passing or gone from the English of her time and country—words like crock and stillroom and buttery.

After the eighties she never changed her style of dress, and because hers was a tradition of good stuff, expensive and durable, her clothes never wore out. On weekdays she wore dresses of black stuff made with a very full skirt which descended from a tight basque fastened at the front by innumerable tiny buttons. On Sundays, when she went to weddings, funerals, and christenings, she had a dress made of some stiff rich material brocaded in satin and covered with tiny embroidered flowers. She always wore a little bonnet, like the one in her wedding daguerreotype, tied coquettishly at one side under the chin. Her Sunday bonnet had a slightly-worn aigrette which sprung from a little wreath of pansies. She had never, like her sister Jane, had a taste for horses, and fiery animals gave her no pleasure, so she had a horse of her own different from Jamie Ferguson's other animals, that was pure white, plump, and docile. His name was Doctor and he drew a phaeton which also belonged to her, and it was behind him that she rode when she went visiting or to parties and funerals, trying the patience of her big husband, who could not abide Doctor's comfortable disregard of all noises and strange vehicles capable of throwing an ordinary horse into a fine display of rearings, buckings, and prancings.

For Johnny, the memory of his grandmother was forever associated with the buttery. This was a big dark cupboard in the very center of the old house near the dark room and at the top of the stairs which led down into the cellar. Here were kept the pies and cakes, crocks full of cookies or apples, cider, maple sugar, butter, and stone crocks of buttermilk in which little bright gold globules of butter hung suspended. Here it was that she led her grandchildren when they arrived. Sometimes there was a whole procession of greedy little monsters who clung to her full skirts while she opened the door. And the small mouths watered at the complicated perfume of cider and pies and cookies and apples which swept over them as the door was opened. It was an aroma which Johnny never smelled again for the rest of his life, an odor which has disappeared in a world where foods come in tins or wrapped in sanitary paper, yet years after his grandmother had died he could not think of her without sensing faintly the ghost of that delicious complicated perfume. She would stand there, surrounded by clamoring children, and sometimes she would tease them by pretending that, to her astonishment, the cookie jar was empty or that some tramp must have broken in and stolen all the maple sugar, but they came to understand her teasing, and the delay only made the treat the more delicious. And sometimes toward the end of her life, when she had mellowed and abandoned even her old-fashioned ideas about the feeding of infants, she would slyly and with a mischievous look dole out pieces of pumpkin pie or maple cake. The wicked act was in itself a pledge of secrecy, and none of her grandchildren ever betrayed her, even when a pain in the stomach was a penalty. When she sinned thus the children had to remain in the dark room until they had finished the poisonous offering and had their mouths wiped, and when all was in proper order the procession with its stomachs filled with pie would emerge, with the Colonel's daughter Maria bringing up the rear, all as innocent as cherubs.

By the time Johnny was old enough to notice the bobolinks in the hayfields and hear the jangle of sleighbells, the Colonel had been dead for half a century and the green locust shoots which he had planted with Jed and Henry to make an avenue leading to the cabin were great shaggy trees with trunks three times as thick as a man's body. They stood in a double line on either side of the long lane, and in late spring their small scraggy branches, out of all proportion to the ruggedness of their trunks, broke out in garlands of white and pale yellow flowers, and as one bumped along the lane over the roots the air above was filled with the humming of thousands of bees swarming down from the hives near the farmhouse to gather honey against the winter.

From the highway, long before you turned in at the lane, you caught a glimpse of the rambling low white house spread over the top of the hill and enveloped by big trees, as if it had grown there and not been built at all. At the front of it, so dark that it appeared almost black against the fresher green of cottonwoods and lindens and lilacs, appeared the long hedge of pruned Norway spruce which served in winter as a windbreak and in spring sheltered from the late storms little flocks of nuthatches and crossbills and the patches of daffodils, crocuses, narcissuses, and grape hyacinths which drifted across the lawn.

High above the shingles of the gabled roof rose a huge cottonwood tree. It had the air of protecting the house from the elements, and twice at least it had been wounded by lightning of a midsummer thunderstorm. It was a great burden to Johnny's grandmother, for from late August onward it began shedding its leaves, twigs, and branches and little tassels of cotton wool over the neat pattern of her lawn and garden, but although Jamie proposed it nearly every spring, she would not consider cutting it down, because it had been planted by Pappy when the forest was cleared away.

If the cottonwood tree was the bane of Maria's existence, the lane was the curse of Jamie's. It was built in the soft rich clay soil of the countryside, and as it went uphill and down, the torrents made by midsummer thunderstorms were forever washing gullies and ruts in its surface. The roots of the locust trees, ancient, tough, and gnarled, came through the surface and sent up tough green shoots which no amount of traffic was ever able to kill, and in spring, when the snow broke up, the brook became for a time a torrent which threatened the foundations of the little bridge and sometimes swept over the roadway itself.

Yet it was the pleasantest of lanes, wild and a little disordered, with here and there a big locust tree scarred by lightning which countryside legends said such trees attracted. On either side the elderberry bushes spread panicles of white blossoms and black fruit, and underneath grew tiny wild strawberries which were white and almost transparent and very sweet.

In those days the county had not yet been invaded by Czechoslovak and Silesian peasants, nor by ideas of "scientific" farming, and the farms had less the feeling of orderly checker-boards imposed upon the earth than of little colonies which had grown out of the earth and belonged to it. There were no straight bare fences of galvanized wire. The fences of pickets or rails seemed to be a part of the earth, and in summer they stood half-hidden by the growth of blackberries and bracken, hazel bushes and hawthorn, which grew up about them. For children the fencerows were jungles filled with excitement where rabbits hid and thrushes built their nests, and for Johnny's grandparents they provided elderberry wine, nuts for the cellar, and jams and jellies made of wild blackberries and strawberries. They sheltered coveys of quail and occasionally gay-colored pheasants which destroyed the insects in the cornfields. And in autumn, when they turned crimson and gold and purple and the little husks of the hazelnuts began to burst open, they had a romantic beauty which disap-peared when Czechs began to cultivate every inch of the fields and allowed no clod of earth to go without producing.

Near the bridge, leaning over the brook, there was a colossal ancient willow in which tramps had once set a fire. The tree did not burn, but inside the hollow trunk there was a great charred cavern big enough to conceal three or four children, and there Johnny and his cousins played at robbers on hot summer days when the cows stood knee deep in the pool beneath the drooping branches, chewing and swishing their tails. They were Jersey cows, small, sleek, and golden,, with enormous udders and shadows of deep brown about their big brown eyes and their silken dewlaps. In spring the willow tree furnished shoots from which whistles were made on which one could play real tunes by pushing the wood up or down inside the slippery bark. Beyond the bridge the lane mounted upward on the steep slope which led to the house, the great barn, and the outbuildings clustered about them. In the spring when the mud was deep the shining rumps of the horses went into little ripples as they plunged forward to drag the carriage up the hill.

At the top you arrived precipitously in the quadrangle surrounded by linden trees which the Colonel had planted to feed his bees when the locust blossoms had faded and which in June filled the air on the hilltop with their odor. The whole of the quadrangle, save for those parts inclosed by the buildings themselves, was surrounded by a fence made of chestnut staves woven together with wire. On one side, where the fence separated the quadrangle from Maria's dooryard and garden, the pickets were of pine, carefully planed, neat and coated each spring with whitewash. In the fence there was a lych-gate garlanded with roses which swung closed with the aid of a heavy weight made from the worn cog of an old cider press. It was Maria's invention against the irresponsibility of her grandchildren, who might leave the gate ajar and admit calves and colts to wander among her choicest plants. Opposite the white fence stood the bulk of the great barn.

It was a vast barn, wide and solid and high, with enormous lofts above and stables and stalls for the cattle below. It had a roof of shingles, and for some reason, despite the advanced ideas of Jamie, it had never been painted, but for that same reason it had a beauty, and above all a dignity, which neatly painted barns never achieve, and there was about it none of the toy-like appearance of the classic red-painted barn. Beneath the assaults of the violent Middle Western climate it had long since turned silver-gray. The sides and the shingled roof were spotted with golden lichen, and over one end of it there sprawled a Concord grape vine of fabulous age from which the fruit was stolen every year before it ripened by the birds which nested in the eaves and on the big hand-hewn rafters of the mows. From the crannies in the sides of the mows wisps of hay protruded, giving the old barn an air of bursting with plenty. It had the beauty of an ancient barn in the fertile Ile-de-France. It seemed to have been there forever and to have grown out of the earth itself, and about it there was a legend. Because it stood on the watershed, people in the county said that if a bird stood on the rooftree and shook the water from its wings, the water which fell on one side of the roof would flow into the Ohio River and from the other side into the Great Lakes. When Johnny was a little boy learning geography he traced with fascination the progress of those drops of water from the one side into the vast Mississippi and the hot Gulf of Mexico, and on the other into the St. Lawrence and the North Atlantic haunted by whales and icebergs. It was fascinating to follow the journey of drops of water shaken from the wings of a swallow on the rooftree of your own grandfather's barn.

Near the barn, so near that one could step from the roof of one to the other, stood the fruit-house, a great, blind, windowless structure whose eaves were frequented by clouds of pigeons. It was the father of cold storage in all the state, having been the idea of the Colonel and carried out after his death by Jamie Ferguson. They were both curious about new things and were forever trying them. The upper part of the structure was a single loft half filled with sawdust. Its walls were double, and in the space between was packed the ice which was cut during the winter in the woodlot pond to last until it disappeared at length beneath the heat of an August sun. Under the loft there were three or four big rooms lined with bins filled with apples and pears and hubbard squashes, which, inclosed by walls of ice, lasted each year until the new crops were gathered. Always just inside the door hung a kerosene lantern, by whose light you found your way about the windowless interior. On the hottest of summer days you could enter the cool darkness and bring forth a basket of apples still bearing the bloom of last year's harvest. The fruit-house had an unforgettable smell of plenty and it had a great deal to do with the vast feasts which came out of Maria's kitchen.

In another corner of the quadrangle stood a gray unpainted structure known as the wagon shed. It sheltered the farm wagons and machinery, and on the upper floor there was a workshop with a vast tool chest filled with planes and saws and other more complicated tools. It smelled of paint and clean pine wood, and in one corner were stored broken bits of furniture to be repaired during the long months of winter. Among them stood the spinning wheel and carding machine, long since abandoned, which had been brought over the mountains from Maryland by the Colonel. Just beneath the windows of the wagon shed stood the corncrib, a slatted,

V-shaped structure mounted upon stilts made of hollow tiles to prevent the raids of hungry rats. All the year round the golden corn peeped through the slats, growing lower and lower as the spring and summer advanced, until in November it was filled again to bursting with the new crop. It gave a sense of richness to that small landscape and of a life which went on and on like the earth itself. When he was small Johnny would go to the corncrib with his grandmother to fetch in a basket of corn and turn the handle of the sheller which was too heavy for Maria's frail arms, and at the sound of the sheller stripping the yellow grains from the ears, the chickens and ducks, the geese and the guinea-fowl and turkeys, would come running from the fields and the barn, the poultry houses and the wagon shed, to crow and gobble, quarrel and quack, while she scattered the corn about her on the ground.

All the year round the quadrangle bordered by linden trees was a scene of noise and activity, for through it passed all the whole life of the Farm. The farm beasts crossed it on their way to and from the fields, stopping on the way in the shade of a big Norway spruce to drink at the wooden trough made of a single hollowed log filled with cold well water and covered with moss. In the mornings and evenings there was a clamor of cows and horses, pigs and colts and sheep, running before the excited barking of the big dogs. At harvesttime the huge wagons, creaking under the weight of timothy and clover hay or sheaves of wheat and oats, crossed it on the way to the mows. At threshing time it was filled with engines and farm teams, buggies and wagons, and the whole life of the Farm became disordered and exciting. The farm animals found their inclosure occupied by a great snorting engine attached by a whining belt to another engine standing on the floor of the mows, spouting straw for winter bedding into a great stack in the middle of the barnyard on the other side. And when the cows entered the barnyard on the evening of threshing day, it took all the dogs to force them into their stalls for milking, for at the sight of the mountain of new straw they seemed to go mad, running round and round it, rubbing their backs and sides against it, to scratch themselves and drive off the worrying flies.

Beyond the house lay more fields like those which bordered the lane from the highroad. The "back" lane ran from the quadrangle between fields and orchards to the woods and the sugar-camp and Finney's thicket, and for a child it was a path which led from all that was peace and security to all that was mystery and adventure. Again and again in his childhood Johnny escaped to run away down the "back lane," for in him there was, even then, a wild desire to know what lay beyond the next gate, the next fence, and the next hedge.

On the way one passed the big orchard which was Jamie's pride, and beyond one came to the field where the big hickory tree stood. It was a memorable tree, famous in the countryside for bearing enormous nuts with shells so soft that the faintest tap of a rock or a hammer would lay open the bisque-colored kernels. It had been there forever and, like the old willow tree, it served as a shelter for the cows against the angry sun of August. In each field there were big trees left to shelter them against sun and tempest, and hedgerows against which they might brush themselves to drive off the flies.

At the end of the lane one came to the woods, a patch of many acres where the Colonel had left the trees of the primitive forest when he cleared the rest of the land for cultivation. They were enormous trees, mostly beech, oak, and maple, and beneath their thick shade grew the dogwood which in spring turned to cloud-drifts of white. In the very midst of the wood, on the edge of the pond where the ice was cut in winter, stood the sugarhouse where in March, while the melting snow still littered the earth, the boiling down of the maple sap took place. For the grandchildren this was a season of festival when they were allowed in pairs to spend a whole night beneath the blankets of the bunk in one corner while Jamie sat up tending the fires and watching the sap which boiled in big iron tanks. You went to sleep only when you could no longer keep your eyes open, and sometimes in the night the hooting of an owl wakened you, terrified, to find that you were safe and warm, with your grandfather sitting in a big easy chair by the table, reading farm reports by the light of the kerosene lamp. And in your nostrils was the scent of burning hickory logs and of maple sap boiling in the vats. In the daytime the fat horses dragged up the sap in hogsheads on a sled and sometimes you made the round of the trees, helping to collect the buckets of sap which hung against the trunks. When the sap at last had boiled into thick syrup, Jamie would throw a ladleful of it on a snow bank outside, where it hardened into thick toothsome candy.

Beyond the woods lay Finney's thicket, a big abandoned jungle of a place which did not belong to Johnny's grandfather, but to a neighbor who long ago had cut down the forest and allowed the saplings and underbrush to take possession. In parts it was a tangled jungle of willows and wild grape vines and birch trees, and in it, two miles or more from any highroad, the shrubs and wildflowers, the wild birds and animals, lived unmolested either by Jamie, who was no hunter, and by the children of old Job Finney, who was a Quaker and would permit no one to shoot the birds on his land. In the thickest part the grandchildren built cabins and played at Indians, dividing into two parties in a game, the goal of which was for one side to discover, surround, and capture the camp of the other; but so thick was the underbrush and so vast the thicket that more than once the game ended at evening without discovery of the camp.

~⊘~

In the big sprawling white house the only rooms which had a fixed and sacred character were the dining room, the kitchen, and the bedroom of Johnny's grandparents. They remained unchanged from the day Jamie and Maria were married until the day they died. The others were always in a state of change, due to the number of relatives "visiting" at the moment, so that sometimes you arrived to find what had been a common living room occupied by two or three beds filled with cousins. Because the house consisted almost entirely of "wings" growing out of the ancient central cabin, it was in reality three or four small houses and sometimes it housed two or three families. The restless sons of Maria and Jamie had a way of departing suddenly for the West to look over some new country with an eye to settling there, and when they left, the wives and all the children were deposited at the Farm, and sometimes one of the eight sons and daughters would suddenly return from the West with a whole family to "visit" indefinitely. There were moments when even the parlor was occupied by sleeping children and when it was necessary even to consign an unfortunate sleeper or two to the stuffiness of the big dark room with the Colonel's collection of fossils.

The furniture was an odd mixture, ranging from patent rocking chairs upholstered in plush and crude split hickory chairs to the fine clocks and rosewood chairs which the Colonel and Susan had managed to bring across the mountains from the East. When Johnny was small there were two pictures in the house which had for him a sinister fascination. One was the oleograph hanging in his grandparents' bedroom, which antedated the days of Currier and Ives and depicted Pocahontas in the act of saving the life of John Smith. The Indian princess was an extremely buxom young squaw wearing a headdress of ostrich plumes and attired in what appeared to be a coat of mail like those worn by Roman legionaires, and she knelt by the side of John Smith, equally stalwart but heavily bearded, encircling his neck with a pair of the mightiest arms ever bestowed upon a woman. But her gaze was turned away from John and directed a little upward toward the raised tomahawk of one of Powhatan's menials, who, like the redskins in the plays of Voltaire, was decorated with the plumes of the ostrich. It was scarcely a tomahawk, but rather a spiked bludgeon such as the Crusaders carried in their combats with the infidels. John Smith's head rested upon a huge boulder, and Johnny, before the candle was put out at night and in the morning when the sound of cowbells, at the watering trough wakened him and the sunlight came through the shutters, lay in the big bed speculating upon the horrible mess which would result if the raised bludgeon ever fell. When the bliss of spending a night at the Farm descended upon him, he begged permission to sleep in the Pocahontas room, where he occupied a kind of trundle bed in an alcove a dozen feet from the great bed of Jamie and Maria's. Until he was eight or nine years old the picture exerted over him a fascination compounded of mingled delight and horror.

The other print was a huge engraving depicting all the stages of Pilgrim's Progress. It had the fascination of a picture which was always new, for in a way there was so much of it that you were always discovering details which you had never seen before—imps and devils, strange plants and fat cherubs. It was composed of a series of small pictures in each of which Christian appeared in one of the stages of his long journey through Vanity Fair and the Slough of Despond, past the cave of the giant Despair, to the glory of the gate where he was received by hosts of angels all blowing upon trombones. It hung on the wall of the dining-room above an old and massive Victorian sofa upon which the grandchildren were allowed to stand while Maria explained the horrors and delights of the story. The sofa long since had been abandoned to the children and was upholstered in carpet so that they might slide and jump on it until exhausted.

The "Pilgrim's Progress" was a companion piece to Foxe's *Book of Martyrs* which stood on the shelf among the other books of the Colonel's library in the dark room. This horrible tome was forbidden the children, and was at last destroyed by Maria in the kitchen stove when she discovered that it had been stolen by Johnny and his cousin Sam and removed to the hayloft, where they might study its dreadful engravings undisturbed. Among them one remained forever stamped on the two childish minds; it was the picture of "Maria Henshowe being delivered of a living child while being burned at Smithfield with two other women."

For half a lifetime after the Colonel's death his daughter succeeded in preserving intact the little museum of fossils and arrowheads and glacial stones in the cabinet in the dark room. Valiantly she managed to protect it from the raids of her own children, but by the time her grandchildren began to arrive in force, her strength gave way and she allowed them to take the arrowheads and make arrows with them and the round stones to play with at bowls or duck-on-a-rock, always exacting a promise from them that the things would be returned to the cabinet; but one by one the arrowheads were lost and the round stones left in the quadrangle before the barn, until at length nothing remained but the dried botanical specimens pasted to leaves of brown paper. One by one, like the Colonel himself, they returned to the earth of the Farm.

The children of the Colonel went to the Congregational church. None of them, brought up with the Colonel's philosophic ideas stamped upon them, was really religious. They went to the Congregational church for social reasons, because that was where they met their friends; but none of them was troubled as to beliefs. They were inclined, like their father, to accept a natural world which they found good and full of pleasures. But Jamie had been brought up as a Presbyterian, and when he married Maria there still lingered in his youthful soul the ghosts of Calvinistic superstitions regarding heaven and hell and predestination and original sin, and so Maria had yielded to his desire and abandoned the easygoing Congregational church for the sterner delights of violent sermons thundered out Sunday mornings by the Reverend McPherson from the pulpit of the Presbyterian church. The thunderings neither convinced nor frightened her, and for four or five years she endured them, sometimes dozing quietly while the Reverend McPherson shouted and shook his fist. But it all came to end abruptly one Sunday morning when in a wakeful moment she heard the preacher roar out that "the floor of hell was paved with the skulls of unbaptized infants." This, she told herself, had passed the borders of nonsense into idiocy, and being the Colonel's daughter, she rose quietly in the midst of the sermon and walked out of the church, never to enter it again.

Nor did Jamie ever go into a church again until the day he was buried, when they carried him in, dead. Somehow, perhaps, because some power of the Colonel's and of the eighteenth century still lingered in the farmhouse as it lingered in all his children, the old Calvinist superstitions died out of him and in their place there came a sense of rebellion and a conviction that although parsons as individuals might be good men, parsons as an institution were a plague. His attitude toward the church as he grew older was both less intellectual and less indifferent than the Colonel's. He had a simple conviction that no priest or parson knew any more about God than himself, and so could tell him nothing, and he believed that Sunday morning spent in going about his farm did more good to his soul than sitting in any church. Yet he always had a genuine religious feeling compounded of a delight in nature and a respect for God as the mystery which stood behind nature. It was almost a pagan feeling which was associated with his fields and his cattle and which caused him to offer up a prayer of thanksgiving vaguely directed toward the heavens when he sat down to a vast meal surrounded by his children and grandchildren. With his prize cattle and sheep, his orchards and vineyards, grafted by his own hands, and all his experiments with new plants and varieties of grain, he was nearer to God than most priests and did more good for man than most parsons.

⊸

The garden of flowers and herbs which lay on the gentle south slope between the farmhouse and the brook was, next to the grandchildren, Maria Ferguson's great delight in life. For her it was what theater and clothes and parties were to most women. It was her great amusement, and working in it, even when she was a bent old lady, after a day of hard work, seemed not to tire her, but to refresh her spirit and charge her frail body with new strength. She had the strange tenderness for plants which any good gardener must have, and she never allowed anyone to work in her garden save under her supervision, for she was unwilling to see her plants mauled by clumsy hands. For her, it was as if she saw her own children being tormented before her eyes. Her gardening differed from that of the Colonel because she cared more for the beauty and color of her garden than for the variety and strangeness of its specimens.

Some of the plants had long, long histories. The Colonel had left her a great collection, most of them unique in that part of the world, and from these she was forever giving seeds and cuttings to the wives of other farmers who liked flowers. Long after she was dead and the Farm was no longer the Farm, her great-grandchildren had in their gardens dwarf irises which were the descendants of roots brought from Scotland the year Lord Baltimore came to Maryland. There were new plants, too, for Johnny's grandfather as well as his grandmother had an interest in new plants and shrubs. They came from all parts of the world and few of them survived long the bitter winters and the ferocious summers of that Middle Western county. There were two cedars of Lebanon which managed to struggle through one winter, wrapped in straw and burlap, but did not survive a second. And the big catalpa tree which shadowed the front stoop was the first tree of its kind in the county. But most of the plants were old-fashioned flowers like bleeding heart and grape hyacinth. There were armies of daffodils and a ragged hedge of lilacs separating the flowers from the vegetables, and beneath the window of her bedroom a bed of small white English violets whose perfume scented the air on blue evenings in May. And there were, of course, stock and spice pinks and countless varieties of campanulas. And in the midst of the lawn, away from the flower garden, there were beds of begonias and geraniums grown from the slips of the plants which she had cherished all through the cold months.

In winter in the warm rooms of the house there were wire stands covered with rows of pots which contained geraniums and begonias, amaryllis, wandering Jew and saxifrage, and a dozen other tender plants. There were geraniums of an immense age with wooden stalks which climbed with tropical exuberance up and up toward the ceiling. Something in the delicacy and the ardor of Maria's thin, veined hands made her flowers grow fantastically. Under the hand of one gardener the strongest plant will wither and die, and beneath the touch of another the frailest seedling will grow into a great hardy plant. The bungler has no place in a garden, and only those with a passion for plants ever succeed with them. It was said in the neighborhood that Maria Ferguson could plant a splinter and it would burst into bloom.

Because the Colonel chose a hill for his cabin, there was no spring near the house, and so its place was taken by an immensely deep well. It was no mere shaft sunk by a gasoline drill, but a great tunnel, five feet across, which to a child seemed to pierce the center of the world. If one stood on tiptoe it was possible to look down it and see far at the bottom a mirror of cool water that reflected the sky and the clouds and the silhouette of a small head. Its walls were made of uncut field stone and in the chinks moss and ferns grew luxuriantly. They were always dripping with moisture, for the bucket on its way up splattered water over them. The well pierced one of the subterranean streams with which the country was crossed and recrossed, and the water was always changing, cool and fresh. It served not only as a well, but as a refrigerator, for there was, besides the bucket for drawing water, a great wooden bucket on a rope which could be raised and lowered just to the cool level of the water. In very hot weather the meat and butter and the cream were kept there. From this well Johnny's grandmother watered all the young plants she set out.

Beyond the borders of the flower garden lay the vegetable gardens, with their rows of sweet corn, carrots, beets, and crisp celery and the neat little hills where muskmelons and cantaloupes grew far separated from the spot where their incestuous cousins, the cucumbers, grew. And at the edges, sprawling luxuriantly against the picket fence, grew the enormous rambling vines of the Hubbard squash with their big rocky fruits ripening, to be put away in the fruit-house against the long winter. And there was always at least half an acre of strawberries with their runners each summer put symmetrically into place to make a little circle about the parent plants. The strawberry patch was always weedless and the berries ripened on a thick carpet of yellow wheat straw. In summer Maria allowed her grandchildren to go out in the morning and select their own dishes of strawberries, fresh with the dew still on them. Always she gave instructions that the berries were to be picked as they came, but she never said anything when the children returned boldly bearing a bowl filled to the rim only with dark-red prize berries.

The work in the vegetable garden was done by her sons or by the men who worked on the Farm, but she supervised it all and selected the prize melons and ears of sweet corn which were to be kept for seed. The vegetable garden was of the greatest importance. Out of it came not only all the vegetables for the summer, but for the winter as well, for Maria would have considered it a disgrace to have bought food of any sort. It had been part of the Colonel's dream that his farm should be a world of its own, independent and complete, and his daughter carried on his tradition. The Farm supported a great household that was always varying in size, and in winter the vegetables came from the fruit-house or from the glass jars neatly ticketed and placed in rows on shelves in the big cellar. The sweet corn was dried in the sun instead of being preserved, pasty and insipid, in tins, and not only did it retain much of its own delicious flavor, but took on something from the sun itself. And the strawberry jam never knew a vulgar kettle. It too was made by cooking it on the roof of the woodshed in the glare of the hot July sunlight.

At the far end of the garden on a little mound beside the brook there was the graveyard grown over with ivy and periwinkle. There were ten or twelve graves in all. Beneath the blanket of periwinkle lay two old men, a little girl of three, and a woman of thirty-seven who, her tombstone said, had gone out of the world in bringing a child into it. The rest of her story was not recorded on the tombstone. Her name, I remember, was Hannah Wells.

Here beneath an old apple tree, perhaps one of those planted by Johnny Appleseed on his demented wanderings, lay Susan and the Colonel, buried side by side. They had the most imposing tombstones of all. They were of white marble, and the others were only of poor sandstone and were slowly crumbling away with age. In

Johnny's childhood most of the inscriptions had become illegible. By the time he was a man they were gone forever, chipped and melted by the frosts of a hundred winters.

It was a perfect grave for the Colonel. He lay in the very heart of the land which he had wrested from the wilderness, only a little way from the house which he had built with Jed and Henry. All around him his grandchildren and great-grandchildren worked and played, stirring the fertile soil each spring not a half dozen feet from his head. And his daughter had only to cross her garden to tend his grave.

If it was a Sunday in summer, the buggy stopped in the quadrangle carpeted with pigweed at the front gate (the one weighted with the cog of the worn-out cider press) and all the family climbed down there to enter the garden and walk along a path made of moldering bricks sunk deep in the grass. Johnny's father, aided by one of the uncles or by old Jamie himself, left the buggy under the linden trees, unharnessed the horses and turned them loose to run madly round and round the great pasture. They were town horses and a day in the country grass was as much a lark for them as coming to the Farm for any of the younger generation. The arrival was always announced by the welcoming barks of the farm dogs, who ran down the hill as far as the bridge to greet all visitors. Sometimes if you arrived early you got down from the buggy in the midst of an animal bedlam, to discover the cows, having been milked, were being turned out again to grass. The barking of the dogs warned Johnny's grandmother of the arrival, and sometimes, if the breakfast was well in hand, she would come out of the house and halfway down the path to greet you. She was always dressed in her full-skirted black, partly hidden beneath a spotless gingham apron. If it was a Sunday in winter when the snow covered the ground, she stood waiting for her grandchildren in the doorway of the dining room with her delicate hands clasping a corner of the apron, folded at her waist.

The dining room was a large room with four big windows and in one corner an old-fashioned cast iron range which kept it warm in winter and was put out of sight during the summer months. In the front of it, surrounded by a nickel frame, there was a big piece of isinglass which permitted you to watch the flames inside. At two of the windows stood wire contrivances covered with pots of begonias, geraniums, amaryllis, and wandering Jew. Almost the whole room was taken up by a great dining table. The number of chairs varied according to the number of offspring in the county at the moment. Sometimes there were as many as twenty or twenty-five chairs and never were there less than ten.

The kitchen always seemed a very small place, considering the quantity and the quality of the food which came out of it. Like the dark room, it had its disadvantages because it, too, was part of the original log house which had come to be hidden as the house grew wing after wing. It was dark, with only a door and a small window which did not give into the open air, but into the big woodshed where the wood, carefully split to fit exactly her stove, and thoroughly dried to give the best of heat, stood neatly piled. All around the edge of the shed was a platform, and in the center an open space a foot lower, where the chipping and splintering was done in bad weather. The center part was always filled with dried chips which were used for starting fires.

In the little dark kitchen there was a colossal iron range with a great tank of hot water at one end and an oven which swallowed up two fat turkeys at a time. It was always scented with the faint delicious odors of cloves and cinnamon, and at one side there was a door which led down to a cellar fabulously stocked with pickles, sauerkraut, preserved peaches, quince jelly, and Damson-plum jam, all of which had been made in the little kitchen abovestairs.

With Maria and with her grandchildren Sunday was a great day when the house was filled to overflowing and the odors of turkey and sausage, waffles and coffee, filled the whole east wing, and after the Sunday dinner the beds were filled with grandchildren taking their "naps." On Sunday the children and grandchildren came from every part of the county. At dawn Johnny rose with his brother and sister in order to arrive at the Farm in time for breakfast, for in the small frame of their grandmother was a determination that Sunday should be a long day. For this the grandchildren had no regrets, since on Sundays they were never told, when they wakened, that they must be quiet and good until the grown-ups were stirring, and at eight in the evening they were never told that it was long past their time for being in bed. They fell asleep at last, one by one, out of weariness brought about by a surfeit of delights, and when the time came for the family gathering to disperse, they were dressed, still half asleep, for the homeward journey. And the next morning they wakened at home in their own beds.

Sundays at the Farm had a special glow and excitement which nothing else—not even the arrival of the circus—ever surpassed. It happened Sunday after Sunday, year in and year out, but the sense of excitement endured. Always, it seemed, there was something new. Sometimes it was a calf or a litter of puppies, sometimes a rat-hunt with the big sheepdogs among the standing shocks of corn, sometimes it was maple sugar making, and sometimes a whole troupe of new cousins appeared suddenly from the West on a visit. There was about those Sundays something splendid and matriarchal brought down from Scotland, and after the grandmother died they were never the same and presently they came to an end altogether.

In spring and summer and autumn Johnny and his family made the journey to the Farm in a buggy drawn sometimes by one, sometimes by two, horses, according to the state of the family fortunes, which were always up and down, or the quality of the horses his father was forever buying and selling and trading with a passion which amounted to a mania. They drove along the yellow clay roads at an hour when the meadowlarks were swinging on the elders and the fat thrushes rustled in and out of the dry leaves in the fencerows. In the early mornings of summer the bobolinks haunted the fields of timothy, filling all the air with their friendly cries. In winter, when the frozen ground lay hidden beneath a foot or two of snow the buggy was abandoned and the journey made in a sleigh where you were tucked in with blankets and old fur robes, with your feet resting on hot bricks placed in ankle-deep clean straw. The bells jingled and the horses trotted and the snow fell, melting upon cheeks and nose and lips, and in the evening when the moonlight struck the banks of snow they were no longer banks of snow, but of diamonds.

The winter journeys were the best of all. There was excitement even in the preparations for departure, with a great hubbub and laughing and chatter. There were mufflers and overcoats and mittens and caps, and if you were very small and the night very cold, a soft shetland scarf had to be tied across your face so that you did not breathe too deeply of the frosty air. And there were the hot bricks and buffalo robes to be arranged while Johnny's father held the impatient horses and the bells jangled and sang. Old Jamie, the grandfather, was always there, standing coatless and vigorous in the snow, to see that everyone was tucked in properly; and at last the horses sprang off down the lane under the locust trees, and the last thing you saw on looking back was your grandfather standing at the gate, waving farewell.

In those days there was not a road of concrete or asphalt in all the county, and in summer the hoofs of the horses beat not harshly against a hard slippery surface, but softly against the good yellow clay. In the ditches and along the edge of the road the wild sweet clover grew waist-high, giving off a thick perfume and a sound of humming. By the time you had arrived at the end of the long lane which led from the highroad to the farmhouse, the dew had begun to disappear from the glistening spider webs in the cloverfields and the appetite grew colossal.

On arrival there was always a great deal of kissing and greeting, and on the occasions when the family gatherings were larger than usual, Johnny had the sensation of being lost in a forest of long legs and big bosoms, for all his aunts and uncles and grown cousins were very big men and women with emotions in proportion to the size of their bodies. They did everything with violence. They were like Jamie in their size and their violence, and not at all like the Colonel. In the midst of them, Maria, so tiny and frail, the mother of them all, seemed preposterous and comic.

When the hubbub had subsided a little, Johnny's grandmother would emerge from the emotional disorder of her gigantic offspring and kiss each of the grandchildren delicately. Then Johnny's father would arrive from the barn, dressed in city clothes and bearing the Sunday papers, for he was a city man and the Sunday papers were his classic contribution. He always got them late Saturday night so that the early-morning start would not be delayed. There were bundles and bundles of them wrapped in the bright-colored comic sheets, damp and stained by the melting snow, which became at once the possessions of the clamoring children—the *Cleveland Plain Dealer*, the *Chicago Inter-Ocean*, the *Chicago Tribune*, the *Cincinnati Enquirer* and the *Columbus Dispatch*. They were always filled with political news which provided material for wild arguments and denunciations among the men and some of the women during the rest of the day, for the family was as violent in its opinions as in its emotions, and at times, especially during the Bryan campaigns, the arguments achieved the quality of bitter denunciations.

When all the wraps had been put away in the dark room, the grandmother returned to the kitchen and, aided by her daughters, prepared to serve the breakfast, while the men and the children seated themselves at the table.

When the breakfast was ready the food was brought on the table—sausages, waffles, and maple syrup from Jamie's own maple grove, fresh strawberries or peaches if it was summer, coffee, hot fresh rolls, and sometimes chicken and mashed potatoes, home-dried corn, and an array of jams and preserves. Everything on the table came from the Farm itself, and it was only the beginning of a day spent in high feasting. On Sundays Jamie suspended all labor except the milking of the cows, and spent the day walking over his land, examining the fences and the state of the crops. Johnny's father, released from city life, wandered about vaguely, starting up rabbits and pheasants which his dogs never captured. After lunch there were a great many sleepers scattered through the house or beneath the trees on the grass in Grandmother's garden. It was a day of festival given over to plenty. It began with old Jamie's prayers to the Deity of plenty and over it all presided Maria, a kind of priestess who stood apart with a queer little smirk of pleasure and satisfaction at the sight of her offspring eating the things she had prepared.

More often than not there was a stray tramp or two seated in the woodshed, enjoying what was borne away untouched from the overladen table in the dining room. Less than a mile from the Farm the main line of the Erie Railroad climbed a long hill where all eastbound freights slowed down, and tramps could leap on and off with ease. In time Maria had become a marked woman, and in the mysterious gastronomic guide of hoboes her kitchen was three-starred. They came and went on their way from the East. Sometimes one of them stayed a week or a month or a season to work on the Farm. There were among them some remarkable characters. But most of them were a bad lot who came to eat and run. She never turned them away. It was her way of giving thanks for the plenty she had always known.

The place had no name of its own. Among all the descendants of the Colonel it was known simply and regally as The Farm. In that rich county there were hundreds of other farms, but for the Colonel's children, grandchildren, and great-grandchildren, for a great many neighbors and friends, and perhaps even for the tramps, there was only The Farm.

THE COLONEL'S DAUGHTERS

THE GREAT-AUNTS JOHNNY KNEW AS OLD WOMEN WHO WERE eternally visiting.

His Great-aunt Jane was the most imposing and the least human of the Colonel's daughters, although in her old age one felt a pathetic desire on her part to escape from the shell of hardness which shut her in, to reach out and touch those who were near to her yet tragically distant. She it was who made the great match of the family, for she married the mysterious Dr. Trefusis of Trefusis' Castle, and she it was, of the four sisters, whose marriage was tragically unhappy. She it was who had the carriages and horses and dogs and fine furniture and a great house in the style of Strawberry Hill Gothic. But she married a fantastic man, fascinating and a little sinister, whom she suspected of being unfaithful to her from the first week of her marriage.

Before their marriage Dr. Trefusis came often to the Farm to see the old Colonel, whom he regarded as the only gentleman in the county, and when Jamie Ferguson married a daughter of the Colonel's, they, too, became friends. All three had a passionate interest in horses, although with Jamie the interest was more utilitarian than in the cases of the Colonel and the doctor.

It was horses, too, which brought together the Doctor and the Colonel's daughter Jane who had frightened Jamie by her proud air

on the first day he ever came to the Farm. She was a noble horse-
woman, slim and delicately built, and once she was in the saddle, a
face which many people considered plain became distinguished,
fierce, and even beautiful. She was one of those women made to sit
on a horse, who seem to lose some quality of beauty when they put
foot to the ground. Johnny never saw her riding, but his earliest
memories of her were of an old lady very stiff and proud and bitter, with a fine Roman nose, riding in a phaeton and capable of
managing any horse, however wild. She used to ride the Doctor's
fine horses, and, I fancy, he was caught by her appearance seated
on a favorite mare and married her without considering that the
iron will and the fierce character which made her unafraid of any
animal might also make her willful as a wife.

Dr. Trefusis died before Johnny was born, yet in a strange fashion he lived on. All through Johnny's childhood he was aware of a
personality called Dr. Trefusis, or Uncle Doctor, whom he had
never encountered but who was, nevertheless, one of the countless
relatives, only more aloof and more elusive than the others. He was
always there, just around the corner somewhere, the husband of
Great-aunt Jane and the father of the six cousins all so much older
than himself. I do not think that it was only the children who
thought him still alive. Even the men and women of the family
sometimes spoke of him, without thinking of what they did, as if
he were still living. It was perhaps because you were aware of him
in the bitterness of Aunt Jane, in the morbidity or hysteria or wildness which touched his daughters. He might have died a thousand
times, but none of them were ever able to escape from him until
they were in their graves. As for Johnny, he never really believed
Uncle Doctor was dead until after he had grown up and left the
Town, never to return.

Perhaps he lived on because throughout his lifetime he existed
in a fog of mystery which never lifted and continued to shroud his
memory after he was dead. In the big Strawberry Hill Gothic house
there were old photographs and daguerreotypes, and in the library
a large portrait of him standing by a mahogany table with a gold-
en setter at his feet. Physically he was an ugly man, thin and wiry,
with straight black hair which he wore falling to the line of his thin,

hard jaw, but there must have been about his personality a singular fascination, for it was one of Great-aunt Jane's burdens that he
had a great success with women. His manners with them was bold
and cynical and flattering, and in the beginning he must have dazzled Great-aunt Jane, who was more accustomed to the coltish
admiration of the strapping boys of the county. In his pictures he
has burning black eyes and the wild look of a gypsy. The secret of
his nationality went with him into the grave. The county knew
only that he had plenty of money and that he made a great deal
more by backing the enterprise of a doctor friend who invented a
panacea for women's troubles. It knew, too, that he spoke English
elegantly and that he spoke French, in which language he always
conversed with the first priest who came into the county to shep-
herd the families of the Irish workmen. At that time it was scandal
enough that the Doctor should have a friendship with a Roman
Catholic priest who spoke French, but to hold a conversation in a
foreign tongue on Main Street was "showing off." Stories persisted
long after his death that he was really Spanish in origin, which
seems to have been the likeliest guess. Once a Miss Trefusis, his sister, a grim, dark, proud spinster, came from New Orleans to
inspect his wife and castle. She remained for two days, and after
quarreling with her brother, set off to make the journey down the
Mississippi on a steamboat and was never heard of again.

He was a man of great cultivation, and immediately after he
married the Colonel's youngest daughter he decided that, although
she had had an education suitable for a woman, there were certain
things which she did not know and that she must learn in order to
be a wife worthy of him, and so he sent her East to Philadelphia to
a finishing school for young ladies, where she might learn music
and French and deportment. But he disposed of Jane MacDougal
without reckoning upon her character. He fancied weak dependent
women, and perhaps could not believe that his wife was different
from all the other conquests he had made. But Jane, who had been
educated by the Colonel as a boy and treated by him as if the feminine intelligence were as great as the masculine, had no stomach
for the curtsying and pretty speeches of a school designed to make
girls into wives whose only defense was to faint. She remained with

the more docile young ladies but a week or two, when she disappeared one night out of a window and returned to the Castle. There she learned that her bridegroom was in Cincinnati, and leaving by the first train she arrived early the next day and, without being announced, went to his hotel bedroom. She found him there, but not alone, for on the bed lay a parasol and a pair of lace mitts. On the balcony, pressed behind one of the shutters, she found the woman.

She never returned to the finishing school, but went back to Trefusis' Castle, where the next year she bore her husband a daughter, whom he named Azalie, although no one could ever discover why. From the moment Great-aunt Jane discovered the parasol and lace mitts the marriage grew stormier and stormier. They had violent quarrels and violent reconciliations, and after each reconciliation another child was born. But they were all daughters, and after the sixth was born there was a gigantic scene, followed by no reconciliation, and from that day on they never addressed each other. For twenty years they lived in silence which was not broken even on the Doctor's deathbed. When it was necessary for them to discuss business or servants, the conversation was conducted through the daughters, Aunt Jane saying very stiffly, "Tell him so-and-so," and the Doctor responding likewise. But the silence had no effect upon their relations with the rest of the family and they went visiting together and always on New Year's Day gave a vast family dinner. They came to see Jamie and Maria at the Farm, driving in the same carriage behind the Doctor's spirited horses without ever addressing each other. On one occasion they arrived both dishevelled and covered with mud, for the dogcart had overturned in the ditch. Great-aunt Jane, her clothes in disarray and her dignity outraged, made only one triumphant comment, "I never spoke to him."

Except for Jamie and the descendants of the Colonel the Doctor had few friends, and in his arrogance he came, before he died, to draw upon his head the enmity of a whole county, even of the men and women with whom he had never spoken a word. He was an eccentric, but in a day when eccentrics were plentiful and conformity was not the goal of good Americans, it was not so much that quality which set him apart from the others as a contempt he had for most of his fellowmen which he made no effort to conceal. In a world which tried, no matter what it practiced, to believe in democracy, that was an unforgivable crime. He made no concessions. He was not, like the Colonel, a relic of the eighteenth century. The quality of the Doctor was feudal.

But he was immortal, for he lived on in the memory of the oldest inhabitants and in legends carried on by those who had never seen him. Long after the Town had grown into the City, and few traces of the old life remained, long after Trefusis' Castle had disappeared, the legend of Dr. Trefusis and the Strawberry Hill Gothic house lingered on, sinister and mysterious, known to strangers who had never seen either the man or the house. During his lifetime fantastic stories were whispered about to explain his wealth and his character and the mystery which surrounded him. Because he always wore gloves when he drove his handsome horses, people said that he wore them because he was a professional gambler and that he wished to keep his finger tips soft and sensitive in order to manipulate the cards. His frequent absences they explained as trips where he passed about the steamboats of the Ohio and the Mississippi, fleecing the passengers. There were ghoulish stories of grave robberies and of Burke and Hare activities and reports that the cellar of Trefusis' Castle was filled with the bones of bodies he had stolen and dissected. Among the more ignorant citizens there were even stories that he was in league with his own farmer to steal pigs and cattle and disguise them by changing their color with dye. They were the stories circulated by a community in which action was everything and idleness a scandal. It hated a man who did no work. There was truth in none of the fantastic legends. There was truth only in the mystery which enveloped him even after his death.

Great-aunt Jane never knew who he was nor whence he came, and it was a subject for family discussion which was never old nor stale, and in the midst of the wildest speculations her sister, Great-aunt Esther—the Mrs. Widcome who upset Jamie by her mockery on the first day he ever came to the Farm—would put an end to the talk by chuckling mysteriously and interrupting with the assertion that she for one was convinced that he was the Lost Dauphin.

❧

The other two daughters of the Colonel, Great-aunt Esther and Great-aunt Susan, both married building contractors who had come into the new country to make their fortunes. Neither of them made a fortune. Indeed, talent and even desire for making money never appeared in any member of Johnny's family nor in any of those who had married into it. In none of them was there either shrewdness or its more sordid twin, thrift. If any of them came into money it was spent at once, as if having it in hand made them uneasy. With all of them living well was a necessity, and it was always possible to live well even upon a modest income in a rich country where there were not too many people. Yet comfort bordering on luxury constantly devoured income and earnings. The great-uncles and great-aunts had a good time in life, all save perhaps Great-aunt Jane, who was the richest of the lot.

Great-aunt Susan was a small woman very like Johnny's grandmother, and the nearest to her in affection of all the sisters. She alone of them all could ever have been called thrifty, but I think she was moved less by actual thrift than by the fact that the idea of thrift gave her an excuse to keep all sorts of budgets and ledgers and diaries. She had a passion for detail and for writing down the purchase of a spool of thread or a quart of peas. In the end, despite all the paraphernalia, she appeared to have made no economies and died no richer than the others, save that she left behind piles of ledgers and account-books. It may have been that she found satisfaction in knowing where her money went.

She and her sister Esther married their contractor husbands in a double wedding, and went off to live in the northern part of the state; but absence and matrimony made no difference to them in the attractions for the Farm and the hospitality of the Colonel, and they were forever returning on long visits, making the long journey partly by train, partly by coach, and sometimes, in a pinch, even on horseback. Both husbands died before Johnny was born and they left behind them no legend. I think they must have been dull fellows and that their dullness was the reason for the long visits made by Susan and Esther in the gayer atmosphere of the Farm and the more worldly one of Trefusis' Castle. Both men were employers, but they knew their business thoroughly, and if workmen failed them they were able to build a well or construct a whole house with their own hands. The family saw very little of them and thought of them as indistinguishable. Usually they were referred to as a pair, like a music hall team. The family always spoke of "Ben and Harry."

Johnny's grandmother and the three great-aunts preserved until the end of their lives an intense intimacy, constantly visiting one another, criticizing one another's households, and suggesting reforms in the upbringing of one another's children and the discipline of one another's husbands. And in those days visits were not made with an overnight bag. They were accompanied by large trunks of tin or cowhide and they lasted for weeks and sometimes for months. The Colonel's daughters were powerful women, and all save Maria long survived their husbands. There were times when beyond all doubt their intimacy and their passionate interest in one another's affairs became too intense to be borne, and then there followed bickerings and scenes and hurt feelings and sudden departures in a flurry, followed by the most complicated intrigues in which each sought to win the support of the other sisters. And then quite suddenly there would be a dramatic reconciliation with tears and emotion, and the little comedy would begin all over again. There was in their blood a strange hankering for the dramatic, and in the intense narrowness of their lives it broke out in the most absurd quarrels. Life never seemed passionate or dramatic enough to satisfy them.

When Johnny was a child and they were old ladies, in little black bonnets and spriggled black and purple dresses, the drama still continued endlessly. Johnny's mother was their favorite niece and one of them was forever calling to enlist her sympathy against the others. Johnny's grandmother was the least dramatic of the three, perhaps because she found enough drama in the responsibilities of her great family and husband and the care of the garden and kitchen, and so she suffered appeals from them all and became the center of their intrigues.

As far back as Johnny could remember, Great-aunt Esther—the Mrs. Widcome who had upset Jamie on his first visit—was blind from cataracts; but despite her blindness she was the jolliest of the three. Like her brother Jacob, she had a quality of puckish mischief. Her face was rather broad, with an expression of great brightness and charm, and out of it her blind eyes seemed always to be smiling. Her old-fashioned false teeth she regarded as an indignity, for, even blind, she was vain of her appearance. They were constantly displaying themselves in a double row of tombstones when she laughed. She was a master gossip with a novelist's sense of a good story and a rich streak of humorous malice and mockery, and if she found one or two scraps of good scandal she did not hesitate to reconstruct the missing parts, either motives or actions or results or all three, embroidering the whole tale with a lavish imagination and a sense of the classic unities. Her gossip usually lacked an air of authenticity because it was *too* good and *too* artistically complete. More than once when one of her sisters trapped her in a falsehood concocted for the sake of art, she laughed and, admitting her embroidery, said, "Well, it *might* have happened that way," or, "Well, it ought to have been like that." She was no realist and had a romantic's proper scorn for the unadorned truth.

Perhaps her long blindness and the tragedy of her life (her husband and children all died before her, leaving her blind and alone in the world) bore in the end a philosophy which consoled her. Certainly she possessed the detachment without which no philosopher can exist. Shut in behind her blindness, she regarded the world, her sisters, perhaps even her own husband and children and herself, as parts of a spectacle. But she was a mischievous philosopher, and now, looking back upon the memory of her sprightly figure, I think that she may have been quietly the instigator of most of those dramas which perpetually disturbed and embellished the lives of the sisters. I suspect that she sat back and enjoyed them more than any of the others.

In her old age she shared a house with her widowed sister Susan (an idea of the mock-thrifty Susan, who saw an added pleasure in keeping ledgers and budgets and diaries for two rather than one), and I think that she sometimes tormented the slower-witted sister, for now and then one or the other of them, with great amounts of baggage and sometimes a bird or two, would suddenly arrive to stop for an indefinite period, with one of the other sisters or with Johnny's mother. The visit was always accompanied by the public announcement that either Esther or Susan, according to the identity of the visitor, had become insufferable, and that the visitor was only remaining until she could arrange to set up an independent establishment. Always in the end there was a reconciliation and the two aunts settled down together once more until there was a new explosion. It went on indefinitely and I fancy that they became so charmed by the drama and so accustomed to it that it was impossible to do without it. Great-aunt Susan died first and Great-aunt Esther followed her within four months.

The visits of the blind Great-aunt Esther were always welcome. She had a sense of fun which children appreciated and she could play the piano and had an endless number of stories about her childhood and the Indians who at that time still escaped from reservations and wandered across the state from time to time, a drunken, degraded crew with their morals and traditions gone the way of their hunting ground. Now and then they set upon some lonely farmer and tomahawked the whole family. That much is history, but most of Great-aunt Esther's stories were, I am afraid, gravely apocalyptic, though none the less exciting.

She did, however, remember well that strange figure of Western Reserve history known as Johnny Appleseed. He existed. He was no invention of Great-aunt Esther. He lives in the traditions of the whole Western Reserve—a voice crying in the wilderness, unkempt, unshorn, and unwashed, a demented fellow who in the Palestine of two thousand years ago would have been honored as a prophet. Like John the Baptist, he lived on locusts and wild honey, clothed in the skins of wild animals and bits of cast-off clothing. He wandered from settlement to settlement and cabin to cabin, preaching and singing, never staying more than a night. Winter and summer were alike to him. He gained his name from his habit of planting, wherever he roamed, on hillsides and in valleys, by streams and on the edge of virgin forests, the seeds of apples which settlers had brought from the East. When the trees they brought with them began to bear, he begged for the seeds of their first fruit, and the Colonel and his family used, half-humorously, to save the seeds of the apples they ate in the long winter evenings and put them into a paper bag to give to Johnny Appleseed when he came in one night at sunset to sleep in the mows of the great barn. Wherever he went he planted, too, the fennel, esteemed as a cure for the fever and ague which rose to attack the settlers' families when their plows turned for the first time the rich black virgin loam of all that fertile country.

His whole existence was a fabric of delusions, and among them was the belief that he had befriended the king of France, Louis XVII, the child of Marie Antoinette. For his life had crossed now and then the path of another life equally bizarre—that of a young white man brought up among the Indians and known only as Lazare. The younger man was handsome, too handsome, indeed, ever to have been a Bourbon, and no one knew anything of his origin save that he had been left among the Indians as a scatter-witted child of ten or twelve. In the simple life among the Indians he had recovered his wits and remembered a little of his early life, such details as vast gardens and big mirrored rooms and mobs with torches. In Canada and in the Western Reserve he became famous as the Lost Dauphin, and a committee of Royalists came all the way from England to see him, but the Duchesse d'Angoulême and Louis Philippe (perhaps for good reasons of his own) repudiated him, and at last he disappeared again into the world of Indians and trappers with an apathy and a talent for obscurity which were perhaps a better claim to Bourbon blood than all the nightmare memories of his childhood. But for a time he was a romantic figure, and there were certainly many strange and almost inexplicable proofs that he was the little boy who was shut up to die in the temple. Sometimes Johnny Appleseed and the Dauphin wandered through the Western Reserve together, a strange, incongruous couple, living peacefully with Indians or whites, sleeping at night in the open or in the mows of a barn.

Johnny's Great-aunt Esther always said that she had seen the Lost Dauphin, but I think that was one of her stories, for he vanished into obscurity soon after she was born. But true or not, her story was a good one. She made him a handsome, glamorous figure, a lost romantic prince, and although she began in mockery she came in the end to believe, like many others of her day, that he *was* the Lost Dauphin, cheated of his inheritance by the son of the wily Egalité. A hundred years have passed since Lazare vanished into obscurity, but no one has ever proven that Great-aunt Esther was wrong. He may have been the Dauphin. No doubt she believed that he should have been for the sake of her story. As for Johnny Appleseed, he lay down one night to sleep in a thicket and never wakened again. He was, in his way, the prophet of the New Country. He preached always that it was the promised land and that one day would be the richest spot on God's green earth. He was vindicated, but centuries sooner than he had believed. His legend lingered after him, and in one of the pretty parks of the Town there is a little obelisk raised to his memory. But there are other monuments, too, for in the hedgerows here and there all over Ohio and Indiana there still linger ancient apple trees, old, rotten, worm-eaten, hollowed by flickers and woodpeckers, sometimes blackened by the smoke of factories, grown from the seeds thrust into the rich earth more than a century ago by Johnny's crazy hand. And on hot summer days when one can see the corn pushing its tall tassels upward, the smell of fennel is everywhere.

✥

The two great centers of family hospitality were the Farm and Trefusis' Castle where Great-aunt Jane lived surrounded by the rugs and pictures and statuary her husband had collected in the East or in Europe during the middle of the nineteenth century. Christmas dinner was always held at the Farm, and New Year's dinner at Trefusis' Castle. It is difficult to imagine two houses more different, the one rambling and of an architecture without style or any charm save that subtle but powerful one acquired by houses which have grown without forethought, out of necessity; the other was pretentious and constructed in the oddest of styles. At the Farm the furniture was worn and shabby and nondescript and placed where it was most useful and convenient. It was always being moved about from room to room, according to the demands of necessity.

In Trefusis' Castle there was an immense long drawing-room, a small drawing-room, a vast hall, a sun parlor, and a library. In the drawing-room each piece of furniture had its place. At the tall Gothic windows, ornamented by little inset panes of blue and red glass, there were enormous curtains of crimson brocade surmounted by gold baldequins and tied back with gilt cord. In the gardens and the surroundings there was, too, a difference. At the Farm, Maria's flowers merged almost imperceptibly into the big vegetable garden, and here and there in the lawn grew clumps of flowering shrubs. At Trefusis' Castle, one entered through a gateway of wrought-iron and gilt, to approach the red brick house with its ornate roof-line and Gothic windows and big chimneys, by an avenue of clipped Norway spruce with niches cut into it to shelter classic statues made of cast iron and washed each spring with white lime. There were avenues and trellises, and behind the house, the big stables grown over with wisteria and ampelopsis. Everything was pruned and clipped and formal.

Both places had a fascination and a charm, the one real and earthy and human, the other romantic and literary and in its gloom a little Gothic. The Farm Johnny loved as a child. Trefusis' Castle he did not love, but it fascinated him because he felt that the great world outside the county, the world of London and Paris and New York, must be like this; and when he went there to spend the day amid the strange hodge-podge of beautiful and ugly things—the things of the eighteenth and early nineteenth century all mixed up with the heavy horrors of the mid-nineteenth—he used to pretend to himself secretly that all the uncles and aunts and cousins were persons of fashion and distinction and importance. Long afterward he discovered that such persons were not very different and frequently enough less interesting than those who sat in the big dining room hung with pictures of birds and fish at Trefusis' Castle.

There was no gaiety in Great-aunt Jane's big house. There were mountains of food, a wonderful Swiss music box that played twenty tunes, and the stables with the negro boys, and among the six daughters there was one, years older than Johnny, who had as much charm as any woman he ever encountered. She was a beautiful, willful girl with the most gracious manners, and she had ideas of the independence of women far beyond her time and generation. She had been her father's favorite, and when he died he had left her rich in her own right, and from that day she led her own life, spending years in Europe and even going alone to the Orient. In those days her behavior created a scandal in the Town, but I fancy she never gave the disapproval of the Town much thought. She led rather the life of a man. She had both the recklessness of her father, the Doctor, and the pride and independence of her mother, Great-aunt Jane. She came to no bad end and late in life she married an Englishman and settled down to being the best of wives and the happiest. Sometimes she was in Europe on the occasion of the great New Year's dinners, and sometimes she was present, and her presence made the most enormous difference. I think that all through his childhood Johnny was in love with her, not alone because she was charming and beautiful and kind, but also because she knew what the great world was like. She had been everywhere. When she entered a room the whole air of the room changed. The conversation grew more lively and Great-aunt Jane's temper grew better. Johnny, watching her, grew fascinated, tongue-tied, and silent, and when she spoke to him he blushed and could think of nothing to say, and he never knew that when she was an old woman he would still, in his deepest heart, be aware of her charm and good nature and poise and her soft voice as a standard by which to measure all other women.

When she was absent the New Year's dinner was inclined to be a pompous affair, with much eating in silence and a long period of coma after dinner in the drawing-room. Of the other daughters, one suffered from melancholia, and one early in life acquired a religious mania. It was altogether a strange household in which one felt forever, even long after the Doctor's death, his presence and the sinister shadow of the unhappiness of Great-aunt Jane's marriage. I think that the greatest tragedy lay in the fact that she was always in love with him and that he had only loved her as much as his philandering and reckless nature would allow; and that was not enough.

At last, late in the afternoon after a great hubbub over wraps, the family was packed into sleighs to drive through the winter dusk down the avenue of Norway spruce and through the iron grill into the sordid streets lined with humble houses. For by the time Johnny was old enough to register impressions of the life about him the mills and factories had already come to the marshes and Trefusis' Castle and the park around it stood isolated from the respectable part of Town. The railroad passed just beyond the iron fence, and the smoke and soot of scores of chimneys drifted over the garden. All around it were the houses of the mill-workers, abandoned respectable houses belonging to another day, used now as rookeries and falling into ruin, or cheap new dwellings surrounded by patches of yellow clay. Leaving the park, that bleak area always gave Johnny an odd, indescribable sensation of uneasiness and fear. The two warring elements, the old and the new, sat embattled side by side. Through the pretentious wrought-iron gateway, the eighteenth century looked out upon the twentieth. Indeed, by the time Johnny was ten years old the new had entirely surrounded the Strawberry Hill Gothic house, so that it was in a state of siege. But Great-aunt Jane refused to surrender. This was her house and in it she would stay until she died.

But the presence of the mills and the sordid houses and the looks of the dark alien faces peering from windows as the sleighs drove over the dirty snow did nothing to make the New Year's Day any gayer.

-ᴏ-

Great-uncle Jacob, who married the daughter of the banker, begot nine children by his first wife before she died. She must have been a woman of small personality or perhaps, due to the arrival of nine children in twelve years, she had neither the time nor the energy to assert herself, for no legend of her survived in the family and Johnny never heard her spoken of, so that he grew up with a vague impression that the children of Great-uncle Jacob had been generated spontaneously. Most of her offspring seemed to have inherited a little of her talent for obscurity. They were sober, earnest, and quiet, good citizens in an inconspicuous fashion, rather like plump birds whose protective coloring made them indistinguishable from their background. But in that great, sprawling family one needed eccentricities and extravagance of character in order to be noticed at all, and Uncle Jacob's children seemed the proper children of a banker's daughter, conservative and sound and perfectly unexceptional. To Johnny they never quite seemed to belong to his family, and he had to pinch himself and think twice before he recognized Josephine and Andrew, Harry and Margaret, and all the others and their children as his own cousins. They appeared at family funerals and weddings and then retired again into the solid respectable houses which they occupied.

Great-uncle Jacob was not only blessed in his first wife by an abundance of children, but by a fortune, as well, which permitted him to live in a large brick house with a fanlight and a white marble stoop near the center of the Town, and to keep horses and continue experimenting with his fantastic inventions. He did not, as the Colonel feared, go over to bankers and the Hamiltonian party after his marriage. Indeed, neither politics nor banking interested him at all, and after a few years of pretense at working in his father-in-law's banking-house he gave it up altogether and abandoned himself simply to the delights of living.

Like his blind sister Esther, he took what Jamie, the good citizen, considered "a light view of life. He had a great deal of the terrifying Mrs. Widcome's spirit of mockery, but very little of the gall with which it was sometimes mingled. He had an airy, fantastic spirit which marked him as the child of the giddy Susan, and an overwhelming curiosity and interest in everything in life—the weather, his children, the affairs of his neighbors, the stray dog in the street and the color of the eyes of a new-born baby. Despite the fact that for half his life he never worked at anything, his days were crowded, and no day was ever long enough to encompass all the delights that were to be explored. He inherited all the enormous curiosity of the Colonel without any of the Colonel's capacity for intellectual organization. In its place, he had the frivolity of his mother Susan, with none of her vanity. He had no sense of responsibility, and when his first wife died, he even turned over his accounts and the housekeeping to the offspring who were still children. Perhaps his own giddiness made them sober, for he always remained more their child than their father. Even them he looked upon, I think, as acts of God for which he was duly thankful to nature for having made the task of begetting them a perfectly pleasant affair.

Yet these sober children were far more fortunate in their father than most children, for his faults were charming, human, and comical and more delightful than the virtues of duller parents. Of all the Colonel's children, the spirit of the eighteenth century, gay, interested, earnest, and mocking, survived purely in him alone. All the others, even Great-aunt Jane, were tainted by the sober earnestness of the nineteenth.

Yet he was in himself a link with the twentieth, for in the clever, superficial brain were born a half-dozen contributions to the age of the machine. If genius follows that dullest of definitions—an infinite capacity for taking pains—then Great-uncle Jacob had none of the quality which characterized earnest and impassioned inventors like Edison. He did not plod. His inventions came as inspirations. And he was no business man. He was invariably swindled out of all the profits—for his bicycle brake, his cash-carrier, his primitive elevator, his patent rocker; yet I think he was entertained even by the intricacies of the swindling process of which he himself was the victim. He was, altogether, a horrible example of another adage—that money will take care of itself and that the first thing in life is to enjoy it.

Fifty years after his death there still stood in the woods on the Farm a great machine of cast iron with which Great-uncle Jacob planned to solve the problem of perpetual motion. It was placed there with the greatest secrecy one summer day before an audience of three—old Jamie, Dr. Trefusis, and the inventor himself. Before starting the machine Great-uncle Jacob warned Jamie and the Doctor to select each one a solid oak as protection, for once the machine was started, he warned them, it would go faster and faster until it flew to pieces. Cautiously they peered out from behind their trees while Great-uncle Jacob approached the machine in a gingerly way and set it in motion with a few turns of a crank. Then he too ran for shelter, and while the three men watched, the governor of the machine turned more and more slowly until at last it stopped.

Again and again Great-uncle Jacob started it, each time with less
caution and more contempt, and again and again it revolved slowly to a dead stop. When at last he felt he had given it a fair trial he
shouted, "Come on out boys; the damned thing is a fake!"

Late in life he married a second time, a lady far more sprightly
than his first wife. She was large and plain, with great intelligence
and cultivation and a Rabelaisian sense of humor; and Great-uncle
Jacob, who never took much notice of the banker's daughter, could
go nowhere without her. They never had any children, but she
made a good stepmother to Jacob's large family, who found her
more entertaining than their own mother had ever been. The two
of them knew everyone in the county, because there was no one,
however dull or horrible, who failed to arouse curiosity and interest in the hearts of Jacob and Malvina. Sometimes their speech and
their jokes scandalized more sober and respectable members of
society, but they had no enemies, and as they grew older most people in the county came to refer to them behind their backs, and
with a kindly respect, as "Jacob and Malvina" as if, they, like "Ben
and Harry," were a music-hall team. Together in a trap behind two
horses they explored the whole county, stopping wherever fancy
dictated for dinner, and always they were welcome. He had qualities and a gift for friendship which would have been golden treasure to any politician, but with them went none of the politician's
insincerity nor the suspicions which the antics of the politician
aroused in the hearts of intelligent men and women. Everybody in
the county knew that Jacob MacDougal had no ambitions and
wanted nothing of them but their friendship and a good time. In
that sober country and that serious community he was a waster all
his life, careless and good-humored and irresponsible, and he
should have brought down upon his head the condemnation and
contempt of the world in which he lived, but somehow he did not.
People respected him without quite knowing why. He was a relief
to a dull life where the only other variations for most citizens were
camp meetings and torchlight processions.

Among the friends of Jacob and Malvina was a queer old
woman with the lovely name of Anne Condon, who lived on the
edge of the highroad within sight of the Colonel's Farm. When

Jacob was thirty she was already an old woman. Although she was a spinster and unprotected, she demanded of her nephew on whose land she lived, a home of her own, and he gave her a little house of two rooms where she lived surrounded by goats and rabbits, chickens, three or four mongrel dogs, and a cow. She had come from Lancashire as a girl and always spoke with a Lancashire accent which to half the county was a foreign tongue. By some of the ignorant and superstitious she was regarded as a witch, but she must have been a very strange witch, for, excepting her appearance, there was nothing in the least sinister about her. On the contrary, she was a clown and had a broad, low sense of humor. In her younger days when doctors were scarce she had been a midwife and she knew all sorts of strange remedies for rheumatism and brain fever, congestion and fever and ague. In her ragged garden she grew dozens of herbs for the concoction of her brews—plants with lovely names like hyssop and rampion, thyme and marjoram.

She shared Great-uncle Jacob's sense of the absurd and the ridiculous, and it formed a bond which bound together an old woman and a young man in a preposterous friendship.

In her little house she used to sit and watch for the passing of Great-uncle Jacob along the Onara Turnpike on his way to the Farm, and when she saw his wagonette and black horses coming over the distant hills she quickly donned her best clothes, scrambled down the high bank covered with sweet clover, and was waiting by the roadside when he arrived. They had an absurd game, begun by accident, which went on endlessly. Across the sides of the wagonette, behind the driver's seat, Uncle Jacob placed a fitted board which he used when there were more passengers than the wagonette could hold properly. On this Anne Condon, in her best clothes and bonnet, would seat herself with great dignity, never smiling or giving any sign of being aware of what was to follow. Then cracking the whip, Jacob would set off at full speed up the road as if to show her how fine his horses were (he always drove at full speed as if going to a fire). The board seat was insecure at best, and with the jolting of the swiftly-moving wagonette it sometimes slipped its fastenings and gave way, depositing Anne Condon in her best clothes unceremoniously upon the floor. The game consisted of seeing whether Anne

Condon could keep her seat or whether Great-uncle Jacob could succeed by fast driving and seeking the worst places in the road in jolting her to the floor. She always hailed him, whether he was bound toward the Farm or toward the Town.

At the Farm she was always welcome, for when she and Jacob arrived together an epidemic of practical jokes broke out at once, jokes which the sober Jamie did his best to appreciate and enjoy. They always knew, on the arrival of Anne Condon, by the state of her clothes and the position of her bonnet, whether she had won or lost the game. On the way to the Farm she nearly always lost, for locust roots in the bumpity lane and the planks of the bridge over the brook provided Herculean jolts which Great-uncle Jacob unfairly took at full speed. Usually old Anne arrived at the top of the hill laughing, clinging wildly to the sides of the wagonette, and attempting to adjust her bonnet at the same time. The only visits she ever made, save as an herb doctor and midwife, were to the Farm with Uncle Jacob. She must have been an exceedingly limber old lady, for when she played her rough-and-tumble game she was well past sixty and she never appeared to suffer any ill effects. She swore freely and magnificently with a fine vocabulary which came out of eighteenth-century Lancashire.

One day Great-uncle Jacob passed the little hut and Anne Condon did not appear. On his way back to the Town she still did not appear, and outside the door her great mongrel sheepdog sat on his haunches, his nose in the air, howling. Great-uncle Jacob found her inside, lying on her bed. She had died in her sleep. Fifty years later her little house, abandoned since her death, still stood on the high bank covered with sweet clover and rugosa roses. It slowly fell into bits and returned to the earth, for no one ever took the trouble to pull it down. Long afterward, when the Town had become the City and the fields of Job Condon's farm had been broken up by a real estate allotment, there were still traces of an old garden lost among weeds and rubbish—patches of periwinkle, wild fennel, and here and there an herb, gone wild, and some scraggly roses.

BETWEEN TWO WORLDS

WHEN JOHNNY WAS BORN THE TOWN WAS NO LONGER A VILLAGE and not yet a city. It lay somewhere between in that dishevelled, disorganized period of growth where hovels stood side by side with pretentious new buildings and empty building lots littered with rubbish and weeds spread their desolation beside the newly built palaces of merchants and manufacturers. It was the desolation of a great prosperity when change and decay ran side by side, the new arose from the ruins of the old and there was no time for clearing away the debris of progress.

The square which Jamie saw when he looked out of the window of the Weiler House in 1852 had gone the way of the log houses set in the clearing in the forest. Where the old brick courthouse with its seemly white columns once stood there was a new one, vast, ugly, and monstrous, with a cheap tin cupola surmounted by a figure of Justice, which the Town knew cynically was worth $10,000 and had cost five hundred thousand. The old trees still filled the center of the square, but in their shade rose a fountain surmounted by the cast iron figure of a soldier in the uniform of the Union Army. At one corner of the square, opposite the new courthouse, stood the old Presbyterian church, long since abandoned, its auditorium occupied by a bustling firm of plumbers, its basement by the courthouse saloon. On the third side stood the bright new building which housed Bentham Brothers' Department Store, built on the site of Silas Bentham's "Great Bazaar. Household Goods, Hardware and Miscellany." The old houses built in the style of Salem or Germantown had long since vanished, and in place of their marble stoops and oriel windows there were rows of shops and banks and the mosque-like structure which sheltered the Pentland *Daily Gazette*. The old charm and beauty of the square had gone and the bright newness of a modern square had not yet come to take its place. The whole façade was an odd hodge-podge of architectural styles and building materials, ranging from the solid simplicity of the disemboweled old church to the rantings in stone of the rococo courthouse. Farmers still weighed their hay on the scales before the courthouse door and the hitching-rails still surrounded the little park. Sometimes in the big space before the courthouse a carnival company raised its tents and a high diver regarded the figure of Justice face to face before plunging into the tank below. Lions howled, and once a female leopard-tamer was mauled for the benefit of the charity fund of the Reindeers' Lodge.

In the middle of one side of the square there was still a building called the Weiler House, the third generation descended from the log cabin in which the Colonel had spent his first night in the new country. It was built of soot-stained yellow brick, with an ugly roof and a façade designed and ornamented in the Byzantine manner with enormous plate-glass windows. The proprietor was the grandson of the first Weiler, but he was as different from the first innkeeper as the new hotel was different from Weiler's Tavern. The rooms of the new hotel were uniform as to painting and decoration, and each was equipped with all sorts of modern comforts, which somehow made them less comfortable than the old rooms with their gigantic beds and feather puffs had been. The blankets were dead pancakes, and no longer did the host come to your room at night with a pan filled with coals to warm your bed, and no longer did he pass from table to table in the dining room to see that the food was as it should be. Dishes were thrown on the table by impudent waitresses, who removed them without interest or comment if they were left untouched. The Weiler House had a poolroom and cigar store on one side, and it was the mecca of traveling salesmen in that part of the state. In the evening they sat on the piazza, smoking cheap cigars and telling dirty stories and making comments on the women who passed along the sidewalks. There was a word for them. "Drummers" were a part of the changing pattern and they fitted admirably into the strange, muddled, tasteless façade of the square. They were the small vulgar forerunners of the New Day that was dawning when they would no longer be "drummers," but high-powered salesmen. The time was not far off when they would be regarded as the heroes of a new crusade whose goal was to sell things to people who did not want them and could never pay for them.

No longer did the presence of the farmers dominate the square. Their hay wagons still stood in line before the courthouse, and on Saturday nights their horses and "rigs" were still tied at the hitching rails while the women shopped and the men drank beer in the courthouse saloon, but they were lost now among the citizens of the Town and among the dark people who came up out of the Flats on Saturday nights to stare in the shop windows. The dark people were strangers and spoke an alien tongue. The men had ferocious black mustachios and sometimes their faces were blackened by soot and smoke. And the women wore dozens of petticoats and on Saturday nights wore bright shawls over their heads. They brought a sinister brightness with them into a country which had never known multiple petticoats and brilliant shawls. They were the first peasants to come into that world, but they no longer tilled the earth; they worked in the swarming factories and mills which had covered the marshes.

The dark people and the "drummers" and the mills were all a part of the New Day. No one in the Town, save Great-aunt Jane, any longer spoke of the marshes or even of the great swamp, for the marshes had long since been drained and Toby's Run induced to follow a straight and orderly channel, save in the spring of the year, when it suddenly went wild and flooded the cellars of the old houses in the lower streets, carrying garbage and sewage everywhere. The brook in which the Delaware chief had found a drunken death was now only an open sewer. The marshes had gone and the Flats had taken their place. No longer did Great-aunt Jane sit isolated in Trefusis' Castle mocking those who speculated in real estate and boomed the Town. In the end they had won and the evidence of their victory lay all about her. She might have the cast iron statues whitewashed once a week, but they were still streaked with soot. The trees of the park, suffocated by smoke, had begun to die, and sometimes at Trefusis' Castle one did not see the sun until long after noon.

In the upper part of the Town, along Elm Street and Maple Avenue, the wooden sidewalks were gone and the trees planted long ago by homesick New Englanders were enormous and made great tunnels of shade and the Virginia creeper and ampelopsis had climbed to the top of the tall spire on the Congregational church. Near the center of the Town the old New England houses still stood, set back a little from the street, but the trees were no longer saplings and the lilacs and syringas hid the windows of the first floor. Those houses had a look of having been there forever, and to Johnny it seemed that nothing could possibly be older than their cold, rather grim façades, nothing unless it was Trefusis' Castle. And the people who lived in them seemed all to be old women who were widows. Sometimes they came to call on your mother, sometimes you encountered them opening the front gates of their dooryards, solid, respectable, prosperous, clad in durable black or purple, living lives in which there was never any change. They were the daughters and the widows of the first men who came into the new country and prospered. They were the relics of the first bankers, and lawyers, and shopkeepers. In their generations all the men seemed to die soon after middle age, but the women went on forever.

A mile from the square, in a part of the Town which had been open country in the seventies stood the only "property" which rivaled in size and splendor the house of Dr. Trefusis. It stood in the middle of a park, with stables and outbuildings and a crescent-shaped avenue bordered by buckeye trees. But it had neither quaintness nor beauty nor charm. It was built during the Grant administration and, like it, was uncompromisingly ugly. Johnny's grandfather and his father always asserted that it was built from the profits made during the looting of New Orleans. How else, they asked, could such a house have been built by a man who began his career a little while before as a penniless lawyer? Why should he have been any different from the other looting friends of Grant's? Why should he, too, not have shared in the profits of the Republican Party during the Reconstruction? Why should he alone have escaped unscathed from friendship with scoundrels like Jay Gould and Jim Fiske and Old Drew and Oakes Ames?

But Old Jamie was a Mugwump and Johnny's father was a Democrat and they may have been prejudiced.

It was a big square house with a square cupola and a heavy bracketed piazza and a vast lawn ornamented with iron dogs and deer, each surrounded in summer by a hard bed of brilliant begonias or geraniums or salvias. The house was painted an ugly chocolate brown, and from the street the whole place seemed done in hard colors, like a bad oleograph. For some reason even the trees and grass appeared to be an unnatural, hard emerald green. Centuries could not have endowed the place with quaintness or charm. It was uncompromisingly ugly, and although it might stand for centuries, no one could imagine it having ever been occupied by anyone more romantic than pigeon-breasted "statesmen" wearing frock-coats and beards. It belonged to the period of the Reconstruction and was forever stamped by it.

The house belonged to the brother of William Tecumseh Sherman, whose soldiers burned and looted their way through the South to the sea. The owner lived always in Washington, and his whole life was spent in politics. He was responsible for a great many of the banking laws passed during the eighties and the nineties, and he knew how to promote tariffs which helped overgrown "infant industries." He made a great fortune, but when he died he left nothing to the Town which he had called his home. For a long time after his death the gaunt ugly house remained, an empty and pompous eyesore, but when at last it was pulled down and the estate broken up into building lots, all trace of John Sherman and John Sherman's Place vanished from the Town which all his life he had used as a political convenience. There were some in the Town who sarcastically regarded the disappearance of the chocolate brown house as regrettable, for it would have made a splendid monument, in all its tasteless and pretentious ugliness, to the era out of which it was born. Over it hung the shadow of men like Gould and Fiske, Drew and "public-be-damned" Vanderbilt, who had contempt for the common people whose judgment Jamie and the Colonel honored, and believed that the country should be ruled by men who knew how to make money.

When Johnny was a small boy the Sherman Place still existed and the house was inhabited by an ill-tempered caretaker and his wife, whose only diversion was the pursuit of small boys who climbed the fences to steal the grapes and apples and pears that grew on John Sherman's land. For Johnny the raids held a special excitement because he was never quite sure that he might not be pursued by the devil himself. Out of all the fierce political arguments he had overheard he had come to believe that John Sherman and the devil were one and the same.

Beyond the Sherman Place there were no old houses and the street belonged to the New Era. The houses stood side by side, each surrounded by a big lawn planted with shrubs and sapling trees, for few of the houses were more than a dozen years old. There were turreted castles and Gothic fortresses and moated granges made of granite and sandstone, each surrounded not by fields and forest and mountains, but by a tiny strip of carefully watered lawn, the bastard offspring of strange matings of styles which took place in the brains of the architects of the day.

Unlike the worn, dignified old houses near the center of the Town and the rambling old white house at the Farm which had an air of belonging to the earth itself, they were boastful houses conceived by childish minds and executed in children's blocks. They made a fantastic collection in which Tudor and Byzantine ornamentation bedecked the same doorways, and vast sheets of plate glass destroyed all privacy and revealed the inmates like goldfish in a bowl. Plate glass was a sign of prestige. It was expensive, and the larger the windows the more prosperous the inhabitant of the house. One or two of the houses—the least offensive of all—were born of no style whatever, but were simply the efforts of small-town architects to create something which had never existed before—phantasmagorias of gables and pinions, oriels and turrets, strange openings and fantastic doorways, all massed in a frozen agitation. These new houses were built of coal and railroads, politics and public contracts, like that which set the absurd five-hundred-thousand-dollar tin gazebo atop the monstrous courthouse on the square. Just as the John Sherman Place was a monument to the Reconstruction, so were most of these houses monuments to the era of McKinley and Hanna, Aldrich and Foraker. The strange mongrel fortresses were the strongholds of men who lived by the faith that any man was a fool not to make as much money as possible, no matter how he made it. In them dwelt a band of men who sought to become the new aristocracy of the country, men like Bentham, the peddler, who carried his background, his tradition, his responsibilities, his ideals in a pack. Mostly they were common, undistinguished men, differing from their fellows only in their shrewdness, which all too often slipped over the borderland into the realm of the unscrupulous and the criminal—the strange fruit of the brilliant *arriviste* Hamilton's doctrine of privilege in a democracy.

On the corner of the street opposite the Sherman Place stood the turreted red sandstone palazzo of Senator Bentham, the grandson of the peddler. It had vast sheets of plate glass which were the largest in the Town and a vast Byzantine piazza ornamented with rubber plants and Aspidistras. He still owned the dry goods store which had descended from "Bentham's Great Bazaar. Household Goods, Hardware and Miscellany," but he allowed others to run it and scarcely ever entered its doors. He had a business much greater than that. It was politics. He could deliver votes and bully lawmakers, and he came more and more to live in Washington, where he had a house with even bigger windows of plate glass. He was descended from those men who long ago met in Essex County to lay the foundations of New England fortunes by swindling the veterans of the Revolution out of their rewards.

⊷

The house where Johnny was born stood on the edge of the Sherman Place. It was built in the eighties and had very little of beauty about it. It occupied the center of a town lot seventy-five feet wide and a hundred feet long, raised above the level of the street on a bank six or seven feet high. It was tall and narrow and had a slate roof. Once it had been painted a gaudy yellow and white which gave it a kind of bedizened gaiety like an ugly woman too much painted, but by the time Johnny was born it was slate gray because that was a color which did not show the ravages of the soot which sometimes drifted from the Flats into the "decent" part of Town. For ornamentation it had a great deal of bracketing and tiny gables growing at random out of the steep roof. Like the house of John Sherman, no amount of age could have made it any lovelier.

The only softening influences were the masses of clematis and honeysuckle and old-fashioned roses called Baltimore Belles which covered much of the offensive jig-saw work and bound it to the earth. The roses grew in clusters and were pinkish white, with a musky odor, and the buds were sometimes eaten both by birds and children. The lot was divided by the house into a front and a back yard, and at one side there was a carriage drive which led to the stables, which were happily painted red. The front porch was so overgrown with a tangle of flowering vines that one could sit there all day watching the passersby without ever being seen. The back porch was partly closed in, and in hot weather was used as a kitchen, and beyond it there was an arbor covered with Concord and Niagara grapes which never ripened, because the children ate them all before their time.

Beyond the arbor there was a big rose garden and borders given over to flowers, and at last a vegetable garden. Here and there stood fruit trees, one of sweet cherries which, like the grapes, were never allowed to ripen. There were pears and peaches, and against the red barn a tree which bore enormous red plums. In October there always stood beneath the grape arbor a whole hogshead of sweet cider, sent in from the Farm by Jamie, to be drawn upon by Johnny's family and half the neighborhood until it had turned hard and Johnny's mother emptied into it the remains of last year's vinegar and had it put away in the cellar. Before it turned, gallons of it went down the throats of neighborhood children who at night preyed upon the hogshead armed with bits of rubber tubing.

The inside of the house should have been as ugly as the outside, but it had beauty, the kind of beauty which comes to a house which has been lived in for years by a hospitable, noisy, and happy family.

There was little in it of value, and even that little was never spared nor allowed to interfere with the enjoyment and hard living. There were many things which were monstrously ugly, not because there had been any special bad taste employed in its choice, but because the taste at the end of the nineteenth century was monstrously bad over all of Europe and America, and so a modest family in a small city in the Middle West had small chance of escaping it. Some of the furniture had been chosen by Johnny's parents, but a great deal of it was made up of wedding gifts and inheritances and odds and ends left behind from time to time by Johnny's migratory uncles and aunts. Due to their restlessness and adventures, the furniture was always in a state of flux. All of them sought to leave as much as possible with Johnny's parents in order to save storage costs, and usually there was enough furniture for a house and a family three times as large as Johnny's. In all the strange assortment there was not one piece with the grace of eighteenth century or the heavy elegance of the early nineteenth. As in the architecture of the John Sherman Place, the ugly times were reflected in the ugliness of the furniture. It was only when old Jamie came to live with the family, bringing with him the Colonel's chair and cherry bed and one or two tables, that any beautiful furniture found its way into the house.

One entered the house by a hallway from which a stairway led to the upper rooms. Beneath its curve stood a strange fat-bellied piece of furniture known as the "hall seat," which for some reason guarded all the family photographs and daguerreotypes within its abdomen. Beside it hung a mirror left behind permanently by one of the wandering aunts who found its cumbersome gold-and-black curlicues too fragile to stand the rigors of her endless travels.

On the right of the hall was the parlor, a room which, contrary to all custom of the time and the country, was in constant use, due, I think, to the fact that there were always so many people in the house that there was an overflow from the other rooms. It had a figured green Axminster carpet and elegant dark-red wall paper heavily embossed with a design in gold. But the furniture achieved perhaps the greatest peak of elegance known to the civilized world. It was intensely individualistic, the conception of some workman

who held all styles and periods in indiscriminate admiration and
sought to combine the more elegant points of all of them into one
great masterwork. It was a mahogany "suite" and the chairs had the
appearance of very fat elderly women suffering from arthritis who
had tiny feet and ankles of which they were excessively proud. The
most agitated rococo in the same room with those chairs would
have seemed of a delicate and classic purity. There was a mantel-
piece in golden oak with a mirror above and a gas grate below in
which the flames licked a waterfall of asbestos and gave off phos-
phorescent colors. And in one corner there was a huge engraving
in a wide red plush frame (a wedding gift) of a young woman in
nondescript peasant's costume in the foreground resting a jug of
water on a stile. In the distance appeared the towers and spires of
a town which greatly resembled Oxford. The picture was called "A
Dream of the Future," although what the title meant Johnny had
no idea. The problem tormented him for years, and long after the
house had been sold and the picture had disappeared he would
wake up in the night and suddenly remember it and puzzle over
what the title could possibly have meant.

At the end of the hall was the dining room, which was furnished
in a gold oak suite very nearly as eccentric as the parlor chairs. It
had yellow wall paper, and at the top of the wall was pasted a frieze
of Japanese irises which had been cut from a horticultural catalogue left behind by the husband of Aunt Bertha, who for a brief
period had worked for a company of bulb and seed growers. The
irises were twice their natural size and exquisitely painted in water-
color on rice paper by some Japanese craftsman. They were cut out
and pasted on the wall by Johnny's older sister in a sudden burst of
creative expression, and they were always a source of uneasiness to
Johnny's mother, who knew their value and feared that their right-
ful owner might some day track them down and claim them. The
dining room had an air of gaiety about it, due, I think, to the fact
that it had a bow window and an open fireplace which gave it a
charm the other more "modern" rooms never achieved.

The living room was a big worn room which adjoined the dining room, and in it, closed in a vast bookcase, were all the books
upon which Johnny and his brother and sister fed as children. They
ranged in rows—all the writings of Dickens and Thackeray, George

Eliot and Walter Scott, Fenimore Cooper and Trollope. All the solid Victorians were there, each with his great shelf of achievement, the joy and wonder of childhood and early adolescence. And there was Ridpath's *History of the World* with the most fascinating pictures of life in prehistoric times, "The Battle of Marathon" and "The Baptism of Clovis," and four immensely heavy volumes profusely illustrated called *Characters from Fiction, Poetry and the Drama.* This was a kind of encyclopedia of literary characters, and its delights were inexhaustible, if somewhat patchy. It, too, had wonderful pictures. There was "Boadicea and Her Daughters" and "Meg Merriles Before Her Cave" and "Jane Shore Driven from London."

It was a singularly comfortable room, worn and cheerful, with a "secretary" at which Johnny's father, horribly bored, sometimes went vaguely over his accounts, and at which his mother was forever writing letters to her wandering sisters and brothers. Off it there was a big room with a bow window and a huge tin bathtub, so large that a child could swim in it. When Johnny was ten years old, a modern bathroom was installed upstairs and the old bathroom was converted into an alcove off the living room and ornamented by innumerable copies of Gibson pictures made and offered by an admirer to Johnny's older sister.

But the kitchen was the most important room in the house. In it were cooked the puddings, the pies, the cakes, the waffles, and the pancakes which filled the table meal after meal. The *cuisine* was a purely traditional one, preserved and carried on through generations. Because Johnny's mother had lived for years in the same house with her mother-in-law she knew all the dishes which had come down from Elvira van Essen, as well as all those which she knew as the child of one of the Colonel's daughters. With each generation and each marriage new recipes had been added to those already established, and there were many, too, which came into the family through the Negroes who from the days of the Underground Railroad had always been friendly with the family of old Jamie Ferguson.

So there were dishes which had come remotely from Holland and the Rhine country, from Scotland and Shropshire, from Maryland and New England and the far South. Some of them were so special that after Johnny left home he never again encountered them.

Johnny's mother was an excellent cook and, like all good cooks, had a passion for the- art. It was her greatest means of expression. She came of a family which had always been accustomed only to the best of fowls and finest of cuts and the most succulent of vegetables and fruits, for they came from the family's own barnyards and gardens and orchards. In the richness of the bounty, only the best parts of the sheep and pig and beef were eaten. The rest was sold and the "innards" were considered worthy only of the dogs. It was a family in which the tradition persisted that in hard times one might wear shabby clothes in a pinch, but one could never go without good food. In the kitchen, even at the most precarious financial moments which in Johnny's family came all too often, there was never any economy.

At prosperous moments, when it was possible to have a servant or two, Johnny's mother concocted the more important dishes and surveyed the cooking of the others. When there were no servants, she did it all herself. In her kitchen there was always a crock filled with cookies to be raided by the children who came to play in the back yard, and there were always slices of pie and cake which might be stolen between meals. In the kitchen took place the great family rite of making Christmas candy, which must have been German in origin and came down from the Rhineland country through the van Essens. It was a business which continued for days before Christmas, for candy had to be made not only for the whole of a large family, but for friends as well. Most of the recipes had been handed down for generations, and although from time to time experiments were made, the new candies were almost always rejected in the end. A good many of them had as ingredients the hickory nuts and black walnuts of the countryside, which the children gathered on brilliant October afternoons on long excursions across country.

Somehow, perhaps from out of the old wilderness tradition, wild nuts were never looked upon as private property in the county. Few farmers protested at trespassers who came to gather nuts. If the owner objected, he was regarded as cranky and eccentric. At the Farm there was never any question of driving away strangers who came to gather nuts and mushrooms unless they came too near to the farmhouse and violated the privacy which old Jamie cherished. It was only when the dark people came to the Flats that the old generosity came to end, for with them the manners changed. Fences were cut, songbirds were shot, and sometimes even sheep and calves. And when one by one the old farms began to pass into the hands of Czech and Silesian peasants, every nut and mushroom was gathered and sent off to market, and the old expeditions came to an end forever.

Upstairs in the house where Johnny was born there were a half-dozen rooms. One belonged to his parents and one to his sister and one to his brother and himself. There was the "spare room" and the "sewing room"—a big room at the back of the house which was a fine place to play on rainy days. Opposite it there was a smaller room which was occupied by a servant during periods of prosperity, and when the day of servants passed altogether, it was occupied by Johnny's Grandfather Willingdon.

But of all the house the attic and the cellar were the parts full of enchantment for the children. The house was gabled, and each gable made a nook in the roof of the attic which might be used as a wigwam or a fortress. And the attic was full of old trunks and discarded mattresses and bits of old clothing which could be used for dressing up. It was a dark place and there were corners where the mice scuttered about which were full of mystery and horror. In the middle of it there was a vast square tank of zinc used as a reservoir for rain water and when anyone downstairs turned a tap the tank gave out sinister gurgling sounds which seemed mysterious and supernatural. If one stood on an old trunk one could peer over the edge into black water which seemed as bottomless as the subterranean pits of *Pelleas and Mélisande*.

Paradoxically, there was nothing dark or sinister about the cellar. In winter and in bad weather the children gathered there after school. It was divided into two parts by a stone wall and on one side was the furnace room, and on the other the cold room where meats and vegetables and canned fruit were kept. The cold room was a dark, damp place with a little trench along the walls, which was nearly always full of water which seeped in from a spring long ago buried as the Town had spread out over the countryside. There were great bins filled with potatoes and Hubbard squash and apples, and from the beams hung hams and flitches of bacon which had been cured according to family recipes in old Jamie's smokehouse at the Farm. In the center stood an instrument of torture and boredom known as "the pump." It forced the rain water from the cistern in the garden to the tank in the attic, and when Johnny and his brother grew old enough it was their task to keep the tank filled. This meant pumping half an hour at least four times a week, and a hatred for the pump darkened all their childhood.

The furnace room was quite a different place, warm, dry, and friendly. In it there was a tool chest and a workbench and great boxes and bags of butternuts and hickory nuts and black walnuts which the children cracked with hammers from the tool chest and ate all during the long winters. There was always a supply of fresh, clean pine wood put in by Mr. Willingdon, and from this the boys fashioned all sorts of toys. Johnny's own products were invariably ships—rowboats, sailing boats, liners, and battleships. Even as a child there was in him a desire to escape the Town and see the world, and somehow the ships gave him satisfaction. Launched in a pool or in a gutter or even in the vast zinc bathtub, they magically grew into full size. The gutter became a vast river and the bathtub a shoreless sea.

In the furnace room the dogs had a corner to themselves behind the clumsy hot-air furnace where it was always warm. There was a long procession of them. Sometimes there were three or four and never were there less than two. There were two collies and a bulldog, a hound, and a nondescript animal called Tuck. None of them ever knew leash or muzzle. They ran free wherever they chose over all the Town, but almost always they stayed in the company of the neighborhood children, taking part in all the games, barking and wagging their tails, going on swimming expeditions and on those long, aimless, rambling excursions which took place in spring and autumn up and down hill across country. One or two of them came to tragic ends. Two were poisoned and one, a puppy, was run over by Stuhldreher's delivery wagon. Most of them died quietly of old age, but not the least of them was ever forgotten. There was Schwartz and Laddie, Budge and Champ, Dash and Wilfred (named after a remote family cousin whom he resembled). Each guarded forever, long after his death, his own charm and individuality, and no other dog ever took the place even of Tuck, the shabbiest and worst bred of the lot, who looked like an overgrown beagle, but had long hair like a collie.

⊙

Beyond the Sherman Place there was an expanse of land where once there had been farms, but by the time Johnny was born the land had long since been bought up by speculators and turned into building lots. But the boom had come too soon and the whole expanse, crisscrossed by weed-grown streets, had become wasteland. Here and there among the goldenrod and the elderberry bushes and the burdock were remnants of old orchards or an old brick farmhouse or the new modest wooden house of a shopkeeper. On one side of the road which led through the expanse toward the Farm rich men from the fantastic houses on Elm Street and Maple Avenue were constructing a golf course, one of the first in all that part of the country. It was a modest affair, but in a curious way it was linked with the turreted houses. Their owners had begun by wanting to live grandly. The golf course was the next step. They wanted to learn how to play as gentlemen and rich men should do. Besides, it was a good investment. It carried implications of wealth and credit and leisure.

Beyond the wasteland and the golf course were the parks. There were South Park and Middle Park and Casino Park, and they came into existence through the efforts of old General Vandervelde, who fought for them at a time when booming cities were disposed to think more of profits than of spending money on parks. Actually they were three sections of the original forest, with streams of water running through them. They were filled with oak and beech and maple trees, and in spring and early summer the earth beneath the trees was covered with spring beauties and violets and wood anemones.

In those days there were no automobiles, and on a hot summer night when the corn grew and ripened in the damp tropical heat it was the custom to harness the horses and drive out to the parks.

Under the great trees there were tables and benches, and on some nights all of them were filled with families who had come to spend the long summer twilight in the open air. There were always plenty of children with whom you might play prisoner's-base and hide-and-seek. Sometimes you were allowed to play late, and then sometimes in the darkness you came across couples lying in the grass and the sight filled you with awe for something you did not understand.

No one ever picnicked in Middle Park where the monument to Johnny Appleseed raised its modest obelisk, and there was always an exciting choice between South Park and Casino Park. South Park had its own special and undefiled rustic charm, but as one grew older its sylvan attractions faded before the more worldly glory of Casino Park. Here there was a casino—a rambling wooden building with a theater upstairs and a huge ice cream parlor below. And close at hand there was a ferris wheel and a scenic railway and a swimming pool. In those days the Town was still small enough for one to know almost everyone who frequented Casino Park. In the theater there was always a stock company which performed most of the old-fashioned plays and some of the newer melodramas. One could see "East Lynne" and "Camille," "The Adventuress," and a strange Biblical piece called "Salome" which had nothing to do with the preciosities of Oscar Wilde and was regarded as a "spectacle."

The actors lived in cheap boardinghouses in the Town and one had the added glamour of knowing them by sight and seeing them both in real life and on the stage. Most of them were past their prime or at least past the age when all save themselves knew there was no longer any hope of playing on Broadway. They were a queer battered crew, rather like those immortal troupers, the Crummles. As a child Johnny had felt awe and affection for them, and as he grew older the awe lessened but the affection increased. There was always a "juvenile" well past forty who on the street appeared to be an old man, but on the stage became miraculously rejuvenated by thick applications of "hero flush," and there was an *ingénue*, likewise rather battered by her long experience with life, who invariably had the most astonishing peroxide golden hair and wore high buttoned shoes of *glacé* kid. And there was the "heavy man" and the "heavy woman" and the "character man" and the "character woman," who had already known long, rich careers as juvenile and *ingénues*. By the time they attained character parts they appeared older than God.

At the first performance of the spectacle "Salome" the *ingénue*, perhaps having read of Mary Garden, created a scandal by doing "The Dance of the Seven Veils." Johnny was taken to the performance as a treat by Great-aunt Jane, who believed the piece to be a kind of religious mystery, and as such indeed it had been advertised. No hint of the dance had been given out until the program was distributed among the audience. In it there appeared the legend, "The Dance of the Seven Veils will be danced by Miss Lilli de Lisle, who created the role of Salome at the first world performance in the Newark (N.J.) Opera House." Newark, I suppose, was as near as they dared to aspire to Broadway. One by one Miss Lilli de Lisle cast aside the seven veils, appearing at the end clad in a flesh-pink union suit over which she wore a kind of corset cover ornamented with passementerie and a long skirt made of fringe. After letters of protest appeared in the local papers and the subject was mentioned by the Baptist preacher, the dance was suppressed by a management eager to preserve the reputation of the casino as "a family theater."

But Great-aunt Jane was indignant over the protests. To Johnny's mother she said, "Why, she showed nothing at all, not even a pimple. At her age she couldn't afford to show anything. I could have done as well myself." And for days Johnny was haunted by a vision of Great-aunt Jane clad in a pink union suit with a corset cover of passementerie.

There were no picture-houses and the Casino Stock Company did a thriving business. The best seats cost thirty-five cents, and the poorest but ten. The sides of the theater had enormous shutters which opened outward, thus permitting you to sit in the open air on those hot, still Middle-Western nights. But this form of ventilation had one great disadvantage. It lay in the fact that the tracks of the Baltimore and Ohio railroad ran past the casino at a distance of less than a hundred yards, and when a long freight train groaned and snorted up the long hill, all action and dialogue had to be suspended, so that on the stage one had the effect of a moving picture suddenly arrested. One night in the course of a melodrama the evening freight chose to arrive at a moment during the big scene of the play when the "heavy," having been double-crossed by the "heavy woman," was throttling her. She lay across a sofa with her head toward the audience, her henna-mahogany hair flowing loose, while the villain knelt on her stomach, choking her. The "heavy" had gotten "into the part," and rather than spoil his effect by suspending the action he continued throttling her until the train had passed. It was a long freight train and he must have shaken her for fifteen minutes, his face streaming with perspiration (for she was heavy not only in her art, but in her physique) before he was able to toss her aside, exhausted and black and blue, with the cry, "Never cross my path again unless you want a worse fate"—something which at that moment it would have been difficult to imagine.

But to a small boy none of this seemed ridiculous and to a small nineteenth-century romantic like Johnny who all his life found glamour and charm in any actor no matter how bad he was, the "heavy" might have gone on strangling the "heavy woman" while all the freight trains in America groaned up the long hill, and the scene could never have been ridiculous.

But, alas! there was in the family of old Jamie and Johnny's mother a shadowy Calvinist distrust of the stage and everything which had to do with it. They went to the theater, but they sat there uneasily, faintly suspicious of everyone from the star of the piece down to the man who sold tickets at the door of the Soldier's and Sailor's Memorial Opera House. In that family there had never been Bohemian tradition. Actors had no homes and therefore were not responsible citizens. And indeed among those who played year after year above the noise of the passing freight trains there were few for whom any case could be made against such accusations. They had not the discretion which must accompany intrigues in a smallish city. Always from the middle of the summer on there was a small crop of scandals centering about the Casino Stock Company. The character man got drunk. The juvenile and the "heavy woman" were living in sin. Usually eight or nine months after the casino had closed and the trees of the park were bare of leaves, one or two stage-struck girls who lived on the wrong side of the railroad tracks had babies by one of the troupe, and once one of the respectable families on Elm Street was shattered when the middle-aged mother conceived a passion for the man who played "The Little Minister" and eloped with him.

He was a singularly repulsive fellow, with a stomach, a big nose, and enormous calves which he displayed in silk stockings in "The Little Minister." (It was one of the plays considered pure enough for Johnny to witness.) After the elopement there was much talk in the Town and some of it Johnny overheard. Eavesdropping, he heard a middle-aged friend of his mother's say, "I can't see what she saw in him. He was too virile-looking," and from that day the word virile always meant to Johnny huge calves, a big nose, and a stomach.

Because of the family feelings toward actors they became doubly exciting to Johnny, so that if ever he encountered any of the stock company in the street he could not resist following them at a distance for blocks, sometimes even waiting outside shops until they reappeared. He did not know what he expected of them— perhaps that they would suddenly display horns and hoofs and a tail. It may have been that the fascination arose from the restlessness and hunger to see what lay beyond the borders of the Town. Actors traveled. They had no fixed homes. They had been everywhere. They knew the world.

Actors fascinated Johnny as a little boy and they never ceased to fascinate him. Much later in life he came to understand the fascination and to know that of all the professions none contained people so human, so generous, so preposterous and so lovable. The "artistes" in the poor defeated troupes which played in the casino while the freight trains passed were very like a good many of the great and successful ones. They were all geniuses and a little vain, good-natured and easy-going, egotistical and fantastic, and although most of them had no talent whatever, the theater was a living place to them and something to which they sacrificed fortune and respectability and a settled, comfortable life. It was a good ideal, but one not much understood in a world where success or defeat and even life itself was often enough a simple, uncomplicated affair of outward sexual respectability and dollars and cents. Yet those troupers were able to create something for which the stolid audience was hungry—an excitement and gaiety and glamour which was never to be found among the battlemented houses of Maple Avenue and Elm Street.

In the Town, twenty-five cents was a good deal of money for a small boy, so that going to the casino was something to be thought of twice, especially in a family which knew moments when twenty-five cents was a considerable sum; so for Johnny there was never any danger of becoming satiated with the drama. But on the nights when Johnny had no spending money or the play was considered improper, it was possible to stand outside the theater and listen to the dialogue, especially the dialogue of the most exciting parts which were either thundered or uttered in prodigious stage whispers. He would stand beside the goldfish pond littered with old newspapers and torn and empty crackerjack boxes, listening to the heroine denouncing the villain. For the rest of his life he remembered exactly how the gravel looked underfoot and how the water trickled into the pool and the spots on the mottled trunk of the old sycamore tree which rose high above the casino roof, while he stood listening to the rantings of the villain hurrying to finish his speech before the arrival of the evening freight train.

At the tables in Casino Park there were always dozens of other families, and sometimes there were card games which continued in the open air until late at night. On most of the tables there were big steins of beer, but never were there any on the table occupied by Johnny's family, for his mother was the daughter of the first Prohibitionist in the county. When the twilight was gone people played by the light of the arc lamps. It was all neighborly and everybody knew everybody else. There was something Germanic and *gemütlich* about it all.

A little way from the casino there was a tiny artificial lake with swans, and a little island with a belvedere, and the greatest possible treat was to rent a boat and row about the lake, a journey which took at most ten minutes. But time had nothing to do with the excursion; one was on the water and on the water anything might happen. The water in that silly little lake eventually reached the ocean by way of the Ohio and the Mississippi, and the ocean meant escape and adventure. The lake itself was never much of a success, for every two or three years it filled up completely with mud.

Casino Park was where that great institution known as a family reunion took place. It was, I think, an affair which belonged especially to the people of the country beyond the Appalachians, for it served to reunite, every few years, all the descendants of the original families who had come across the mountains a hundred years earlier. They came, the descendants, from all parts of the county and the state, and sometimes whole prosperous families returned from the Far West on the occasion of the tribal gathering. The festivities began early in the morning and continued far into the night with masses of pie and cake, roast turkey and ice cream, and afterward in the Town newspapers there was always a long account of the speeches and the singing and the reading of the family records, with a complete list of all those who attended. Sometimes the singing had a great wild beauty. Sometimes a very old lady would stand up at the table beneath the trees to sing, in a cracked voice, a whole collection of the old English songs brought across the mountains long ago.

As a child Johnny sometimes stood on the outskirts of these vast family gatherings, wishing that he belonged to a family which had such merry gargantuan conventions once every few years. His father's family never had much taste for keeping up family ties. His father and grandfather Willingdon were, in different ways, both passionate individualists—cold toward ties of the blood and soft toward their friends from the world about them. And his mother's family always had the Farm to go to. At the Farm there was a perpetual reunion, but in the eyes of a child it lacked, by its very usualness, the pomp and ceremony of those vast tribal gatherings in Casino Park.

The parks have lost their place in the sun. No longer does the old air of festivity exist. The stock company no longer suspends the action of "East Lynne" while the B&O freight train passes by, and the vast family reunions are almost a thing of the past. If anyone frequents the parks now it is the factory workers who are not rich enough to own automobiles and whose children, brought up upon the anemic movies, will never know the glories of the Casino Stock Company whose actors were on view in the daytime on Main Street.

⟿

Beyond the parks one entered the open country with a sense of freedom and escape. It was not very wild country. The fields were all neatly hedged and fenced, and in Johnny's childhood the farmhouses along the road were still fairly prosperous in appearance and well painted. Here and there on the rolling landscape there was a hillside still covered with a patch of forest left uncleared out of the first wilderness. It was not very wild country, but here there was room to breathe. Here there were no untidy vacant lots and crowded houses. There was no smoke or soot or any sound of rolling-mills. Once you had passed the parks you were in the open country. You were free!

Johnny knew each farm along the road which led at the end to his grandfather's house. He knew them as they were and so they will always exist for him, no matter what has happened to them since.

One crossed a little valley through which ran the brook called Toby's Run. Beyond the bridge there was a hedge of osage orange which, long left untended, grew high above the top of the buggy and dropped by the roadside enormous green oranges which the children gathered to play with. Then one crossed the Baltimore and Ohio tracks, a haunted spot at night because a whole family returning from a Fourth of July celebration had been killed there and because an old woman called Janes, returning to her farm, had once been robbed and beaten by the tramps who hid in the ragged hedge of osage orange.

At the top of the hill just beyond stood the farmhouse of the Ernsts. He was an immigrant from Germany. He had come over when a boy and he was at that time perhaps the only farmer of foreign birth in all the county. As such, he was always regarded as a little strange. He never exchanged visits, perhaps because no one wanted him or his wife. He was rather hard-faced and dour and

sometimes one saw him in the distance in passing, at work repair-
ing a fence or clearing a fencerow. His wife one never saw save from
a long way off working in the bright peasant's garden which she
had created about the ugly house. I do not think there were many
festivities in the lives of the Ernsts, nor much that was bright. They
were the first to bring with them into the county the peasant traditions of Europe, and the first who rose at daylight to work until
dark, the first to cultivate every inch of fencerow and to plant fruit
trees and berries in every inch of available space. I think that
toward the end he was disliked because he worked so hard and was
prosperous, while in the shadow of the growing factories in the
Town the old native farmers fell slowly into bankruptcy.

Just beyond the Ernsts, on the opposite side of the road, stood
the house of the widow Mills, and the contrast between the two
places could not have been more violent. The Mills homestead was
built of brick and covered with flowering vines, and it stood back
from the road, with a wide garden in front which was filled with
syringas and lilacs, weigelia and laburnums, and in summer
against the brick wall of the house in neat rows stood pot after pot
of geraniums and heliotrope and begonias which in winter she
kept inside. It was as English as any place could have been—a
house and garden which one might have found in Sussex instead
of in the Middle West. An orchard surrounded the whole house,
and under the drooping boughs bees hummed about a dozen
hives. The widow Mills' sons did the farming and at that time they
were still prosperous. She was a small, rather withered woman with
bright blue eyes and a hard mouth, and she lived very much to herself in the way of people who have a passionate love for flowers and
trees and gardens and spend all their days among them.
Occasionally when Johnny's grandmother passed she would come
out of the orchard and stand leaning with her elbows on the fence
to talk with Maria Ferguson about the better days which had
passed and to make bitter comments about their neighbors.

Farther along there was the township schoolhouse, long disappeared, and then one came to the house of "the Peckham girls."
When Johnny was a child they were already old maids past fifty,
but in the family they were always known as "the Peckham girls."

They were called Mary and Martha and were very different in appearance and personality. Their father had been a great friend of old Jamie's and so Johnny's family rarely passed the Peckham place without stopping to exchange gossip. Martha was a little birdlike woman with a merry face covered with fine wrinkles, and in the division of duties she it was who ran the house and had charge of the chickens and bees and pigeons. Of the two, Mary was vastly more imposing. She was a big, handsome, mannish woman who dressed severely and walked with a slight limp. She managed the farm labor and sold all the produce, and a hard bargainer she must have been. They belonged purely to the old tradition and so neither of them did any work about the place save in the house and garden. There was no peasant in them. The Peckham place was in the tradition neither of the Ernsts nor of the Mills, but belonged to the eighties. The house and barn were always kept brightly painted and in excellent repair, so that, although they were at least forty years old when Johnny first knew them, they still had an air of neat old-maidish newness. Every tree and shrub was meticulously pruned and there was never a blade of grass out of place. The whole house and garden and barnyard had the air of a chromo. But Mary Peckham had trouble finding labor, for the tradition got about that she was stiff-necked and much too exacting. Yet she had a prevailing charm and a good sense of humor. For Johnny she had a special fascination because she was the first person he had ever seen with one blue eye and one brown.

Beyond the Peckham place one descended a low hill between enormously high locust trees, and came to the little hollow where the yellow-and-white cottage of the Lunts' sat with an orchard on one side and a barn and horse pond on the other. It was the horse pond which Johnny envied the Lunts, because at the Farm there was no pond where you could sail boats, but only the swift-running brook. All the Lunts were old. Johnny never knew how many of them there were. The youngest generation had all gone off to Town, and as the carriage drove past the Lunts' place one had the impression of thin old people peering out of the doors and windows at the sound of hoofbeats on the road. Usually old Mrs. Lunts came out and stood on the little piazza, staring wistfully at the passersby. No one knew how old she was, but she must have been one of the early settlers in the county. I think that in her old age she was lonely. Sometimes she smiled and nodded and sometimes she gave no sign of recognition at all. She was very thin and brittle. She had no teeth and her chin and nose very nearly touched each other. She always stood with one thin hand wrapped in her clean apron and the other pressed against her thin lips. She gave the feeling of an old woman who was awaiting some one. She was so very old that it may only have been death she was awaiting.

Beyond the Lunts' came the twin farms of the Condons. They were owned by two brothers, the nephews of old Anne Condon, who long ago had gone bumping along the road in Great-uncle Jacob's buckboard. Her deserted little house still stood on its high bank by the roadside, half-buried in a tangle of flowers and vines. Frank Condon, the older brother, never married and always lived alone in a low brick house lost in a thicket of sassafras trees. He quarreled with his brother and with all his neighbors, and as he grew older he no longer cultivated his farm but let the fields disappear under waves of goldenrod. In passing one sometimes caught a terrifying glimpse of him as he peered, bearded and hostile, through the branches of the sassafras trees which surrounded the house. Children ran past the place when they came to that part of the road. People said he had been disappointed in love as a young man and that he never recovered from the shock. A few mangy chickens scratched about the door, but what he ate always remained a mystery. He died at last with only his dog in the house. It was the howling of his dog and the fact that for three days no smoke came from his chimney which led his brother to enter the house for the first time in thirty years. He had died in his sleep.

One crossed the tracks of the Erie railroad and on the tracks one caught a faint distant glimpse of the Farm with the big low white house pressed close against the hill beneath the dark Norway spruce. At sight of it the children grew restless, squirming and begging to be let down from the buggy. Sometimes they ran beside it and sometimes in summer they ran across the fields. It was the end of the journey, and at the end there was a whole life which was different from the prosaic life of the Town, a life filled with exciting adventure which centered about Maria standing at the gate in the whitewashed picket fence to greet her grandchildren.

For a child it was a fascinating journey made with impatience to reach the end, and in his impatience and his childishness Johnny never saw the signs of change which were taking place day by day before his eyes. He did not know, like his grandfather, old Jamie, that not one of the farms along the way, save that of the Peckham girls, was what it had been during his youth and middle age. Johnny never saw that some of the houses were in need of paint and that here and there a fence had been patched once too often. Nor did he notice that there were almost no young people and that as soon as the children grew up they disappeared, nor that there were no longer any good "hired men," but only wastrels and vagabonds who worked for a few days, and then went into the Town to spend the money on drink or to disappear forever. And as he could not see inside the farmhouses, he knew nothing of the mortgages made again and again in the hope that next year they would be paid off, nor of the falling prices of cattle and grain and the rising prices of clothing and farm machinery and furniture and all the things manufactured and marketed by business men. Week after week Johnny made the journey to the Farm, and week after week, year after year, life grew a little harder for the farmer and the farms changed a little, always for the worse.

‹∘›

In the Town, the church was still a force which concerned itself with preaching and missionaries and made no pretense at being "modern." The preacher did not attempt to be just another business man, and simple faith had not yet been compromised. Religion was religion. Philosophy was something else and no one had attempted to make the lion and the lamb lie down together. The church was a center of social life and so it had a profound influence upon family life. The Strawberry Festival, which took place under the trees of the Congregational churchyard, the weekly high teas of the Missionary Society, the quarterly supper of the Ladies Aid Society organized to pay off the church debt, were events in which every solid respectable family took part. It was about the church that the Town organized itself socially. When a good citizen died, the obituaries always said that "he had been a practicing Christian and a lifelong member of the church." The country club had not yet been born.

The social layers into which the Town settled were smaller but no less complexly organized than those of London or Paris or New York. It was society *in petto* with all the banal and classic prejudices and virtues, mockeries and successes. In the Town Proust could have found all the Guermantes and Charluses and Swanns. One could have found Odette and Albertine. There were Democrats and Republicans and a little handful of Socialists, Jeffersonians and Hamiltonians, Rooseveltians, Bryanites, standpatters and Progressives, just as there were in Paris Royalists and Bonapartists, Radicals and partisans of the Third Republic; and the shades of political opinion were felt sometimes openly, sometimes subtly in the social contacts and ambitions, for ever among the "self-made men" and the "business men" there was a faint social itch, which in their wives broke out often enough into an angry rash.

Each church had its place in the scheme, and one's affiliation with this sect or that made one's success difficult or easy. Now and then a Baptist or a Methodist family became members of the Congregational church for the "sake of the children," and more often when parents chose to remain faithful to a less fashionable sect the children became Presbyterians or Congregationalists or Episcopalians. Just as the Town itself was a transplanted New England town with secondary Scottish characteristics, so the Congregational church was *the* church, with the Presbyterian a close second. The Episcopal church came into importance with the rise of the turreted baronial houses when, mysteriously, the wealthy, finding its conservative doctrines sympathetic, clustered together under its new slate roof to worship the God of the privileged. But there was always something faintly vulgar about it, something which had the odor of great wealth recently acquired, often enough by methods that were none too scrupulous. To the old citizens it was always spoken of as the church which belonged to the "new people." The Town, if questioned, would have professed to be what it had started out to be—a Republican and Democratic community, free of snobbery or ideas that any man or woman was better than another; but no one ever questioned the Town, and certainly no one ever discussed without self-consciousness such a thing as one's position in society. Yet the thing existed. One was aware that being a Baptist was a handicap and that Lutherans were excellent citizens but never lived on Park Avenue or were seen at fashionable weddings or funerals. It was better to live on the wrong side of the railroad tracks and be a friend of the Congregationalists than to live in a house filled with plate glass on Elm Street and go to the Methodist church. Sometimes great wealth could be of help, but even wealth was useless if you had an accent. There were a thousand other complications lying beneath the surface of a hypocritical simplicity.

Nearly all the old families lived in the big houses near the center of the Town, where they dwelt entranced, living off incomes which each year grew a little smaller, just as each new generation seemed to grow a little less vigorous and capable. The whole scene was forever changing and families were always at some stage of the progress from shirt sleeves to shirt sleeves. The picture was classic to the point of banality. And alone on the wrong side of the railroad tracks in Trefusis' Castle, surrounded by mills and factories, Czechoslovakians and immigrant Italians, the local Duchesse de Guermantes, Great-aunt Jane dwelt entrenched amid her prejudices and contempt. People sometimes mocked her and her old-fashioned ideas and furniture. She had nearly all the qualifications. She was rich. She had a big house. She was a Congregationalist and belonged to the oldest of families. She failed only in living on the wrong side of the tracks. But she had a standard of her own which was both older and newer than that of the crude world spread upon the hills about her, a standard that was eternal. She did not ask people whether they were rich or poor, whether they lived on the right or the wrong side of the railroad tracks, or whether they were Congregationalists or Roman Catholics. She demanded only that they be intelligent or distinguished or entertaining. She was rich. The exact amount of her wealth troubled the Town, but no one ever knew until she died, and left almost nothing, how rich she had been—not even her own lawyer ever knew. The mills pounded, the soot gradually killed her trees and stifled her flowers, the aliens stared at her when she drove in or out her big wrought-iron gates, but she stood her ground and remained in the saddle to the end, a daughter of the Colonel who had known civilization so well he had sickened of it. She could, I think, have lived in a muskrat's home in the middle of a swamp and still have dominated the community.

The Congregational church was new when old Jamie had come to the county, but by the time Johnny was born it had almost a look of antiquity. Its bricks were weathered and more than half hidden by ivy and ampelopsis and Virginia creeper, and the trees whose big branches brushed the big Gothic windows were enormous. Children—even children to whom sermons were tiresome—loved it, and it must have given Johnny a great deal of pleasure, for as he grew older he came to think of it more and more frequently and to feel a desire to recover somehow some of the beauty and simplicity of the life which centered about it. When he thought of it, he saw it nearly always on a bright June day with the congregation gathered on the long wide flight of stone steps, gossiping before returning home to roast beef and the Sunday newspapers.

His earliest memory was of what was called "the primary room," where at the age of five he committed his first assault upon another individual. It was a large square room with the tiny chairs arranged in a circle intercepted by two thrones, on one of which sat Mrs. Mack, who taught the infants' class for forty years. On the other sat her adjutant, a pretty, faded old maid called Miss Hallowell. If one behaved well, one was given the privilege of sitting once a month beside one or the other. To sit on the right hand of Mrs. Mack was to sit on the right hand of God. At one end of the room were enormous Gothic windows, and on the other three walls hung enormous and brilliant oleographs from the Old Testament. There were the scene of "Jacob and the Heavenly Ladder," "The Arrival of Sheba" to visit Solomon, with Sheba borne in a litter upon the shoulders of six stalwarts who were neither black nor Hebraic, but resembled young Germans on a walking tour, and "The Return from the Promised Land," with Joshua in the foreground, bearing a bunch of grapes each the size of a Nonesuch apple. Beside them, the most gigantic Homburg grapes were no bigger than currants.

From her throne at one side of the circle Mrs. Mack told biblical stories. From her throne on the opposite side Miss Hallowell,
who had a powerful voice, led the piping sopranos in singing "Jesus
Loves Me" and other childish hymns, and outside the circle, rather
with the air of animal trainers, lingered two or three young women
whose duty it was to suppress quarrels, quiet tears, and now and
then remove a child to the lavatory nearby. One of the assistants
played the piano, and when at the close her powerful hands struck
a chord all the children rose and marched twice about the circle to
the accompaniment of "Onward, Christian Soldiers." It was during
the singing of "Jesus Loves Me" that Johnny committed his assault.

The victim was a little boy called Bennett who had sandy hair
and was mean and a bully, and the assault came at the end of
months of hatred suppressed week after week for the reward of
being allowed to sit on the right hand of Mrs. Mack. Chance on
this Sunday morning placed Johnny and the little Bennett boy side
by side in the infants' circle. Throughout the Bible stories Johnny,
plotting, struggled with murderous desire, and with the hymn-
singing inspiration came. Johnny had a handful of pennies destined to save heathen souls in China and a pair of woolen gloves,
and placing the pennies in a finger of one of the gloves, he constructed a murderous blackjack. The assault was the matter of a
second. While the Bennett boy sang "Jesus Loves Me" very loudly
in order to display his devotion, Johnny got in two or three blows,
and then the singing turned into loud wails and Johnny was
snatched from his chair by one of the animal trainers and impris-
oned in the lavatory. Behind him bedlam broke loose, for the
smaller children, frightened by the screams of the Bennett boy,
began, one after another, to scream, and in order to drown the
uproar the assistant banged louder and louder at the piano. It did
no good. The noise penetrated to other rooms and one by one
older children, old gentlemen and ladies, mothers and fathers,
flocked into "the primary room," until at last it was filled with a
confusion of parents comforting their children, of aunts and
uncles spiriting their nieces and nephews to safety and old ladies
all talking at once. In his lavatory prison Johnny sulked alone and
forgotten. It was the greatest scandal ever created in the Sunday

school and never again did Johnny sit on the right hand of Mrs. Mack, but on that day he achieved the greatest fame he was ever to know in the Town.

Most of the entertainment to be had in the Town came through the church. Besides the festivals and missionary teas and Ladies Aid suppers there was always a vast entertainment on Christmas Eve, when all the congregation and Sunday school were present and there were net stockings filled with poisonous dyed candies for all the children. And there were always tableaux and perhaps a Christmas play, and children dressed in starched frocks or velvet suits recited "The Soldier of Algiers" or sang "Good King Wencelas" in voices trembling with fright or brazen with the confidence of a "show-off."

Occasionally the church even undertook theatrical entertainments for the benefit of the church debt or the suffering heathen in far-off China and Africa. When Johnny was three or four years old there was a great fashion for staging "Gibson pictures" as tableaux, and while he was still too young to protest he was chosen to take the role of Cupid, which he enacted modestly clad in a union suit. The fashion lasted several years, so that each year there was a new series to be presented. There was great rivalry in the congregation among the pretty girls who sought to pose in the more attractive scenes. Fortunately, when Johnny was five he had the measles and emerged a thin, lanky child with an overlarge head. His lugubrious appearance unfitted him for the role of Cupid and a plumper and more rosy child was chosen.

Much later he played Marley's Ghost in "A Christmas Carol," in a costume made of black muslin draped with old pump chains to which books had been tied. And once he played the name part in "The Private Secretary" and gave a performance so vile that he was nearly asked to withdraw from the cast on the morning of the performance. And once he played in German in a piece called "Karl Hat Zahnschmerzen," the lines of which he remembered for years afterward, so great was the mingled vanity and horror at appearing before the public in a foreign tongue. Those premature appearances as Cupid gave him a fixation which to the end of his life forced him to look even upon such harmless entertainment as charades with horror.

To a child the church itself seemed a vast place, especially at
night when after church suppers in the big basement below, the
children escaped their parents and ran upstairs to play in the darkness of the big auditorium. This was not easy to do, for there was
always the sexton, filled with suspicions born of long experience,
who had to be avoided. His name was Henry Krebs and he was
German by origin, spoke with a German accent, and had a black
beard and a thunderous bass voice. Immediately after the supper
was finished downstairs, he began to prowl about, casting suspicious black eyes in the direction of every group of children. I think
he enjoyed the game, but he never gave any sign of it, maintaining
always the grimmest of faces and the most savage look in the black
eyes. He could have sat for a portrait of any fairy-tale ogre. The
game was to escape his vigil and run upstairs into the vast darkness
of the auditorium, the big halls, the belfry attic, and the organ
room. In these parts of the church there were never any lights, and
save in the auditorium, where the faint light of the Town itself
came through the big Gothic windows, they were black as the
depths of Hades. By that time it was an old church long since
impregnated with the memories of countless weddings, christenings, and funerals, and in a curious way I think the children were
aware of these memories and that the vague consciousness of them
made the nocturnal ramblings profoundly exciting. Only the brave
ones ever penetrated the morbid depths of the organ-loft, a vast
cavern of a place filled with treadles and pipes, and only the most
daring ever climbed the ladder into the belfry where the pigeons
lived. In the hall there was a great double stairway where on
Sundays parents and children descended sedately from the services
upstairs. In the darkness these stairways took on a different aspect,
for they had rails of polished mahogany which for sliding were a
delight, and here after the church suppers the children congregat-
ed to slide until interrupted by a bellow from Henry Krebs, at
which they scattered like mice into dark corners to wait until they
heard him grumbling to himself, pass them by on a patrol, which
rarely ended in the region of any of the miscreants.

As the children grew older, the dark auditorium became also a
place where a boy and girl could sit together undisturbed in the

darkness of a high pew. I know much courting took place there, and more than one proposal.

It was curious that this church, Congregational, Anglo-Saxon, set down on the eastern borders of the Middle West, should have had so much the character of a church in an Italian village. There was no more mysticism about it than there is about an Italian church. It was the center of social and family life. Its entertainments were communal entertainments, and if children thought of God at all it was as rather a pleasant old man, much as Italian children think of Him. In it took place weddings and funerals and festivals and even courtings.

There was none of the mysticism one finds in the church of Spain or the chill formality of the Church of England or the hysterical atmosphere of revivalist churches. It drew its character more perhaps from the community than from any tradition or ritual, for as its name implies, the Congregational sect is an intensely individualistic one, each congregation conducting itself as it pleases and determining its own creeds. There was, therefore, no stamp upon it of an organization of bishops handing down laws received secondhand from God himself, and so the character of its individual churches has always veered from an intellectualism which was almost Unitarian to the hysteria of the reforming evangelical churches. It must have been a superior community with more than the average share of good American qualities and less than its share of the bad ones.

As a small child Johnny overheard whisperings of various scandals which only later became wholly clear to him. There was the story of a servant coming unexpectedly into the study of the Parish House to find the clergyman holding on his lap in a tight embrace one of the most respectable old maids of the congregation. Looking back upon it long afterward, Johnny found something infinitely pathetic in the picture of a clergyman of nearly sixty, a figure set up by society not only as a model but as a spiritual healer, making love to a dowdy old maid of forty-five who had just lost the father to whom she had given up her whole life.

The story got about. The clergyman protested to the deacons who came for an explanation that he was only consoling Miss

Wilkes, which may well have been true, but in the end the situation grew out of hand and the clergyman's position impossible, and he left under a cloud. He was an old man. I do not know what became of him. I think Miss Wilkes rather enjoyed the scandal. At any rate, she came to church brazenly as regularly as before, and for the rest of her life she could cherish the knowledge that not only had she been attractive to at least one man, but that all the congregation and most of the Town knew it.

There was another clergyman who was asked to leave because he married eighteen months after his wife died, a fact which his deacons and some of his congregation felt called upon to denounce as fleshly and undignified in a man who was supposed to be all soul and no .body, especially since the new wife was both young and attractive.

And there was the scandal between one of the deacons and the female leader of the choir, which everyone, due perhaps to the character of the lovers involved, treated as a comic episode. The deacon was a dandy in a small-town way—middle-aged, plump, and given to wearing white waistcoats. His plump figure passed the pew of Johnny's family when he carried the collection plate on Sundays, his pink, shiny double chin pinched by the starched points of his collar. He was never seen without a flower in his buttonhole. The inamorata was a gaunt horse-faced woman of forty-five who had a booming contralto voice which was the loudest Johnny ever heard. At prayer meetings, at Sunday school, in church, it always boomed out full and clear like the roaring of the sea, leading the way for more timid voices to follow. Their sin was discovered by a stable boy at the John Sherman Place, who for reasons which have never been quite clear found himself one June night in a buckeye tree above their heads. They were caught in *flagrante delicto* and the stable boy, delighted, told all the Town.

And there was the scandal of the Presbyterian elder who was caught in the back room of Mrs. Mallop's millinery shop. In those days there was always something glamorous and wicked about small-town milliners. Certainly there was a succession of them in the Town, sometimes two in business at once, and always they seemed to be "widows" and always they suffered from suspicion. As a small boy the house of Mrs. Mallop and her sister in the millinery trade held for Johnny the same exciting awe and mystery as the row of shuttered houses in the Flats which were always being open or suppressed, according to the moral tone of the community, but which were always there. To the end of his days Johnny will always think of milliners as a little fast.

❧

By the time Johnny was born the "hired girl" had gone the way of the "hired man." No longer did she occupy the old position of frontier equality with the family which employed her. No longer did she sit at the table after she had carried in the food. No longer was she married, perhaps to a neighboring farmer, in the house of her employer. If she existed any longer it was as a servant who had little more than a servant's dignity and a little more than a servant's intimacy with the family for which she worked. The old easy manner of democracy was gone save on distant farms and small villages where among eccentric old people it still lingered, cherished rebelliously as something precious. The Town wanted to grow up. It wanted to be like the East. It felt, a little self-consciously, that there was something vulgar about the institution. In the big houses, the very expression "hired girl" began to go out of fashion. It was more "refined" to speak of servants. But it was not only that the attitude of the employer had changed; the quality of the "hired girl," like that of the "hired man," had fallen into decadence. No longer were they young men and women who had come, intelligent, independent, and ambitious, over the mountains to make their way in a new world filled with opportunities; they were of a different sort now, more often than not shiftless, ignorant, ill-educated, and resentful. The grandchildren of those first "hired girls" and "hired men" who came from the East now paid young men and women to work for them, but the relationship had undergone a change. Very few among them were any longer of American stock, and although the immigrant girls and men went often enough by the old name, the name no longer meant anything. Domestic service, like manual labor, had fallen into disrepute among Americans, and if the "hired girl" was an immigrant, the whole relationship was hopelessly different, for all the community looked upon immigrants as a race apart. The immigrant, on his side would have been uncomfortable in the old relationship, even if it had been possible for him to conceive it.

Of all the procession of "hired girls" who passed through the little room over the kitchen before Grandfather Willingdon came to live there, only one was American. She was perhaps the last servant of American lineage in the whole county, and something of the old democratic friendliness persisted in her relations with Johnny's family. She was a daughter of a farmer who had fallen upon evil days and she was a tall, thin girl with dark hair and eyes and a heart-shaped face. She had a long thin neck and resembled one of the women of Modigliani. For the children she was a great friend, and in Johnny's mother she confided everything which happened to her and from her she sought advice whenever a problem arose.

She stayed with Johnny's family longer than any "hired girl" who came to work in the Third Street house, and in the end she left only to be married to a young man who presented himself to Johnny's mother before he asked Mary herself. They were married in Johnny's house and went to live in Pennsylvania, and long afterward came back, bringing two small children, to spend a two-day visit. She had weak lungs and until she was married was threatened with tuberculosis, against which she dosed herself with a ferocious concoction known as "skunk oil" which she kept on the sill of the kitchen window. Its smell more than fulfilled the implications of its name, and how Mary Crane was ever able to swallow it remained one of the family mysteries. It may have been that the skunk oil was psychological in its effect, but whether it was the oil or matrimony which cured Mary's lungs no one ever knew. When she returned to visit the family she was cured and resembled a Rubens rather than a Modigliani.

Out of all the girls who passed through the little room, only Mary Crane "fitted" into the family. Behind her lay the same blood, the same traditions, the same standards. When you talked with Mary Crane there were no gaps in the understanding, no moments when on one side or the other there was bewilderment and sometimes even resentment. Her father was one of the first of the old line of farmers to go down before the hopeless conditions of the

New Day, the millennium of prosperity. She was the last of the "hired girls." All the rest were servants, and none of them could have fitted into the Colonel's dream of an agricultural democracy. The stuff for Utopias was not in them, nor was the fault their own as individuals.

The other girls came from the Town itself, from those parts so remote, spread out in the shadow of Trefusis' Castle, over the marshes and the surrounding *terra firma*. They were the new parts of the Town and they went by two or three names. There were the Flats, the Syndicate, and the Additions, and their nucleus was the area taken over by factories, blast furnaces, and rolling-mills.

The Flats were the oldest of them all. They covered the area of the marshes and the bordering flatland, where, among the furnaces and millyards there still lingered a few old houses built half a century earlier by prosperous, respectable citizens who dwelt in them until the noise and smoke became intolerable. Most of them were ugly wooden houses with vast piazzas, and the passing of the years and increasing neglect had not made them any more beautiful. Long ago they had been painted in "wearing" shades of chocolate brown or slate gray, and over these dead colors the rain and soot had superimposed long streaks of black. When the owners deserted them they were converted into rookeries for immigrants and never painted again. Dining rooms and parlors were divided by partitions into cubicles, and houses which once sheltered families of nine or ten in the old heavy elegance of the nineteenth century now sheltered fifty or sixty men, women, and children living in the industrial squalor of the early twentieth. On Whitmore Street four of them in a row had been changed into brothels. They had a sinister fascination for Johnny, and sometimes in summer, when he drove through the Flats on his way to Trefusis' Castle, he saw slatternly women clad in flowered wrappers, rocking and screaming at one another like parrots from one piazza to another.

Afterward Johnny came to know many kinds of ugliness, but none that was more uncompromising and abandoned than the hideousness of the Flats. Long ago the old shade trees had died in that atmosphere of soot and carbon dioxide, but instead of being cut down and mercifully removed from sight, they remained to contribute their share to the desolation. In the old dooryards behind the rotting wooden fences, the grass turned yellow and died, until where once there had been a green lawn there were only trampled patches of yellow clay littered with old newspapers, tin cans, and even garbage. Whatever sanitary arrangements had once existed soon became clogged and abandoned, and the immigrant tenants, pleased to be free of such civilized affectations, set up makeshift privies in the desolate back gardens. Once, on his way to visit Great-aunt Jane, during an epidemic of typhoid fever, Johnny passed through streets where the sewage and bedpans of the ancient rookeries had been dumped into the open gutters. Sometimes in the spring, behind one of the rotting fences, a lilac still persisted and sent forth a cluster of sickly blossoms.

Occasionally certain women of the Town, moved by indignation, set about cleaning up the district. The brothels were suppressed for a few weeks and the dooryards were cleared of their litter, but beneath the surface everything remained the same, and in a month or two the brothels opened once more and the dooryards looked as dreary as ever. The courageous women had no votes and they had no business men to support them. The business men were too busy. It was the moment when America's prosperity was moving toward its peak and it did not matter what happened to the animal population which was being imported by shiploads to make wheels turn and fill the pockets of the men who were building turreted houses on the other side of the Town, as far as possible from the Flats; nor did it matter to those other men who had gone to the East to live in palaces furnished by picture dealers and to buy what they wanted in Washington. Privilege was everything. The class fit to rule the interests of the county was in power. Even the panic of 1907 did not jar their sense of infallibility for long. There were always excuses to be found for clay feet. They are still finding them.

The Syndicate was a part of the Town which lay beyond the Flats to the north on the side of the open country. It got its name from a syndicate of citizens who with the rise of the mills bought up a dozen farms and made rudimentary streets which were no more than paths of mud, and built match-box rookeries to house the newly arrived immigrants. The whole affair was a speculation contrived with the smallest possible investment, to yield the largest possible return, and the objects of the exploitation were the mass of workmen arriving each day and each week from the old country. The usual procedure was to rent a house to a steady worker who had already been in the country for a few years and spoke a little English. So long as the rent was paid—and a good fat rent it was, too—the owner turned his back and closed his eyes. The tenant in his turn took in boarders, as many as he could squeeze into the dwelling, setting up mattresses side by side on the floors and even in the cupboards. Nearly always the lodgers worked in shifts, so that the same beds were occupied at night by one set of workers and during the day by another.

At one period two of these houses came into the possession of Johnny's father for a short time and Johnny was allowed to go with him occasionally to collect the rents. The tenants knew that the owner objected to overcrowding and always they kept some member of the family on watch throughout the day on which the rent was due. When Johnny and his father arrived they sometimes saw a whole procession of men moving out of the back door of the house to disappear among the neighboring dwellings. When they entered there was every sign of bustle and excitement and one caught glimpses of mattresses stuffed hastily into cupboards or tossed down the cellar steps out of sight, and one knew that a score or more of workmen who had just finished ten or twelve hours of grueling work had been roused from sleep and hurried out of sight. There was no time lost by them in dressing and undressing.

In all the district there was perhaps not more than one woman to every fifteen men. From time to time the Town brothels were either closed entirely in some transient wave of reform or closed against immigrant workmen upon the grounds that their presence excited disorder, so that in the depths of their oppression even the most fundamental of human functions was stifled as far as it was possible. It did not matter that they slept in filth and were overworked and underpaid; it did not matter that sometimes a single woman was the mistress of a half-dozen men or that children were debauched and perversion common enough. It did not matter, because all these things were hidden. One could not hide brothels. The surface must be bright and moral, regardless of natural and human needs. Nothing must interfere with the business of making money. One must keep shop open and attend church on Sunday. Those were the fundamental principles. The Town was, after all, the child of New England.

Johnny's clearest memory of the Syndicate was of arriving with his father one winter evening after sundown to find one of the houses in immense confusion. In the darkness the lodger on guard had failed to notice the approach of the owner, and as Johnny and his father entered the house other lodgers were climbing out of windows and doors. The only ones left undisturbed were a dozen who had come in off the day shift at the mills and were around a table eating supper. They were all dark men, of every age, with enormous melancholy eyes. They were unshaven and covered with sweat and soot, and the smell in the room was nauseating. The whole supper was an enormous common bowl of soup filled with bread from which they all dipped with huge ladles, sucking the soup with loud animal noises. Johnny was only nine or ten years old at the time and the sight of them terrified him. They were all Bulgarians from a village on the Turkish border where their women and children had all been massacred a few years earlier.

It is tragic to return from the fields to find that your wives and children have been massacred, but I am not certain that the men Johnny saw seated around the table had exchanged their old life for a better one. Even in the new country they saw their wives and children starve in time of strike. They saw them beaten and shot. For a Russian serf, either under the Tsarist regime or under the worst conditions of Soviet rule, life was scarcely more miserable than for the immigrant workman in "free" America during its great industrial growth. It would, I think, be impossible for men to have lived under worse conditions of oppression—economic, political, or spiritual—than the immigrants of the Flats and the Syndicate. They died of epidemics and overwork, but it did not matter, because ships hurried back and forth across the Atlantic bringing fresh loads of fodder to be fed to mills and factories. The spiritual mortality in the slums of our cities and factory towns was even higher. It was, I think, almost one hundred per cent. The Town, the county, the state, the whole nation were destined to pay for the spiritual slaughter, and neither Johnny nor Johnny's children will live to see the end of the retribution. But it did not matter then—the business men were making money and because they made money the shopkeepers' tills were full each evening. That was the important thing. That was why men like Aldrich and Lodge and Smoot sat in Washington making certain that no one should interfere with the business men. The privileged ruled and took the profits. Men like Frick grew rich and filled houses with Fragonards and Vermeers. Business bribed and stole and corrupted. One dared not interfere with business and prosperity.

Neither Johnny nor his father, nor old Jamie, in his indignation, understood the spectacle, because they knew nothing about "business" and there had never been any "business men" in their family. It was a tradition which they could not fathom. They failed, too, because it was beyond the comprehension or credulity of any simple man. It was not until Johnny was grown and had left the Town forever that he came to understand it and to see that it was a strange compound of dishonesty and sharp dealing, of stupidity and ruthlessness and bribery, shot through with rare occasional flashes of genius. For half his life he stood in awe of big business, thinking that big-business men had some quality or genius which set them ahead of other men. It was only when he began to grow middle-aged that he understood the whole picture and saw that a man needed only mild shrewdness, vitality, and a lack of scruples to have succeeded in that new world where every element contributed to help him. Luck was on his side, and opportunity and a government which he owned. Perhaps the American people, preferring wealth to decency, were his greatest allies. When he was forty, Johnny knew that what he had seen in the Flats was only a tiny corner of a vast incredible spectacle, a whole nation debauched by the mean instincts of the unscrupulous village shopkeeper.

But Johnny never forgot for the rest of his life the Flats and their tragic inhabitants, nor the look in the eyes of those haunted, exploited Bulgarians ladling soup greedily out of the bowl in the middle of the table. Since the frosty evening when the Colonel and the Jesuit had looked out over the marshes toward the Indian mounds, less than a hundred years had passed. The black slavery which troubled the old philosopher and his son-in-law Jamie was gone forever, but something else had taken its place, worse in the fundamental greed of its motives. Old Jamie himself thought the slaves had been happier and better treated than the workers in the mills.

The people in the Flats were untouchables and so one never saw them. They never entered the life of that comfortable prosperous world save as a dim, distant cloud upon the horizon which was always there, menacing, like the cloud which threatens all the day given over to a picnic. But above them, of a higher caste, were the Jews and the Germans and the Irish whose children one sometimes met in school and whose paths in business or in politics sometimes crossed the paths of the *Brahmins* in the old houses beneath the elms or the *Bunyas* who lived in the monstrosities beyond the Sherman Place.

In that changing world there was no prejudice against Jews. One sat beside them in school and sometimes they came to supper and often enough to play in the vacant lots or in the skeletons of houses in the process of construction. If you were aware of anything which set the Jews apart from yourself, it was a difference in tradition, for the rich, colorful, sensual tradition of the Jews was doubly exotic against the thin, meagre background of that transplanted New England town. As a child, Johnny knew that the Jews observed Saturday as their Sunday and that on Friday nights some of them placed candles in the window, and he knew, too, that in one or two of the Jewish houses which he entered there was a richness which elsewhere one seldom encountered—a richness of food, of custom, of music, of books, of hospitality. One never encountered that strange atmosphere of emptiness, of thrift, of barrenness which was so prevalent in the Town, even in the houses of men as rich as the peddler Bentham's grandson. When one went to play in a Jewish house one found it filled to overflowing with warmth and kindliness. One never left without receiving a gift, sometimes a worn toy to which you had taken a fancy, sometimes a bouquet of flowers for your mother, sometimes a piece of *apfelstrudel*, still warm from the oven and rich-scented with spices. In the plate glass, fake Byzantine pretentiousness of the Bentham house, there was an atmosphere of desolation, a kind of life in death which in childhood Johnny could not have analyzed even if he had attempted it. At the Benthams, the furniture was never worn or scratched and it always sat in the same place. The shades were drawn in mid-summer "to save the carpets." You could not play boisterously for fear of damaging the chairs. Long afterward he came to understand what it was that blighted that whole household. It was something which the peddler Bentham had brought with him in his pack from New England as surely as he had brought bone buttons and "fine silk for gentlemen's waistcoats." Long afterward Johnny found it again in New England houses, again and again—meanness and thrift, security and fear. It was never like that in a Jewish household.

There was another difference of which he was aware—that Jewish children did not play as wildly as the other children in the Town. They were always a little shy and self-conscious, as if they were afraid of putting themselves forward or were oppressed by an indefinable melancholy, as if nine hundred years had passed since they had been able to play like other children.

If there was no prejudice against Jews, there was an immense one against Roman Catholics, and under that head were lumped all the Irish, for in that world you were not considered Irish, no matter what blood you might have, if you were not a Roman Catholic. An Irish Roman Catholic was something to be feared, because the Irish were believed to be wild, drunken and disorderly and the Roman Catholics were all servants of the Pope and traitors to every country which gave them shelter. The feeling permeated the whole life of the Town. As a small boy Johnny encountered it in the livery stables, the undertaking establishments, the police station—wherever idle citizens gathered to chat. And now and then as a boy, he found lying about in livery stables copies of a newspaper called The Menace which was filled with stories of rapes by Roman Catholic priests and whole illegitimate families born to nuns. It was a paper which served, I suspect, a double purpose—that of providing an unlimited amount of salacious reading under the virtuous guise of an attack upon the Scarlet woman of Rome.

There was no Roman Catholic church in the Town until the Irish came in with the railroads. The first edifice was a simple enough structure, a mere shack, replaced by a brick structure, but during Johnny's childhood, the Catholics built an enormous handsome Romanesque structure of Indiana limestone which in size was the only rival of the ancient Congregational place of worship. I think that most of the ignorant and prejudiced citizens of the Town looked upon St. Vincent's as an affront and a piece of arrogance and their resentment gave rise to an outburst of feeling and to new sets of incredible and dirty stories. It was said that there was a secret passage connecting the house of the priest with the convent a block away, so that he might visit the nuns at his convenience, and that the cellar of the church was filled with arms to be used when the Pope gave the signal for an uprising which was to subdue the whole country and bring it beneath his power.

There would have been in these stories the fantastic humor which touches the preposterous but for the fact that hundreds and even thousands of people in the county really believed them. When Johnny was a small boy the murders and violence, often enough justified, of the Molly Maguires, were still only a little way off and over the Flats there still hung the shadow of brutal beatings and assassinations which had occurred during the cowardly secret warfare between Mollies and members of a fiercely anti-Catholic organization called the American Protective Association. For Johnny the stories had a sinister and foreign character which made the dark alleys and the houses where the crimes had occurred seem doubly fearsome. Those assassinations and mob attacks, secret and often cowardly, seemed as unreal and as exotic as the dark stories of Renaissance Italy which he sometimes read, terrified, by candlelight in the sewing room. It was all very puzzling to a boy who was a grandson of the bluff and straightforward Jamie, for the old Scot, with all his hatred of priests, never forgot that even Roman Catholics were human.

Johnny puzzled his head too in a desperate effort to reconcile families like the O'Sheas and the Siegfrieds with the livery stable tales of plots and rapes and assassinations. The O'Sheas, he knew,

because Esmond O'Shea was a Democrat and one of his father's
stoutest henchmen in the wards on the wrong side of the Town
where the Irish lived. They were a family whose beauty and charm
should have earned them forgiveness on earth and in Heaven for
all the crimes attributed to Roman Catholics at the most rabid
conferences held under the sycamore trees in front of Robinson's
livery stable. Esmond O'Shea himself was a man of forty, with
black hair and blue eyes, spare and finely built with a mouth which
curled up at the corners. Around his bright eyes there were little
crow's feet which came from much laughing. He had very beautiful hands of which he was proud and a laugh which passed
through a room like an epidemic. He had come to America as a boy
and when he was twenty-two he sent to Cork for his two younger
sisters. Esmond had married when he was twenty-one and by the
time he was forty he had eight children.

About a visit to the O'Sheas there was all the quality of a lark
and for Johnny there was no better treat than the privilege of driving across Town on a summer evening to call on Esmond O'Shea
and talk politics. The O'Shea children were allowed to stay up late
and only went to bed when they were too sleepy to play any longer
at "Run-sheep-Run" or "Duck on Rock" up and down the block
under the street lights. Sometimes one of Esmond's sisters came in
for the evening and brought her children. There was a merry
happy-go-lucky air about the household which Johnny never
encountered elsewhere in the Town. The O'Sheas, like his own
people, were poor but it never seemed to trouble them, perhaps
because, living in the wrong part of Town, they had no appearances to keep up and no pretenses to make. Beneath the lack of
respect for material success which colored the whole life in
Johnny's family, there was always the desperate, tragi-comic strain
of gentility. The O'Sheas simply enjoyed life and let the devil take
the hind-most. They were not brought up to gentility, yet they had
charming manners and all the generosity of the reckless. But
underneath their gaiety and their wildness there lay tragedy, for the
whole family was touched by tuberculosis. The mother was already
dead and the oldest son could do no work. Before Johnny was
grown, three of the children were buried in the Catholic cemetery.

The O'Sheas, from Esmond, who was one of his father's best friends, to little Michael, who was six when Johnny was ten, were hard indeed to reconcile with the stories of Catholics which appeared in *The Menace*. For Johnny they provided delights so ecstatic that when at last he left them to return to the right part of Town for his own respectable bed, he was overcome on the way home by a profound feeling of melancholy and depression. At ten years old he did not understand it, but when he was a man he looked back upon that indefinable deflation of the spirit and understood that it was born of envy and of a feeling which no child who grew up in the shadow of New England and Scotch Calvinism would ever escape—the feeling that there was something wrong and sinful in enjoying oneself too hilariously. The O'Sheas, even in the shadow of death, never knew that feeling.

The Siegfrieds also lived in a wrong part of Town but not so wrong as the part in which the O'Sheas lived. Their quarter was merely nondescript and colorless, neither fantastic and spectacular like the houses of the newly rich nor mysterious and sinister like the Flats. Nobody from the right part of Town ever knew exactly who the people were who lived out by the cemetery nor how they gained their living. They were simply a vague amorphous mass, all save the Siegfrieds who occupied an enormous house with a big lawn on which there were cast iron fountains and grottos made of cement with imitation stalactites covered with moss and tiny ferns. When Johnny was a boy they were rich and still possessed the profits of an oil business which was squeezed out of existence by the lawless operations of the pious Rockefeller octopus. It was a business built up by Johann Siegfried after he had come from Germany during the troubles of Forty-Eight and the loss of it broke his heart, for he was very proud of having come to America a penniless revolutionary student, to make his own way up to wealth. He died of it, but he left a son and two daughters who lived in the big house with their children.

The Siegfrieds had two great handicaps in the society of the Town. They were Roman Catholics and they lived out by the cemetery and save for music Johnny might never have known them, for they did not meddle in politics. Wherever music was concerned the Siegfrieds were not to be ignored. They it was—Louis Siegfried and his old maid sister Bertha—who provided most of the guarantee fund whenever any good musician or orchestra came to the Town. And in that world music had a hard struggle, for it was in the blood of few of those who dwelt in the turreted houses. Slowly as they raised themselves a little above the peddler stage, they came to see that a taste for music was a sign of civilization and more than that, that it was a social asset, and then their pockets were loosened a little; but when Johnny was having his introduction to Mozart and Brahms, music was left to the Siegfrieds and a few people without money like poor Miss Ainsworth who had spent the savings of a lifetime on a good piano.

The inside of the Siegfrieds' house was different from that of any other house in the Town. There were tapestries and a great deal of carved wooden furniture and oil paintings, very sentimental most of them but very beautiful to Johnny's eye, of South German meadows blue with cornflowers and peasant girls and cattle standing in pools. It was a heavy richness which was strange in the Town, even in a house like Trefusis' Castle. And in the parlor there were two superb grand pianos, at one of which Johnny's sister sometimes played symphonies and concertos with Johann or Bertha Siegfried at the other. When Johnny was old enough he was allowed sometimes to go to the Siegfrieds in the evenings to listen to the music. All the Siegfrieds, including the children who were old enough, played two or three instruments and among them with the aid of Johnny's sister they were able to arrange trios and quartets and quintets. Very often they came to play in the Willingdon's small, well-worn parlor and evening after evening Johnny, when he was still too small to go out in the evenings, went to sleep to the quartets of Schumann, Mozart and Brahms and sometimes, an experience even more wonderful, he was wakened slowly in the night by the sounds of the music downstairs, coming distantly to his bedroom. Then he would lie awake, listening, in the magical realm between consciousness and slumber, with the agreeable melancholy pleasure of imagining that he had died in his sleep and was awakening in Paradise. Sometimes, if he did not fall asleep again too quickly, he became a spectator at his own death and funeral, seeing himself lying in his coffin with his face washed and an angelic smile already on his lips. And he watched his aunts and uncles and the neighbors as they walked past and heard them say, "He looks as if he had just fallen asleep. Perhaps he's better off than the rest of us. Think of all the trouble he's missed," and, "Probably he's with the angels now." Aunt Hattie would be sorry she said he had bad table manners and his mother would be sorry for all the times she had punished him. Unconsolable and dressed all in black, she would say, "If I'd only known that God meant to take him from us so soon, I'd have let him go to the round house or go swimming or anything." Sometimes under the stimulation of Mozart or Brahms the scenes at the funeral became so moving that even Johnny found a lump in his throat and tears in his eyes. Music and drowsiness provided a wonderful release to the imagination.

There was a double pleasure in going to the Siegfrieds' great house overlooking the cemetery, for there was not only the mystical pleasure of the music but there was also the material one of a big South German supper of cold meat, sardines, sandwiches, sausages, sweets, beer and cider. The Siegfrieds were a handsome family, big in the Wagnerian way. Louis Siegfried, who was middle-aged, had brown eyes and blonde hair and he played the more thunderous piano parts of a concerto magnificently. Brahms was his hero. Miss Bertha, who was a spinster of thirty-eight and always dressed in black with a high collar held up by whale bones, thought Brahms alternately too academic and too overwhelmingly emotional. She had a theory that as a man he had not lived enough and so the emotions he suppressed sometimes got out of hand and ran away with him in his music. She preferred the more stern and ordered beauties of Bach and in her more emotional moments the pure, lovely baroque of Mozart. Mrs. Brandt, the married sister, was a romantic and loved Schumann.

It was the Siegfrieds who set Johnny's feet on the paths which long afterward led him to Munich and Salzburg and Vienna and it was the Siegfrieds who helped him to understand the ultimate glories of German music. It was perhaps due to them that almost all other music would forever sound thin and artificial and trivial by comparison. They were a charming and sympathetic family, as different from the O'Sheas as it was possible to be, for the charm of the O'Sheas was on the surface and brilliant and that of the Siegfrieds had to be explored. Perhaps of the two it was the more profound and lasting. The charm of the O'Shea family left nothing behind once you were out of their presence. The charm and the memories of the Siegfrieds, their music and their heavy suppers, was destined to endure forever. Long afterward when Johnny had passed by and finished with adolescent cynicism, he came to guard and cherish even their sentimentality.

⤌

The "hired girls" for all the Town came out of the Flats and the Syndicate bearing unpronounceable names and still sometimes clad in innumerable petticoats. They spoke little English and could be had for a few dollars a month, and the sudden change from the squalor of the Flats even to the comfort of a modest lower middle-class house worked strange results. When first they came they were dirty as they had to be, and surly, which was not surprising. And some of them were dishonest, having already imbibed a little of that lawless philosophy which arose partly from the sordid poverty of their lives, partly from the idea that in this new "free" country small dishonesties would go unpunished, and a little, perhaps, from what they had heard of the lives of the men who owned the mills and factories. Once a week they returned to the Flats to spend an hour or two with their families, and on these occasions they bore off in the pockets of their voluminous petticoats eggs and sugar and delicacies which had no place in the meals of the dreadful rookeries. Sometimes they even made off with valuable articles which later they attempted to sell. Some of them did it with a kind of wide-eyed innocence, and were astonished and hurt when they were sent away or threatened with punishment, and always they had excuses. A silver pitcher was scratched or a tablecloth had been darned and therefore no one who lived in a fine house could have any use for them. Nearly always they took away, like magpies, articles that were less useful than dazzling.

In the Town they were an institution. Every house in the street where Johnny lived had one or more of them—clumsy, hulky peasant girls with great legs and arms, cowlike and rather stupid, well-meaning but undependable, and often enough without morals of any kind. Frequently in their direct, animal simplicity they came into conflict with the standards of those solid middle-class houses, filled with families of Methodists and Baptists so fanatically strict that they would not suffer the melancholy strains of a concertina played on the back porch after nightfall by some lover come up from the Flats into the respectable part of the Town to court one of the "hired girls." Frequently they were cruelly treated and made to sleep in cupboards or in the cellar, for in a good many households "Hunkies" and "Polaks" were regarded as a little less worthy of comfort than the family dog. On one occasion Johnny's mother became involved in a neighborhood feud because she dared to rescue a Czechoslovak girl called Eppa who for weeks had been sleeping on a piece of carpet on the back porch of one of the near-by churchgoing ladies. Other women said that she was ruining the new class of "hired girl" by being too soft with them. Her critics were not women bitter and hardened by poverty. They were the women of prosperous shopkeeping citizens who went to church on Sunday and read papers at women's clubs on art and literature.

There was no such thing as a girl being able to quit one job and find another, for there was an abundance of labor (due to the propaganda of the mill owners and to the hard-working ocean liners) and the absurd wages which they earned, three or four dollars a week, were precious to the countless smaller brothers and sisters in the Flats who had not enough to eat. But even Johnny's mother, who was good and generous and armed with her father's fathomless capacity for moral indignation, never felt quite the same toward these immigrant girls as she felt toward the girls like Mary Crane or the Negresses who were so much a part of the Town life and were looked upon always with affection. Perhaps it was too much to ask that these rawboned girls, speaking an outlandish tongue, untidy and often unable to read or write, should have been accepted as the old servants had been.

Yet they were pathetically human, and sometimes one of them, like the rescued Eppa, found her way into the family's affections. Eppa had come from a country where for centuries her ancestors had been no more than serfs. She was little used to kindness, and

when she felt its warm glow turned upon her she became a different girl, growing pretty and neat and clean and full of spirit. But,
alas! kindness very often achieved an utterly different result, leading to thefts and impositions and insolence. I think that some of
them, born in the squalor of Europe and transferred to the squalor
and oppression of America, had come to believe before they were
grown that it was only possible to live by making constant warfare
in a million ways upon the classes above them. And some of them
had a conviction that the classes which exploited them were as nat-
urally their enemies as that the sun made darkness and daylight.

There came a time, much later, when most of them were
absorbed in factories, and then it was that their pathetic ambitions
came to know realization. In a way the machine brought them a
better and more independent life. No longer were they constantly
in the presence of some hard-faced middle-aged woman who
watched their every move and endeavored to spy upon their
thoughts. For the machine they worked so many hours a day and,
if inadequately paid, were none the less paid more than they had
ever earned in domestic service, and when their work was finished
they were free. And with that freedom they became American.
They threw off the shawls and the multiple petticoats in which
they had come to work as "hired girls" and appeared in shirtwaists
and hats with plumes. Quickly they forgot their old tradition of
economy and saving. They forgot the old sense of duty toward
their parents and families. They learned to spend all that they
earned and to go at nights to movies and dance-palaces and sometimes on the streets or into brothels. It was their first pathetic gesture toward assimilation, and their impulse was not well received
by the community in which they found themselves. For all their
pathetic finery and independence they were still "Polaks, Hunkies,"
and "Dagoes." They still lived in the segregated districts of the Flats
and the Syndicate. When they went to school they still went to the
city schools of their own district, where it was considered among
the school teachers a punishment to be sent; but all about them
they were picking up ideas of independence and even pride and a
lawless insolence which arose out of an imposed sense of their
inferiority and out of a consciousness of their fantastically increas-

ing numbers. The Flats and the Syndicate became unwholesome districts into which no American chose to go after nightfall. The citizens of the Flats often enough were lawless, but scarcely more lawless than many of the citizens on Maple Avenue and Elm Street and those who had gone to Washington on "business"; and when one analyzed the lawlessness of the Flats one found its roots in oppression and ignorance. The roots of the lawlessness in the big turreted houses were embedded in greed.

There was in the Town another sort of servant, more numerous than the vanishing "hired girls" of American stock, but infinitely less common than the immigrant girls from the Flats. These were the Negresses who had abilities and a character and position all their own. There were a great many of them, the children and grandchildren of the escaped slaves who had swarmed through the county in the days when old Jamie and Job Finney and Great-aunt Martha were "conductors" on the "Underground Railroad." On the eve of the Civil War a good many of them had stayed in the Town, protected by abolitional sentiment, troubling to go no farther; and after the war a great many, with sympathetic memories of the place, returned from Canada. In this town which had never known slavery there was a whole colony of Negroes with its own shops, its own music, its own social life, and its own African Methodist Episcopal church. To the white population the colony bore a relation wholly different from that which existed between the two races in the South or between those in communities like Harlem which grew up out of the great northward emigration of Negroes in the nineties and the early part of the twentieth century. The tradition of slavery had never existed. On the contrary, this essentially New England community had been trained to look upon the Negro as a fellow citizen liberated from bondage. There lingered much of the old sentimental, slightly hysterical, humanitarian spirit of the abolitionists, and the Negroes themselves by their very character roused a feeling of affection which the alien immigrants never knew. In the days of Reconstruction, when the Republicans waved the bloody shirt up and down the state, politicians had even been applauded for asserting that any Negro was as good as a white man and that some of them were superior. By the time Johnny was born, no politician any longer made such statements, and there had entered into the relationship between the two races a patronizing sense of good-natured superiority on the part of the whites. The little colony on Otis Avenue had been there for nearly half a century and their history had been a peaceful one. There was no case of miscegenation and there had never been the faintest suspicion of an attack upon a white woman and only one or two cases of quarrels between men of the two races. A bad negro called Tom Scott had murdered an old couple named Barnes for their money which gossip had it was hidden in their house. He was hanged in the jailyard in the year 1874. But four white men had been hanged in the same jailyard for similar crimes. The little colony had become not only a part of the Town, but in a curious way necessary to it. It was a part of the life and the color of the place, and in the older families established before the War of the Secession there was a close bond with the Negro colony which had persisted through two or three generations. At Trefusis' Castle the stables were always full of negro boys of all ages. Most of the men supported their families by working as butlers or gardeners or coachmen, and the women worked sometimes as laundresses and caterers and "accommodators," but the Negroes who worked regularly as domestic servants were a rarity. One saw them everywhere and some among them became close friends. There were a half-dozen who fixed themselves in the memory of Johnny forever.

Aunty Walker was rich and had a house with a big garden outside the Negro quarter on Elm Street. She had money made out of a catering business which had engaged her energies for forty years until she retired at last, a capitalist, to live upon her income. She was an octoroon who must have been handsome in her youth, with the slow, beautiful animal charm which many octoroons possess. With her the charm had persisted even into her old age, for when Johnny first saw her she had countless wrinkles and grizzled hair. She had great intelligence and during a lifetime of hard work had educated herself by reading in her spare time, and like old Jamie, whose education had been cut short in his youth, she had a reverence amounting to awe for books. For the merry and undignified antics of the other Negroes who were members of the African

Methodist Church she had an attitude of good-natured condescension. She herself was the only colored member of the important and fashionable Congregational church.

The Civil War is a long way off now and the passion which
moved the abolitionists has faded, so that it is difficult any longer
to understand that there was a time when the members of that
church regarded the presence of Aunty Walker in their midst as a
sign of grace and honor and distinction. She had her own pew and
on the occasion of the great church suppers it was Aunty Walker,
experienced as a cateress, who took charge of the big kitchen with
its rows of spotless pans and kettles and its two immense shining
coffee urns. She understood managing such affairs and I think she
regarded her task as the bit she might contribute toward the work
of the Kingdom of Heaven. She was amiable and gentle, with a
loud laugh which one could hear all the way from the kitchen to
the distant assembly room, and from her the white women of the
church took their orders.

She had no children and no relatives, having lost all trace of her
family during the confusion which followed the Civil War, but she
had a passion for children and spoiled them when they went into
the church kitchen before the hour for serving supper. She fed
them with bits of cake and even dishes of ice cream passed with a
secret chuckle out of the back window while mothers and aunts
were not looking. When she died she left all her little fortune to
establish a library for the children of the Sunday school, uniting in
this final act her love for children and her reverence for books. Her
picture, an enormous enlarged photograph taken when she was
middle-aged and handsome, still hangs in the library room,
framed in old-fashioned gilt, almost the last reminder of the days
when to be a Congregationalist was to be an abolitionist, almost
the only memento of the days when the Town and the county were
bitterly divided into abolitionists and Copperheads. So long as the
church exists the picture will hang there and Aunty Walker will be
remembered by the Children's Library, which each year grows a little larger on the benefice of the little fortune she left a long time
ago. It was due to Aunty Walker that Johnny discovered at the age
of eight or nine the limitless beauty of the Greek and Norse

mythologies and later the sober splendor of Plutarch's *⅝IVES*. The library and Aunty Walker and the First Congregational Church were profoundly American and profoundly New England.

And there was Miss America, who was a beauty specialist long before the days of Elizabeth Arden and Helena Rubenstein. She was a tiny, very black Negress with an enormous mouth and a wide smile which revealed two rows of shining gold teeth. These and her fine kinky black hair were her pride. She it was who washed the hair and massaged the faces of the ladies in the Town, and one might meet her on the streets at any hour of the day, accompanied by her mongrel terrier, hurrying along on her short legs and carrying a little bag which contained her toilet preparations. She was always hurrying, for she was in great demand, not alone, I suspect, for her services as manicurist and shampooer, but for her talents as a gossip. She was the Saint Simon of the Town and always brought with her a long catalogue of news and gossip which she had collected on her rounds. She knew everybody and everything which had happened in the Town and she always had more details, sometimes, I suspect, fictional, than anyone else. She carried about with her the faint aroma of a witch doctor, for her creams and lotions were concocted of herbs and simples according to secret formulas which could not have been dragged from her by wild horses.

What her name really was, or whether she had any other name than Miss America, Johnny never knew, nor did anyone else. However she came by it, she was christened long before the days of international beauty contests. On her rounds she was always accompanied by a dog as black and as merrily ugly as herself. It must have been of a fabulous age, for, so far back as anyone could remember, she never had any other. When Miss America arrived in the house life became a little more exciting. When there was a wedding of importance, the bride was given into the hands of Miss America to be shampooed and manicured and made ready for the sacrifice. It was Miss America who helped the bride into her wedding dress, pinning it in here, letting it out there, standing off to survey the product of her skill, flashing her wide grin of ebony and gold while she made clucking sounds of admiration. Miss America was supposed to understand "chic," and for forty years she groomed every bride in the Town and went with her in the cab to the church. In the end it became almost a rite. No girl was respectably married without the expert aid of Miss America.

But best of all was Big Mary. She was as huge a Negress as Miss America was small. She was taller than the six feet two inches of Johnny's father, and she was generous in her proportions. She must have weighed nearly three hundred pounds. She was a black Venus Genetrix, for she was a handsome woman and had countless children and grandchildren, so many that it was impossible to know them all or to keep their individualities separate. Some of them were named for Greek divinities, and in his childhood Johnny played with two pig-tailed goddesses called Juno and Athena. Big Mary and her capable daughters never worked out regularly. They belonged to the aristocratic and expensive category of domestic servants known as "accommodators." Whenever a servant left or there was need of extra help at a funeral or a wedding or a family reunion Big Mary and her daughters were called upon, and they came good-humoredly but with a certain amount of condescension to "help out" until the crisis was passed, but no amount of money could bribe them to sink from the level of "accommodators" to that of ordinary servant. With her children and grandchildren Big Mary constituted a whole catering establishment. They were all excellent cooks and laundresses and as good in one sort of crisis as in another, but best of all they were all big, strong, good-natured sensible women whose presence added gaiety to the household, whether the occasion of their ministration was a wedding or a funeral.

Her daughters went wherever they were summoned, but Big Mary as she grew older chose her places and would go only to the families for whom she had a fancy. Luckily, she had a fancy for Johnny's mother, and so whenever there was a funeral or a wedding she would come in and take charge. She was not an economical servant, for she cooked in the lavish manner and tradition of the old South and herself had a gargantuan appetite which needed a whole chicken at a meal to satisfy it, and she clung to the old southern tradition of "totage," which meant that when her work was finished she had a right to carry home with her all the vegetables and fruit and potatoes she could "tote." As she was a big woman of enormous physical strength, I think that perhaps she held the record of all time for "totage."

When she came to work she arrived in clean gingham with a clean bandana tied around her head, and her arrival meant that so long as she stayed the family would feast upon delicious and indigestible delicacies covering the whole range of the Southern kitchen. But for the children the range of her delights was not confined merely to food. She had an inexhaustible collection of songs, stories, and legends which she poured out lavishly while she worked. Unlike most cooks, she did not banish the children from her kitchen; on the contrary, she welcomed them, and as long as he lives Johnny will remember the big kitchen filled with children eating cookies and listening to Big Mary talk or sing while she mashed the potatoes or basted a turkey. While she was there the kitchen became an enchanted place.

It was always said that Big Mary was the child of a Negress slave and a plantation owner, but Big Mary never gave out any hint as to her descent, although she did admit owning six hundred acres of land on the borders of West Virginia and a whole village from which she drew rents. But she was an absentee landlord and never visited her property. She need not have worked, but she did so, I think, out of primitive wisdom and a liking for a contact with human affairs. She understood the value of things in life and appreciated the happiness which came out of her own peculiar position, a position in which she was honored and respected. She knew, I think, that the position grew out of the old abolitionist traditions of the Town, and that her relation to the white people of the Town was a peculiar one, which could never exist in the South nor in the cities to which the "new negroes" were migrating by the thousands. She knew the whole of Johnny's family intimately, being associated in all its major joys and sorrows. I think there was nothing which one concealed from Big Mary, for, unlike Miss America, she was not a gossip. And she was aware that there were occasions when her advice was sought, and that her wisdom and experience had a value. But she stood in this position not alone to one family which would have implied a kind of servitude, but to half a dozen.

⇔

Johnny went to school for the first time when he was not yet six years old. It was a big building, square and built of red brick and only a few years old, for it was one of the monuments of the growth and progress of the Town. It was a simple building, neither ugly nor beautiful, but it had an engaging look such as many plain women have.

It was the Fourth Ward school and in the scale of the Town growing snobbery the Fourth Ward meant something. It was in the Fourth Ward that the important families lived, and more and more the expression "important family" came to mean "rich family," or perhaps more exactly "successful family," for the word "success" had come to have but a single shade of meaning. It meant "rich." But the Fourth Ward was not only the most prosperous one. It was on the right side of the railroad tracks and as far removed as possible from the Hunkies and Polaks, the smoke and the filth of the Flats. It included the John Sherman Place and those rows of turreted structures being erected constantly by the newly successful. It was the district which became more and more "the place to live."

But when Johnny was a small boy, there was still strength in the old democratic tradition and everybody went to the grade schools and the high schools. Fashionable boarding schools and rich Eastern colleges, if they were ever spoken of at all, were still regarded a little as institutions of some foreign country. The commercial-industrial junto was still feeling its way toward a consciousness of self. It was still sprawling and rather half-baked. No one had begun to talk loudly of the valuable contacts in business and society which a boy might make while attending an Eastern boarding school or college. Education had not yet come to be looked upon largely as a stepping-stone to new opportunities for selling bonds and making financial alliances. One was not likely to go to college unless he went seeking an education. Already there were signs of a change. There were boys who went to college because they were good football players, and others who went because it would be a help in business, and even one or two, like the great-grandson of Bentham, the peddler, who were sent by parents who were looking toward Washington and the East and thought it a good thing for their son to meet the sons of other "important" people like themselves. But on the whole young men usually went to college in order to lay up for themselves a treasure or to fortify themselves against whatever disappointments and tragedies life might bring.

The idea of boarding school was considered affected and pretentious, and a large part of the Town long criticised Great-aunt Jane with bitterness because she sent her six daughters to the East and later to Paris, where they learned to speak French and paint watercolors of bowls of fruit and flowers. As a child of that world one played alike with the children of the rich and of the laundress and the immigrant gardener and sometimes with the grandchildren of black Big Mary. That much remained of the Colonel's democratic dream, but that little was already fading. In a little time when wealth grew a little more self-conscious there would be an effort by rich men and their wives to segregate their children. They would seek to make them believe that because they were born rich they were also born of a superior caste, and in the attempt they would surround them with the trappings of aristocracy, with motors and antique furniture and pictures bought from shrewd dealers, and so bring on the first step in the famous American progression from shirt sleeves to shirt sleeves. All too often there would be no core to that spurious aristocracy, but only the trappings which make a shabby enough disguise. In Johnny's childhood the men, and especially the women, who lived in the ugly houses along Maple Avenue were already growing restless and uneasy because so much money set them apart so little from the people on the wrong side of the railroad tracks. But the Fourth Ward was still a fairly democratic American community, following directly the line of an old and honorable tradition, and still almost uncorrupted by a desire to imitate the East and Europe. It was still a small world which sought to imitate no other and was still content to stand upon its own.

If Johnny had been a supernaturally clever child he would have found all about him on the playground of the Maple Avenue school the seeds of the change which was to come so quickly. They were the children who played with him day after day when classes were finished. They existed already in the brains of the spinsters who taught them and in the parents to whom they returned after school hours.

Surrounding the schoolhouse there was a great space shaded by trees where the grass was worn away by the feet of the children playing at recess time. On school days beneath the trees there was much shouting and screaming and laughter, and one might have stood watching the spectacle thinking all sorts of sentimental banalities about youth and children and gaiety. The surface looked all right. It was only underneath that one came upon the rottenness, the cruelty, and the heartbreak.

Long afterward, when Johnny had come to know many kinds of cruelty in the world, he never discovered any worse than he had found on the playground which surrounded the Maple Avenue school. Because he was awkward and shy and bad at games he came in for a good share of it himself, but what he suffered was nothing by the side of some of the others. He came of an old and respectable and outwardly prosperous family, and so he was never an outsider and the hardships he suffered were nothing extraordinary and did him no harm. There were times when his father was poorer than the German gardener who sent his children to the school in patched clothes, but few ever suspected it because his family was a thoroughly middle-class family and long ago had learned the American game of pretending to be richer than it was, even though the effort was at times desperate. Only once did Johnny know what it was like to be tortured on account of his poverty. It occurred one morning when he appeared at school in a pair of trousers cut down for him by his mother from an old pair of his father's. They would have passed unnoticed save that instead of buttoning down the front they buttoned at the side. One boy made the discovery, and then another and another, until at last, in a corner of the schoolyard, he was surrounded by a mob of boys jeering at his homemade pants. There was more in their attack than the mere savagery of schoolboys. Somewhere in their childish minds they were aware that not only was poverty a disgrace, but that poverty in one of their own kind was an unthinkable crime. Johnny never wore the pants again, but he knew for a few minutes the torture which a dozen other children went through day after day in that schoolyard.

Once or twice he defended one of the children when their torture went beyond endurance, but on the whole he accepted it and did not at all understand what lay at the roots of it. Thirty years later he began to understand that what he witnessed was not simply a manifestation of childish cruelty which might have happened in any nation at any time; he came to understand that it was American. It was something which these children had picked up at home from their own fathers and sometimes from their own mothers. It was the shadow of a philosophy which often enough took the place of religion. It was the principal motive of existence in a good many of those families who sent their children to the Maple Avenue school. One had to be successful, no matter how success was achieved. One must make money, no matter how one came by it. The only hell was poverty and lack of success, and the only heaven was material.

At home those children were accustomed to hearing their parents speak with reverence of Judge Wyant because he was rich, although they must have known that at the same time he was guilty of enough crimes to have kept him in prison for a lifetime. Bentham, the grandson of the peddler, who everyone knew was guilty of bribery and fraud and even perhaps of murder, was looked upon cynically as a clever fellow who knew how to get on in the world. The boys who played at recess under the maple trees of the Fourth Ward schoolhouse were a generation which was growing up to believe that Christ was the first business man and that God must be a banker or a broker. Their religion was profit and prosperity and for it they would be willing to sacrifice every other principle. Most of them never got beyond being members of Rotary Clubs and optimistic boosters in the Chamber of Commerce. In their small way they were destined to go on and on, poorer in this life than the sons of the laundress and the immigrant German gardener had ever been, tending the altar of wealth and privilege, flattered and oily, if one of the high priests deigned to drop them a word of recognition.

It was not only the children in rags and cast-off shoes who suffered, but the immigrant children as well. If a child came to school who spoke with an accent he was set upon at once and tormented by all sorts of cruelties. Luckily, since the Fourth Ward was the "right place" to live, there were very few immigrant children in the school, but sometimes, since the dozen who went there were poor as well as foreign, they suffered from a double dose of cruelty. There was one boy called Herman who wore cast-off clothes and shoes given him indiscriminately by more prosperous families. They seldom fitted him and sometimes they were ragged at the elbows. Most of one winter he had to wear a pair of women's shoes with pearl buttons, run down at the heels, and these were seized upon as a special incentive to torment. The small boys were not merely content with tormenting him at recess time, but when classes were over they followed him home, running all the way and pelting him with sticks or snowballs. Herman was guilty of no crime save that he was poor, and that because he could not speak English without an accent he did not conform. What has become of him I do not know, but he had every reason and every right to become an anarchist, a Communist, a Bolshevist. Perhaps he has become one and is still being pelted by little boys whose bodies have grown up and whose minds remain still capable of schoolyard brutalities. They are still chasing Herman.

In the day of the Colonel and even in old Jamie's prime nonconformity had never been a crime. Indeed, eccentricity had been admired and individuality encouraged. Men and women passed through middle age and grew old, mellowed in the possession of their own particular flavor. But by the time Johnny was born, non-conformity was coming to be regarded as a dangerous thing. A person who behaved in an eccentric way, or had opinions not universally regarded as respectable, was a danger not only to the state, but to prosperity, which was far more important. Even a man who disclosed corruption in the government was often enough regarded as unbalanced and dangerous. Certainly he had no chance whatever in politics. The religion of business required conformity, else how was the country to prosper?

And in a good many houses in the Fourth Ward there was at that moment a new kind of Americanism, like neither that of the Colonel nor that of old Jamie, nor that of Thomas Jefferson, but strident and bullying. The War with Spain had just been won. The Spanish fleets were beneath fathoms of water at Santiago and in Manila Bay. Everything was "bully" with the colonel of the Rough Riders, and Senator Lodge was weaving a mesh of chicanery and bad faith to force the American people into a wild career of imperialism. It was a crude decade and not a very pretty one, and perhaps the boys in the schoolyard were no worse than their elders. Certainly there were plenty of models about on whom to pattern their behavior. Perhaps there were in the Town too many of those dark people imported from Poland and the Mediterranean to work in the factories and the mills. Perhaps America had indigestion from trying to swallow too much cheap labor. Perhaps here and there there were citizens who were sometimes frightened. Every schoolboy knew that it was the immigrants who made strikes and hurt business. They all knew that the Hunkies and Polaks were only animals, anyway.

But none of these reasons made the lot of Herman any easier.

Long afterward, when Johnny's own children went to school in foreign countries, they were received in a kindly fashion and were neither mocked for their accent nor for their manners. Long afterward in those same countries Johnny was forced, until he was weary of it, to defend American children against accusations of atrocious manners and American business men against accusations of brutality, ruthlessness, and sharp dealing; and at last, thinking of these things, it seemed to him that the trail of those

accusations led back over the years to the schoolyard of the Fourth
Ward school. It was not, he thought, that American business men
were any worse than those of other countries. Often enough they
were more honorable, and even when brutal more straightforward
than the others. It was rather that America itself, from the children
in the schoolyard to the greatest of the bankers, was, above all the
others, a nation dominated by a passion for business and success;
and neither the one nor the other has ever made good manners, or
fineness of thought or of feeling.

In that Laurel Avenue school Johnny was taught an incredible
number of lies about the War of the Revolution, about the War of
1812, about the Mexican War, about the Spanish-American War. All
redskins were cruel savages who preyed upon innocent, generous,
well-meaning settlers. All British were oppressors and tyrants. Very
little attention was directed toward the achievements of which
Americans might well be proud. It was as if all the energy of those
men who outlined the history books was expended in glossing over
the depredations and dishonest acts of the American government,
so that little was left to discern and describe the more gracious
achievements. Johnny was taught that the Spanish were a decadent
race addicted to the most fiendish cruelty, that the Spanish-
American War was one of pure altruism, that the imperialist
manipulations of men like Lodge and Roosevell were motivated
only by Christian charity. He was even taught that there was no
virtue in the southern states, and as a child he had the idea that half
the southerners were the direct descendants of Simon Legree and
the rest of Benedict Arnold. Once a month, at the behest of some
female crank, each class of children was called upon to stand and,
placing one hand over the heart, and then raising the right hand, to
parrot in piping voices, "I give my heart and my head and my hand
to my country." There was also something idiotic about my country
right or wrong, but that, fortunately, Johnny forgot. I do not know
what good this special piece of asininity was to accomplish, but I
suppose it was to fill the budding citizens with a blind enthusiasm
for a government (and so for themselves) regardless of its folly, its
corruption and hypocrisy. There was even an effort made to make
us believe that the President was a sacrosanct creature, incapable of

wrong, yet at home Johnny had heard of McKinley and Hanna and he knew that his own state had produced a whole crop of feeble Presidents and crooked and scoundrelly politicians. When I think of it now, it seems to me that more good would have been done if, instead of all the lies we were taught and the parrotings we were put through, there had been a large sign hung in each schoolroom with the words of Dr. Johnson, "Patriotism is the last refuge of the scoundrel." Certainly the loudest patriots in the world of Johnny's childhood were also the greatest scoundrels. And the political bosses and the big business men who honored the flag and shouted the loudest at gatherings of veterans were at that moment stealing from the people at whom they shouted, sweating and red-faced, in shirt-sleeve oratory. The men, like Grandfather Willingdon's friend, General Vandervelde, who had given his whole life to the welfare of his fellow citizens, never spoke of patriotism at all, or if they did so it was with a fine blush of self-consciousness.

❧

Johnny was seven when the incident of the pants occurred and he understood for the first time that his family was poor. All poverty is relative, and unless a man stands naked before his God there is always another man in the world who has fewer possessions. And so Johnny's family was much better off than hundreds of others in the Town, but it suffered from perhaps the worst of all poverties— the variety known as genteel. There were times when the family was even affluent, but most of the time Johnny's parents had much less money than the people of their own small world. They lived well and were never without one horse and sometimes two or three in the stables, but in order to keep up a front it was necessary to deny themselves things which their friends had as a matter of course, and to make petty economies and makeshifts which were unceasingly annoying. Most of it was done in secret, but sometimes one of the family got caught out, as in the case of the home-made breeches. There was, of course, no reason why they should have kept up a bluff except that in that Town and in the then existing state of civilization in America it would have been impossible to have done otherwise. I think that if Alexander Hamilton had looked ahead he would have had the American dollar stamped with the motto, "Nothing succeeds like success." It lies at the root of the average American's incapacity to understand and appreciate life, of his habit of living always to the limit of his income and often beyond it. It lies, I think, at the root of the American passion for speculation, and for the abysmal helplessness of the American in a financial depression—the American who does not own his own home, although he has his automobile—the American without enough saved to support his family for six months. One has to keep up a false front, and a good many Americans worry themselves into the grave struggling to maintain that bogus façade.

And so Johnny's family wwas always pretending to the world that they were better off than they really were. It was not so bad when he was small, but as he grew older he became more and more aware of the strain. I think it was his mother who bore most of the burden of worry on her strong shoulders, for she was one of those made to worry and who, seeing a responsibility in the distance, ran to meet it and place it on her own shoulders. Her whole life was spent in anticipation of calamity or in the expectancy of some stroke of fortune which would make them all rich forever. Johnny's father was inclined to take things calmly; at least one never saw any sign of the vagaries of life disturbing him, unless it was in the wild outbursts of temper which sometimes seized him. The horror of that respectable poverty colored all of Johnny's childhood and left upon him marks which he was never able to destroy. As a man he came to live from day to day in horror of being poor, but at the same time he could not resist living extravagantly as if he were compelled to do so in a wild effort to destroy those childhood impressions; and he acquired a horror of borrowing, and a terrible self-consciousness about money which made it impossible for him to bargain, so that he always came out worst in every deal he ever undertook, and could never ask for the payment of a loan he had made. Even to talk about money was painful to him.

THE OLD MAN

WHEN JOHNNY WAS SEVEN YEARS OLD HE SAW HIS GRANDFATHER Willingdon for the first time. There had been a good deal of mystery before the old man actually appeared. It began with a letter which arrived one morning and was opened by Johnny's father, who read it through to himself once, then twice, and handed it silently to his wife. She did not read it twice. She did not even read it through to the end, but tossed it into the middle of the breakfast table and said, "It's come at last."

For the moment they said nothing more on the subject nor did they speak of anything else until Johnny's father rose and said he must be off to the office, but in the days which followed Johnny overheard them talking now and then and heard his mother say, "I suppose he can have Mary's room," for Mary Crane had just been married and because the family fortunes had gone into one of the periodic doldrums no "hired girl" had been engaged in her place. His father said, "Yes, I think that will suit him best." And Johnny was left floundering in curiosity. For days he tried to imagine what his Grandfather Willingdon was like, but he could not make any progress with the puzzle, because he knew nothing at all about him. No one had ever spoke of him. Johnny only knew that he was always traveling in some remote part of the earth and that two or three times a year a letter came addressed to his father in minute handwriting, and that sometimes the letter had foreign stamps on it. The last one had come from San Francisco, and the one before it from China. It was difficult to imagine Grandpa Willingdon because there was something about Grandpa Ferguson, some vigor of personality, which got in the way. For Johnny Old Jamie seemed the model of all grandfathers and whenever he tried to think what Grandpa Willingdon might be like, the figure of that huge muscular old man of eighty somehow obscured and blurred the picture.

And then one morning Grandpa Willingdon arrived in the most unexpected of ways. The station express wagon from Thompson's livery stable stopped before the house laden with three big wooden boxes and a tin trunk, and on the wagon seat beside Ed Thompson rode a tall lean old man with a pepper-and-salt beard. He was dressed rather like a preacher, in shabby black clothes and a wide-rimmed hat of black felt, with brilliant grim eyes which were so deep a blue that they appeared to be black. He was Grandpa Willingdon, the son of the Methodist and the Congregationalist, the child of Thomas and Marianna Willingdon.

He had come home to die. The trunk was carried up into the "hired girl's" room, and the boxes were unpacked under the arbor in the back yard. They contained nothing but books, and whether they had accompanied the old man on his wanderings or whether they had been kept somewhere in storage no one ever discovered. Shelves were built in his room and they were carried up and put in order by the old man himself. They were to be his only companions for the rest of his life.

It was not easy to receive him into the midst of that noisy family. The first greetings were cold and awkward, but the awkwardness never wore away even after the family had long grown accustomed to his presence. He was the strangest of strangers, but even if he had lived all his life in the ugly house, I think the relationship would have been no different. Johnny's mother had seen him but once, and Johnny's father had not seen him for seventeen years, but his strangeness arose not so much from his long absence and the mystery which surrounded him, as from the character of the old man himself and in the terrible coldness which appeared to incase him like a shroud of ice. It was ice which did not even melt in the ardor of a family which long ago had capitulated to the domination of that other grandfather, old Jamie.

He asked that he might have his meals in his room, and Johnny's mother did not protest, for after he had had a half dozen meals with the family, she was delighted at the prospect of never having him again enter the dining room. It was like having a ghost at the table. He sat there cold and silent, save that once or twice during the meal he opened his thin lips to utter some bitter remark which chilled all the others as if a door had opened suddenly and a blast of icy air had come up out of some subterranean place. Arguments and even quarrels were frequent enough at the table, especially when the aunts and uncles were "visiting," but they were hot-headed and wordy and usually concerned with politics, and suddenly they would be finished in a gale of laughter, and good feeling would return as if nothing had ever happened. But of cold bitterness and cynicism there had been none, for it was a family in which there were no doubts nor any talent for satire. The presence of Grandpa Willingdon was wrong, and even Johnny's small brother felt it, although he could not possibly have understood it, and twice burst into tears for no reason at all, only calling out amid his wails, "I'm frightened! I'm frightened!" while the old man glared fiercely at him.

He came to be known as "The Old Man," not only in the Town but in the family as well. There was, I think, nothing of disrespect in the title. It was somehow appropriate and inevitable, like the names of Toby's Run and Trefusis' Castle. He was very straight and very lean and brittle and spry. Yet one had the impression that he was immensely ancient and had always been so, like the prophets of the Old Testament. It was impossible to think of him as ever having been young or gay. One could not imagine what it would have been like to hear him laugh. It would, I think, have been terrifying. If there was any shadow of contempt in the title "The Old Man," it lay in the mystery which always surrounded him and in the knowledge that he had never worked at anything. In the opinion of the Town, the neighborhood, and even the family, a life without work was a damned life. It was the old sin for which Dr. Trefusis had never been forgiven.

From the day he arrived, eccentrically, upon the seat of the baggage wagon instead of a cab, he was accepted by Johnny's parents as a cross to be borne. He had written to announce that he was returning to make his home with them, inclosing no address which would have allowed a protest. There was nothing to be done. It was unthinkable that he should have been sent into an asylum, and impossible to have paid for his lodging and board elsewhere, even if a boarding-house keeper could be found who would support, at any price, the perpetual chill of his personality and his strange disordered habits of life. But in the end the family came to accept him, and in the exile of his room above the kitchen, he became a part of the establishment. But there grew up about him a protective wall of tissue, such as the flesh builds up about foreign matter lodged within it. In that noisy overflowing house he was forever isolated.

The children came to accept him as a phenomenon which had intruded suddenly within the borders of their existence. Blindly they felt his strangeness. They knew that he was old, but also that he was different from the other old people they knew. He was not like the great-aunts who were always visiting, and he was as different as it was possible to be from Grandpa Ferguson. And after a time they came no longer to notice him any more than if he had been a new chimney on the house. It was only when they encountered him at dusk and found his sharp eyes staring at them that the old terror seized them. For none of them save Johnny did he ever show the faintest interest or affection. Johnny was the exception, and Johnny it was who carried his meals up the narrow dark back stairs and lighted his kerosene lamp at dusk. And slowly in Johnny there grew up an impression and a memory of The Old Man which was destined never to leave him. It was of a room smelling of kerosene and apples and dusty books and old age, and in the midst of it the squeaking of the rocking chair in which The Old Man sat as the darkness fell and he waited for Johnny to light his lamp.

He had a faint liking for Johnny, which embarrassed and troubled the boy, for it was not pleasant to have a ghost touch your head or ask you what you had learned in school. He responded, politely as he could, for he was well brought up, as a grandchild of old Jamie's had to be, but there were times when he could not control his limbs, which would, in spite of everything, shrink away a little. And as he grew older he became dimly aware of something pitiful in the groping efforts of the lonely old man with the bitter brilliant eyes which made him ashamed that his body rebelled as if from death itself.

As a child Johnny had no great curiosity about Grandpa Willingdon, nor any impulse to inquire into the reasons for the bitter loneliness of the old man, nor for his own feeling of distaste and even horror. But The Old Man became a part of him forever, fixed in his memory with a vividness which his agreeable memories of old Jamie never approached. It was only after he was grown and had children of his own and there were moments when he felt The Old Man in his blood, that he began to wonder about him and to understand him a little through his own self. Twenty years after The Old Man died, he came to live again with a strange vividness in the memory and even in the blood of Johnny. It may have been that The Old Man preferred Johnny to his other grandchildren because even then, on the evenings when Johnny climbed the dark stairs of "the back way" to light his lamp, he had been aware that in Johnny alone he would live on.

In him mingled the hot blood of Jorge and Elvira van Essen and the cold sensuality of Thomas Willingdon, the New England emigrant, and it may have been that in his veins the two bloods congealed. He was the son whom the passionate Marianna had overwhelmed with love, setting him against his father, pouring out upon him the affection for which she had no other outlet. She it was who kept his very soul in subjection all through his childhood and adolescence, using whatever means she found at hand. For she belonged to the unscrupulous women of the nineteenth century who, denied suffrage and divorce and sometimes even the rights of property, found weapons of their own to gain what they wanted in life. Like them, she could faint at will and summon to her aid the most spectacular hysterics. She was not above the most petty intrigues, even setting her husband and her children against one another. She was capable of raising a hurricane of emotion which wore the nerves of others to rags and filled the whole house with unhappiness for days but somehow left her miraculously untouched, standing in the center of the storm, a martyr and a saint. But fate had sent her the one husband who was able to ride untouched and serene through tears and screams, through fainting fits and hysterics, to emerge perfectly calm and wholly cold with the remark, "Mrs. Willingdon has had another attack," or "You had better go in and look after your mother; she is beside herself again." It was a hurricane wasting itself against a wall of flint, and when at last, baffled and furious, she gave up all hope of ever dominating her husband, she turned to her son.

When she began her attack he was a soft, rather timid boy, and in the end she succeeded only in turning him into the flint his father had been before him. When she came to die at last he was a man of sixty-five, but she had done something to him for which he never forgave her. He had the news of her approaching death in San Francisco and could have returned, but he wrote coldly that the journey was too long and, anyway, she might be dead before he arrived.

But while he was still a boy he had loved her passionately, so deeply that he existed only in relation to her. He thought her the most beautiful woman in the world and the most charming. He knew, like herself, that she was martyred, and he hated his father who lived in the same house, cold and aloof, untouched by the emotional tempests which were forever sweeping over him. Marianna was a primitive woman, and her instinct must have been to save her son for herself and to keep him bound to her for as long as she lived. She called him "my boy" with a glow of affection and tears in her eyes, and she taught him, insidiously, that other women were to be despised and that girls were evil creatures with only one thought in their minds. Out of her Methodism and her own baffled passions she led him to believe that whatever had to do with love or sex was filthy. There was only one life which was pure and good. And so, under her spell, he went off when he was seventeen to a Methodist seminary to become a preacher.

He was a handsome youth, looking very like his father, the handsome New Englander with a head like a Greek bust, and in the picture taken the day he set out for the seminary the face is of a boy who knew nothing of the world. It is the face of a frail, emotional

boy of seventeen, touched by a look of unearthly purity and asceti-
cism. It was the first time the two had ever been separated, and
they wrote each other every day long emotional letters, his touched
by naive religious sentiments and hers filled with insidious emotional phrases. She urged him "never to forget the one person in
the world who would give up her life for him" and to remember
that "in her sad persecuted existence he was all that she had in life."
A half dozen times during the first awful year of their separation
she left home without warning and made him hysterical visits
drenched with emotion.

The second year at the seminary was easier for him, but he still
remained dependent upon Marianna. One could see it in the letters which Johnny found long after The Old Man was dead. They
were filled with doubts and timidity and homesickness, and here
and there, most terrible of all, there were the faintest insinuations
of his doubts of God Himself; but Marianna, possessive, affectionate, determined, overwhelmed him with new outbursts, and for a
little while the doubts would vanish, stifled more by her violence
than by any change of belief.

And then in the third year he discovered a friend. It was another boy come up from a farm to be a preacher like himself, and
slowly he began to discover what he had never known before—the
pleasure and beauty of a companion in whom one could confide,
who understood one's doubts and fears and the very terrors of life
itself. It was the first friend he had ever had, and into the friendship he poured all the emotion which slowly he had come to with-
hold more and more from the overpowering Marianna; for as he
had begun to doubt in God he had begun to doubt in her as well.
Slowly as he grew used to the separation he began to doubt that she
was infallible, that she was saintly, even that she was a noble martyr. He lived away from home now. He saw perhaps that other
mothers were different. Now that he had tasted freedom, the world
began to open up before him. The name of the friend was
Chauncey Knox, and presently they took a room together in the
house of the professor of theology, a man named Roscoe Bates.

It was then that Marianna grew suspicious. Perhaps she felt
from the tone of his letters that he was slipping from her. Perhaps

she felt, with that intuition by which she lived, the coolness that crept into the words set down with a certain perfunctoriness that turned them mysteriously into formulas. Once more she descended upon the seminary and did her best to destroy the friendship which she suspected was weaning her son from her. And for a time she succeeded, but Thomas, the son, had caught a glimpse of other horizons and there must have been in him, even as a boy, something of his father's quiet craftiness and of his mother's overwhelming willfulness, for quietly he returned to his friend. He returned in secret.

So passed the year, and presently the time for his ordination as a preacher drew near, and Marianna came once more to the seminary and his deception was uncovered. There was a fresh hurricane, more terrible than any which had gone before. There were wild tears and reproaches, and the storm fell alike upon the son and upon his friend. What she said no one will ever know, but three days later Chauncey Knox was found drowned in the little river which ran past the seminary. Her son Thomas was ordained a preacher, but he never preached a sermon and Marianna lost him forever.

He disappeared, and for more than two years there was no news of him, and then one day he returned quietly and went to work reading law in the office of a friend of his father's. Thomas Willingdon knew that his son had returned, but it was a week before Marianna discovered it. She wrote to him and came to see him at the law office, but he would not return, and when she threatened to create another storm he walked out of the room as he had seen his father do so many times. Marianna went home and took to her bed, where she remained until her twin sister, the tiny, capable, business-like Sapphira, left her farm and business and fourteen children and routed her out.

A year after he returned to the Town young Thomas married a girl called Ellen Winchell, the daughter of a man of English descent who kept a drugstore on the square. Marianna came to the wedding, and as the last words of the ceremony were being spoken she fainted dead away and had to be carried to the "spare room" and fanned and fed with blackberry cordial. But neither her husband nor her son came near her, and in the end she recovered her senses and ate a hearty dinner.

The bride was a handsome girl with dark hair and eyes, modest and possessed of a strong character and a quiet philosophy of resignation, two weapons of which she had great need in the years that were to follow. She had been brought up simply by her father, the chemist, who was a quiet fellow given to experiments with a bent toward science rather than shopkeeping. I think she must have been deeply in love with her morose, emotionally unstable young husband, and that it was a love which endured through all the long years of their married life. It survived neglect and long absences and coldness. She had a faithful heart.

Her trials began a little more than a year after the marriage, when suddenly he abandoned her and his law studies and disappeared into the West. From time to time she received a letter from him, but she was never able to write him, because he never sent any address. Sometimes the letters came from California, sometimes from New Mexico, sometimes from Nevada, and in none of them was there any hint of his returning home. She returned to live with her father in the big brick house of which the drugstore occupied the ground floor, and the burden of her support fell upon her father and old Thomas Willingdon. Eight months after her husband disappeared a son was born. He was five years old when his father returned suddenly and learned of his existence.

He had a way of disappearing and returning thus. It happened a half dozen times during Ellen's life. She would find a note and discover that he had gone away, and then, after three or four years had passed, the bell at the door of the drugstore would ring one evening and Ellen would go to open it, thinking it was someone in need of medicines, and there she would find her husband. He would come in and eat supper and return to her bed without comment on his absence, as if he had never been away at all. There was no question of divorce and I do not think she would have divorced him even if she had lived in a day when divorce was a conventional affair. She never questioned him about his long absences and he rarely spoke of them, so that she never really knew where he had been or what he had been doing. It appeared to have troubled Ellen's father no more than herself. He was a vague old gentleman and scarcely noticed whether his son-in-law was in the house or not.

On his first return he remained nearly a year, and then one evening, on the eve of the Civil War, there was a note left on the dining room table and he was gone again. This time he went to Montana, where he fought Indians and prospected for copper, traveling from settlement to settlement spending weeks alone in the high mountains. He had a mule and a pick and a shovel and a big pack filled mostly with books. He never discovered any rich mines, although vaguely he staked out a few claims of which he afterward lost the papers. But I do not think that it was gold or copper that he really sought. No man, to the misfortune of his family, ever held wealth in less esteem. Gold and copper were simply excuses for solitude, without which he could not have lived.

It was during the second absence that Johnny's father was born. The Civil War was over and Johnny's father was four years old when the wanderer returned again, took off his hat, and sat down to supper to find that he had two sons instead of one.

His sons knew him scarcely at all, for out of their whole youth he spent altogether not more than two or three years in the house with them, and even when he was at home he remained remote and showed little interest in them. There must have been something about him in his youth and manhood which his wife alone knew and understood, some sympathy, some occasional burst of warmth, which was revealed to her alone. She stood by him, and when her father died she kept the drugstore as a means of supporting her two children. The business gradually failed, and when Johnny's father was fourteen she sold what remained of it. And when that money was gone, Johnny's father at eighteen went to work in a bank. Old Thomas Willingdon helped them, but the elder son was no aid. At nineteen he too had gone off to see the world.

Ellen, who was Johnny's Grandmother Willingdon, died before he was born. One day when she had pains she refused to send for the doctor and took some strong physic. She had appendicitis and the physic killed her when she was still a strong woman of sixty. Her pictures are those of a woman with a fine, good-humored face who never made any attempt to escape her responsibilities. When Johnny's father and mother were married, they went to live with her because there was not enough money for two households, and mother-in-law and daughter-in-law dwelt together in peace and deep affection until Ellen died. And Johnny's mother was no weak, small woman without a character of her own. But she adored her mother-in-law.

All his life The Old Man was unhappy save perhaps for those times when he escaped into utter solitude. He was, I think, incapable of giving or receiving warmth. Something at some time had hurt him, so profoundly that from then onward until he died he was afraid of being hurt and so withdrew more and more into himself. He possessed a profoundly emotional nature and the character to control it, and always he was driven, I suspect, by a horror of unbridled emotionalism. The scenes and quarrels and swoonings of Marianna left a mark on all her children, and the memory of them left her son frozen forever, incapable of showing any feeling. Her two daughters died as old maids in their eighties, too frightened ever to have married. But the case of her son Thomas was more complex than that of her daughters. Somewhere, deep beneath the icy surface, there flowed the currents of her own hot blood and of old Thomas Willingdon's cold sensuality. But for them there was no outlet and their flames burnt themselves out at last in the furnaces of a fierce interior life. In the end, I think he found that the only means of enduring life lay in utter detachment from it.

He had not the blessings of a man of action, never having known that curious animal vitality which drove old Jamie to create and achieve, to breed and to mingle with his fellow men, leaving him no time in the day's short span for morbid introspection. Whatever joys and sorrows he knew, occurred not in the market places, but in the fastnesses of his own soul, concealed there so proudly and so profoundly that none could ever divine when he was happy or sorrowful. And so he became as detached physically and spiritually from the whole human spectacle as it was possible for any man to be.

Johnny's mother, who was for all the world like her father, old Jamie, had a contempt for him which he in his turn reciprocated. For years they lived in the same house, hating each other with an inevitability which was Greek and classic. To her, his worst vice was what she called his laziness. Being all that was positive and active herself, she could not fathom the paralysis of a tormented divided soul; nor could she ever forgive him his detachment or the profound mystery which prevented him from ever doing a constructive action in all his existence. She did not understand that laziness was not his vice, but a paralyzing cynicism, nor that his aloofness was not a thing of his own choice, but imposed upon him tragically against his will. His soul, I think, existed in a perpetual state of interrogation—a ceaseless questioning of the value or the reason for everything about him. It was a soul which was profoundly sick, and his hysterical wanderings were born as much of a frantic effort to escape from himself as from his fellow creatures. He lived to be eighty-three years old, and save for a few illumined, mysterious moments, life was forever intolerable to him.

He had in all his life, so far as Johnny ever knew, only one close friend. This was a man of his own age, the most distinguished man in all the Town and county, perhaps even in all the state. He was a General Vandervelde, a man of Dutch ancestry who had served both in the Mexican War and in the War of Secession. He was a tall man, very straight and military in appearance, yet by nature too much of a gentleman to have acquired the brutal manners and gaucheries of the usual professional soldier. His blue eyes were merry and his beard the whitest Johnny ever saw on an old gentleman. His complexion was very fair and pink. In Johnny's memory he remains as the cleanest, merriest old man he ever saw. Like the Colonel, he belonged more to the eighteenth century than to the nineteenth. His whole moral attitude, his liking for the good things of life, his poise and detachment, his humor and charm, his tolerance and the extraordinary distinction of appearance, were all in direct antagonism to the sour respectability and bad taste which colored so much of the community and the century in which he lived. He brought to the Town and the county a distinction which was rare in that time and place.

Throughout the years that The Old Man lived with Johnny's family the old General came three times a week to climb the dark stairs of the "back way" to the room above the kitchen. He walked with a stick, very straight, his white beard blowing over his spotless shirt front. His carriage was very different from that of The Old Man. He moved with the dignity and assurance of a man who had done his duty and earned the respect of his neighbors and his nation, a man who knew exactly what he believed and in his rationalism felt the earth solid and fine beneath his feet. He was never troubled by cynicism or doubts nor by the terrible, morose, sentimental, Gothic temperament of The Old Man, his friend.

It was a strange friendship which must have had its roots in the liking of the two men for books and for interminable philosophic discussions. In the room above the kitchen the two would remain closeted, talking and smoking and eating apples for hours on end. The General also lived to an immense age and died a few weeks after The Old Man. I should like to believe in heaven, if only to know that they are now sitting somewhere together smoking and talking philosophy. I think the General understood the lonely Old Man who lived surrounded by books, in exile from all the Town and even from his own family.

In the end, as he grew older, Johnny came to understand him a little, for there were moments, unwanted and even terrifying, when he felt creeping over him a strange weariness of the world, a hunger for solitude, and a desire to hide away like a hermit in the

desert. And there came, too, that awful mood of doubt and questioning and hated cynicism and bitterness, and a sense of disap-
pointment and disillusionment with all the world about him. It
was like a horrible disease which Johnny came to fight whenever he
felt it stealing over him, for he had memories both of The Old Man
and his grandfather Jamie and he knew that the man who had lived
by action was the happy one of the two.

In his old age, The Old Man had been bitter and tragic, yet one
felt that there were things he knew which none of the others had
ever imagined. Behind the burning eyes and that air of immense
age one suspected that it was better never to penetrate. It was perhaps that quality which made his presence in any group of people
disturbing and gave you the feeling, when the brilliant eyes looked
at you, that he saw through all the defenses and hypocrisies and
knew you at once completely, with all your sins and vices, petty
dishonesties and evil thoughts. There was something intolerable in
the gaze of The Old Man which made people hate him. He had
been born understanding too much, and out of his own bitter suf-
ferings I think he came in the end to know things of men and
women which they themselves dared not to face.

‑‑Θ‑‑

A little while after The Old Man came to live in the slate-gray
house, Great-aunt Sapphira, his mother's twin sister had her hundredth birthday and all the descendants were invited to the first
reunion of the descendants of Jorge and Elvira to be held since the
days when Elvira, as an old lady, gathered her sons and daughters
and grandchildren about her in the big house at van Essen's mills.
She had been dead now more than half a century and her daughter Sapphira was the oldest living member of the family. At the age
of a hundred, this old lady herself addressed letters of invitation to
the heads of each of the now countless branches of the family. And
so a letter in Sapphira's tremulous, scratchy handwriting came to
The Old Man, who was past eighty, asking him and his sons and
grandchildren to come to Spring Hill Farm in Oswego County on
the old lady's birthday in June.

But Thomas Willingdon had finished with traveling. His wanderings were at an end and he had come home to die, and nothing
could stir him from the security and solitude of that room above

the kitchen. In his son's family one of the periodical financial crises was in progress, and it was therefore impossible that all of them should make the long journey into the southern part of the state. So after a conference it was decided that Johnny and his father should be sent, one to represent the fourth and the other the fifth generation to have been born since Jorge and Elvira came into the new country.

It was Johnny's first long train journey, and the excitement was so great that during all the hot journey he was sick. They arrived in Williamsburg to find that in the small town every hotel and boarding-house was already filled with the descendants of Jorge and Elvira, and in the end they threw themselves upon the hospitality of Great-aunt Sapphira. Her own house was filled to overflowing and at length they were given a room in the stables which was usually occupied by one of the farmhands. It was a small room built of fresh unpainted pine and it smelled of horses and harness and soap, and when one wakened in the morning one looked out over a paddock filled with colts and yearlings. For a small boy it was a room finer than any palace. For Johnny's father, with his passion for horses, it was paradise. Together, father and son fed the colts sugar and examined the brood mares and rubbed the sleek withers of the two big stallions, Jereboam and Achilles. There were horses everywhere. One saw them, one felt them, one smelled them—big fine Morgan stallions and mares and colts.

The old lady still lived on the farm to which she had come as a bride more than eighty years before. To arrive at the farmhouse one turned in off the highroad from Williamsburg through an archway on which was painted in golden letters *Spring Hill Stock Farm*. Beyond the archway there was an avenue of maple trees between pastures where mares and foals of all sizes looked up and galloped wildly around as one drove past. At Spring Hill Farm they had bred Morgan horses since the stock came into existence. There were always a score or more colts of various ages, two stallions, and a dozen brood mares. The horses which drew the carriage of the old lady on the rare occasions when she left the farm were always the pick of the stable.

The house, like that built by the Colonel, was large and rambling and white, and stood on a slight rise in the land. At the foot of the slope the big cool spring welled up to water the pastures and give the place its name. In the beginning its waters had been forced up the hill into the house by an old-fashioned ram, but the old lady, believing in progress, was always interested in the latest inventions and had long since installed a gasoline engine to take the place of the ram. There was nothing picturesque about the place; it was far too prosperous and modern. The fences were all of wood, and big barns and stables were painted a cheery banal red. At each corner of the cow barn stood the first silos in all the state.

Sapphira was a rich old lady. From the days when she had run beside the wagon train along the trail from Maryland, collecting bluejay feathers and bright stones in a cloth bag, she had gone on acquiring possessions. In her youth and in her prime it was her shrewdness and energy, operating through a bewhiskered Victorian husband, which had built up the stock farm and guided all manner of shrewd speculations and wise investments. And when he died of pneumonia, caught at sixty-seven from driving all night in a sleet storm, she carried on. After his death it became apparent that he had never really counted at all save as the begetter of Sapphira's fourteen children. Sapphira, everyone saw, had always been the real source of brains and shrewdness, for she not only kept the fortune which she had made through her husband during his lifetime, but she continued to add to it. For nearly forty years she had been a widow and for nearly forty years she had continued to grow richer and richer.

On the day of the reunion there were four enormous long tables placed on the lawn beneath the trees and all of them were filled with the descendants of Jorge and Elvira van Essen. In all there were more than fifteen hundred, but a few hundred of them had been unable to attend. Some lived in California, and some in Washington and Oregon, and some in Europe, and one great-grandson with a family of five was consul in Singapore. There were Patersons and Butterworths, Willingdons and van Essens, Joneses and MacDonalds, mostly modest, sober citizens ranging from one who was a blacksmith to the old lady's eldest son, Eben, who had been a congressman, and her grandson who was a state senator. Of her own descendants there were one hundred and eighty-six and some of them had not been able to come. Jorge and Elvira, the patriarch and matriarch of long ago, had done well. In that new country they had left enough descendants to populate a town.

For the feast there were three barbecued oxen and five lambs, as well as countless chickens, roasted with sweet corn and potatoes in the ashes of a fire which consumed several whole trees. There were cider and beer and cold water from the springhouse, and scores of pies. Sapphira's daughters and granddaughters and great-grand-daughters served their relatives. There was even a great-great-grandchild of eleven who had a place beside that kept for old Sapphira at the head of the most important table.

Under the trees and about the fires gathered uncles and aunts, cousins and nephews and nieces, children and grandchildren and great-grandchildren who had never encountered one another before. There were some who until that moment had not known of the existence of the others. They gossiped and chatted and exchanged stories and planned visits which in the end were never made. Only one person present knew who they all were or that they existed at all. He was Eben, the congressman, Sapphira's eldest son, who was himself eighty-two years old. The family was his hobby and he had a great ledger in which he had all the descendants filed and ticketed neatly.

At last, when everything was ready and the oxen and sheep roasted to a turn, old Sapphira, accompanied by her son Eben, came out of the house.

She was a tiny old woman, who looked scarcely bigger than a bird. She was dressed in purple (for she detested black) and wore a bonnet covered with sequins and ornamented with ostrich tips. As she came out of the door and moved across the lawn, the news of her arrival was whispered from group to group under the trees and a silence fell like the shadow of a cloud over the whole big lawn, as one by one and in little groups the descendants of Jorge and Elvira van Essen turned toward her.

As Johnny turned he was overcome suddenly by awe, almost by terror, at the sight of anyone so old, and slipped his hand into that of his father. Near him someone said, "The old lady's very spry for a hundred," and another cousin murmured, "But for her, a hundred and eighty-two of us wouldn't be here." Someone laughed nervously, and then out of the silence someone cheered in a far corner of the yard and the cheer spread from group to group. The old lady, as if surprised, turned and stood leaning on her stick, looking about her. Then slowly she understood and her ancient face softened. She smiled, and raising her stick with the friendliness of one sure of her importance and accustomed to authority, she shook it in a gesture of greeting to all the descendants of Jorge and Elvira. Someone started "Auld Lang Syne," and when the singing was finished everyone moved toward the tables.

But there were even more descendants than the honorable Eben had counted upon, and some of the lesser ones had to eat their dinners sitting on the grass beneath the trees, because there was no place for them.

The feasting lasted until the late afternoon, when old Sapphira took her leave and retired to the parlor to receive certain chosen members of the family. She asked for her nephew, Thomas Willingdon, and when she was told that The Old Man had not come, she sent for Johnny and his father and together they went in to speak to her. She sat in a big armchair, rather like an elderly bird in a nest, smoking a pipe now because her son Eben no longer allowed her to smoke cigars. Lately she had become absent-minded and sometimes left them, lighted, here and there about the house.

There was something hard about the old lady which frightened Johnny, and he held back shyly. As they crossed the room her son Eben, who sat beside her, shouted, "Here's Thomas's son and grandson," and a look of understanding came into the dark old eyes. For a moment she regarded the pair standing before her, up and down, as if they were children, and then said, sharply, "Where's your father?" and Johnny's father explained that The Old Man was too ill to come to Spring Hill Farm. It was a lie and the old lady knew it. She said, "Well, I never expected him to come, anyway. He never put himself out for anybody. He always was queer."

Then she took Johnny's hand and said, "You've never seen anybody so old, have you, lad?"

But when Johnny tried to speak, he could find no words, and the old lady said, impatiently, "What's the matter? Cat got your tongue?"

"No."

"Well, it's all right," and turning toward Johnny's father, she asked, "Do you remember my father, Jorge?"

James Willingdon said that Old Jorge had died long before he was born.

"Aye, that's true," said the old lady. "I forgot you were one of the youngsters." Then, dismissing the two of them, she said, "Tell Thomas he should have come. Yes, I've got it right now. You're the grandson of my sister Marianna. Marianna always was a fool!"

It was the first and last time Johnny ever saw Sapphira who had run beside the wagon train coming over the mountains from Maryland. She had borne fourteen children, all of whom were healthy and lived to great ages. She played the piano and sang and smoked cigars. She had built up a fat fortune and refused ever to leave the farm to which she had come as a girl. In all her life she never weighed more than ninety-eight pounds. She lived for four more years, and to the end she treated her son Eben, who was eighty-six when she died, as if he had never grown up.

⤙

Besides The Old Man there were two other grandchildren of Jorge and Elvira in the Town who did not go to the reunion at Sapphira's. Both of them were old maids. Indeed, they were more than old maids, for they were so ancient that long ago they had reached the age when neither virginity nor sex had anything to do with them. To Johnny it seemed that they had been there forever. He was aware always that in some way they were related to him, but no one in the family ever thought of addressing them as Cousin Zenobia or Cousin Susan. Perhaps it was because they were, both of them, caricatures of women, and so were unconsciously regarded by the family as creations of a God with a talent somewhat like that of Dickens. They were always spoken of as Zenobia van Essen and Susan Wilkes, as if the family had washed its hands of them.

Zenobia van Essen lived in a house outside the Town which stood in the shadow of the hard gray walls of the State Prison—a house which was very much like the castle of Mr. Wemmick in *Great Expectations*. It was a miniature house with countless tiny gables and turrets and castellations, with doors which seemed scarcely large enough to pass through. Surrounding it was an acre or two of garden which simply was a tangle of flowers gone wild. Honeysuckle, wisteria, and eglantine climbed over the whole cottage, devouring the jigsaw bracketing. In the corner of the garden there was a miniature ravine shaded by huge willow trees, and at the bottom of it there was a deep cold spring. An ornamental wooden fence also in the process of being devoured by honeysuckle and trumpet vine, surrounded the place, and at a little distance from the house there was a gazebo in which Zenobia sometimes sat in hot weather. Chickens and turkeys and ducks wandered about the doorstep, and exotic ducks and geese with strange-colored feathers and tufted heads swam on the miniature pond below the spring. Whole families of cats slept in the sun by the doorstep. Instead of the cannon and the moat which Mr. Wemmick used as defenses against invasion, Zenobia van Essen had an old white horse, which was far more effective. He had never known saddle or harness and had passed his whole life comfortably guarding Zenobia's property as a watchdog. At the first click of the gate he would come running, ears back and teeth bared, to attack. At a word from Zenobia his whole aspect would change and he would turn into an amiable old dobbin and wander off to nibble the grass and the flowers. But Zenobia seldom gave the word of restraint, for as she grew more and more ancient she also became more and more solitary. The old horse was called Robin.

The garden of Zenobia van Essen was an island in the thousand acres and more of the land used by the prison for a farm which was worked by the prisoners. Long before Johnny was born the state had condemned Zenobia's little piece of land and ordered her to move out of her cottage, but the state did not know Zenobia. She stood on her rights as a citizen and an individual and for months she refused to leave the place for fear that she would return to find it in the process of being pulled down. She began a series of lawsuits which dragged on for years, and in the end the state, wearying of the contest, abandoned it and allowed her to remain in the midst of the prison farm, with only convicts for neighbors. She had a reputation for being the stubbornest woman in the county and there was nothing which she enjoyed so much as complicated interminable battles in the courts.

When Johnny first saw her she was already an old woman well

past seventy, tall, vigorous, straight, and dressed in the fashion of the early eighties. She had brilliant black eyes and her hair was still black, although whether she dyed it or not Johnny never knew. She was a distant cousin of Johnny's father's because she was the child of Jacob van Essen, the son of Jorge and Elvira, who had married the granddaughter of a Wyandot Chief. In Zenobia the Indian blood returned in full flower. She had a bronze skin and high cheek bones and always walked like an Indian, as if she wore moccasins instead of shoes. None of the family ever did very much about their relationship to Zenobia because she was an extremely uncomfortable relative who would file a lawsuit at the drop of a hat and the less one was noticed by her the better. She always wore a purple dress with a bustle and a skirt so long that it appeared to be a train, a large plumed hat with a veil which she wore thrown back from her face, and lace mitts. So long as Johnny knew her, she never had any other costume. In it she walked the two miles from her cottage to the Town, never troubling to lift the train, but allowing its ruffles to swish behind her in the dust, an eccentricity which always gave her the air of a tragedy queen. As she walked along the road on a hot summer morning her ruffles raised as much dust as a flock of sheep. There was something in her carriage, the proud turn of her head, and her old-fashioned clothes which was very like the Carolus Duran portrait of Sarah Bernhardt.

Over her eccentric figure and the fantastic little cottage hung an aura of genuine melodrama. Zenobia, as a young girl, had been left an orphan, and something of an heiress as well. Also she was handsome. And when her father died and her younger brothers and sisters went to live with uncles and aunts, Zenobia refused to leave the lonely cottage and sometimes, to the scandal of the community, received there unprotected the suitors who came to woo her for her looks and her fortune. Not all of them were welcome, and sometimes she had trouble in ridding herself of the undesirable ones. One of these, a young man called Zachariah Betts, showed an unusual ardor. He would not be dismissed, and when she would no longer open the door to him he came at night to wander about the garden, calling out his admiration and attempting now and then to force the shutters. If he had had greater powers of penetrating the character of Zenobia, he would have abandoned her and sought some other heiress, for Zenobia, even as a girl, had no great gift of patience, and after a time the visits of the ardent Mr. Betts began to get on her nerves. There came a summer night when she heard him trying the shutters and calling out to her amorously from the garden, and, her patience at an end, she shouted that if he did not go away she would fire her pistol through the window. Still Mr. Betts lingered, begging her to let him in, until at last the exasperated Zenobia took aim and fired through the shutters from which the sound of her suitor's pleadings had come. She was troubled no more that night, and in the morning she discovered the reason. Outside in the flower bed under the window she found Mr. Betts lying dead.

There was a trial and Zenobia would have no lawyer. She defended herself and was acquitted, but afterward she refused all suitors, and after Mr. Betts's experience none of them attempted to force their attentions upon her. The trial seemed to have given her a liking for the courts, and after that she took up the study of law and installed a whole library of law books in the cottage. In all her suits later in life she never engaged a lawyer, and in the end she came to know the law better than a good many of the lawyers in the Town. In a way her tragedy was that of a woman born at the wrong time. She had intelligence and independence and great force of character, but in her day and situation there was nothing left for her to do but become an eccentric and to end her life as the prey of small boys who came to the cottage to torment her and the old white horse.

Of about the same age was Susan Wilkes, who was the daughter of another of Jorge and Elvira's children. She was a leading Congregationalist and all her life was troubled by transcendental yearnings and plans for the reform, but more especially, I think, for the refinement of mankind. In appearance she was not the typical reformer of her day. There was nothing of Carrie Nation about her. On the contrary, she had an air of meekness and Christian humility which was utterly deceptive. Behind it lurked a will of Bessemer steel. Beneath the quiet velvety voice there lurked the tenacity of a bulldog. She was a leading member of the Anti-Saloon League, the

Women's Christian Temperance Union, the Anti-Tobacco League, and half a dozen other organizations. She was of the breed of Frances Willard and Mary Baker Eddy.

She had a horror of untidiness and of germs, and it troubled her, I think, that her fellowmen should be gross and untidy. Her horror of drink was founded less upon moral grounds than upon the fact that occasionally a citizen returning from a spree was sick on the sidewalk before her house, and she condemned tobacco less because of its depraving influence than because of the cigar butts which vulgar men left about. On a big elm tree before her door she had a carefully painted sign put up which read, "Please do not spit or leave cigar butts on my sidewalk," with the result that many citizens who had no desire to spit at all managed to do so as they passed her house, and others cherished cigar butts all day long in order to drop them on her sidewalk on the way home in the evening. In her horror of germs she used to go twice a year into all the schoolrooms (a favor granted her because she was rich and was also somewhat feared even by tough politicians) in order to lecture the children upon the peril of communicating germs to their interiors by touching their faces with their hands.

She was a strange figure with a long thin neck which curved upward and outward, and she had a little the look of a secretary bird. Johnny knew her for years and he never observed the slightest change in her costume. Always she wore a long skirt of black material as durable as iron, a shirtwaist, and a shawl thrown round her shoulders. She never wore a hat and when it rained or snowed she drew the shawl over her head. Her skirts were made exactly the same, back, sides and front, with an elastic at the top, so that as the portions on which she sat wore out she could turn them around. It may have been that she never had but one skirt in all her life, or that she was born in a skirt—a phenomenon which, considering her refinement and modesty, was not impossible.

She was given to rather flowery language, and on the sign which she placed over the gate to her orchard was not the familiar "No Trespassing," but, "These are not public ways." She had a brother much younger than herself whom she guarded as closely as her own canaries, but somehow at some moment when she was not watching him he must have put his hand to his face, for a germ entered his body and he was stricken with a long illness from which he died. He was a deacon of the church and on the day of his death members of the congregation telephoned Susan for news of him. She herself answered all the telephone calls. All hope had been abandoned, but instead of saying simply that her brother was dying, she replied, "Mr. Wilkes is just passing through the gates."

Johnny entered her house but once, when he was taken there as a small boy by his mother, and out of the visit he carried only the memory of a huge bust of Napoleon, more than twice life size, which dominated a long drawing room stuffed to capacity with furniture. Why Miss Susan Wilkes had chosen Napoleon for her hero Johnny never understood. She was very penurious and it may have been that she inherited the bust and kept it because she could not bear to waste or throw away anything. She saved the cards left by the people who called upon her, and when she returned their calls she brought the cards with her so that they might use them again.

She lived to be nearly a hundred, and when she died she disappointed her relatives by dividing her fortune among the Anti-Saloon League, the Anti-Tobacco League, and a home for dogs and cats which was to be called by the terms of her will, The Susan Wilkes Cat and Dog Hostel and Asylum. How she was able to reconcile her hatred for germs with her solicitude for cats Johnny was never able to discover, but there was something magnificent in her final gesture and in the name she chose for the animal home. It was as if she appreciated her own flavor and was determined that it should go on after she died.

AND POLITICS

O NE OF JOHNNY'S EARLIEST MEMORIES WAS LIKE THOSE OF "THE Dauphin," of mobs and torches.

It was a cold clear November night and he had been in his bed for hours when slowly he wakened out of a confused dream to hear the barking of dogs and the shouts of men and the sound of a brass band. Outside in the street there was a fire and scores of torches and flares whose light filled the bedroom. He was eight or nine years old and too big a boy to cry, so he pulled the bedclothes over his head and lay there, hiding and comforting his younger brother, until the door opened and his mother came in. She told Johnny to put on his flannel dressing-gown, and wrapping his brother in a blanket she took them in to another room to look out of the window.

Below, the street and the front yard was filled with men and dogs. In the street they had built a great fire. A band, the players recruited here and there, played "Hail to the Chief" discordantly. Men shouted and dogs barked and fought. It was a terrifying spectacle in spite of its friendliness. They had come only to congratulate James Willingdon on his election as county treasurer. It was one of the rare elections when the Democrats had won, and they wanted him to buy them a barrel of beer so that they might continue the celebration.

In all the Town and the county and the state, there was nothing of such palpitating interest as politics. Kings might be assassinated, wars occur, ships sink at sea, and whole cities like San Francisco fall into ruin overnight, but none of these things really touched that rich Middle Western country very profoundly. One talked of them for a day or two and then forgot them. Europe and China and South America were equally remote. It was politics, always politics, which provided excitement with a genuine flavor. On the eve of an election, families were divided by strife, brothers ceased to speak to each other. In the schoolyard enemies became friends for a few weeks because they came from Democratic families, and friends became enemies because their fathers belonged to opposing parties. Every small boy bedecked his coat with rows of celluloid buttons bearing the images of his party's candidates from the President to the county sheriff. There were fist fights and black eyes, and on election night the children were allowed to stay up till midnight to hear the first returns. In that Middle Western county one breathed politics. From childhood one knew about party bosses and the sanctity of one's own party and the corruptness of the other; for there were only two parties. On the wrong side of the railroad tracks a little cluster of German Socialists held a meeting now and then, and in the Flats and the Syndicate there were perhaps half a dozen Anarchists and Syndicalists, but none of these counted. Their candidates did not even appear on the ballots. And, anyway, few of them were citizens. They did not matter. One was a Democrat or a Republican. In Johnny's childhood the parties were evenly divided in local elections and one never knew for certain which side would win. It was inevitable that such an atmosphere should produce weak presidents like McKinley and Harding, dictators like Hanna, and cheap bosses like Cox and Harry Daugherty. It was inevitable that the politics of that county should always have a tremendous influence for evil as well as for good, in Washington and at any national convention. Every schoolboy was an apprentice at politics. By the time he was old enough to vote he knew all the tricks.

Although Johnny's father was elected to office two or three times and all his life remained a small political figure with a devoted following, he was a failure in politics. He was a handsome man, gentle and simple, with a charm and an honesty which led many men to support whatever he undertook, but he had one great failing. He had no gift for compromise nor the chicanery which was necessary in a political life that was highly organized and all too frequently dominated by unscrupulous bosses or business men seeking privileges in return for money. The reproach was never made against him that he was dishonest or even sharp, accusations brought often enough during the heat of a political fight against every candidate. The politicians had small use for him because he was too honest. Sometimes they said, as if it were a reproach, that he did not know how to make money, and in the eyes of certain citizens that was the worst fault of all.

He would have liked a gift of a million or two dollars from the blue, but he had no talent for making it. The fundamental fault was that he was simple in all his tastes and had no very great passion for money. If he had had the million or two, he would scarcely have lived differently, save perhaps that he would have had a stableful of trotting-horses. All his life Johnny heard Americans say that they could not imagine a life in which the economic necessity for making money was not present. It was a statement which, upon examination later in life, seemed to reveal a singular poverty of spirit and imagination in a world so filled with possibilities of diversion, enjoyment, and even service. His father was one of those who, without the necessity for work, could have made for himself a full, rich life. The gift was born not of the complexity of his nature, but rather of its simplicity, for his tastes were for the fundamental things of existence—for land, for animals, for his children, and for the endless enjoyment of friendly contact with his fellowmen. He was a philosopher and had a deep romantic love of nature which, except for a few rare moments in his existence, was tragically unsatisfied. These things all made him a friend to the farmer, and although he failed on the one occasion when he turned to the land, his friends and his political following was always among the men who cultivated the soil.

His earliest memory was of sitting among the flowers of his mother's back garden while a dozen women of the Town, come in to seek the advice of his calm and sensible mother, discussed the chances of Morgan's Raiders, who were burning their way north, descending upon them. Nearly all of the men were at the war and the women talked wildly of organizing the old men and the boys into a militia of defense. The Old Man, then a young man, was somewhere in Idaho, prospecting and helping to fight Indians. But the Raiders never reached the Town, because the wild and gallant Morgan was defeated and captured in the battle of Buffington's Island.

From the time he was a child until he was forty James Willingdon was forced by necessity to undertake work which he did not like. As a boy he worked in the failing chemist's shop which had belonged to his grandfather, and when that was sold he went to work in a bank, and although he rose to be cashier and director, he never had any talent nor liking for either shopkeeping or banking, and when the chance came to enter politics he escaped and never returned. Although he had none of the Colonel's blood in his veins, he was in his tastes and character very like the old philosopher. In life, however, they had fared differently, for the Colonel had been born well-off with every opportunity for satisfying his tastes and desires, and Johnny's father had been born poor, with the necessity of working to provide for others, for his mother and father and even at times for his own brother, for his own wife and children, and for relatives who were forever coming to him for aid. It was a necessity from which he did not escape until he was old and his own children grown and gone away. Because he was always too friendly and too generous he was forever lending money which was never returned to him.

He was a gentle man with fair hair and very bright blue eyes. In him the almost pure Willingdon English blood, come down through New England, asserted itself. There was about him none of the Scot's tough boniness nor the broad fleshiness which somehow seemed to claim most of those descended from the first settlers. About the corners of his eyes there were crow's-feet which came of good humor, but as he grew older little lines came about the corners of his mouth and a shadow of bitterness into his laugh. They came, I think, from the long, slow process of disillusionment.

He had begun by liking and trusting all his fellow men, but at the end, I think, he only trusted those who were simple and without worldly ambition.

Like a good many fathers and sons, James Willingdon and his son Johnny were shy with each other, although the shyness disappeared as Johnny grew older and wiser and came to understand that much of it arose out of the long contact of a sensitive personality with insensitive and sometimes brutal people. He was shy because he was afraid of being hurt and unwilling to expose himself to abuse and ridicule. There was a great deal of poetry in his nature and in the world in which he moved, poetry was largely represented by Ella Wheeler Wilcox, James Whitcomb Riley and Edgar Guest. Living with him day after day, one had the feeling that circumstance and a hard life had suppressed something fundamental in his nature. It was only when one saw him in the country talking endlessly with the farmers or in those moments when he would escape from the Town to wander over the fields, that one felt he was himself, full-grown, unhampered, and happy.

He was content to run for hours across snow-covered fields, following his dogs in pursuit of some rabbit which they never caught, or to sit all day in the shadow of a willow, catching suckers and sunfish and silversides. The blood of his ancestors from the English countryside was strong in him. He should have been born in England, for in England there was a place for him. In that Middle Western county in his youth there was really none.

Yet he was a man without resentment. The scornful, acid bitterness of his father, "The Old Man," who had turned his back on the world, never touched him. I do not think that it ever occurred to him that there was anything at fault in the materialistic world about him. If he did not fit, he assumed that the fault was his, believing that he should have adjusted himself somehow to a society for which he was unsuited.

Because Johnny shared his liking for nature, it was on their expeditions into the country that the shyness between father and son was dissipated. It was not that they talked much. Sometimes they must have ridden side by side in a buggy or sat fishing together for hours with scarcely a word spoken between them. It was unnecessary to speak, for if a swallow skimmed low or a kingfisher darted over the water in a flash of gold and blue, they both saw it and they knew that they felt the same about it. If the wild irises were especially vivid or the willows a superb green, it was not necessary for one to tell the other. His delight at catching a half-pound sunfish was unforgettable. He was never rich enough to know the tarpon fishing of Florida or the salmon fishing of Nova Scotia, but I doubt that they would have given him more excitement than the fishing below the dam at van Essen's mill.

Sometimes Johnny and his father went alone on these expeditions, but he liked best the great family excursions which took place on holidays and sometimes on Sundays. On those occasions the whole family rose at dawn, taking a vast lunch prepared the day before, and set out in a surrey with two horses and never less than two dogs. Sometimes the goal was a spot along the Black Fork where the fishing slowly became ruined by the contamination of factories; and sometimes the family went to Onara or to Belleville, villages where there were fishing streams.

But the favorite spot was van Essen's mill where Jorge and Elvira had settled long ago. It no longer belonged to the family, for it was sold in Thomas Willingdon's old age, and The Old Man's share of the money had long since been spent during his restless wanderings. The big house and the mill still stood, reflected in the waters of the milldam. They were built of sandstone from a quarry in the hill beyond the flat land of the valley, and with the passing of a hundred years the red stone had lost its first rich brightness and was tawny and stained with moss and lichens where it was not hidden by ivy and Virginia creeper. Along the edge of the stream beneath the willows grew great clumps of blue and yellow wild irises and wax-leaved buttercups. The land all about was low-lying and damp and in the fields nearby the corn grew twice as high as a tall man. Its ribbons of leaves were the deep rich green of corn which grows under a hot sun in rich, black, deep soil. The sight of it so rich and flourishing gave one a deep feeling of pleasure. Below the dam among the water lilies, the fishing was excellent.

Part of the big house was closed, and the farmer who lived there chose the rooms which faced the river. He was a solid, middle-aged man who even on his own rich bottomland had to work hard to stave off mortgages. He and his wife were friendly to Johnny's family because the house had been built by Jorge and Elvira. The mill was nearly always silent. Its vast granaries were empty and here and there among the cobwebs there were still traces of flour milled years before. By the time Johnny was born, farmers no longer came there to have their flour ground from their own wheat. They sold the wheat and bought the flour in the Town, and in the vast difference in the price which they received for their wheat and paid for their flour lay the roots of one aspect of their constantly increasing troubles. The old-fashioned machinery was kept oiled because it had a certain value and because the farmer who owned it stubbornly cherished a hope that some day the big millstones would once more grind out flour for half the county.

The expeditions in other directions each had their particular charm, especially the one to Onara, where one drove through the village into a countryside of wide green meadows and pastures to unharness the horses by the roadside and follow all day the banks of a meandering stream, fishing hole after hole under the willows. It was a landscape soft and green like the loveliest English countryside.

At that time there was no such thing as private fishing. In all the county there was only one stream owned by a club of which Uncle Harry was a member. Men went there to eat and drink well, and fish from a clear green river filled with sinuous weeds. The stream sprang, full born, cold and clear as crystal, from out of the ground where it had traveled hidden away for two hundred miles or more through limestone caverns. The streams, like the nut trees, belonged to everyone and a fisherman could wander where he would, unmolested by farmers crying, "Trespasser!" Only a few miles from the Town one found lonely and remote country hidden away along lanes bordered by witch hazel and elderbushes and wild irises where streams of water ran singing secretly beneath the arched willows.

In the end the automobile destroyed the remoteness of those streams and removed the sense of adventure and the aroma of wilderness. With horses it took two hours to travel the ten miles. Two hours in a motor now only brings one through half a dozen

towns and villages, all situated in time (which, after all, has become distance) side by side. There is no longer any wilderness between. Van Essen's mill is only half an hour from the Town and the pretty village of Onara a mere twenty minutes. In a few years the whole county shrunk to a third of its old size. Mystery and adventure, even for children, disappeared. And the automobiles, filled with marauding parties who tear blossoms from trees and steal fruit from the orchards, have put an end to the old freedom to roam. Where once you could wander where you pleased there are now "No trespassing" signs everywhere, and farmers on the watch for thieves and vandals.

In those days, so near and yet so remote, the villages had a special charm of their own, as half-forgotten relics of a life which even then had nearly disappeared. A hundred years earlier they had been settlements begun here and there in fertile spots along an Indian trail by the side of a little stream, and within half a century their whole destinies had been changed by railroads. Here and there a village had luck and remained a small market town and shipping center, but most of them were passed by, left to loneliness and decay as the new generation deserted them for towns which had the fortune to be blessed by a railroad. By the time Johnny was old enough to visit them, the forgotten ones were half-deserted and the old New England clapboard houses stood with windows broken, doors ajar, and shutters hanging from their hinges. The orchards had been abandoned to goldenrod and the lilacs had grown into jungles, and here and there against the rotting picket fences lingered the remnants of an old flower garden—a few hollyhocks standing like sentinels, a clump of purple campanulas, and a little patch of bleeding hearts slowly being choked to death by fennel. The only inhabitants were those who were too old to go away, and they sat in the doorways or in the sun and pottered about the old gardens. One had the impression of a world in which everyone was old. In the square or at the crossroads there was always a watering trough made from a hollow log and overgrown with damp moss beneath a clump of willows. Always it was cold, clear spring water which ran from the rotting wooden pipes, and there on a hot summer day one got down from the buggy to drink with the horses.

When the old people died the houses in which they had lived all their lives died with them, for they had no value. There was no one to buy them or rent them, and in some of the villages only two or three old men and women lingered on, surrounded by empty, decaying houses, haunted by the ghosts of the past, until they too died and there was no one.

At Onara there was one house more terrible and sinister than any of the others because of the tragic story told of it. When Johnny first knew the house no one had lived in it for fifty years. It stood on a low hill beside the brook, a little apart from the rest of the village, surrounded by old apple trees and heaven trees and a thicket of candleberry bushes gone wild. A locust tree grew straight through the roof like a sword piercing a heart. It was said to be haunted, and no one, I think, ever had the courage to disprove the story, for there was something strangely terrifying in the atmosphere of the place even in the daylight of a hot summer afternoon. Once it had been owned by a man named Billings, who lived there alone with his daughter, a girl of nineteen. She loved one of the village boys, but her father, an eccentric man, would not allow her to see him. His harshness accomplished nothing, for one day he found that his daughter was having a baby and she confessed to him that her lover was the father. In a fit of rage he beat her so brutally that she died and, terrified, he did not leave the body for days. At last, after placing it in a box he hid it under a bed and ran to the lonely house of a farmer in the valley three miles away. There he confessed to the crime and disappeared, never to be heard of again. From that day on no one ever lived in the house. It had no owner. Even when it was put up for sale for the taxes, no one bought it.

I do not know whether the old house is standing, but I know that the rest of the village has been changed. Now it is only twenty minutes from the Town by a wide road of cement and it has been reborn, settled this second time not by frontiersmen, but by men and women who work in the shops and offices and mills of a town which, only a hundred years ago, was half a day removed from it by a journey through a forest over rough trails. Most of the old houses have been pulled down, and the academy founded there by old Jamie and his friends has disappeared. There are new houses and some of the old ones have been done over, and at the corner where the watering trough stood beneath the clump of willows there is a filling station and an ice cream parlor.

⊸

Johnny's father would have liked fine horses, but since he rarely had any money he had to satisfy himself with the best he could get. He knew all the famous trotting-horses and would drive any distance to see a race. He had an adoration for two famous trotters called Maud S. and Dan Patch. The horses he could afford to buy or acquire by trading always had something the matter with them. All of them had the makings of racehorses, but each of them had some illness or was hard-mouthed or possessed a devil's temper. He always hoped miraculously to cure them of their faults and win a great race with one of them, but I do not remember that any of them ever grew any better for all the care he took with them, or that any of them was ever placed in a race. When they were ill he sent them to pasture at the Farm, and if they were hard-mouthed or ill-tempered, he tried to cure them himself and sometimes he allowed his sons to try it. He was forever buying and selling and trading, and his strange assortment of horses was the greatest pleasure of his life.

The able-bodied horses his family used as carriage and saddle horses, so that the only horses Johnny knew as a boy were the ones with hard mouths and bad tempers. In the carriage they would balk or run away, and sometimes Johnny's mother, tried beyond endurance by her means of transportation, made scenes and demanded a decent animal to drive. At last she won out and a horse called Sunny Jim became her special property. He was a docile, intelligent horse and perfectly sound, but he had so strange a build that buyers regarded him with mirth and suspicion. He had the small head and arching neck of an Arabian. In the shoulders he was hackney, and the rest of him was polo pony. Sometimes in a pinch the children used him as a saddle horse, but none of the children really wanted to ride him, for there was no fun in it. By the time Sunny Jim came into the family the children had acquired a strong taste in horses and Jim seemed a boring, pedantic animal of no interest whatever.

Much more fun was a hard-mouthed, long-legged Kentucky running-horse who would go splendidly until he became bored and decided that the moment had come to return to the stable. Then he would stop abruptly, hurling you forward onto his neck, and begin a series of remarkable buckings. If you were able to keep your seat, this performance would sometimes continue for five or ten minutes, and then suddenly, as if he were the sweetest tempered horse in the world, he would canter off with a comic air of perfect amiability.

In one of the fields at the Farm, Johnny and his brother constructed hurdles from fence rails and endeavored to teach this strange assortment of horses to jump. Sometimes they succeeded and sometimes they did not. It was there that Johnny received a dislocated shoulder which he was able to dislocate at will for the rest of his life. And on the calf of his right leg he bore forever the scars of a vicious bite given him by a horse who decided he was tired of jumping and simply turned his head and bit his rider. And once the long-legged Kentucky horse, galloping at top speed along a country road through the woods after dark, slipped and did a perfect somersault, with Johnny underneath, bursting the girth and losing the saddle blanket forever. And there was the day when, driving home with his father behind a team which he had been able to buy cheaply for some mysterious reason, the team suddenly revealed the secret by clenching the bits between their teeth and running off. The mad lark continued for two miles, finally ending in the destruction of a hundred feet of wire fence and a buggy smashed to splinters. Johnny's father landed on his head, unconscious, and Johnny found himself, a boy of ten, careening down the road on the frame of a buggy from which the body had disappeared. Not knowing what else to do, he clung on until the team smashed a gate and came to a stop.

Because of this passion for horses and because he was in and out of politics James Willingdon knew all the drivers and owners and trainers in the state, and with him Johnny came, as a small boy, to know them along with dozens of horse dealers and livery stable proprietors. The livery stable has vanished and I cannot think of any difference so symbolic of the change of the times as the difference between a livery stable and a garage. The divergence in tempo between the two institutions is perhaps the greatest of all, for about the livery stable there was always an air of leisure and sleepiness.

The proprietor and the stable boys always appeared to be dozing in their chairs when there was nothing else to do. Either they slept or gambled at cards and dice. For a small boy the livery stable was a cavern of enchantment, filled with the odors of horses and ammonia, hay and soap and harness leather. There was always a bitch and a litter of puppies somewhere about, and a fat sleek cat or two to keep away the rats which lurked in the mows among the cobwebs. And there was something about a livery stable which molded the character of the proprietor and the stablemen, giving them a picturesque character and a poetic flow of indelicate language. In a livery stable a small boy could learn about life in a fine, free, Rabelaisian manner. Perhaps there was something mellow in the leisurely life which livery men led. To Johnny it seemed that the livery stable men never worked, but always sat with chairs tilted back in the shade of the big elm and sycamore trees and in winter about the big iron stove, drinking coffee and gambling with a greasy pack of cards. They were not always clean and more often than not they smelled of the stables. Most of them chewed tobacco and were great spitters, but they were always good-natured and they possessed the lazy wit and the racy humor which goes with much "setting." From farms and livery stables Johnny learned the facts of life and it was not a bad way of learning, because the attitude toward it all was big and hearty, and if minds dwelt upon sex a trifle too much, how could it have been otherwise when there was so little else to occupy them? In most families, livery stables were regarded as dens of idleness and iniquity where all manner of vices were to be acquired and boys were forbidden by their church-going elders to hang about them. In Johnny's family, perhaps because of his father's passion for horses and racing-men, there were no restraints placed upon the frequenting of livery stables, and whatever he picked up there was more wholesome and less vicious than much that was whispered about in the locker rooms of the Young Men's Christian Association.

I think Johnny and his brother must have known every livery stable in the Town and the county, and more than once, driving across country with his father during a political campaign, Johnny spent nights, wrapped in a blanket saturated with the delicious smell of horses, sleeping in the big mows or on a cot by the big iron stove.

There were three great stables which always filled Johnny with wonder and delight. Not far from his house stood Painter's Stables in an alley lined with enormous sycamore trees. It was a great center of gossip and it supplied cabs for weddings and funerals. If there was a murder in Town one heard of it at Painter's in all its gruesome details. At Painter's there was always an immense amount of information regarding the amorous propensities of certain whited sepulchers among the citizenry. If a son of a deacon was arrested in the Railroad Hotel with a waitress and gave a false name in police court, the whole story was known at Painter's as soon as it happened.

There are no more horses there and the stable itself has been pulled down. With it have gone those wonderful, dark, smelly conveyances known as cabs which conveyed the citizenry with dignity to and from funerals and weddings. Gone with them is much of the dignity which belongs to death. When Johnny was a small child there was always great excitement in the house when one of those dark, upholstered cabs arrived at the front door and the family set out for the station to visit Great-aunt Esther or Great-aunt Susan. Something of the mystery of death clung to those pompous old hacks, accumulating a little more with each successive funeral. They smelled faintly of death, just as they smelled faintly of ammonia. They were exciting.

Wilmerding's Ten Cent Barn stood a block from the courthouse, near the center of the Town. It was a vast structure of wood built soon after the Civil War and it survived long after the buildings of the same era had been pulled down all around it. In winter and in bad weather when farmers could not leave their teams at the hitching rail on the square, they went to Wilmerding's, where for ten cents they could stable the horses for the whole day. It was built with huge sawn beams and had four floors, with wide steep ramps leading from one to another, so that one could drive a team right to the top of the building. On Saturdays and market days in bad weather it was filled, and in the big room near the entrance there was always a little group of farmers discussing crops, prices, and politics. It was a place much frequented by Johnny's father when he represented the farmers of the county in public office.

Then there was a vast livery stable called "Grimses" where twice a month a great horse-fair took place, attended by horse dealers and farmers from the surrounding counties. In the vast open space, littered with tanbark under the high roof, there was a constant procession of stallions and mares and geldings, Percherons and Clydes, Morgans and hackneys and trotting-horses, all prancing and neighing and stepping nervously as if they were on springs, while Joe Burns, the auctioneer, a thin man with a roaring voice, who looked like Uncle Sam, stood in his pulpit beside the tanbark, calling for bids. Johnny's father was always there, watching and hoping for a bargain, and sometimes his own horses, fat and sleek and fairly sound after months at the Farm, were placed on sale. At one end of the big barn there was a lunch counter where one bought hot dogs and ham sandwiches and baked beans and beer and hot coffee, and when Johnny's father was afraid of missing a bargain, he and Johnny would eat there, but more frequently they went to the Crescent House, a couple of blocks away, where they had lunch sitting on high stools at a counter.

The Crescent House was one of the relics of the past, for it had been built in the days when the Irish descended on the countryside to construct the railroads across the rich Middle West. It had been built in haste and it was a huge square box of a building without a vestige of ornamentation. Because it stood at the crossing of the Erie and Pennsylvania lines and there were always locomotives on the siding beneath its windows, it was given a coat of liver-colored paint every few years. It was a shade unaffected by the soot. Before the door there was a little patch of sickly grass and a few shrubs half suffocated by the smoke, and from the big glass windows of the lunchroom one had a view of Trefusis' Castle sitting on its hill above the Flats. It still served as a hotel frequented by firemen and engineers and brakemen who ended their runs in the Town, but no longer was there the wild drinking and gambling and occasional shootings which colored its early days. It had the best food in Town and there were epicures who came all the way to the Flats to sit at its lunch counter. It was owned and run by Mrs. Sten, a fat, solid woman who had entered its doors for the first time as a waitress during the Irish invasion and when the invasion ended she came by virtue of her talents as a cook, to own it. When Johnny was a child Mrs. Sten was already a rich and handsome old lady living in a fine brick house with big plate-glass windows, in the most fashionable part of Maple Avenue. She never entertained anyone in the big house and she never left it save to visit the Crescent House every day in order to see that the food was always as good as it should be. The rest of the time she sat in a rocking chair at the plate-glass window, half concealed by an enormous Boston fern, watching the Town go past her house. To go to the Crescent House was always an occasion of festival, for Johnny's father allowed him to eat the things children are not allowed to eat—great slices of cake and pieces of Mrs. Sten's famous lemon pie. There were things to be had at that lunch counter, such things as oyster stew and fried chicken, which Parisian gourmets have never known.

For Johnny the company was as exciting as the food. Soldiers and policemen never fascinated him, for in the Town the only men who ever became soldiers were black sheep or boys who were stupid and good-for-nothing, and there was no special glamour about policemen when you knew every one of them by name. The heroes of Johnny's childhood were the engineers and the firemen who drove the great locomotives on the Erie and the Pennsylvania and the Baltimore and Ohio through the Town on their way from the West to New York. To Johnny locomotives were the most beautiful things in the world, not only because of their power and their strength and the beauty of their lines, but because they were the engines which could take you out of the Town into the world. He knew every type of locomotive from the doddering old switch engines to the great Moguls which pulled the Erie freights up the long hill toward the West and the big high-wheeled greyhounds which drew the eight-thirty-seven, the only train which did not stop in the Town, over the rails of the Pennsylvania from Chicago to New York.

When he was old enough to go off by himself he spent nearly every Saturday afternoon in the Pennsylvania yards where the big engines came in off the lines to the roundhouse to be examined and repaired. He never told his mother or father that the round-house was his destination, for he knew he would be forbidden to go there on account of the danger. A dozen times he was ordered out of the yards by watchmen, but always he returned, until at last he made the acquaintance of the railroad detectives and the men who worked in the repair shops and they no longer objected. I think they looked upon Johnny's obsession as a joke and presently they came to consider him as one of themselves. He shared their lunches, so excited by the honor on the first occasion that afterward he was sick; and presently he was allowed to go where he pleased, wandering over the whole yards in and out and under trains. Nothing ever happened to him and he was as happy as it was possible to be. He was content to sit on a greasy stool for hours, simply watching the repair men at work, and nothing gave him such excitement as to see one of the huge locomotives, oiled, repaired, and ready for the line, start off from the roundhouse as easily and as smoothly as a toy. There was a beauty in it which was indescribable and which for Johnny remained forever a living thing.

Sometimes he lingered about the yards until after dark, and then slowly out of the fog and steam and smoke the signal lights would begin to appear here and there, ruby and yellow, mauve and green, like jewels, and then when a long train with all the windows lighted slipped past, a lump would come into Johnny's throat. And always he said to himself, "Some day I shall get aboard one of those trains and go off and travel and travel and see everything and at last find the place where I want to live forever."

When he was grown Johnny traveled and traveled, but he never found the place, or perhaps he found too many places. But great locomotives, like great ships, remained for him the most exciting and beautiful things in the world. They helped him in a strange way to understand the restlessness of The Old Man who had been a mystery to him all through his childhood.

⊸

James Willingdon left the bank for politics when two of the political bosses in the northern part of the state persuaded him that in politics there was a great future for him. Three things, I

think, led them to believe that he was the material they sought—
his charm, his easy-going ways, and his wide acquaintance among
the farmers. The Republicans already had such a man—handsome,
simple, and willing to compromise. He came from the next county and already he had done much to help the "party," which meant
that he voted as he was told, by men who seldom held any office
but stood in the wings, prompting and directing the performers.
His name was Warren Gamaliel Harding. The Democratic Party no
longer held to its old-fashioned principles. In it too there were men
who believed in tariffs and believed that "business" should be
helped now and then discreetly and judiciously.

But the men who sought out James Willingdon failed to count
upon his what they later called eccentricity and pigheadedness.
They did not understand that "honesty" meant one thing to him
and another to themselves, nor that he was a man so fantastic that
he could not be tempted either by money or by the political honors which could be bestowed through the mechanical operation of
a political machine which was not above making bargains with the
opposite party. Nor did they comprehend a man who never
allowed ambition to become an obsession, and saw success and
money not as the whole of life, but only as a part of it. It was, in
their opinion, simply mad for a man to prefer respect for himself
to money and renown.

He was elected at once, and no sooner was he seated in his office
in the big courthouse than certain rich men came to him separate-
ly and in groups to demand reductions upon the valuations of the
mills and factories and houses which they owned. It was scarcely a
shameless procedure because the question of shame was not
involved. They had supported him and given money toward the
expenses of his election, and now that he had won they were enti-
tled to their rewards. It was all a part of the game of politics and
not very many citizens troubled to consider the ethics of what they
were asking. Not very many of the citizens who elected Johnny's
father could even have defined the word "ethics." The Republicans
had had their innings and had their properties undertaxed, and
now it was the turn of the men who had succeeded in driving them
from influence. A poor man had no chance of having his taxes

reduced, but the rich man who contributed to the party fund could have what he wanted. It was simply a question of "business." Why should anyone drag in a question of honesty in government? The contributions were investments and now the men who made them had a right to a return. Subtly the government itself was being taken over by business men. Subtly government was being put on the level of shopkeeping. It was a rule which worked in Washington as well as in a moderate sized town in the Middle West. They had plenty of Senators like Aldrich and Hale and Payne and Foraker and Hanna who saw the point clearly and made no trouble. Often enough because they too were business men they were helping themselves as well.

When Johnny's father refused to lower tax assessments and alter valuations his career was doomed. He liked politics, but he was not a politician in the meaning imposed upon the word by the New Era. His supporters, bewildered, stormed and fumed and argued, and one of them, himself a judge of the Court of Appeals, sat up all one night trying to make him see that times had changed and that politics had to be "practical" if business was to go ahead and prosperity bless the country.

When his term of office came to an end James Willingdon stubbornly refused to disappear from the picture. There was a fight within the party organization and again he was nominated and elected. The farmers were behind him and in the Town there were old-timers who believed it was better to have him in office than a Republican. At least, if he were elected it would keep the Republicans out of the benefits. But it was the last time he succeeded and his career came abruptly to an end. Long afterward, when the administration of county offices became a scandal, there was a wave of reform and a half-dozen men went to prison. But they were only the good-natured "agreeable" men who had been placed in office because they "understood" politics. Among them were none of the business men. Somehow in American life bribe-giving had come to be accepted as conventional. Bribe-taking was a different matter, but not very much different.

The "agreeable" man from the next county had a great success within the Republican Party, rising from office to office, without ever making trouble for anyone until at last Senators Lodge and

Penrose and a Republican boss named Harry M. Daugherty arranged for him to be nominated and elected as President. In the end he died suddenly because there was nothing else for him to do. But the rule still held. None of the bribe-givers went to jail. It wasn't quite possible to send a big business man to prison, when the government was no longer government, but only a business.

When Johnny's father campaigned for office automobiles were still curiosities, and as most of the villages and all of the farms could not be reached by train, the electioneering had to be done in a buggy behind a team of horses. Sometimes it was a dreary business and Johnny's father took him along on the trips and for Johnny each trip was a fresh adventure. He saw new country and new farms and occasionally a village he had never known before, and always the heaviest campaigning took place in the month of October when the days were brilliant and the nights frosty and clear. The trees had turned to brilliant reds and yellows and purples, and the corn was being shocked in the fields. Johnny always went with his father on Saturdays and Sundays and on week days when he had been good at his lessons and was allowed a day or two of holiday. Together father and son covered the whole country and in the end Johnny came to know every road and lane and stream and to visit every farm.

They always set out in the early morning just after daybreak when the October air was still frosty, in order to get a good start on the long journey. Warmly dressed, they sat covered with a horse blanket and an old buffalo robe, the last of its kind, rather mangy, with great patches where the hair had been worn off and the hide showed through; and when they had passed the last house on the outskirts of the Town an intoxicating sense of delight swept through them. With each mile the country grew less familiar. There were new pastures and woods, new brooks and farmhouses, new valleys and hills Johnny had never seen before, all illumined by the brilliant October light. The trees and houses cast the long blue shadows of early morning.

At each farm they stopped to chat for a while. Sometimes the men had already begun the winter plowing and were in the fields, and sometimes they were husking corn from the fodder-shocks.

Johnny and his father always took a hand in the work. Sometimes they assisted at hog-ringings and butchering. They husked corn, carted in winter squash and apples and potatoes. They milked cows and held the milk pail while the greedy calves buried their heads up to the eyes in the warm foaming milk. They did a hundred things which were fascinating to a small boy, and at noon they were always invited to stay for dinner at the farm they were visiting when the clock struck the hour.

Usually there was a delay, and Johnny and his father always knew that it had occurred because the farmer's wife was making a special effort for visitors and was piling the table high with food. They were enormous meals at which Johnny was allowed to gorge himself, for what is the digestion of a small boy weighed against the votes to be won by pleasing the farmer's wife? The more they ate the more popular they were. Until Johnny was twenty-five he had recurrent indigestion caused, I think, partly by the gorgings of pie and cake which took place at the Crescent House on the day of the horse fair, and partly because he had been made a political sacrifice in his childhood.

Usually there was fried chicken or tenderloin of fresh killed pork with mashed potatoes and fried sweet potatoes, beans and turnips, cole slaw, sweet corn, pie, cake and coffee. But what Johnny liked best were the arrays of fatal side dishes like small bird baths by which your plate was surrounded. These were filled with lima beans and dried corn, piccalilli and succotash and gherkins and dozens of other things which have been forgotten. I think the tradition of side dishes found its way into the Middle West from Germany by way of the Pennsylvania Dutch country. After that early training Johnny never learned to like one thing served at a time in the French manner. Later in life nothing, it seemed to Johnny, could be more unappetizing than a few string beans set down in barren loneliness on a large, cold, white plate. But then, he was feasting in those days in a land of plenty and not in a thrifty country where a green vegetable is regarded as a luxury.

When the lunch was finished the two always sat a spell, and raspberry cordial or elderberry wine was brought out and Johnny's father and his host talked politics and farming. They made their departure at the moment James Willingdon thought tactful. After dinner they continued the journey from farm to farm until night-fall, and if they were not too far away from home they returned for the night, but more frequently they stayed at a farmhouse or at a village hotel and sometimes at the livery stable. It was a wonderful moment when Johnny's father said, "I don't think we'll try to get back tonight."

Whenever there was a family reunion or a "homecoming" Johnny and his father were present. A "homecoming" was a cele-bration given by one of the villages for the sons and daughters who had gone away to live in the cities. A great many returned, and on the occasion there were barrels of free beer and cider in the square and oxen and sheep were roasted whole, over huge fires. The fire department gave an exhibition and the local band a concert, and the old people in those dying villages sat about watching the young ones who had returned, amusing themselves until far into the night. But the next day they went away again and the dying villages were left to the old people.

UNCLES AND AUNTS

IN THE MIDST OF THE CAMPAIGNING AND POLITICAL UPROAR THE
Old Man sat aloof in his room over the kitchen, taking no part
in any of it. Sometimes he must have been drawn into discussing
politics with his friend, the General, for the General, like old Jamie,
had a crusader's spirit and he spent much of his time trying to kin-
dle a feeling of indignation against the mockery of government
which surrounded him; but he was alone, like Canute ordering the
waves to come no farther. He died before the worst of the Ohio
gangs was elevated to Washington. The Old Man probably mocked
him if he discussed politics at all. He was older than any of them,
not only in years, but in cynical wisdom. Beside him the General
and old Jamie were little boys full of faith. It was as if The Old Man
belonged to a much older civilization and all those who surrounded him were crude, enthusiastic, optimistic, and unmoral, believing only in one faith—the inevitable success and prosperity of the
United States in general and the state of Ohio in particular. In the
midst of all the political hubbub there was something Godlike in
his detachment and cynicism.

　　Old Jamie never remained aloof and found satisfaction only
where the fight was most fierce. He fought until he was too feeble
and childish to fight any longer. Once he had been a Republican
because he was an abolitionist, but by nature and principle he had

always been a Jeffersonian Democrat, and once he left the Republican Party for good and found himself allied with the party which professed to follow the teachings of Jefferson, he felt freer and more happy. When Johnny was born the battle was no longer over secession and abolition, but a struggle between farmer and industrialist, the county and the city. He must have known that he fought on the losing side, but, like a good many other Americans belonging to the nineteenth century, he went on fighting gallantly. On the other side there was power, wealth, dishonor, corruption, tariffs, and all the instruments of great manufacturers and bankers, many of whom, in another time and in another country, would have been judged criminals. But in the nineties and the beginning of the twentieth century there was no one to judge them save a few conscientious men within the Republican Party and the mass of Americans belonging still to a dying tradition who saw political power slipping farther and farther from them. It was the epoch, too, of jingoism and fantastic talk of an American Empire.

Out of it all came the "Populist" Party and the "Granges" and the free-silver movement and other efforts to help the farmers. Old Jamie was one of the first Populists and he organized the Patrons of Husbandry in his county to fight against the thievery of the railroads. The opposition brought out its time-worn weapons and denounced all Grangers as "enemies of society" and above all else of prosperity. At that time they had not yet the words "Red" and "Bolshevist" to cast about carelessly in the direction of anyone who threatened the strongholds of money and privilege.

The menace of the "Grangers" was pitifully small. What could a million and a half citizens accomplish against the interests intrenched in Washington and the State Capitols where legislators were always in the market to sell their services? In some of the western states which were purely agricultural, the Grange did succeed in passing laws establishing railroad rates, and the cry went up from the big men of the New Era that this was Socialism, which was the worst word they could think of at that time.

But that was an era of despair when few citizens, I think, ever hoped that men like Rockefeller could be made to behave decently and that men like Fall would ever be brought to justice.

The Patrons of Husbandry faded into obscurity as a political force, and in the county, where it still remained alive for a time as an organization, it came to be a society for spreading information and education about crops and markets among the farmers. No one objected to farmers meeting to discuss such harmless subjects as grafting and the cinch-bug. And it endured as a social organization serving to bring together once or twice at great picnics the farmers and their families. When Johnny left the county forever, the old Grange Hall was still standing, but no one had come there for years and the roof was falling in. The old farmers had gone, and with them their tradition, and in their place there were only immigrant peasant farmers who had never heard of the West, the frontier or Jefferson or the Patrons of Husbandry.

It was always the name of Bryan which caused the greatest rows on the occasions of big family dinners. On the subject of Bryan there was an impregnable alliance between Johnny's father and old Jamie, for James Willingdon was an unregenerate Democrat who would vote for anything which was not Republican, and old Jamie was a Mugwump and regarded Bryan at the beginning of his career as a kind of messiah come into the world to save the farmers. For Bryan these two held the fort against most of the others in the family. Old Jamie believed in the Populist Party as he believed in the Grange, and although he had doubts about free silver he was willing to give it a try; at that time things could not have been much worse and any change might turn out to be an improvement. He had no faith in the mystical omnipotence of bankers and felt that they knew no more about economics than preachers knew about God. He could virtually recite the whole of the Cross of Gold speech in his great chesty voice, and he respected the young Bryan for one quality which he himself possessed—that of placing faith and conscience and ideals, however faulty their dictates, above bargaining and compromise. And he believed that Bryan, even as a thinker, was superior to most of those who in one way or another ruled the country. Bryan's sincerity, he would shout, was no mean quality in a country cursed with damned pussy-footing, pocket-picking politicians. Even later, when he began to believe that Bryan's limitations would forever prevent him from really achieving anything, he never confessed his doubts in the presence of his Republican sons. Bryan raised the only standard about which the farmers and the last of the frontiersmen could rally. Johnny's father, having once worked in a bank, privately thought Bryan's free-silver platform dangerous, but in the presence of the enemy he never admitted his distrust. On the contrary, he unscrupulously used his banker's patter to confuse and confound his less techni-cally informed brothers-in-law and prove that free silver was sal-vation. However upright may have been the public political prin-ciples of old Jamie and James Willingdon, in a family political argument they became crafty and unscrupulous and used any weapon which came to hand. In a family political quarrel, quarter was neither asked nor received.

Old Jamie's children, all save the youngest who died when he was twenty, were big men and women with great chests and bosoms and stentorian voices, and a political argument about the patriarch's groaning table quickly became a thunderous affair. Everyone talked at once, and more often than not the debaters placed faith in the loudest voice rather than the best argument. As a child Johnny grew impatient at never being able to speak or, if he spoke, to be heard. In the heat of those arguments the requests, the desires, even the bodies of the grandchildren were trampled under foot. So far as Johnny could see or remember no one of the debaters ever had his convictions altered in the least. They were a very American family, endowed with a goodly share of hysteria. Passions ran high and logic and facts counted for little. Prejudices always won out when at last, overcome one by one with the drowsi-ness which follows overeating, or exhausted by the violence of the argument, the discussion finally died away and each one of them remained as fixed in his original beliefs as when it all began. But a fine time was had by all.

Sometimes the heat of the discussion attained too high a degree and one of the brothers or sisters became personal and bitter, and then one or two of them would rise and leave the table angrily with the superior manner of one finding the discussion beneath his intellectu-al level. Immediately he would be followed in a body by the women seeking peace and reconciliation; but the ensuing conference, like so many others of infinitely greater importance to the world, would end only in spreading trouble, for Aunt Ruby would assert that her husband, Uncle Herbert, had been insulted and was perfectly right in leaving the table, and at that remark Johnny's mother would say that Uncle Herbert was a fool and that he had been quite wrong in all he said, and the other women would take sides, and so it would begin all over again. The peace conference came to nothing because each of them demanded peace and victory without concession, and each woman had the conviction that her husband was really a great statesman whose talents had not been recognized and that all the others were merely fools.

All those uncles and aunts were as unlimited in prejudice as in vitality, and in the spectacle they created before Johnny throughout his childhood there was much which explained to him later on the peculiar quality of American life. They were intelligent, exceedingly healthy, passionate people of colossal vitality, scarcely educated at all in the classical sense, but full of practical education. One is tempted to say that they possessed Yankee common sense, but on examination one discovers quickly that this was not true. One was misled by the solidity of their physical appearance. They all looked, like most Americans, as if they should have had common sense, but the fact was that they had very little and that at heart they were incurably romantic, all of them, and Johnny's mother most of all. Common sense, thrift, practical qualities, despite legends to the contrary, do not go with frontiersmen, and they were all children by blood, tradition, and experience of the frontier. If the men who conquered the wilderness of America had been thrifty and cautious shopkeepers, they would never have adventured into the wilderness. If they had had common sense and been interested first of all in putting away money beneath the mattress, they would not have been forced, like so many defrauded Revolutionary veterans, to seek salvation in the hardships of the frontier. The qualities of vitality and endurance, of resourcefulness and romance, they had in abundance. Of the shopkeeper or the settled peasant there was nothing in them. Few things could be farther apart than the European peasant and the American farmer of old Jamie's day.

It never occurred to any of those uncles and aunts to take a shop or a piece of land and stick to it for the rest of their lives, building up a small fortune through solid economies. They were always seeking the end of the rainbow and all of them died or will die some day in the belief that one day they will strike it rich. And so they were possessed of an undisciplined restlessness which drove them from place to place, from adventure to adventure, from one undertaking to another in all parts of the country. If one thing failed, they abandoned it and set out to try another in some other place. They never had the faintest attachment to any house or piece of land. They married and some of them brought into the world large families, but even seven or eight children did not succeed in settling them. The disease of wandering continued with all of them until long after middle age, when at last, one by one, they settled, most of them in the Far West where there still remained a sense of space, of freedom, and of adventure. Uncle John once wrote to Johnny's mother from the mountains of Oregon, "You should come out here and let your children grow up where there is still elbow room and where they won't grow up just like everybody else."

Uncle John married a woman who had one child after another, so easily that the aunts said when her pains came on that it was impossible to get her to a bed before the child was born. She was a strong woman and she gave birth to ten strong children, all of whom grew up to be as big and as powerful as their uncles and aunts. Considering the life they led as children, they had need to be vigorous. As a child Johnny envied them, for they seemed to him to lead the most romantic adventurous life, always traveling, never remaining long in one spot. Between adventures they returned to the Farm, sometimes with one parent and sometimes with both, to pass an interim in the house of old Jamie until some new plan was undertaken. When they arrived the character of the big farmhouse was changed and for the time of their visit the sacred parlor was defiled by being made into a bedroom to shelter two or three of them. It was no simple problem to feed and shelter twelve people who descended upon you without a word of warning, but Johnny's grandparents accepted the erratic visitations without complaint

and even with pleasure, for I think they would have liked it if all
their children and grandchildren had remained with them on the
Farm until they died. The arrival of Uncle John's family always
meant delight to the other grandchildren, for on visits to the Farm
there were always armies of children to play with. Their mother,
Aunt Hilda, was a romantic woman and consequently a rather slatternly housekeeper, and she brought with her to Jamie's and
Maria's house not only the burden of her family but of her incor-
rigible untidiness as well. Perhaps if she had been able to lead a
more settled life she would have been a greater success as a housekeeper. There was much to be said in her defense against the perpetual criticism of the energetic sisters-in-law to whom she was a
scandal. Her children suffered from her romantic nature, for they
were all named after characters in the novels of Walter Scott. One
was called Rob Roy, and another Rowena.

The children of Uncle John were the only descendants of the
Colonel who carried out the pioneer tradition to the very end.
They all settled at last in the state of Washington, where they married farmers or established themselves as farmers, all save two sons
who became engineers and gave up their lives to building roads
and dams and subduing the rivers in the remote mountainous
parts of the far Northwest and Canada, living the year round in the
open on horseback. Sometimes in the East and in Europe, filled
with a hunger for a country "where there is still elbow room,"
Johnny as a man felt an obscure envy of them and experienced a
sense of having taken a wrong turning somewhere long ago when
he was too young to know better.

The second uncle, Harry, was a great sport and the blood of the
family. He was the biggest of seven big brothers and sisters, both in
height and in girth, of a boisterous and Rabelaisian personality,
and of them all Johnny's memory of him always remained the
clearest. He too led a roving life, but in a financial way he was
always more successful than the others. It seemed to Johnny that he
had been everywhere and had seen everything, and he had a gift
for telling the stories of his adventures and describing the wonders
he had seen to the stay-at-homes of the family. The news that
Uncle Harry was to appear for a visit raised the whole tempo of the

family life, for he was one of those personalities who on entering a room seemed to bring into it a curious current of vitality which charged all the others present. Even the children, who understood nothing of "personality," were aware that here was someone who "lived" in a large way. Johnny's mother and his aunts were intensely respectable women, critical of any laxity of morals on the part of others, but with them it appeared that Uncle Harry was *hors de concours*. They knew he was licentious, they knew he had lived with actresses, but it seemed to make no difference. It was as if men like Uncle Harry had a special power even over respectable women which set them apart in a privileged class. I do not know how it was that he alone of all the children in a respectable Presbyterian family should have escaped a consciousness of sin. But he had none. He just lived. It gave him a great charm and an attraction for others who tormented themselves. He may have been a throw-back to the old Colonel who came out from Maryland, bringing the end of the eighteenth century with him. But he had, too, the colossal vigor and physique of old Jamie.

Uncle Harry liked rather flashy clothes and dressed with the exuberance of one who enjoyed life and found satisfaction in being a big handsome fellow. Johnny's clearest memories of him were always associated with his arrivals, when the children ran to the door to meet him and receive the extravagant presents he always brought in his big valise of crocodile skin. Coming up the path to the slate-gray house, you could hear his shouted greetings before he reached the door. In winter he wore a brown derby hat and a yellow covert-cloth box coat which ended just above his knees. He liked fancy cravats and wore a big diamond pin in his tie and a diamond ring on his big carefully kept hands. He ate enormously and smoked excellent cigars, and the aroma of tobacco smoke was inevitably associated with the memory of him. Despite or perhaps on account of his shortcomings, he was the favorite brother of Johnny's mother, and I think that part of the reason for her devotion to him lay in the vague glamour which he had for a woman who by circumstance and a rigid sense of duty was condemned to a routine humdrum existence in a small town. Of all her family she was the only one who did not roam and see the world.

As Johnny grew a little older he became aware that there was a
scandal about Uncle Harry which the children were not permitted
to know and which was discussed only in mysterious whispers.
Sometimes the children overheard their elders talking about some-
body called Eva who had something to do with Uncle Harry. The
mysterious Eva was always spoken of in tones of condemnation
and scorn. Then one day Johnny discovered what the scandal was.
Uncle Harry was divorced! When Johnny was much older he
learned the whole commonplace story. Eva was a pretty woman
and Uncle Harry was always leaving her alone in Indianapolis, in
order to go to San Francisco or New York. One day he returned
unexpectedly and found another gentleman's hairbrushes "stained
with macassar oil!" (as Johnny's aunts described them scornfully)
in Eva's bedroom. In the bosom of Johnny's mother and her sisters
there was no forgiveness for Eva nor any charity regarding her sin
on the grounds that her husband himself was licentious and left
her much alone. To them it was simply unthinkable that any
woman could have been unfaithful to the handsome Harry.

For a long time Uncle Harry was the manager for his brother
Robert, who was first amateur and then professional sprinting
champion in the world of bicycle racing. It was before the days of
automobile racing and baseball and a bicycle champion was as
much a hero as Babe Ruth. Together the brothers traveled all over
the United States making century runs and winning sprinting
races. Johnny's memory of Uncle Robert was dim save for the fact
that he was handsome and an athlete and that when he returned to
the Town, celebrations and receptions were given in his honor. It
was his melodramatic death and the effect it had upon all the family which fixed him forever in the gallery of uncles and aunts. He
was killed in a railroad accident worthy of the great moving-pic-
ture spectacles, when the train on which he was traveling from San
Francisco plunged, during a wild thunderstorm, through a
washed-out bridge into the bottom of a ravine two hundred feet
below. The children were told none of the details directly, but,
overhearing them, they pieced them together from sentences and
phrases picked up here and there until the parts reconstructed
themselves into a whole which was fantastically picturesque and

dramatic. Johnny re-created the whole scene in his imagination with such vividness that thirty years afterward he still had a perfect picture in his memory of a place which had never existed but which he could describe in detail. It was a deep canyon, narrow and dark, with a black rushing torrent flowing at the bottom, and at the top, a narrow arched bridge which gave way, crumbling, to drop a whole train of sleeping passengers into the dark waters below.

He remembered Uncle Harry saying, "If only Robert had taken my advice and gone to bed with his feet toward the engine, he would be alive today." Uncle Robert's body was found in the berth where he died in his sleep. His neck was broken from the shock of having been thrown against the end of the berth. Otherwise he was uninjured. The speech of Uncle Harry haunted Johnny ever afterward, deranging every voyage he ever made on a night train. Always he debated whether or not he should change the berth and sleep with his feet toward the engine. And always, thinking, "If I don't do it just this once, something will happen," he changed the pillow and bed clothes in order to go to bed traveling feet first.

Uncle Robert was a champion and he was handsome, and a good many women tried to marry him, but in the end he married a beauty, one of two sisters famed for their looks in the San Francisco of their day. They were the daughters of a man named Hackenschmidt who came from Germany during the troubles of 1848 and found his way to the Gold Coast, where he opened the most spectacular bazaar and jewelry shop the world had ever seen. It had nuggets and bars of gold and real jewels set into the wall, and in the great days of California Hackenschmidt did a huge business selling diamonds to gamblers and men who came down from the mountains with great bags of gold dust. One of the sisters was blond and the other brunette, and they were inseparable. It was said that people turned in the street to look at them, and that strangers were told that they had not seen all the wonders of San Francisco until they had seen the Hackenschmidt sisters. Both of them had clothes from Paris and dressed always in the latest fashion, long before the new styles had reached American small towns. There still exists a wedding picture with the two sisters, Greta, whom Uncle Robert married, and her sister Jo, both dressed in the height of fashion with enormous sleeves and tiny waists and aigrettes in their hair. Aunt Greta was looked upon by Johnny's mother and her sisters as a little "fast," but even this was nothing to the sin of having married Uncle Robert, the baby of the family. So the visits of Aunt Greta to the Willingdon household were always marked by a certain coldness, which she either failed to notice or ignored. It was whispered among the aunts that she was horribly extravagant and made dreadful hysterical scenes, behaving altogether like a professional beauty and ruining the life of Uncle Robert. I think the powerful aunts were as unjust to her as they were to the romantic, untidy Aunt Hilda. She was beautiful with a quality of brilliance in her beauty which made her seem hard, and undoubtedly, because she was a spoiled beauty, there were times when she seemed selfish and imperious, but I cannot see why she should have married Johnny's Uncle Robert, save for love, because she could have done far better for herself.

She was accused of "putting on airs" and of deliberately trying to shock the people of the Town when she came on a visit, but for that crime, if it was ever a conscious one, she must be forgiven. She came from San Francisco at a time when San Francisco was perhaps the most civilized and fascinating city in America, where conformity was considered mediocrity and extravagant individualism was encouraged and applauded. Grown up overnight of citizens from every country in the world, San Francisco had a wild, reckless, and generous character of its own, far removed from the desiccated propriety of Boston or the English mold which New York society attempted to ape. And out of this colorful background Aunt Greta stepped into the midst of a solid Scotch family in a community molded by New England tradition, to find herself surrounded by the hostility of disapproving sisters-in-law. It was a community wherein the mention of physical love was commonly regarded as shameful, wherein respectable women were supposed to submit themselves with distaste to the desires of their husbands, and a woman who found pleasure in love was no better than a trollop. To all this Aunt Greta, who was a South German and a San Franciscan, would never have subscribed, and I think that unwisely, either by inference or with a horrifying directness, she let the women know of her passion for the handsome Uncle Robert.

The sister Jo was more beautiful than Aunt Greta. She was dark and tall, with a superb figure, and looked rather like Anna Held. Once or twice she accompanied Aunt Greta on a visit. Johnny always remembered her as she was at Uncle Robert's funeral, seated in dazzling contrast beside her blond sister, both of them dressed in black clothes which were denounced as "freakish and undignified" because they were smart. A little black veil covered her eyes and the tip of her upturned nose.

When they appeared on the streets of the Town they never failed to create a small sensation. Women gathered disapprovingly to stare after them and whisper, like hens when a hawk appears in the skies overhead. I think they both enjoyed the excitement, for neither of them was above liking to attract attention.

Afterward Jo became an actress and died a tragic death when she slipped on the floor of a bathroom in a Chicago hotel and fell into a tub of scalding water. There was a full page in the magazine section of the *Chicago Record-Herald*, with the story of her life and her love affairs and pictures showing her beauty.

Aunt Greta's colorful life began in San Francisco. After Uncle Robert died she came back once or twice to visit Johnny's mother, and then no more was heard of her. She simply disappeared and whether she was dead or alive no member of the family knew for nearly thirty years. Then after she had almost been forgotten Johnny's mother went into a shop on Fifth Avenue to buy a hat, and the saleswoman who came toward her was Aunt Greta. She was no longer rich, and what had happened to her during all those years, save that she had married again, no one ever discovered. At fifty she was handsome and as smartly dressed as ever, but all the luxury which surrounded her in her youth had vanished forever.

It was not dreams of New York which fascinated Johnny in his childhood, but of San Francisco. Uncle Harry and Uncle Robert knew every big city in the country, but for them there was only one which stood apart from all the others by its glitter and charm and color. Uncle Harry looked upon New York as a rather drab provincial town compared to San Francisco, and I suspect he was right. New York, whether it was the New York of Henry James or of O.Henry and Madison Square Garden (which was probably the one Uncle Harry knew best), must have been a stuffy place beside San Francisco.

New York, the uncles said, had nothing which could equal the picturesqueness of the Barbary Coast, or the brilliance of the Cliff House or the luxury of the Palace Hotel, nor was there a single restaurant, even Delmonico's, in New York which could compare with any one of a half dozen in San Francisco. As a child Johnny longed to go to San Francisco as a Calvinist longs to go to heaven. The Cliff House with its seafood, and the sea lions on the rocks outside, and the carriages drawn by high-stepping horses and filled with beautiful women, seemed to him the apotheosis of all that was worldly and beautiful and exciting. When he went there for the first time twenty-five years later, on a sentimental visit, nothing remained but the sea lions. In place of the high-stepping horses there were only a few dreary taxicabs. The Barbary Coast had vanished and Chinatown was a cluster of tourist shops. Most of the famous restaurants were gone, slowly throttled by prohibition. Yet something remained—something which had the softness and the color of a city which was not American. In the south of California there was a great boom city, born of the New Era, but nothing could have been more different in charm or beauty or tradition.

Aunt Ruby was a big, powerful woman who married a little man and dominated him for the rest of his life. He was a quiet, docile fellow and would have liked, I think, to settle down in a corner and remain there, but that was the last thing Aunt Ruby had in mind, and so he was dragged and buffeted back and forth, up and down around the whole of the United States until Aunt Ruby felt she had seen and experienced all she desired and settled down at last in Oregon. In all their restless life he was never given time to establish himself anywhere, for Aunt Ruby was always seeking the foot of the rainbow and hadn't the patience to stick with any economic experiment long enough for it to prove either successful or unsuccessful. Hers was a nature which demanded either immediate success or the excitement of travel and adventure. As she never achieved immediate success, her life was given up entirely to travel. It always seemed to Johnny that somehow the sexes had become confused in the case of Aunt Ruby and Uncle Herbert. She should have been dressed in trousers and he in petticoats. It was a happy marriage and finally burned itself out into the peaceful companionship of old age. Aunt Ruby's husband scarcely ever spoke without glancing deferentially at her as if to ask for permission, and in the end he came to have no opinions which were not pale shadows of her own violent prejudices. I think that he was one of those feeble men who would always have been timid and wretched without some powerful woman to make his decisions, order his life, and arrange his day for him. The relationship used to puzzle Johnny; he was only a child then and knew nothing of theories of sexual compensation.

Aunt Annie was a slightly paler edition of Johnny's mother, Ellen, and Aunt Ruby. She married a tall, lanky man who was the proprietor of a comfortable small hotel in one of the few prosperous villages of the county. He had inherited the hotel from his father and would have been content to die there. It was a charming old building of brick which stood on the edge of a little river where the fishing was good, and he asked only to be left in peace to look after the needs of his guests and fish from the terrace when he had nothing else to do, which was a great part of the time. But Aunt Annie had no intention of leading so dull a life, and after a few years she persuaded him to sell the hotel, and she, too, accompanied by her husband, took to the road looking for the end of the rainbow. She, too, led him over all the Middle West and the West. She never found any pot of gold, but in the end, after middle age, she settled in southern California, where he promptly died, worn out, I think, from constant traveling and the companionship of so vital a woman.

Johnny's mother, like many Scotswomen, had a fair complexion, blue eyes, and black hair, and like the rest of her family she was built upon magnificent lines. She was one of those people who in this world appear to collect responsibilities as a sheep collects burrs, and from the time she was a child it was always to her that Johnny's grandmother, Maria, looked for aid in everything. She was a middle child in the family, but it was she who watched over her brothers and sisters, even the ones who were older than herself. Even in the cradle there must have been something about her which caused the others to unload burdens and responsibilities on her. She must have suffered countless hours of boredom during her life listening to the confidences of other women, more vain and silly than herself, who sought her advice and sympathy and insisted upon telling her all their real troubles and a great many which did not exist at all. Yet I think that her nature would have been cramped and starved without confidences and responsibilities and burdens, for in a way, as Johnny's father used to say in a rare outburst of acidity, she went out looking for them.

She was the one in Maria's family who helped with the housekeeping and gardening and in the dairy and cared for the younger children, and when old Jamie found that, in the changing times, it was impossible economically to provide the education he desired for all his eight children, it was his daughter Ellen whose higher education was curtailed. She was the one who could be spared the least. She had always a passionate love for music, but there was never either the time nor the money for her to have lessons, and so, while her sisters who had no taste for music were given lessons, she patiently taught herself to play a few tunes on the melodeon in the dark parlor.

She married young and the wedding photograph shows her dressed in a tight basque with innumerable tiny buttons following the flowing lines of an ample figure. She wears a pert bustle and a bang falling to her eyes. She and James Willingdon married for love, since neither of them was rich and there was no other possible reason. He had only his salary as a bank cashier out of which he supported his parents and sometimes helped his brother, who was a wild fellow and uncertain support for a wife and large family. By her marriage Ellen Ferguson escaped none of the responsibilities and burdens of her early life; she only took on a new set which added their weight to many she continued to bear. When there was still very little money she shared a big house with her mother-in-law and with The Old Man on the occasions when he deigned to return from his wanderings on a visit. When, at last, she had a house of her own, it was an extremely rare occasion when she had it all to herself and her family. Almost at once it became a sort of hotel for relatives, aunts and uncles and cousins who were in financial troubles, great-aunts who had lost their husbands or quarreled with one another, and cousins come back to pay a visit to the hometown. Whenever there was a wedding or a funeral in the family it took place in her house. The great-aunts came upon visits which extended themselves for months. When one of the family was ill he or she came to stay with her until he had recovered or died.

There were times when the situation must have been unendurable, most of all for Johnny's father, but in the patience of his nature he never complained, and in any case there seemed to be no escape. His wife was a magnet. She had not the heart to send the relatives on their way, and if she had, I think, something would have been missing from her existence. Her hospitality was her way of expression and she always lived her own destiny to the full. James Willingdon was certainly not a rich man and he had no gift for money-making, but whatever he attempted to save was eaten up by relatives, his own and his wife's.

Money, either in its abundance or in its scarcity, did not trouble him very profoundly, but I think there must have been times when he was driven to distraction by the interference and the unasked advice of great-aunts and sisters-in-law and cousins. His wife's family was not one to hold its tongue or to exercise tact in any circumstance, and I know that if Johnny's parents had taken one-half the advice offered them upon the upbringing of their children, their offspring would have ended in a madhouse.

All her life Johnny's mother had a colossal strength and vitality, but it was an unorganized force which more often than not burned itself out without accomplishing very much. A proper education, or some hard training which would have taught her to think straight and to control her emotions and organize her great powers of intelligence and energy, would have changed the whole course of her existence and made her perhaps a happier woman. She found satisfaction in her children, but she was an ambitious woman and suffered all her life from a sense of bafflement. She did not even have the satisfaction of achieving her ambitions vicariously, like old Sapphira, through her husband; for the life of James Willingdon moved in a slower rhythm, so gentle and placid that at times she grew ill from the accumulated exasperation of attempting to spur his worldly ambitions. It was unthinkable in her day and with her background that she should have gone into business, yet that was where she belonged. She could, like the old Sapphira, have managed her household and brought up her family and still have run a business with more energy than most men.

No woman was a more passionate mother and wife. For thirty years she gave her life to her husband and children. She protected them, cared for them, and made sacrifices for them, sometimes bitter sacrifices. Occasionally she spoiled them and nearly always she allowed herself to be trampled upon by them, although in this again I think that her nature demanded it. She was less like a bird defending her nestlings than a lioness protecting her cubs. Her own children were unspeakably brilliant and good and clever and all other children were inferior beings. She was a great primitive force, like a thunderstorm.

There were times when in the intensity of her devotion she threatened to devour her children without ever having the least consciousness of what she was doing; and if any one of them had been less than a chip from the old block, their lives might have been warped and ruined forever. That was a subtlety of relationship, which I think she never understood and could not have altered even if she had understood it. She was feminine and born of the nineteenth century, and there were times when she donned willingly and with satisfaction the robes of a domestic martyr. It was a role which she enjoyed most when she felt profoundly the overwhelming exasperation and the terrible limitations of being a woman. There came a time when Johnny knew that if he was to save himself he must escape as The Old Man had escaped long before from the love of the stormy Marianna, and the escape caused great agony and suffering for himself and his mother. Years passed before she could understand that a slavish devotion which amounted almost to servitude could be an evil thing in its effects upon a mother and son, but when at last she understood, she was happier than she could ever have been as the devourer.

Her character and her situation in life were both extremely complex and full of baffling contradictions, and even long after Johnny had escaped from the devastating intimacy of her relationship with

her children, he found it impossible to see her justly or clearly and with detachment. The very emotionalism of her own nature, opposed throughout all her life to the philosophic calm of her husband's character, kept her in a perpetual state of irritation. Again and again she saw him accept defeat with a philosophic calm amounting to indifference, when she would have gloried in carrying on a bloody and hopeless battle; and because she was a woman with children and a household dependent upon her, she could do nothing. I know that the irritation was especially severe at the times when the perpetually wobbling family fortunes were at the lowest. The most superb proof of her vitality was that at seventy, after the strain of a long life full of material hardships and spiritual bafflement, she was as strong and as vigorous as most women twenty years younger.

Physical action was an absolute necessity to her existence, and repose was almost beyond her command. It was, I think, a family characteristic—that there were long periods when only physical activity, frequently of the most intense sort, could bring peace to soul and body. There were awful moments when one was aware of slipping into the grip of something far stronger than will or intelligence, with the power of driving one far beyond the limits of normal fatigue. The force was one which gave birth to the most appalling exasperation at others whose tempo was less violent and whose desire to accomplish was less strong.

Her own wanderings began after middle age, at the time when the restless searchings of her brothers and sisters had come to an end and they were settled in the new country in the West. She began to wander when her own restless children left her, and her wanderings, prompted by the old intense desire to keep possession of them, were always made in a vague spiritual and physical pursuit of them. After fifty she set out, unabashed and unafraid, to settle for a time in three different great cities, to make new habits and new friends and create a whole new life for herself. It never occurred to her that these adventures were anything remarkable or that she possessed an extraordinary quality in being able to change her whole way of life and create a new background for herself at an age when most women and men seek only monotony and peace.

Her Scotch blood gave her adaptability, for like all Scotch people she created a world of her own wherever she found herself, instead of seeking, like the English, to carry the old familiar world with them and transplant it into the wilderness. She was not even intimidated by the bustle and the coldness of New York, but made a place for herself there, as if she had never lived anywhere else.

She would have been a better politician than her husband, for even with her emotionalism she was the more practical of the two and, perhaps because she was a woman, she would not have hesitated to use the political weapons then in fashion which James Willingdon refused to touch. She would have fought fire with fire and traded vote for vote and beat the swindler at his own game. In her husband it was always the qualities most honorable and charming in the human race which left him at the mercy of others. Once when he had been betrayed by a corrupt political boss she herself, unable any longer to endure the helplessness of being a woman, went to the office of the man and told him before an audience a great many truths about his morals and character which no one had ever dared tell him before.

Left to himself, Johnny's father would have found contentment in a groove in the small society of the county and the Town, but for his wife no such dull things as grooves were imaginable, and it was her energy and the family passion for finding the foot of the rainbow which kept him perpetually attempting new ventures. None of them ever succeeded, perhaps because he had small enthusiasm for most of them, and because she was never able to work them out directly but only through the medium of her husband.

In the hope of sudden fortune, urged by his wife, Johnny's father speculated in real estate and in stocks. He became involved in that most treacherous of all enterprises, the oil business. He even helped in the exploitation of the Great Northern Railroad and the vast new country which it opened up to settlers.

It was during the Great Northern adventure that the Town saw for the first time the superb apples beginning to be grown in the Northwest. It was long before the days of fruit-shipping companies, and the spectacular fruit, larger and more handsome than the world had ever seen before, was still a curiosity in the East. As part of the propaganda to lure new settlers to Washington and Oregon, James Willingdon received from time to time crates of magnificent Winesaps and Baldwins which were the wonder of the county. These he placed on exposition in the window of the shop, beneath his office on the main street, and crowds collected to observe their splendor. Johnny was allowed to take them to school, where the teacher placed a dozen in a row on the front of her desk as an exhibition of one of the wonders of God's country. And all the Town, save one or two elderly cynics, were so dazzled by their color and their beauty that they forgot to observe that the apples from Ohio orchards, smaller and less showy, tasted far better.

During the Great Northern adventure there were always railroad men coming and going to and from the house for meals, and sometimes to spend a night or two, and all of them were filled with stories of the miraculous Canaan to which the Great Northern Railroad would transport you for a figure which was something like fifty-nine dollars and sixty-five cents. Johnny was allowed to sit up late in order to listen to the wonders—the scenery, the climate, the roses, the waterfalls, the salmon rivers, the magnificent trees. He grew sleepy and yawned as Spanish children must have done four hundred years earlier at the tales of Eldorado brought back by the first adventurers. The whole procession of exploiters were rather jolly, fleshly, hard-living men, in the traditions of the gambling, get-rich-quick American promoters. One of them Johnny never forgot. He was a short, stout, good-natured fellow named Blunt, who incurred the ire of Johnny's mother because he always smelled of whisky.

Mr. Blunt had a loose, free way with waitresses and chambermaids and she felt, I think, that he was a dangerous influence on Johnny's father. Being a powerful woman, she believed half without knowing it, that all the inhabitants of the earth save herself were perilously subject to evil influences. It was very likely the fanatical idealism of the Calvinist in her as well, which sought to correct the ways of humanity and bundle it off to heaven in a single large omnibus. But the smell of whisky on Mr. Blunt only made him the more exciting to Johnny and raised up pictures of the exciting life in the West, aggravating the passionate desire to escape from the Town and the county and see the world. And Johnny liked the smell of whisky for itself.

In the end James Willingdon himself succumbed to the very propaganda which he was spreading. He was a slow man to get under way, but eventually he too was seized with a desire to sell out everything and migrate to the Northwest. There beyond the Rockies lay a new Canaan where he and his family could all make a fresh start, where perhaps they should find sudden wealth. I do not know whether in his heart he ever meant to go. He had a way of creating a dream and living in it without translating it into reality, and in the end I think the proposed great migration was only a dream, and if anyone had forced him to a decision he never would have gone. It was an agreeable dream. He disliked and shunned responsibilities much as Johnny's mother attracted them, and I suspect that the idea behind the dream was one which had motivated a great many earlier migrations. He fancied that by leaving the county for a new country all the troublesome details of life would miraculously be left behind. Two brothers-in-law with their families had already gone, and wrote ecstatic letters home.

It was his active, restless wife who, oddly enough, refused to consider the plan even as a dream. She was always a woman who relied upon "the feel of things" rather than upon logic or reason, and she obeyed the least stirrings of instinct. On this occasion I think there was a little reason mixed with her "hunch." She refused on account of her children. They were growing up and she was full of ambitions for them, none of the ambitions in the least material, and she had much of her father's respect and awe for education and the gentler pleasures of existence. All this, she knew, could be found easily in the East. She had hungrily desired cultivation and a knowledge of music, and those things had been denied her, and now she meant her children to have them. She had no intention of thrusting them into the frontier life of a new country. If they went anywhere, it would be to the East and to Europe, and not to the West. She had had enough of building America and she meant her children to enjoy the advantages which her ancestors had helped to create.

So the idea of the migration died out at last. If James Willingdon and his family had gone, the lives of all of them would have been vastly different, richer in some ways and incomparably poorer in others.

The venture into the oil business did not last very long and it was, I believe, less disastrous than most of the others. Johnny's father did not lose any money and out of it Johnny gained one fantastic memory of the flat, monotonous southern Indiana country. For some reason, and it certainly could not have been for pleasure, James Willingdon took all his family on a visit into the country where he had an interest in some wells. Perhaps Johnny's memory of the country has been warped because the visit occurred when he was very small, but whenever he thought of that country afterward it always seemed to him that it would have served Dante admirably for one of the circles of hell.

It was perfectly flat as far as one could see, without a tree or a hill, and once in prehistoric times it had been a bog so that the soil had a peatlike quality and when it caught fire burned like tinder, sending up thick clouds of smoke which sometimes covered the whole countryside. Either the bog soil had little value or the inhabitants were a listless and lazy lot, for apparently there was no effort made to extinguish a peat fire once it was started. The only ornaments of the countryside were the dreary villages filled with boardinghouses which were inhabited by drillers and their helpers, and the ungainly derricks which rose like desiccated forests in clusters wherever a strike had been made. Yet, like the Flats, another district which was hideously ugly by light of day, that country acquired at nightfall a kind of wild beauty and splendor. The dull peat fires cast a rosy glow on the drifting clouds of smoke overhead, and wherever there was a cluster of derricks there were the wild, torchlike flares of the flames of natural gas which burned night and day. The workmen were mostly Poles, ugly high-cheeked men, always black with oil and smoke. Once, returning after nightfall to the village, there was a sudden terrific explosion which lifted the buggy from the road, and in the distance, miles away, there was a brilliant flash in the sky above that flat country. The next day the Willingdon family learned that a wagon load of nitroglycerin being hauled to the wells had blown up, and they drove to see the vast hole made by the explosion. Not even a hair of the horses which drew the wagon nor of the men who drove it was ever found.

THE TWO GRANDFATHERS

IN THE MIDST OF JAMES WILLINGDON'S ADVENTURES HIS FATHER-in-law, old Jamie, came to live with the family, so that there were two grandfathers living in the house, as different from each other as they could possibly have been. By that time the thin old cynic with the brilliant eyes had withdrawn from all contact with life forever into the fastnesses of the room above the kitchen. Days and weeks passed when no one saw him save Johnny when he carried up his meals, and days passed when there was no sign of his existence except the exaggerated thumpings and bangings which were his only retaliation against his vigorous daughter-in-law's opinions of his selfish uselessness. Sometimes, too, he was heard tramping up and down the floor of the room overhead, wrestling with some problem which concerned his own soul and was doubtless far beyond the comprehension of the rest of a family so charged with action and so little given to reflection. Now and then, after twilight, one surprised him making the rounds of the backyard, and sometimes when Johnny encountered him thus The Old Man would address a word or two to the small boy and make cramped, self-conscious, and rather terrifying gestures toward establishing some sort of a human relationship; but the gestures always failed, and his attempts were awkward, fumbling, and frightening to a small boy. Always Johnny drew away from him, and sometimes, I am afraid, he took to undisguised flight, terrified and at the same time ashamed because, with the simplicity of a child, he was aware of The Old Man's loneliness. And sometimes in the twilight he did not speak at all, but merely glared at Johnny out of his terrible shining eyes, and sometimes he did not see Johnny at all. Once he said bitterly that he detested dogs and music and flowers, but I think he said that only because these were three of the things much loved in the family from which he was forever an exile.

Old Jamie, a man of action, was honored in a household, in a community, even, one might have said, in a civilization where action was the greatest of qualities and virtues. He was given a big mahogany bed in the bedroom which Johnny and his brother had always shared, and they were sent to sleep in the sewing room, which was a pleasant change for them because they could do as they pleased there without fear of scratching the furniture or making too much noise. They could even manage to read by the light of a pilfered candle late at night and never be caught, because their mother had to cross a little passage before reaching the sewing room and could always be heard approaching. In old Jamie there was no bitterness save the crude direct bitterness of a man to whom youth and vigor had been everything, at the knowledge that he was growing old and feeble and useless. But even this bitterness scarcely ever showed itself. He was good-natured and abrupt, opinionated and full of talk and prejudices as a good Scotsman ought to be. His old belief in the infallibility of his judgments in matters of ethics, morals, and even table manners was undiminished by his age. Rather it seemed to increase with the forced inactivity which had been imposed upon him. Over eighty, he still remained perfectly clear-headed.

Until that year, from the day Maria died he had stayed alone on the Farm, fighting a losing battle. All his children had gone away. Not one of his sons remained to inherit and cherish the land which the Colonel had cleared out of a wilderness. The physical work was beyond him or beyond any one man. He found hired men unsatisfactory and scarce, and often they would drift away mysteriously at the very moment they were most needed, and so at length he fell into the last resort of the farmer. He accepted the humiliation of sharing the empty echoing old house with a tenant. The tenants came and went, rarely staying very long, moving on in the belief that the next place would give them opportunities for making a fortune with a minimum of work. Often they cheated and always they aroused his impatience and anger by their insolence and slovenliness. He was a perfectionist and all his life the Farm had been the great object of his perfectionism. Now in his old age, try as he would, he found it no longer possible to keep it as it had once been kept. It must have troubled him, too, to find in the rooms where no one had ever lived save his own people strangers who were not only strangers but shiftless and lazy creatures, for whom he had no respect. Most tenants were men past middle age who long since had given up hope of succeeding at anything, and farmed only because it was the simplest way of providing food for their wives and children. They were the worthless sons of the old settlers or the descendants of the riffraff which had come in after the first migration to make their way as best they could. None of them had ever owned more than two or three broken-down beds and a few chairs. They were undernourished and unintelligent and without the shadow of an ideal or an ambition.

Although the great Sunday gatherings had ceased with the death of Maria, the Willingdons continued to go regularly to see him, and in the midst of all her other work Johnny's mother found time to drive at least twice a week to the Farm to collect the old gentleman's laundry and give his rooms a thorough cleaning. She too, I know, suffered at the sight of the rooms, in which she had spent nearly half her life, turned dusty and ill-kept under the care of drab "poor white" women. She, too, saw the fields which had once been so fertile growing bare and sterile because the tenants would not share the expense of fertilizer nor cultivate them as they should have been cultivated.

But at eighty old Jamie still clung on, aware that the times were changing and that life was no longer what it had once been for an American farmer. Prices were poor and transportation high. Everything was expensive save the wheat and the corn which he grew. Although the butchers grew rich, it was scarcely worth the trouble to go on raising hogs and lambs. Woolen manufacturers became millionaires, but his wool brought next to nothing. He clung on, pottering about his beloved orchards and the big barn. The peach orchard, of which he was extremely proud, he reserved for himself in all his contracts with the tenants, and he picked the peaches himself, handling them with tenderness in order that their bloom should not be bruised. Next to himself he trusted his grandsons with the picking, and to Johnny and his brother fell the task of picking the peaches which were beyond his reach.

There were times of crisis when he helped his tenants with the work, not because he was called upon to do so, but because he grew impatient of their shiftlessness and because he could not bear to see the crops suffer because they had not the energy to harvest and shelter them at the proper time. It was thus that he received the fall which ended with his coming to live with Johnny's parents. It happened on a day when a thunderstorm threatened the newly mown hay lying fragrant and ready for the mows in the open fields. He was eighty years old, but he went into the fields to save the hay. As each load was driven into the barns he climbed into the high mows to pull the trip rope of the unloading fork. Somehow the rope entangled itself round his ankles, and the horses pulling at the other end drew him over the edge of the mow and he fell twenty-five feet, striking his head.

It was a fall that would have killed most men. They brought him to the gray house in Town, where he lay for many days unconscious, and then when he grew a little better and began presently to recover and talk of returning to the Farm, Johnny's mother decided that he should stay on. At first the old man refused even to consider the idea. He could not imagine the Farm going on without him, but as the weeks passed and he began to walk about shakily, one detected a faint softening in his decision. I think that for the first time in his life soft living tempted him. He found it pleasant to be coddled and treated as a patriarch, to be served his favorite dishes, and to have his grandchildren devoted listeners to his long stories. For a long time he had led a lonely life with no companionship in the long evenings but that of the men and women who shared his house and for whom he had, in his heart, only contempt; and now once more he found himself in a house

which was always overcrowded, where there were children and
dogs and where he could receive visits from the few old men who
remained of his generation and had preceded him in succumbing
to the temptations of the softer life of the Town. But in his
Presbyterian heart I think that he felt ashamed of his weakness and
believed that the temptation came from the devil himself. He
would never admit that he liked the new life, or that he had really
decided to live with his son-in-law for the rest of his life. All his life
he had had the strength and the vitality to do whatever he set his
will to do, and now when in the marrow of his bones he began to
feel old and weary he could not admit that he was defeated. He
talked always of returning to the Farm, but fixed no date for his
departure, and there were none in the household who would have
dared to question him on the subject, because they knew that if he
suspected even for a moment that anyone thought him tired and
old he would return out of pure stubbornness to prove the falseness of such an idea. So the comedy went on for months and even
for years. But in the end his terrible will won out and he did return,
to die as he wished in what was left of the "dark room" which had
been the cabin of the Colonel himself.

Although he was old and in his heart disappointed because so
many of his dreams had failed and so many of his battles had been
lost, he never lost the old quality of fierce indignation. He was born
to action, and active people, being driven by a force stronger than
themselves, seldom grow bitter, since bitterness can be born only of
indolence and inactivity and brooding. But slowly as the days and
weeks passed and the weeks became months and the months years,
one became aware that the fire which had always animated him was
growing a little dimmer. He went less frequently on those long walks
through the Town which always had as their goal the feed stores and
warehouses and livery stables where farmers gathered when they
came to Town. Day after day he made the rounds, hoping always to
find an old friend with whom to chat for an hour or two. But the old
friends were dying off. Week by week they grew fewer and fewer. Now
and then Johnny drove with him miles into the country to the funeral of some old man who, like himself, had fought first against slavery
and illiteracy and ignorance and secession and the corruption of

Reconstruction, and later the long losing fight against railroads and banks and commission merchants. They were sad affairs, these funerals. Sometimes the old man had died alone and sometimes he left a widow, old and bent and feeble, but never was there a son or a daughter to succeed him in taking over the land to which he had given all his life. Always the sons and daughters had gone away to the West or to the cities. They came home for the funeral and then went away again. Johnny was not old enough then to understand what it was that was happening all about him. He did not understand that a whole epoch of American life was passing. He only knew that the funerals of these old men in the parlors of empty farmhouses were sadder than the other funerals he had known, and that on the long drive home his grandfather was either melancholy and silent or talked always about the past and the days when he was young.

The deaths of his old friends depressed him, but I think what troubled him most was the boredom of having nothing to do. There was in him little capacity for philosophy or reflection. All his life when he was not working or agitating he slept simply to refresh himself and rise the next day full of strength for new tussles. Suddenly there was nothing to do. He pottered about the garden, digging among the flowers and pruning the trees, and there was something infinitely pathetic in the exaggerated care he spent upon these tasks. He would pass a whole morning going from fruit tree to fruit tree, examining each one with a meticulous care in the hope that it might have developed a sick twig which he might cut off for the good of the tree. When he had finished digging over a flower bed there remained not a single lump; the earth had been worked to a powder. His big muscular figure seemed hopelessly out of proportion to the narrow limits of that Town lot. He was like Hercules working at a piece of needlepoint. Often Johnny drove with him to the Farm, for he went there three times a week to see how his tenants were getting on. But it was always the same story. With each visit the once neat fences were in a little worse condition than the time before. More nettles grew in the quadrangle, once so neat and clean, between the barn and the house. There were fresh gullies in the fields because the tenants had plowed the wrong way. He was forbidden to do any real work, but with his small grandsons he pottered about, picking fruit, pulling up nettles, keeping up the fences, painting the chicken house. It must have been a long agony for him who had so loved the Farm and taken such pride in it.

And at last, slowly, he began, in the fashion of the very old, to substitute the memories of his adventurous youth for the activity of which he had been robbed. He became content to sit for a few hours every day in a rocking chair on the front porch, fanning himself and watching the passersby and talking if there happened to be anyone with whom he might talk. The old fierce indignation over politics and the corruption of politicians faded a little, as if in his heart he was aware that his own day was past and that this day into which he had lingered on was one filled with degeneration and feebleness. In his grandchildren he found an audience for his tales. They heard them again and again, always with the same fascination plus the pleasure which children find in hearing the same story several times, so that they came to know every word of it and corrected the narrative when he went astray. They came to know the tales by heart, but sometimes there were surprises when suddenly in the midst of the California saga (which was always a serial continued from day to day) he would remember a place or a character which would open up a whole new avenue of reminiscence. He was a good storyteller, understanding the importance of building up character and suspense, and he had a way of putting things in their proper sequence. There was something heroic in his storytelling, and passages like the hanging of the peddler near Fresno and the escape of the gold-hunters from plague-stricken Panama were vivid and even poetic. Perhaps it was the Scotch in him which gave his tales the qualities of sagas. Bit by bit he reconstructed for the children the whole of that early life which had gone forever.

Sometimes in the garden at dusk he encountered the wiry old man who lived in exile above the kitchen, but between them there was never any friendliness nor even a word of conversation. They might have passed the long hours gossiping together in the way of old men, but that never happened. It could not have happened.

The one, all action, could see the other only as a useless parasite, and the other, bitter, mocking, and silent, hid his reflections so well that no one ever knew what he thought. Yet mockery and scorn and contempt were written in every line of his sharp, intelligent old face. I suspect that each of them envied the other a little for knowing in life things which he had not known himself and which it was then too late ever to experience. It must have been so for them to have felt so intensely the barrier which separated them.

Then one morning when Johnny knocked at the door of The Old Man's room there was no answer, and when at last Johnny pushed it open he found his grandfather's lean old body lying half in, half out of the huge black-walnut bed. In the bright daylight the kerosene lamp beside his bed still burned feebly, for he had been reading when death came to him.

The bitter philosopher had gone first, leaving behind the man of action.

The funeral was held in the parlor with the rococo furniture which The Old Man had not entered since he came home to die. He lay in a simple black coffin on which there was a single sheaf of flowers, yellow chrysanthemums, sent by his old friend, the General. The rest of the Town and the rest of the world had forgotten him long ago. All his life had been led fiercely inside his own soul, and so there were no tributes uttered and no odes to this "worthy citizen." In life he had dwelt utterly apart and in death he was alone. In the newspapers there was only a simple notice of his death.

Johnny must have been twelve years old when he died, and he had a dislike for the sight of a dead person, but before the services he forced himself to go into the dark parlor, where he sat alone on a stiff chair, looking at his grandfather in his coffin. Something Scotch in him made him conceive the idea that contemplation of the dead would be good for his soul. In death The Old Man seemed, in a strange way, real to Johnny for the first time. The boy was afraid of death, but he no longer had any need to be afraid of the bright, bitter, searching old eyes which seemed to pierce one's soul, discovering even the most hidden things. Thinking of him long afterward, it seemed to Johnny that perhaps The Old Man was one of those who are born burdened somehow by all the experience and wisdom in the world, knowing vice and virtue, sin and tragedy. What was his own life no one will ever know, but I think that he knew all those who scorned him in their very hearts, as he knew anyone he ever encountered, with all their weaknesses and meannesses, their secret sins, their hatreds and their jealousies. There are people like that, and their burden is one sufficient to set a man forever apart from all his fellows in a loneliness which nothing can ever change.

No one came to the funeral except the family, for the General himself lay dying. The Old Man has long since been forgotten. It was the funeral of a failure in a world where for a hundred years the only need and the only test had been that of action.

✧

After the funeral one of Big Mary's daughters came to clean the room above the kitchen and put it in order. In the corners and behind the rows of battered old books there was a vast accumulation of dust, for The Old Man while he was alive had resisted every attempt to root him out and give the place a thorough cleaning. Once he had said, angrily, "I'll be dead soon and then you can sweep it all out into the street and forget all about me." And now that he was dead, Big Mary's black daughter took out all the old books, dusted them and conveyed them to the loft of the barn. Most of them were books on theology and philosophy, of small use to a family whose whole existence was dedicated to the present and to reality—books by Spencer and Montaigne and stiff, complicated treatises by Spinoza and Descartes in which Johnny pretentiously tried to interest himself, leaving them in the end for a game of baseball or a novel by Dickens or George Eliot. And there were scores of books by theologians whose names were forever unknown save to clergymen, and a few books, like the historical works of Mommsen and the worn, massive old edition of Gibbon's *Decline and Fall*, which were salvaged and put in the cupboard of the living room because there was no longer any room in the bookcases. What became of the philosophical and theological library no one ever knew. For years it lay forgotten in the loft of the barn with mice building nests between volumes of Descartes and Herbert

Spencer. They were left there forgotten, to be the heritage of the puzzled drugstore proprietor who came to live in the gray house after the family had left it forever.

The old walnut secretary held in its musty drawers and pigeon-holes treasures of another kind. It was filled with old letters and papers and scores of pages of faded yellow paper written over in the tiny handwriting of The Old Man. But for Johnny's curiosity all of them would have been lost forever, cast by Big Mary's daughter into the fire on the carriage drive which she made to consume all the rubbish carried down from the room above the kitchen—a kind of ritual fire raised to cleanse the household forever of the presence of the idle, sardonic, unhappy old man who had always been a stranger. Johnny, rubbing down one of the horses outside the stable, saw her flinging boxes of papers into the flames. How much she had burned before he saw her no one but God will ever know, for to Big Mary's daughter it was all just so much tiresome rubbish. But Johnny managed to rescue what remained, and out of the lot he discovered a few treasures and here and there a letter or a scrap of paper which illumined for an instant the life and the soul of Grandpa Willingdon. Of the precious sheets of yellow paper covered with the writing of years only three or four were salvaged, and of these Johnny could make nothing at all, for they were full of strange words and phrases. In the end he cast them into the fire, and years afterward, when he would have given almost anything to have the precious sheets once more in his possession, he could remember, try as he would, nothing which had been written on them save one curious, stimulating phrase which had a medieval flavor. Somewhere on those sheets he had seen the words, "the substance of God." He remembered it because for days after the ashes of the bonfire had been washed away from the carriage drive by the midsummer rains, the phrase had troubled him. What could it mean—"the substance of God"? How could God, who was everything and nothing, have substance? For the rest of his life Johnny was destined to be haunted by regrets and curiosity over the sheets of yellow paper which had long ago become part of the earth in that Middle Western country. What had been written on them? Was it an outburst of confession or a book on theology, or perhaps even some new philosophy? Could it have been that The Old Man had been profound and brilliant and intellectual? Had he written down the record of some illuminating experience born of all those rows of books and of his own strange wandering life? Or were those pages the manuscript for a book to which he had given his whole life, only to abandon it in the end through the cursed sense of futility which forever paralyzed his soul? In those sheets of faded yellow paper perhaps lay the whole key to his character and his strange, erratic life. But they were burned. There was no recovering their essence.

In one of the drawers there was a bundle of old letters, a dozen or more, tied together with a bit of rotten string. They were addressed to Thomas Willingdon, Jr. Esq. at the Cordova Theological Seminary, in an emotional, flowery handwriting ornamented with Spencerian curlicues which began in a neat correct flourish and ended in a splatter of ink. Across the face of the top letter was written in The Old Man's handwriting, "not to be forgotten."

They were the letters of Marianna, his mother, written to him when he was escaping from her. They were mostly emotional tirades, full of such phrases as "all I have in the world" and "if it were not for my Thomas, I should have no reason to go on living." Once she wrote, "Your father has been more cruel than ever to me. Surely God made him without a heart." Once she mentions Chauncey Knox, who committed suicide in the little river at Cordova just before Thomas was ordained. She writes of him as "your puny friend Chauncey and his un-Godly ideas."

Like "the substance of God," the words, "not to be forgotten" were destined to haunt Johnny for the rest of his life whenever he thought of The Old Man. Had they been written there by The Old Man when he was old, and remembering his boyhood once more, had softened toward her? Or were they set down in bitterness against the woman who had crippled his soul forever? Why had he kept the letters for more than sixty years, carrying them with him in all his wanderings? Was it because in spite of everything some affection of the spirit and body lingered beneath the surface of his cold intelligence or because he must have them forever with him to harden his soul against ever relenting? Out of the pages there rose the essence of Marianna, old Sapphira's twin sister, the image of Marianna approaching middle age, passionate and baffled, hungry to love and to be loved, stupid and silly, creating evil in the conviction that she was doing good, dangerous because she was all emotion and no intelligence, human and sometimes even lovable—a woman not to be forgotten by any of those whose lives she had touched, because she was, in spite of everything, one of the phenomena of nature itself, like Niagara Falls or a Caribbean hurricane.

And in other drawers there were the old letters of Elvira van Essen which had somehow come into The Old Man's possession from the family of that cousin in Virginia with whom she had corresponded long ago. And there was a single letter written by Jorge van Essen himself to his uncle in Delaware a few months after he had come over the mountains with his twelve children. It read:

State of Ohio, Midland County
Near Pentland, 3rd, July 1816

"Respected Uncle:
We left Anderstown on Monday the 6th of April and arrived here in 24 days much tired as Elvira and myself and the older boys walked almost all the way except while we were on the boat.
Elvira had ninety-nine dollars when we started—one dollar went to pay for mending the tea kettle in Hanover, one dollar for tin cups and one dollar for medicine—$25 for horse hire, as we could not get along with the two horses. Three dollars we paid for a pair of chains and hames which we since sold and with the money bought 400 feet of hewn lumber to lay a floor in our cabin. 17 dollars we had when we got here, 14 dollars of which went to buy a cow and calf and one dollar for a sow and five pigs, the rest of the seventeen dollars to buy some coarse lining and something to put the milk in, the rest of the 99 dollars it cost us on the road for horse feed and provisions.
We laid by on the road 1½ days and got here on Thursday night the 30th of April. And on Monday the 4th of May went to work in the woods and by the 26th of May we had about 6 acres cleared and planted in

corn. On the 11th of June we raised and covered a cabin 1¹/₂ stories high, 18 feet by 22.

Our corn is now generally about 3¹/₂ feet high—Thursday 17ᵗʰ June we moved into our cabin—without a window or chimney and it was not even filled with mud, and only one floor and 25 cents in money. I am now about the chimney. Uncle William's land that we have moved on is very rich chiefly covered with walnut, wild cherry, sugar trees, some white oak & swamp oak and elm & ash wood and a great deal of hickory: the underbrush is ironwood, spicewood, plum, hazel, white thorn hugh-bushes, &c. We have to haul our water half a mile or more.

Hector Blake made it his business to write to his father Heber Blake our situation which arrived here the day before we did—which I believe did us no good. Hector has always been an enemy save within this three or four years past we have made peace. Since then I took him to be a friend but now I believe him to be no friend. A man with plenty has friends—but let him get poor & his friends are scarce. I have suffered more cruelty from the old gentleman than I have from all my creditors. The sons have all been kind.

Should we live to see another harvest after this, we shall have plenty to eat but how it will be until then we can not now see.

I have suffered more since we left Anderstown than I have before in twenty years. We are as poor as those that have but little to eat—in land where there is plenty—our chief living is bread and milk and that sour unless we drink it fresh from the cow. Had I known before I sold the Fort what I now know I think I should have staid upon it until I was driven off of it. Although I must confess if we have our health we can live as well here in two or three years as there in Anderstown, and it may be better here for our children. I am almost sure it will.

I expect to start back about the 1ˢᵗ or 10ᵗʰ of September & I expect to walk as the horses will be too poor to ride for want of feed. The woods does not afford them sufficient pasture to keep them in order and work them.

I wrote you from Wheeling Post Office Virginia.

What things we could not sell were left with Mr. John Hazeltine to

sell and he was to give the money to you—We could not realize half
price for them.
We are now having reasonable health.

Yours &c
Jorge van Essen

"Post Scriptum—Colonel MacDougal of whom you have heard much
back home has settled a few miles to the northward of us."

He lived to see scores of harvests and to enjoy plenty. Out of
that poor cabin came van Essen's mills and tannery and all those
descendants who went to Spring Hill Farm to congratulate old
Sapphira on her hundredth birthday. Out of that last twenty-five
cents came wealth amounting to several millions of dollars distributed through four generations of offspring.

It was indeed a rich country.

And there was another letter written after Jorge and Elvira had
begun to prosper, in which there was a hint of the strange blend of
piety and worldliness which was forever tormenting the Patriarch.
It was a rambling, sentimental letter full of nostalgia for the old gay
life in Maryland. It was a Biblical letter, perhaps more Biblical than
grammatical. It ended:

"Tell my dear old Mother the ferry man is waiting to take her over
if she has not already crossed the river. If she loves such a country, the
people and their King—she need not be the least afraid, the ferry boat
is big and strong and the ferry-men are careful.

My respects to Aunt Robinson and family and all inquiring
friends. Please to remember 21206 in sending claim of the vaccine
institution lottery.

There is no record as to Jorge's luck in the lottery, but his "dear
old mother crossed Jordan's Flood" a few weeks later.

⌐

The ritual bonfire built by Big Mary's daughter did not succeed
in clearing the house of the memory of The Old Man, or of his
presence. No amount of cleaning and scrubbing ever succeeded in

driving away the peculiar odor of the room above the kitchen—a curious aroma blended of old age, of kerosene, of apples and tobacco. From the time he died until the Willingdons left the house the room was never used again save as a place to store discarded furniture, and on the day the key was turned in the lock for the last time by any Willingdon, the room still smelled of Grandpa Willingdon. Sometimes Johnny, going from the house to the stables in the dusk long after The Old Man was dead, suddenly knew that somewhere among the fruit trees he was there, walking up and down, and the old fear of the brilliant eyes returned to him. And after he came to sleep with his brother in the sewing room they never crossed the little passage which divided it from the room above the kitchen without a little shudder. And when one wakened in the middle of a hot still summer night one could smell the odor of The Old Man's room. When at last the family left behind them the house and all its associations they succeeded in shaking off the ghost of Grandpa Willingdon—all but Johnny; for Johnny was destined to be haunted by him for the rest of his life.

THE LAST OF THE FRONTIER

From the time The Old Man had come to live in the gray house the interest of Johnny's father in broken-down horses had extended itself to abandoned farms.

This was not one of those countless new ventures embarked upon in order to support his growing family and the hordes of visiting relatives, or in a vain dream of putting a little money in the bank. It was a passion like his passion for horses. If he had been a shrewd business man he might have used the same capital and the same mortgages to buy land on the outskirts of the Town and resell it to the mills and factories and the builders. He chose instead to buy farms hidden away in remote valleys, for which there was no market at all save among the shrewd immigrants who had begun to seep into the county and reclaim the land left abandoned by the vanishing contemporaries of old Jamie. But I do not think that in his heart James Willingdon ever had the faintest idea of these farms as speculative adventures. He may have said so to calm the doubts and silence the reproaches of his wife, but I doubt he himself ever believed it. The motive was far more romantic and one which in his nature was forever driving him nearer to economic disaster. It was a simple creative desire, in its source the same desire which led to his futile efforts to recondition horses. He wanted to make over and build up. In that world I suppose he never heard the words "creative force," and if he had heard them he would have laughed. Certainly he never recognized the force in himself. He never knew the American passion for gambling, in the belief that fortune lay just around the next corner. The delusion of the foot of the rainbow which had haunted old Jamie's family for six generations said nothing to him. They had come from England and Scotland to a new country, and when that country grew a little crowded they had gone to the Western Reserve, and after that into the Great Northwest, always in the belief that in the new country lay unbounded wealth. If Johnny's father knew that dream at all it was only vicariously, through the extraordinary force of his wife's character. He never believed in it. He would have been content simply to find himself free from debt. He was an artist without ever knowing it, and an artist who never succeeded in finding his *métier.*

Once when he made about five thousand dollars more by luck than by shrewdness, out of the sale of some land, he promptly spent nearly all of it in taking his family on a grand tour of the Great Lakes. Old Jamie, who had no desire to make the trip, was left at home in care of Big Mary, and all the others went to Cleveland to embark on a ship which took them through the straits past a Detroit which was still a sprawling big town with no skyline and only two or three little factories turning out that newfangled vehicle, the automobile. They went north to Kalamazoo, Grand Rapids, and to Mackinac, and finally through the canal at Sault Sainte Marie across Lake Superior to Duluth—through all the country whose names had come into being before the Colonel's Jesuit friend came out from France to the New Country.

There were plenty of forgotten farms in the county, for it was the time when one by one the farms of the original settlers and their sons were falling into the hands of tenant farmers who carried their degradation to the ultimate depths. When a farm became too poor to be worth a tenant's trouble he simply abandoned it and occupied another and farmed that wretchedly until its poor exhausted soil no longer had any value. The Town had conquered in more ways than one. It won not only the economic struggle, but it attracted the sons and daughters who should have carried on the destinies of that land cut out of the wilderness such a little time

before. The immigrants were only beginning to arrive, family by family, to take over the tired land and by work and sacrifice restore it once more to fertility.

Most of the farms lay hidden away from the main road in the half-wild romantic little glacial valleys which furrowed the county. The decaying fences were choked with wild blackberries and elder bushes, the shingles of the roofs rotting away, the windows staring with their panes shattered by tramps and small boys. When you pushed open the sagging doors, the rotten flooring gave way beneath your feet and you heard the scampering of small animals—woodchucks and field mice and chipmunks who had their nests beneath the boards. About them all there was that queer ghostliness which haunts a house in which there is no longer a fire on the hearth or the sound of a voice. Sometimes in one of the upper rooms you would find the remnants of a crude bed used at night by tramps wandering the countryside, and sometimes on the hooks fastened to the moldy wall you might find an old dress or a moth-eaten coat or a faded forgotten sunbonnet. And in the dooryard, half buried beneath the nettles and the flowers of a garden gone wild, there lay rusting bedsprings and broken mirrors and pieces of cracked furniture not worth carting away when the last tenant drove off down the lane, leaving the door unlocked behind him. The poor stripped fields were filled with daisies and goldenrod and sumac, and on the edges of the pasture the trees were slowly advancing to take possession once more of the land wrested from them a hundred years earlier.

As often as not the woodlot, like the fields, had been stripped by the last tenant, and there remained only scarred and rotting stumps of the old trees already hidden by new shoots springing up from the dark ground. In these clearings in the month of May one could always find in abundance the delicious spongy morels pushing their fawn-colored noses through the carpet of leaves and spring beauties and bloodroot, and if it was a hot day in May one was certain to uncover here and there warm nests lined with down and filled with baby rabbits huddled together in a neat bundle. And over it all hung the ghostly beauty of the dogwood, which the last tenant had not considered worth cutting even for firewood. It was a rich land and bit by bit the richness had been pilfered.

Johnny shared his father's passion for these abandoned farms, although the reasons for the delight they gave were different. He had no desire to see them restored to their former neatness and fertility. He loved them because they were romantic and adventurous places and the nearest thing he could find to a wilderness or a jungle, and because there was about them the ghostly fascination, bordering a little upon terror, which haunts places which have once been full of life and are at last deserted. On those farms it was as if the land had reached the end of a cycle and was returning to the savage state in which his great-grandfather had found it. It was too late for Johnny ever to know what the forest was like when it grew close up to the clearing which surrounded the block house, but when he lost himself in the abandoned thickets, listening to the birds and the small rustling sounds made by the animals all about him, a little frightened because he was not sure where his father was or whether he could find his way out, he came a little nearer to that primitive experience than he had ever been before.

I do not think James Willingdon ever saw these places as they really were—bare, deserted, weed-grown, and desolate; he saw them only in his imagination as they would be when he had finished with them and made them livable and fertile once more. Not once was the dream ever realized; not once were the fencerows wholly cleared nor was the fertility restored to the furrowed fields. Not once did he leave a farmhouse as it had been in the old days, prosperous and filled by a sturdy family. The failure was not his fault. It would have required either a fortune in gold or the patient hard work of many years to have realized the dream. He had not the money and he was not a peasant. The best he could do in the end was to get rid of the farms one after another as well as he could, hoping that the pleasure he had had was not too expensive.

But he was never disillusioned, and perhaps he never had any illusions in his heart. Working over one of these wrecked places gave him enormous pleasure and perhaps he thought it worth the money it cost him. One by one they passed through his hands, bought and sold on mortgage, going in the end to some poor bedraggled farmer who was very close to being a "poor white." During the time he owned a farm he sometimes found a tenant for it, and sometimes he installed a hired man to build fences and clear rubbish and care for the horses which were turned loose, to come back at night through the broken fences to the decaying barn. But both tenants and hired men were a poor lot, else they would have gone long ago, like the vigorous men and women of the community, to the cities or the Far West. None of those tenants was drawn to his station by a passion for the earth, but merely because they had been born to it and had not the energy to escape when it became impossible any longer for a man to receive an honorable reward for his labors as a farmer.

Some of the places had a charm and beauty of their own. There was one which had a round stone springhouse with a circular stone trough where once crocks of milk and yellow butter had stood, cooled by the icy water which gushed from the hillside just behind it—a hillside covered with jewelweed where the dogs hunted for gigantic black snakes which they killed by cracking them like whips until their backs were broken. Outside the springhouse watercress grew out of the black soil, green and cool in the icy water, and on the banks of a little pool the mint ran wild among clumps of irises planted long ago. The house had a low sloping roof with gable windows, and wisteria and grapevines disputed possession of it in a tangle of vines. The spring emptied itself into a brook where sunfish and silversides and rock bass darted in and out among the rocks in the shadow of the willows. Johnny always remembered it, too, because in the woodlot he found the biggest morel he had ever seen. It was a gigantic fungus fully ten inches high and ten inches around its thickest part, fresh and damp, with a scent about it which was the distilled essence of decaying leaves and of good earth. He put it carefully into a paper bag and carried it tenderly five miles on his bicycle to show old Jamie, who told tall tales about the morels which grew in the county when it was a new country. When he showed it to his grandfather, old Jamie remembered, with no difficulty at all, a morel he had found in 1867 which was nearly twice the size of Johnny's phenomenon.

Neither Johnny's father nor himself ever belonged by temperament to a new country and both of them found a charm in a house, however dilapidated, which had been lived in and so had acquired a soul of its own. Neither of them by nature was a pioneer. They were, after all, the son and the grandson of The Old Man and they could discover no charm in any new, brightly painted farmhouse. Old Jamie would have torn down the old buildings and constructed something solid and new and practical, but then he, unlike The Old Man, believed profoundly that cream separators and silos improved the soul of man. He could not understand the subtle pleasure of bringing life once more into a dying house, of rekindling a fire on the cold, long-empty hearth and of coaxing back to an ordered beauty the garden too long abandoned by any hand which loved it. He could not understand that the old-fashioned flowers found beside a rotting fence or brought as a gift by some old woman who lived on the next farm were more beautiful than the showiest inventions in the catalogue of the horticulturist. He was always for progress until the day he died.

☙

After three or four years of experience with the farms James Willingdon conceived another of his quixotic ideas and began to buy cattle to turn loose in the empty fields. He had a theory that somehow they would miraculously grow fat feeding upon goldenrod and sumac and milkweed, and that each new pound of flesh meant a profit. It was a theory which might have worked if the cattle had been turned loose in fields knee-deep in succulent grass. Of course nothing came of it save a great deal of pleasure for both Johnny and his father, captured when they set out together upon expeditions into remote parts of the countryside where Johnny's father had heard there were cattle for sale. The excursions were always occasions for Johnny to be excused from school, for in case James Willingdon bought any cattle he needed help in driving them home. The two always took the dogs with them, and when Johnny was old enough he took turns with his father driving the buggy and trudging along on foot to keep the shaggy cattle from straying. Through all sorts of weather they visited distant farms and cattle markets and so they discovered corners and valleys which they had not visited before even during the electioneering journeys. They came to know the country in spring when the streams were torrents and the green of the skunk cabbage (the most fresh and delicious of all greens) was pushing through the

swamps; and in winter when the wind howled across the bare
snow-covered fields, and in summer when they drove along lanes
where the wild grapevines were powdered by the yellow dust of
that Middle Western county and the air was filled with the heady
sensual odor of pollen drifting across the acres of hot green corn,
and the cattle, panting in the heavy damp heat that blessed the
corn, would scent water from far off and run bellowing to plunge
into the streams at every ford. But in that county, as in all fertile
countries, the autumn was the most beautiful season of all. Then
the trees turned to red and purple and yellow and the corn stood
in shocks and the pumpkins made lumps of gold in the wide fields,
and in the orchards the big red apples began to drop. Then the
mornings were blue and frosty and at midday it grew hot as summer again. The winter had its special charm. Then it was more
pleasurable to trudge through the snow behind the cattle than to
ride in the buggy, feeling the slow chill creeping up one's legs from
the straw beneath the mangy old buffalo robe. Sometimes the
snow fell and the wind blew and once they were snowed in and
forced to spend two days with one of James Willingdon's farmer
friends. In winter the charm of a village hotel or a farmhouse was
doubly potent, for then they became refuges from the biting
weather, and the heavy rich food and the hot coffee acquired a
savor which it lacked in softer weather. The food was rarely as good
as Johnny had at home three times a day, but it was seasoned with
the salt of adventure and the spice of strange surroundings.

The great cattle adventure lasted only two or three years, until
it became evident that the fields of those abandoned farms were
too poor even to fatten shaggy half-wild cattle. It ended abruptly,
and as usual Johnny's father made no money out of it.

On Sundays and holidays the lost farms became the picnicking
grounds for the whole family. At dawn everyone rose and set out in
the family surrey drawn by a pair of erratic reconstituted horses,
carrying a huge lunch prepared the day before by Johnny's mother. Sometimes two or three of the neighbors' children accompanied
the party, in the surrey if it were possible to make room, and sometimes on bicycles. When they were older, Johnny and his brother
were allowed to make the trip on "wheels" and there were times

when the procession, made up of the family surrey surrounded by eight or ten children on bicycles, had the air of an expedition going into the wilderness. The dogs accompanied them, running alongside, barking and darting in and out of the fencerows in pursuit of rabbits and chipmunks. They went east, west, north, and south, along dusty roads bordered by elms and maples and locust trees, past damp mills where ferns and Solomon's-seal grew down to the water's edge, stopping to drink in cupped hands from cold springs, each marked by a hospitable roadside watering trough surrounded by mossy willows.

When at last the party arrived at the abandoned farm Johnny's father drove the horses as far as possible along the overgrown lane which led to the inevitable clearing. When he could force his way no farther, everyone descended, the horses were unharnessed and turned loose to feed and roll on the shaggy grass, and the day began before it was yet eight o'clock with a preliminary excursion to explore the clearing and the pastures and the marsh along the brook where one had to jump from hummock to hummock at the risk of falling waist deep into thick black mud and water. The boys killed snakes and uncovered rabbit nests, and sometimes the dogs cornered a scolding woodchuck. If the weather was warm the children went swimming, naked, in pools where sunfish and silversides darted out of their way when they dived.

The morning for the children was given over to play, and the afternoon to work which in itself was play. At noon they returned to the clearing to find that James Willingdon already had two or three great fires burning which he fed with the underbrush cut down during the week by the hired man.

Whatever of the lunch there was to be cooked—the coffee, perhaps a steak and fresh green sweet corn plucked from the garden— was already in the special small fire built for Johnny's mother. The brush-burning had a quality of ritual excitement without which these expeditions would have been incomplete. There was something exciting in the sight of the flames leaping twenty feet into the air as one piled underbrush higher and higher to feed it, and sometimes the fire got out of hand and ran wild in the dry grass and leaves, and then began a battle in which everyone took part, armed with bundles of switches and pails of water and wet blankets, to emerge at last from the fray triumphant, happy, and excited, covered with sweat and soot. At lunch the whole party sat under a wild cherry or hawthorn tree, eating heartily and drinking great gulps of the cold spring water brought up from the foot of the hill, and when it was over at last, the older members of the expedition each found a spot in the thick shade to lie dozing until the worst heat of the day had passed. At that hour, in the thick heat, one could *smell* the trees and the ferns and the fungi. It was a delicious perfume compounded of wild cherry and maple, of pennyroyal and fennel, of toadstools and elder blossoms. Overhead the woodflies danced in the heat, glittering in the watery green light of the thick woods.

The only distraction from brush-burning arose when there happened to be a brook where the fishing was good, and then a part or the whole of the day was spent in wandering along the banks, fishing hole after hole in the clear stream. On such days there were sunfish and rock bass fresh from the water cooked in a frying pan over a wood fire. They had a delicious flavor which no other fish ever possessed, for, as every good cook knows, there is something special about food cooked over a wood fire ... something magnificent and miraculous in the case of steak and fish and coffee and sweet corn; and added to the wood-smoke flavor there was the sunlight and the open air and the wild smell of the abandoned clearing.

Just as the party arrived as early as possible in the morning, so it stayed until the moon had risen and hung yellow and heavy in the heat of the distant horizon. When at last the hour for returning had come there was always the pleasurable chance of an added delay caused by the horses, which could not be found or chose not to be recaptured. But at last everyone got under way, a procession of bicycles following the surrey, and sometimes everyone sang on the way home and sometimes there was a halt made in the moonlight to distribute what was left of the sandwiches and cold meat. The smaller children fell asleep in the surrey, and on reaching home were carried into the house, undressed, and put into bed to wake in the morning with the dazed belief that they had slept all night under the trees of the clearing.

But the best fun of all occurred when a wild thunderstorm arose suddenly on the way home. In haste the side curtains were put on the surrey and inside everyone sat huddled together while the rain fell in torrents and the lightning illuminated the fat streaming rumps of the horses plodding along through woods and fields. Sometimes if the storm was of more than usual violence, Johnny's mother grew frightened and made James Willingdon drive into the barn of some farmer along the road. One never stopped to ask permission. One of the party simply jumped out, flung open the great doors of the barn, and Johnny's father drove in, his way lighted by the brilliant flashes which illuminated the whole countryside as brightly as if it had been midday. There they would wait until the worst of the storm had passed and then set out again on their journey. On such wet nights the surrey was filled with the smells of damp woolens and of dogs and horses, all dissolved in the delicious freshness of air just cleared by a thunderstorm.

I do not think that any one of the excursionists knew exactly what it was that he sought in those holiday expeditions nor what was the true source of the glamour he found in those upland clearings, but I know now that it was the shadowy memory of those long processions of oxcarts filled with women and children and furniture which had crossed the mountains before any of them were born. There was in the excitement of those early-morning departures a hunger for loneliness and privacy—not the aloofness of the European's walled garden, but the loneliness of the wilderness which afflicted the American frontiersmen as a disease.

James Willingdon never had any money to leave to his children, nor very much to spend on extravagant pleasures, but out of his simplicity and his curious romantic love of nature he gave them something which could not vanish in times of crisis or be lost through foolishness. What he gave them was destined to stay with them forever. It was the most precious heritage one could receive. He was a man who knew how to live. He knew the things that count.

The tenants and hired men came and went, quarrelsome, shift-less, and, like most idle men, without vitality, cherishing always the belief that they were perpetually the victims of hard luck and of swindlers. As a class they had a peculiar psychology which was almost universal, and always they were haunted by the same vision which had haunted their ancestors—the belief that just around the corner lay success and fortune. But unlike their ancestors, they did not journey hundreds of miles across mountains and rivers through a wilderness; they were content to move to the farm across the road or beyond the next hill, listlessly taking with them their pitiful household furniture and stringy, feeble children, all in a sin-gle spring wagon. There was a long procession of them, all American of degenerated stock, the children and grandchildren of misfits who had come over the mountains long ago, the dregs of the old stock. And then suddenly out of their midst there emerged a bizarre figure who was unlike the rest and who became a part of the family establishment for years to come.

His name was Hud Williams and he was a small tough little man with a big bulbous nose and a pugnacious manner. In addi-tion to the conditions which made it impossible for a farmer to live decently, he had a long run of genuinely bad luck. Indeed, it was as if he was under a curse, for it was not the hard luck founded upon shiftlessness, which haunted the sagas of the usual tenant and hired man. Once his barn, uninsured, had burned just after the crops had been taken in. Another time, when he took up hog farming the cholera wiped out his whole stock. His cattle acquired hoof-and-mouth disease and had to be destroyed. His one child, a son, was a ne'er-do-well who brought only misfortune to his parents. Yet this modern job had a heroic tenacity of purpose and spirit so that each succeeding calamity left him not whining and weakened and dis-couraged, but more tough and stubborn than he had been before; and he was from birth, I think, a monument of toughness and stubbornness.

Always he was driven by the hope of recovering the indepen-dence he had known as a young man before troubles descended upon him like midsummer hail upon a cornfield, and it was this hope which still drove him when he came into the lives of the

Willingdons at the age of fifty-five, a time when most men are willing to give up and rest. He was honest and dogmatic to the point of fanaticism, and if he was in any way responsible for his own ill luck it was on account of this fantastic characteristic. He had been known to quit the employ of a man on a moment's notice because he disapproved of his ethics or his morals or his philosophy. Bitterly he resented being classed with other tenant farmers whom he regarded as a poor lot, and this long resentment made him even fiercer than he was by nature. At the source of his pugnacity and resentment there lay a profound dignity and a touching uncompromising idealism of which he was a little ashamed, concealing it tenderly and proudly beneath a pugnacious exterior. In this he was like Johnny's father, and the likeness was one of the many things which drew the two men together and kept them friends in spite of everything, in a relationship which was notoriously difficult. It was a bond which they never spoke of. Indeed, it would never have occurred to either of them ever to mention it. But it was there. They were both aware of it. Both of them were by nature openhearted and frank and generous, and both of them had been rebuffed and disillusioned again and again in their contacts with less decent men. Again and again they had been forced to learn that despite their own optimism, there were such things as greed and meanness and dishonesty; yet it was a lesson by which neither of them profited, because it was not in their natures. Hud Williams turned bitter and gruff and Johnny's father simply withdrew deeper and deeper in a world of unreality which had nothing to do with the small life of which he was a part. To Johnny, as he grew older, it seemed that Hud Williams was rather like a good-natured small boy forever expecting and preparing to dodge a cuff or a kick.

He was, of course, a relict of another day. The grandson of one of the earliest of the settlers and the most respected of farmers, he had been brought up in an era when it was easy to be generous and when farmers lived as gentlemen. It was a time when there was room for everyone and no one needed ever descend to meanness and sharp dealing unless it was a part of his nature. Old Jamie was sometimes puzzled and made uneasy by the new world which had grown up around him, and perplexed, too, by the bitter knowledge

that in the county farmers no longer were of importance and no longer ruled the community; but he was too old to suffer very directly and the days of his full-blooded indignation were past. Hud Williams still considered himself in his prime and knew bitterly that he had been caught full in the collapse of the old life.

He had a wife called Melissa, a little, gnarled woman, who appeared much older than her years, and was as thin and dry as Hud himself. She wore spectacles and had a magnificent set of tombstone false teeth. In her there was no bitterness, but only a kind of quiet resignation. Beside Hud she seemed so gentle that before one knew her well one would have said that she had no character at all, and it may have been that the violence of her husband's nature had long ago crushed her own individuality out of existence. I think she had come to accept his sudden quarrels and his sudden indignant flights from one farm to another, packing her furniture quietly and departing without complaint for a new house on a night's warning. She was very clean and neat, and when she arrived at a broken-down tenant farm the neighbors knew after a few days that this was no shiftless creature who had come among them. The house and the garden gradually became transformed. Sagging shutters were repaired, the picket fence was whitewashed, the vines were pruned and new flowers were planted. In her thin old body there still lingered the conviction, come down through generations from England, that no house was decent or respectable which had not a fine garden. It was the last vestige of a profound belief that life was not worth living unless time was wasted upon what pleased the senses, even though there was no profit in it. Her balsams and dahlias and the petunias growing in pots suspended from the fruit trees were signs that, although she had fallen upon evil days, she was neither a "poor white" nor a peasant woman who had no time for such things because she worked all day in the fields. Her chickens and turkeys were well kept and she made excellent butter. Hud's clothes were kept spotlessly clean and patched until sometimes there was very little left of them save patches. She had a quiet dignity based, I think, upon the knowledge that although she was poor, she was respectable, and that in the tiny niche which she filled she did her duty toward her husband, her God, and her neighbors.

Long after they were both dead, Johnny still remembered them as clearly as in a photograph, standing in the doorway of the little house on the Lexington Road farm, their figures mottled by the shade of the cherry tree, Hud in patched, clean overalls and Melissa in gingham or calico, clean and faded by countless washings. It was Hud's big nose and bristling mustaches which one saw first, and then slowly one became aware of his extraordinarily bright blue eyes, at once shining with friendliness and pugnacity, goodness and sly, bitter malice. Melissa always stood in the way of shy, proud women who have worked hard, one roughened hand concealed in her clean apron and the other pressed against her thin old lips to hide the false teeth of which she was always ashamed. One of Hud's baffled ambitions was the desire to buy her a set which looked more "natural."

Far away in the past of these two homely figures lay romance. When young they had loved each other and there was still about them that atmosphere of contentment and peace which surrounds couples whose love has proven sound and right in spite of every hardship and calamity. I am certain that they never spoke of the feeling which existed between them, but the knowledge of it must have been in them both, and the appreciation as well, else they could not have conveyed, without consciousness, that curious sense which they gave of rightness and satisfaction. I am sure that in moments of disaster and defeat there rose in them a precious sense of confidence and oneness.

They were cousins, and they had run off to marry because both their families opposed the marriage on the ground of close kinship, and it may have been that some hidden taint of blood came out in the ne'er-do-well son who brought them no satisfaction, but only anxiety and grief. There were times when Hud was forced to pay out money from his poor savings to keep him out of punishment. Johnny saw him once or twice—a sullen, sly, middle-aged man who returned to see his mother and father only when he was penniless and in trouble, and when he returned they took him in, accepting him quite simply and even with a melancholy pleasure until one morning he would go off again, scarcely taking the trouble to bid them good-by. Long afterward, whenever Johnny thought of Hud and Melissa, a feeling of warmth and kindliness came over him and an indescribable sensation of pleasure, as if the memory of them could make more easy the cowardice and meanness of others. Melissa was almost a relative of the family, for she was the granddaughter of the Colonel's man, Jed, and the hired girl, Maria Savage, who had come over the mountains with Susan.

⊷

The friendship between James Willingdon and Hud brought them both comfort as well as a new confidence and happiness. Hud was an ignorant man, scarcely educated at all, yet intelligent in his understanding of animals and of the earth because for both he had a sympathy which amounted to a passion. It was a passion which Johnny's father shared in a fashion much less immediate and practical and far more vaguely poetic and philosophic. Often enough they disagreed about the moment for planting the corn or whether the wheat should be sold or fed to the hogs because the price it brought made it scarcely worth the trouble of raising, and often enough there were hot words between them, for Hud's temper grew hotter with age; but I do not think it could have been said that they quarreled, because deep in both of them was the knowledge that the other could be trusted and would never be guilty of pettiness or meanness.

One after another Hud and Melissa occupied the deserted farms bought by Johnny's father, moving from one to another as they were sold, always as tenants on shares because that was the only arrangement which Hud, in his pride and dignity, would accept. At one tumble-down farmhouse after another Melissa set up her household goods and planted her flowers. Hud was happy in the knowledge that between him and James Willingdon there was no sense of inequality, no feeling of the landlord and the tenant. They were both democrats by nature as well as in politics, in the old Jeffersonian sense.

For many years, during all the speculations and fantastic adventures which James Willingdon undertook halfheartedly, he had been moving more and more toward the land, and now the discovery of Hud seemed to become a decisive element in his existence. From the moment he and Hud began working together the vague dream which had been in the back of his mind as cashier of a bank, as a real estate agent, as oil-promoter, as a politician, grew steadily more clear.

His friends had nearly all been among the farmers, and so at last the farmers came to him for help. They sought him out to make him president of the Midland County Agricultural Society. It was an organization founded years before the Grange, and in it old Jamie had been one of the moving spirits. For thirty years it had prospered, but lately, for more than ten years, the farmers had fallen upon evil days and the society had come to know a slow decay. The old vigor of the organization seemed to have gone with the old prosperity of the countryside. The leaders were all dead or old men like Jamie Ferguson, and the younger farmers seemed to be of a different breed. A few among them still had the old strong sense of duty toward their state and toward their community, but too many of the new generation had lost their interest, and among the new immigrant farmers there were none who were willing to spend either time or money in behalf of the common good. In Silesia, in Bohemia, in Poland, in the Balkan States from which they had come, exhibitions of cattle and fruit and grain had been the affairs of great landlords and did not concern them. Now in this new country they had become the most intense individualists, suspicious, aloof, and solitary. And tragically many a farm which in the old days had sheltered a prosperous, vigorous family had fallen into the hands of shiftless tenants or stood empty and deserted.

There was honor in the new task, but no money. By now Johnny's mother had come to say bitterly that James Willingdon was never interested in anything in which he might make money and that the only tasks he liked were those which produced no profits. His reply to her was that the new undertaking would not interfere with his supporting his family and that he could do it in his spare time. He had a gift for deceiving himself, although I think the deception always began at first by being directed at his wife; it was only after a time that he began himself to believe the specious arguments he set up in his own defense. In his quiet way he had a stubbornness which must have been maddening to his wife, especially since all her energy and character could not overcome it.

The county fair had fallen upon days so evil that if something were not done at once to restore its old prosperity, the only course left was to abandon it forever. Already the high wooden fence about the fairground had holes in it. The sheep pens were threatened with decay and the grass grew in the dirt tracks where the trotting races, once the glory of the county, had been held. They asked Johnny's father to reorganize the association and restore the interest and fame the county fair had once known throughout the northern part of the state.

No task could have given him more pleasure. It strengthened his old bond with the farmers and it brought him directly into the world of trotting-horses, for the trotting-races played an important part in the revenue of the association. It was no easy task, for the Midland County Fair had come to have a bad name, and a bad name is for a county fair the worst of handicaps. The purses for the trotting-horses had diminished until it was no longer worth an owner's while to bring his horses, and the judging of farm animals had gained the reputation for slovenliness and prejudiced opinion, so that none of the best farmers and cattle breeders in the state troubled any longer to exhibit. Carnival people would not pay big prices for concessions at a fair where the attendance was so small it brought in scarcely any revenue. The fair had fallen into a vicious circle in which it was going round and round, diminishing a little in importance each year.

Johnny's father succeeded in restoring the fair to something of its old eminence among the fairs in the state, and his success was due more, I think, to his passion for horses and everything which had to do with farms, than to any great executive ability. He was better suited to the task than any farmer, for he knew more people in the county than any other man. The townspeople had money and some of the finest cattle, and the best horses belonged no longer to the farmers, but to men living in the Town who, growing richer and richer out of mills and factories, had bought up farms in the county simply for diversion. He made the merchants see that if the fair was a success they in turn would profit from the visitors attracted by it, and so he wrested from them clocks and beds and carpets, as well as money, to be given as prizes for fancywork and canned fruit. Wisely he spent money in advertising the fair throughout the state. The fences were repaired and the stables and sheep pens put in order, and presently carnival people showed an interest in buying concessions for good prices. Always throughout the adventure he had the advice of old Jamie, who in the great days had been president of the Agricultural Association and carried off many prizes with his own horses and cattle.

Besides Johnny's father and grandfather, at least two other members of the family found delight and glory in the undertaking. One was Hud Williams and the other Johnny himself. For weeks before the fair he went each Saturday through Wilmerding's Ten Cent Barn, where the farmers left their horses when they came to Town, and along Walnut Street, where there were lines of hitching rails, distributing handbills announcing the fair as the biggest ever and listing purses and prizes as lures to exhibitors, and when the week of the fair at last arrived he was given a badge of yellow silk on which were stamped in gold letters the words "Aide to the Committee." He helped to drive hogs and sheep into their pens and to direct wagons and buggies to the part of the fairgrounds where new hitching rails had been put up. He haunted the stables, admiring the big Clydesdales and Percherons, and sat in box stalls knee-deep with clean straw, listening to the talk of jockeys and trainers and stable boys. And when he was not busy he wandered in and out of the grandstand to watch the trotting and pacing races. He visited sideshows and shooting-galleries and helped to water the great Hereford and Shorthorn bulls. The sacred yellow badge took him everywhere. It was a week of paradise for a boy of thirteen.

And wherever he went he met Hud Williams, sometimes alone and sometimes accompanied by Melissa. Hud wore the same gawdy badge as Johnny and he carried himself with the air of a bantam rooster. For him, too, it was paradise. It was as if in the end he had been rewarded for all his bad luck by the eminence bestowed upon him by that yellow badge. Now he was a person of importance. Was he not the "partner" of Johnny's father, the head of all this hubbub and gaiety? Was it not his "partner" who was responsible for all the success of the Fair and so in a way Hud himself?

There was a strain of sporting blood in him, and in honor of the occasion he bought himself an ill-fitting new suit of the loudest checks and a new bright green fedora hat. Across his waistcoat stretched an enormous watch chain of what was patently brass. And his poodle mustaches were waxed so that their points were like bayonets.

It was the nearest Hud ever came to the dream he had of being the most important farmer in the county. And for three years, until Johnny's father resigned, he swaggered about during the week of the fair. It may have been that the fantasy of fair week was better than reality to him. It was a handsome holiday during which he play-acted for seven days, spending his money on fancy cigars, neglecting his farm and sometimes overacting shamelessly. He fussed about the cattle barns, patted the heifers with a patronizing air, appraising the points of long-legged Chester Whites as against snub-nosed Berkshires, withdrawing pompously to a little distance in order better to view the animals under discussion. He was always on hand when the trotting-horses were led out to feel their slim ankles and run his huge, work-worn hands (so out of proportion to the small wiry figure) over their sleek withers. He talked big about the glories of those celebrated horses Dan Patch and Maud S., and from time to time with great ostentation he entered the judges' stand in order to be seen from the grandstand opposite by the men with whom he had quarreled at one time or another. And always not far away, in all the places where it was not unseemly for women to go, lingered Melissa, looking very strange in store clothes and a little uncomfortable with a new hat and black gloves, her eyes shining with happiness and pride in the importance of her man. But she always stood with one black gloved hand held before her mouth to conceal the false teeth.

For old Jamie the occasion was a kind of renaissance. Well past eighty, he seemed suddenly to grow straighter and more vigorous. The terrible heat of mid-August weather had no effect upon him. He arrived early in the morning to stay until late at night, wandering about, happy, but also a little sad because there were so few of his generation left. There was no pomp in him because there was none in his nature, and besides to him the fair was an old story.

Had he not in his prime been president of the Agricultural Association when the Midland County Fair was the finest in the state? The new fair, he admitted to his son-in-law, was a great improvement over what it had been for twenty years past, but even so it could never attain the glories of the fair in the eighties. He doubted if such glory would ever return again. In his prime the Town had not counted for anything. It was the county alone which was important. The Town then was no more than a marketplace, and banks could not have existed save for the farmers. Now and then he encountered a patriarch of his own generation and together they talked scornfully of some of the exhibitors at this new fair—men who scarcely knew the back side of a cow from the front and had never turned a furrow, but sat all week in offices in a smoke-blighted Town.

The cattle barns and sheep pens were filled to overflowing. Outside the Hall of Domestic Arts a tent had to be erected to shelter the overflow of canned fruit and pickles and hams. In the Hall of Fine Arts, the walls were hung solidly with quilts and embroidery and watercolors. It was a great renaissance and old Jamie alone saw that it could not last, because its very foundations were no longer there. One thing alone was unchanged from the days when he had managed it all. Old Mrs. Bell, who like himself was over eighty, still won most of the prizes for canned fruit and pickles. There were none among a generation of softer, weaker women who could rival her. It was an open secret that some of the prizes were given to others only because it would have been a scandal if she had won them all.

ELLEN

JAMES WILLINGDON IN HIS QUIET WAY SHARED WITH HIS CHILDREN an intimacy so fragile that it was never spoken of. It was one of those relationships which depend upon a silent acceptance and one knew that one must not betray a recognition of it even by a glance of understanding lest it should alter its character or vanish suddenly forever. Quietly he had an influence upon his children, teaching them, without being aware of it, the delights of small things and the most enduring of all defenses against the bitterness of life—a pleasure in all that concerned nature. Through him they learned, without being taught, the joy which is to be found in a running brook, in a lane shaded by hawthorn, in the wet muzzle of an awkward calf, and in a warm nest of puppies hidden in the hay. What he gave them could never be taken from them save in death.

But it was Ellen Willingdon, their mother, the daughter of old Jamie and Maria and the granddaughter of the Colonel, who determined the concrete facts of the children's existence and the line their lives were to take until they left her and, I suspect, until at last they are in their graves. She was a woman without doubts as to conduct and behavior and greatness and as in the case of her powerful father, morality and ethics sometimes became translated into narrowness and intolerance. Long afterward Johnny was painfully forced to unlearn many things which had been driven into him in youth and became a very part of his nature. Yet there were great virtues in the sureness of her attitude toward life. She knew there were things which no decent person could possibly do. There were thoughts which no decent person could possibly have. She was impatient and even bitterly intolerant of smallnesses and compromise and meanness. She taught her children the satisfaction which only the fanatic and the martyr can know—that of refusing all compromise of an ideal or a conviction. She gave them a force and even a certain ruthlessness which was to be of immense value to them for the rest of their lives. The gifts she imposed (for it could scarcely be said that they were given) were very different from those which came to them from their father, but in a material world peopled by men and women full of human weaknesses they were of a greater practical value. The gifts of Johnny's father were those of one whose whole instinct was to turn his back upon the spectacle and seek refuge in a life in which he could not be hurt, and the heritage come down from Johnny's mother was from one whose whole instinct was to see it through to the end. Yet in the abstract, James Willingdon loved humanity far more than did his wife, who in the primitive directness of her nature regarded all the world save her own family and a few friends as an enemy against which one must be forever armed.

From the day her children were born she set out to arm them adequately with the qualities and convictions which she was certain they should need most. It was inevitable that she should always seek to form the lives of those about her, and hopeless to believe that she would not find in her own children material which was irresistibly tempting, yielding, and impressionable. And she had the peculiar integrity of American women which carries them through to the end of impossible undertakings. So from the moment her children were born, and even before, she determined for them their careers. It was the day when all sorts of mystical discoveries were being made in medicine and a time when the fumblings toward what is now called modern psychology were just beginning to be known. Among the other theories much in fashion was that of prenatal influence, an idea in which Johnny's mother had an absolute belief.

Considering that most of her life had been spent in a struggle against genteel poverty, and that the whole world in which she lived as an American woman was engaged in a mystical worship of material success, she made strange choices for the careers of her children. She sought for them all the things she had wanted for herself and had never known—all save money. She wanted them to have the best of educations, and as careers she chose that of music for her daughter, and for her first son that of writing, and toward the realization of these careers she worked without rest until at last they left her for the world. She wanted them to speak three or four languages and to go everywhere and know all sorts of people. By the time the last of her children were born, I think that she knew it was too late for her ever to achieve any of these things for herself, and the whole tremendous force of her character and her physical vitality was directed toward achieving them for her children. She knew, too, I think, that she would never have the money to buy the opportunities for all these achievements, so she determined to create in her children a hunger, a curiosity, and a determination which in the end proved more powerful than any amount of money.

Before Johnny's sister was born his mother returned again to that thwarted passion for music which had colored a youth devoted to the needs and weaknesses of others, and she spent hour after hour learning to read music and practicing on the piano which she had already bought for the child who was not yet born. When Johnny's sister was six years old she began music lessons with Miss Ainsworth, who was the great goddess of music in the Town. She was a spinster goddess with a great deal of talent for it, who lived in a little house hidden by a tangled garden and filled with birds in cages whose music mingled with that of the Steinway which had cost her years of savings. Whether it was the prenatal influence in which Ellen Willingdon believed or not, I do not know, but Johnny's sister had a talent for music and the temperament of a musician, and by the time she was ten she played Chopin and Mozart, sitting on a stool in the parlor with her blond curls falling halfway to her waist. There were moments when her nature rebelled against practicing, but she had no chance of escape in the face of her mother's determination. On these occasions she was shut into the parlor with the door locked, and despite kickings and screamings she was not allowed to come out until her two hours of practice had been accomplished. Long afterward she was grateful for those hours of torment, and oddly enough she never acquired the hatred of music which such methods are believed to create, perhaps because with each hour of practice she came a little nearer to that perfection of technique which allows the soul to luxuriate and the spirit unhampered to say what it will. Johnny's own gratitude was great as that of his sister, for those hours of work meant that he had a childhood in which the air was forever filled with music. Out of those hours grew others filled with the enchanting sounds of Mozart, Chopin, and Beethoven. Out of them came those evenings when the Siegfrieds came to the house to play trios and quartettes and symphonies and concertos arranged for four hands. Night after night in bed, with the door left ajar, Johnny went to sleep to the music played downstairs in the parlor with the "elegant" furniture, until it became a part of him. Out of those grinding hours of practice when his sister was locked into the parlor came a love and the understanding of music which Johnny was to value far above any of the pleasures or achievements he ever knew.

So in the end, in the strange continuity of life, those hours long ago which Ellen Willingdon spent as a girl picking out the melody of "The Blue Danube" on the melodeon of the parlor of the Farm came to bear fruit in her children.

It was for Johnny before he was born that she filled a whole library with shelves of Dickens and George Eliot, Thackeray, and Sir Walter Scott. From the moment he was old enough to think or to talk she sought always to guide his steps in the direction which she had chosen for him. Often enough it was not a subtle performance, for there was little of subtlety in her nature and always it was the manifestation of a blind and dominating will. When he was a little older he was forced to read a certain amount every day just as his sister had to practice her two hours locked into the parlor on occasions when she did not feel in the mood. But reading, all things considered, was far less tiresome than practicing scales, and even the ponderous works of Cooper and Scott and Stevenson

Johnny was able to struggle through without too much agony, although he did acquire for these writers and their verbosity, and for the historical novel, a distaste which he was never able to overcome. George Eliot he read with pleasure, and Meredith he did not understand, although he was shrewd enough even as a child to resent the all too frequent "smartiness" of his style and peculiar point of view. But in Dickens and Thackeray and Balzac lay Johnny's delight. In them, it seemed to him that he had discovered all that glamorous world which in his childhood he believed was not to be found in the Town or the county—all that world from the brutality of Bill Sykes to the brutality of Lord Steyn, for which he was hungry and thirsty.

That all the stories of Balzac and Dickens and Thackeray were happening in the Town and county all about him never occurred to him. The Town was dull and drab and usual. Only people who lived outside it in the world could be glamorous and exciting and *real* like the people of Thackeray and Balzac. People like old Jamie, the good citizen, and The Old Man, Great-aunt Jane and Uncle Doctor, and his great-grandmother, the stormy, unhappy Marianna, were as near and as usual as the dog sleeping on the rug in the living room.

Of all the novels which Johnny read, *Vanity Fair* remained his favorite, but there were parts of *Cousine Bette* and *Great Expectations* and *Nicholas Nickleby* which became fixed forever in his memory as experiences of his own. Some of those books were perhaps strong fare for a small boy, but they did Johnny no harm unless it was that they gave him forever a rather melancholy "sense of the spectacle" which compelled him to go through life regarding it rather from the outside.

A good part of that early boyhood was spent in the world of imagination, peopled entirely by the characters of the novelists of the great period, and gradually all of that early reading transformed a nature, which was meant by every facet of its temperament to turn in upon itself, into one whose preoccupation was largely with the lives and characters and personalities of others. That, to be sure, was a benefit which Johnny's mother had never foreseen; but she always worked diligently toward the main achievement, overlooking all the side issues. To her and her vigil Johnny remained eternally grateful for having given him an interest in others rather than in himself. Doubt and introspection had paralyzed The Old Man and it would, perhaps, have paralyzed Johnny but for the blood of old Jamie and the determination of his mother.

When Johnny was a little older corruption set in and he read book after book of Henty—*The Young Carthaginian*—*The Lion of St. Mark's*—*With Clive in India*. It seems to me that Henty must have had gifts far superior to those for which he has been given slighting credit, for he managed to create characters which to Johnny remained forever sharp and bright in the memory, endowed even with a sense of reality. I am tempted to say that his minor characters, if not his heroes (who were simply the same young man over and over again), were more real than any of Scott's and most of Stevenson's. Horatio Alger had no attraction for Johnny, perhaps because in his family there was a total lack of that philosophy which applauds the rise of a newsboy to the eminence of a bank president. Johnny lived in what was essentially an atmosphere of gambling, in a family which would have been delighted to win a million dollars in a lottery but saw no virtue in hard work, economy and application which stifled the richness of living. Johnny never believed the Alger books, and the idea of success through virtuous application always seemed to him the last resource of a dullard.

And then for a time during early adolescence he read the books of Ralph Henry Barbour in which boys and girls went off on camping trips together, accompanied by a chaperon who was, considering the purity and virtue of the characters, wholly unnecessary; and he read with delight all the animal stories of Jack London and Ernest Thomson Seton. All of these books came from the Sunday school library endowed by the old mulatto, Aunty Walker, who had been dead for years.

Johnny's mother, alarmed, regarded these digressions as a threat to her plan. In her active life she had never had any time for reading, and by the time Johnny was fifteen he had read more books than she had read in all her life. She had for the classics the same exaggerated awe which she had for the music which had been denied her, and she felt that if Johnny was to admire lower ideals her ambitions for him would be lost. But in the end, when he was seventeen or eighteen, she saw him return to the old high ideals, although she regarded with uneasiness his discovery of strange exotic writers like Tolstoy and Chekhov. For her, of course, the fount of all literature was English and Scottish, and for some reason she made a place for that immoral Frenchman, Balzac. All else must be less good and less moral.

It was in her ambitions for her younger son that Johnny's mother faltered and grew a little confused, perhaps because he was born at the time James Willingdon first entered politics and she was preoccupied by the importance of an election. Throughout his childhood and throughout adolescence he read and practiced on the piano, not sullenly, but in a baffled rage, because neither of these things was in his temperament, and when later he set out into the world on his own he attempted both writing and music, but accomplished nothing in either because his heart was not in them. Mr. Wells and Mr. Huxley assert that there is nothing whatever in that old-fashioned theory of prenatal influence. Doubtless they are right, but I know that of all the children of James and Ellen Willingdon, only the youngest, who was born in the heat of a political campaign, was endowed with the qualities of a politician. He was always easy to approach, agreeable in personality, emotional and persuasive. He grew up to be very like his sporting Uncle Harry, on both the physical and the human side. He was impatient like the rest of the family, but not scornful, and he possessed a wise talent for compromise which is the mark of a born politician. They are traits which must have come from somewhere. He looked exactly like old Jamie, but in Jamie there had never been any compromise.

THE RETURN

So WHILE JOHNNY'S FATHER MEANDERED DREAMILY ALONG HIS PATH in life, his mother pushed energetically along hers, shoving her children before her. Sometimes they wandered from the path into what she *knew* were unprofitable or corrupting areas, but in the end, like a faithful sheepdog, she always routed them out of the moral or artistic underbrush and set them once more on the proper path.

But the family finances went from bad to worse. The ruined farms continued to devour what money there was, and from time to time Johnny's mother rose in revolt. With a fair chance she could have won and put the house in order, but she was alone. Her husband was against her with that quiet stubbornness which was so often undefeatable, and her sons were against her, for to them the abandoned farms were simply a series of small paradises, but most serious of all Old Jamie refused his aid. It was perhaps beyond his power. He had been born on the land. All his life he had lived by it, detesting towns and cluttered communities. Even as an old man he continued to fight the losing battle of the farmer. In the depths of his soul he believed the land to be the finest and most honorable of all that which might occupy the energies of man. And while he sat idle in the Town, detesting it and regarding it as an enemy, he saw his own farm, the pride and the very foundation of his whole existence, slowly falling into the estate of those abandoned weed-grown places which Johnny's father was forever buying and selling. I think the spectacle was a slow agony to him, and each of the melancholy visits which he made to it were the source of an increasing sorrow. In the end it was he who betrayed his daughter by a plan which threatened to wreck the goal to which she had given her whole life.

For a long time the idea had been taking form, uneasily, beneath the suspicious eye of Johnny's mother. Her daughter would have been on her side in the struggle, but she was married now and had gone away to live in the West with her engineer husband, and so brought no help. It took form, the idea, like a cloud forming in the open sky, growing larger until it could no longer be ignored. No one ever mentioned it save by hints and insinuations, by a word, a glance, an allusion. The nearest Johnny's father ever came to recognizing it was to say with a sigh that in his old age he hoped to have a farm where he could retire to live unplagued by people, among orchards and cattle.

In the end the force which precipitated the crisis was the same which always forced action upon a family given to a philosophy of optimism and *laissez-faire*. It was a question of money. There were mortgages to right and left. The real estate business of James Willingdon was not doing too well. I think he found himself bewildered by the methods of high-pressure salesmen in a booming factory town. They were not his methods, but they were the ones which were most effective. It was Johnny's mother who understood suddenly that something must be done if they were to be saved from bankruptcy.

But it was old Jamie who had the solution.

There waiting for the Willingdons, stood the Farm, which was, after all, the home of all of them, much more the home than that slate-colored house on a city lot had ever been. It was from the Farm that they derived their inexhaustible vitality and their physical strength. From the Farm came the hunger for freedom and space which was in all of them. What was more obvious than that they should sell the slate-colored house and pour the little money which remained beyond the rim of mortgages into the Farm?

But Ellen Willingdon rebelled, for the plan fell exactly across the path of the ambitions she had for her sons and so for herself. Her daughter had escaped and her sons must escape as well. The idea of her children returning to the land was revolting, even more profoundly revolting since she knew that it was no longer possible to live on the land decently and with dignity as her family had always done. She saw well enough, and far more clearly than the rest of the family, that the prices of everything had risen save those things which the farmer produced and that there were years when a farmer could not make enough money to keep himself out of debt. You saw wholesale grocers and commission men growing richer and richer, but the only spectacle provided by the farmer was one of increasing debt and poverty. She knew, too, that although it was a good life it was a hard one, in which the smallest misfortunes could take on the proportions of a tragedy. Cholera might wipe out the hogs, or the prize cow might choke herself on an apple, or the hoof-and-mouth disease might suddenly reduce the whole of a fine dairy to a heap of charred carcasses.

But in the end she lost the battle, at least temporarily, not through any yielding or weakness, but because it was the only thing left to do. The Farm was the only sure refuge. There, at least, her children would have good food and a roof over their heads. There they would have the independence without which life was unthinkable. She told herself that it was a step backward in order to make greater progress ahead. And in her heart she loved the Farm as much as the rest of them, but, with the instinct which had always guided her, she knew that it was in the blood of at least one of her children, and because of that she feared it.

In the end the decision was a relief, for from that moment the worries and troubles of the old life ceased to exist and the whole family looked forward impatiently toward the sale of the house in the Town and the escape into the country. It was a fresh start, almost as good as if James Willingdon had followed the examples of the uncles, aunts, and cousins, selling everything and migrating into a new country. Old Jamie saw his land restored, his house once more filled by his own children and grandchildren, himself dying as he had always hoped to die, in the room he had shared for nearly fifty years with the woman who had been everything in his life. James Willingdon and Johnny were filled with the conviction that they should make the Farm prosper by new methods. "Scientific" was a word that they used over and over again. "Modern" became worn and frayed. They were words used by the handful of farmers of the old stock who had stuck to the land, determined to find some way by which it was economically possible to go on with a life which they could not bring themselves to abandon. Father and son had a new dream which was almost a mission. They meant to show the county that it was still possible to live on the land and have a life that was good, comfortable, and even rich. One did not need to rise before dawn as the immigrant farmers did, nor to work women and children in the fields. The adventure became a flight from reality in which the self-deception of optimism, at once a great virtue and the greatest of faults, ran riot. Night after night they sat enchanted, poring over farm papers and government reports, constructing bit by bit a future filled as much with plea-sure as with profits. It was a gathering of innocents, for in those days they had not yet learned that aside from a little band of hard-working scientists, harassed and handicapped by politicians, the congressman cared little what happened to farmers whose vote, divided, unorganized, and unpredictable, was not worth much concern.

It was Hud Williams and Melissa who now lived on the Farm. They were to stay on, occupying one wing of the rambling old house, although how the land with its worn fields and rotting fences was to support them both as well as all of the Willingdons was a point which no one considered. If Johnny's mother had doubts, she kept a grim silence, believing, I think, that the only course was to allow the rest of the family to find out for them-selves. Old Jamie, in his delight at the return, had all the faith of a young man. Everything would arrange itself. Soon the fences would be mended and the fields restored to their old fertility. After all, had he not brought up eight children, not to mention hordes of visiting relatives and grandchildren, in plenty on that same land?

As the time for moving drew nearer the apathy which had set-tled upon him during the hot afternoons on the front porch seemed to disappear. He grew extremely spry, and on the visits to the Farm attempted feats which clearly were beyond the strength of the most robust old man approaching ninety. I suspect that there were moments when quite seriously he doubted the reality of old age and the existence of fact, and believed that by returning to the Farm he would miraculously be made young once more to start life all over again. That there were now moments when he grew a little childish made it all the easier for him to deceive himself. He was happy as a little boy.

And then one morning when he went out to the red barn at the foot of the Town lot he found his old horse, Doctor, unable to rise to his feet. The veterinary was called in, but only told him what everyone in the household already knew—that Doctor was simply too old to go on any longer and that he could never again stand on his feet. For three days the old white horse lay there, eating out of a box held for him by old Jamie, but his teeth were worn away and he had no longer the will even to eat, and on the fourth morning, when Johnny's grandfather went out to the barn, Doctor was dead. Hud came in with the Farm team and he was carted away to be buried in the ravine at the far side of the woods where all the Farm horses had been buried since the Colonel came there a hundred years before. In the midst of the graves lay the bones of the oxen, Buck and Berry, who had drawn the wagon over the trail from Maryland.

The end of Doctor brought back to old Jamie the fact of death. Doctor was nearly thirty years old when he died. Long ago he had been Maria's horse, drawing the old phaeton in which she rode into Town to spend the night with Great-aunt Jane at Trefusis' Castle. I think old Jamie had always half-believed that Doctor was immortal like himself and not subject to the ills and aches of ordinary horses. For a week the old gentleman was silent and depressed, and then all his old spirit returned with the plan which had suddenly come to him.

With his old horse dead, he felt that the trips he made to the Farm with Johnny and his brother had become an inconvenience. It was for him an insufferable situation to be dependent upon anyone, so he determined to go to the Farm at once before the rest of the family had moved there and install himself in his old room. Melissa was there to cook his meals.

His daughter thought the plan was dangerous as well as foolish, for she knew that if there was no one to watch him he would attempt to work once more as if he were a man in his prime. But her opposition did no good. To him she was still his daughter, subject in a stern Scottish fashion to his commands. That she was a woman nearing fifty, with a grandchild of her own, did not impress him. Never in all his life had he taken orders or even advice, and at eighty-three he could not bring himself to change his ways. So in the end, with all his belongings, he was driven to the Farm. With the excitement of a little boy he saw his old room grow alive once more, as it had been in the days when he had shared it with Maria. The house had not changed much, for the procession of tenants had never occupied anything but the wing in which Hud and Melissa were now installed, and most of the old furniture remained where it had always been. "Pocahontas and John Smith" and "Pilgrim's Progress" still adorned the walls, and the great stove, long since soiled and rusty, still stood in Maria's kitchen. When Johnny and his mother left in the evening, he went with them to the white picket gate, carrying a milk pail. He was flushed and happy and, save for the whiteness of his beard and hair, was like a young man. As they drove down the long lane full of ruts, they saw him go into the barn to help Hud with the milking.

⊹

The house in Town was sold to the proprietor of the new drugstore on the square, and the dismantling was begun at once. Now that the time had come, it was a sad business. Even the prospect of living at the Farm could not altogether dissipate the sense of melancholy. I think Johnny's mother felt the departure more than the rest of them, for she had no faith in the new adventure and this house which she was leaving was her own creation. The "feel" of it, the homely atmosphere which annihilated the ugly furniture and the elaborately arabesqued wallpaper, was made by her. She and James Willingdon had come there as a young married couple. In this house her children had all been born. From it two brothers, three aunts, and one or two cousins had been buried. In it there

had been five weddings. No longer would the relatives come there for a breathing space when they were poor or ill.

Before the family left, Hud came with the farm wagon to cart away all the manure which lay outside the stable door, for it was manure that the starved land at the Farm needed most of all. And at last the day arrived and he came with the hay wagon to transport everything but the piano and the hideous parlor suite, which were carried away by professional "movers." Then the door was closed and locked and the key given to Mrs. Hirsh, who lived next door, to be turned over to the new owner. None of the Willingdons ever saw the inside of the house again, and although none of them knew it then, it was the end of the Town in their lives.

On the day of the moving Great-aunt Jane died in the big bedroom overlooking the railroad yards, so that on the night of the moving day, Johnny's mother, exhausted, slept at Trefusis' Castle, for at the end Great-aunt Jane had sent for the niece whom she loved as much as her own children. The old lady died, powerful and rather grim at the very end, in the vast canopied bed which Dr. Trefusis had bought at the Paris Exposition the year he died. She slipped out of life, bitter and tired, to the accompaniment of steam riveters at work on the new mill shed being built against the tall iron fence which marked the limits of the park.

The death of Great-aunt Jane was the end of something. She had, in a way, outlived her time, passing from the day when people were encouraged to be individuals into a day when eccentricity of character and even independence of opinion aroused distrust and resentment; and in the end she had come to be regarded as "queer" because she was not interested in all the noise and boom and speculation and because she preferred to live more and more modestly each year and to die at last in Trefusis' Castle rather than to sell it and its rococo park for a fortune which would have allowed her to build a shiny new house far from the soot and filth of the Flats and end her days among electric refrigerators and mother-of-pearl toilet seats. She was a great character who lived through much tragedy, proud and aloof, and with her died the last faint vestige of that philosophical elegance which her father, the Colonel, had brought out of the eighteenth century across the mountains. She was the last of her generation, for Great-aunt Susan with her erratic economies and blind Great-aunt Esther, with her wit and malice, Great-uncle Jacob, with his airy denial of all responsibility, and Maria, the good wife, had all gone before.

It was a large Congregational funeral, and on the way home from the cemetery, in the old hack smelling of ammonia, Johnny felt a deep regret, not that Great-aunt Jane was dead, for she was an old woman and content when the end came, but because he knew that it was the end of Trefusis' Castle. Never again would there be those great family dinners on New Year's Day when afterward everyone sat in the long drawing room with the Gothic windows. The tradition was played out. It did not go on in her six daughters, for, erratic as they were, they somehow lacked her richness and flavor and they had in them a restlessness which drove them perpetually here and there seeking something which did not exist. No, with Great-aunt Jane Trefusis' Castle had come to an end. Johnny knew then that it was only a question of time until the hedges would be cut down and the statues sold to the junkman, the park itself cut into town lots or buried forever, and the old Strawberry Hill Gothic house pulled down to make way for new factories. Something was ended for which there was no place in the big "decorated" houses that were being built on the other side of Town, nor on the piazzas of the pretentious country club which had grown out of the funny little golf course built a dozen years before by a few business men who needed automatic exercise. It was, I think, the elegance of living which had gone with her, for when she died the last echo of the eighteenth century died with her.

On the day that the Willingdons and old Jamie drove back from Great-aunt Jane's funeral to the Farm they were, although none of them understood it then, driving not into the future, but into the past. The Town, changed and arid, lay behind them, and what they drove toward was something which no longer existed. And so, although at last they turned in the long lane at the end of which stood the big white farmhouse, they never arrived, because the goal was no longer there. Like Great-aunt Jane, it was gone.

‡

In the migration, none of them abandoned completely the life of the Town. James Willingdon kept open his real estate office, although he went to it less and less frequently. Johnny's mother went to church affairs and sometimes to lunch with friends, and Johnny's brother and himself went to school and Johnny worked half of the day on one of the Town newspapers. Only old Jamie never left the Farm, and its care was left largely to Hud Williams and to himself.

It was Johnny's last year in high school, and because he was good at remembering what he read and was taught, at the end of the third year there was not enough left for him in the curriculum to fill a whole day of work. So half of each day he became a newspaper reporter. On Saturday mornings and all day on Sundays he stayed at the Farm, plowing, milking, mending fences, picking apples, doing whatever there was to be done. It was an agreeable combination. As a boy learning to be a newspaper man, he went everywhere in the Town, seeing it as he had never seen it before, learning things about it which he had never suspected, discovering poverty and vice which he had never dreamed existed, returning always to sit about the editorial rooms listening to talk of politics which was cynical and disillusioning. He was not yet sixteen years old, but after a few months he did everything which an old-time reporter was asked to do. He came to know the full horror and misery of the Flats and the Syndicate and the tragedies of the morgue, and to know truths about this or that crime or this or that citizen which were too dark or too indecent to publish. And he came to know all sorts of characters, from Sally Peters, who operated the most popular brothel in the long row on Franklin Street, to that distant cousin, Susan Wilkes, who left her money to a home for stray animals and was a moving spirit in the Anti-Saloon and the Anti-Tobacco league. Oddly enough, Johnny found that Susan and Sally had certain qualities in common. They were dominating and intolerant, and each by her own rights eminently respectable, and they both loved animals and took care of stray dogs and cats, and Sally Peters never took a drink or smoked a cigarette. Afterward when Johnny worked in the city room of a New York newspaper, where all the vice and misery of a great city came in over the telephones each night, he never encountered any vice or any misery which he had not met before in the days when he made the rounds of Joe Sim's undertaking parlors, the railroad station, Hennessey's saloon, the Crescent House, the Flats, and sometimes the police court of the Town.

For six months the illusion of the old life showed no signs of fading. Because every piece of land and every house which Johnny's father possessed had been sold to begin all over again at the Farm, there was cash in the bank and the moment there was cash in the bank all the family, even Johnny's mother, was always seized by the delusion that the mere existence of cash made it inexhaustible. Old Jamie knew well enough that a few thousand dollars were not inexhaustible. He had more common sense than any of the others, but he was old and all the money was going into the Farm he loved. He would live to see it as it had once been—neat, prosperous, well kept—and that was enough. Once it was reestablished he was sure it would be a prosperous affair. And so he did not protest.

So plumbing and bathrooms were installed. Johnny's father went East to New York State and returned with a handsome Guernsey bull and ten Guernsey cows. New floors of hardwood were put in where the old floors had rotted. New fences were built. The dark room after sixty years came into light once more when one side of it was torn out and the original cabin of the Colonel was joined to what had been Maria's parlor, and the two became a long living room.

And then suddenly the money seemed to come to an end. No one noticed that the account had been shrinking until there wasn't any more, and there were still bills to be paid for work that already had been done. Sharply, with a shock of disillusionment, Johnny and his father knew that something had to be done. Either the Farm must be given up forever or they must become real farmers. It was Johnny who, in the end, made the decision. He would become a farmer and somehow or other he would go to an agricultural college and learn how to make a living from the land. James Willingdon was pleased. His wife made a few bitter remarks about Johnny and his father getting it out of their systems and then held her peace. She was the daughter of old Jamie. She knew what farms were, and she knew that neither her husband nor her son had in them the stuff of which true farmers are made. But old Jamie was delighted, for now, like the Colonel who was buried at the corner of the garden, he had a son-in-law and a grandson who would carry on his farm after he was dead.

But Hud and Melissa had to go. Reality had suddenly entered the dream, and no one could imagine that the Farm could support two families.

And then one night, a day or two after Hud and Melissa had packed and gone away, old Jamie rose from his bed to pour himself a glass of water. He tripped over the old rag rug which had been there since he married Maria. He fell and found that he could not rise again. He had broken his hip, and when the doctor came he told Johnny's mother that old Jamie would never walk again. But no one dared to tell him that he would never again potter about the stables and walk through the fields and orchards to which he had returned at last. They all pretended that in time he would be up and about again, and in their hearts they knew that it would have been better for him to have died.

JOHNNY

WHEN JOHNNY WAS BORN HIS SISTER WAS ALREADY TEN YEARS old. His parents looked upon him as a miracle, because when his sister was born, Ellen Willingdon nearly died and the doctors said when she recovered that she could never have another child. For ten years while her baby grew, spoiled and petted by a mother who was meant by God and nature to have a dozen children, Ellen Willingdon had spells of illness and suffered from wild attacks of nerves. Once threatened with blindness, she was forced to spend weeks in a darkened room, tormented and distracted because she had to sit there, useless and helpless, fretting over whether her household was being properly run and whether her wandering brothers and sisters were not in need of help and advice. They were spells of illness which were largely hysterical, born of her fury at being denied more children and out of the genuine weakness which sometimes overcame her as a result of that first muddled childbirth. In the frustration which descended on her there was a kind of classical quality—the fury of a big strong woman, charged with great vitality, whose whole destiny had been muddled by the mistakes of a well-meaning doctor who was not clever enough. To her, it was all the worse because there was not even malice involved, but only blundering. For ten years she lived baffled and furious, as she always was when confronted by a situation which she could neither solve nor destroy by the sheer force of her will.

And then one day she began to feel more uncomfortable than usual, and presently she began to experience all the symptoms of pregnancy, and in delight and excitement she rushed off to the doctor, only to be told again that it was impossible for her to have another child. He told her that she must be imagining the symptoms. The second doctor, a little more clever than the first, even told her that there were cases on record of distracted old maids who in hysteria created for themselves false pregnancies which bore all the signs of real ones and even led them to order perambulators and make baby clothes. No, the doctor said kindly, it was quite impossible for her to have another child.

I do not think that the doctor, even though he was more clever than the first one, ever guessed the profundity of Ellen Willingdon's willfulness and determination. Instead of being disappointed and bitter, she simply told herself that the second doctor, like the first, was a fool, and she went home to have the perambulator brought up from the furnace room and put in order. She started hemming diapers and making baby clothes. The months passed and with the first signs of *grossesse* she returned in triumph to the doctor, who again told her that she was mistaken. This time, however, he said that her pregnancy was merely a tumor (for there were certain evidences which he could not overlook), and that if the tumor increased she should have it removed by an operation.

She was Scotch and she was the daughter of old Jamie who knew when he was right and would never listen to the advice or protests of others less dogmatic, and this was one of the times when Ellen Willingdon *knew* she was right. She continued with her preparations, ignoring all doctors, and five months later, in triumph and in the face of all the protestations of the family doctor, she gave the light of day (as the French say in their fashionable newspapers) to a son. He was named Johnny and his parents regarded him as a wonder, although certain members of the family looked upon him as one more evidence, somewhat comic this time, of Ellen Willingdon's extraordinary determination. Uncle Harry, the blood of the family, even made ribald jokes about her turning a tumor into a baby simply by willfulness. And Johnny,

when he was a man and had come to know the full force of his
mother's will, sometimes believed that she had simply accomplished the impossible because she desired it so profoundly. She
always said to her children, "You can have whatever you want in life
if only you want it hard enough."

Three years afterward another son was born, but by this time
Ellen Willingdon had come to regard the achievement of the
impossible without any sense of triumph, and no one, least of all
herself, was astonished. A second son she accepted quietly and
without any feeling of triumph.

⌖

When the Willingdons retreated from the Town to the Farm,
Johnny was not yet sixteen. He was a tall, lean, awkward boy who in
appearance was an odd blend of old Jamie and The Old Man. He
had the more than six feet in height which belonged to both of
them, but instead of the great bones and muscles of the old Scot he
had the thin, wiry build of The Old Man. His face had the
Willingdon look, at once concentrated and dreamy, a look full of
vagueness and decision, a look full of contradiction. Only in the big
ears and the squareness in the angle of the jaw did one discover the
stubborn willfulness of old Jamie and the mother who had borne
him in spite of every counsel to the contrary. He was a lean, gawky
youth, homely and shy, but less ugly than he had been as a small
boy; for as a baby and as a small boy he had been thin with enormous ears, and a tendency to catch every possible children's disease.
It was as if the will of Ellen Willingdon had succeeded in bearing a
son, but had not been strong enough to make him a fat, healthy
baby. For the first year of his life he cried without ceasing, and for
years afterward he nearly choked to death two or three times each
winter from croup. And so he was coddled and spoiled, and Ellen,
in her passion for the son who had been born miraculously, never
allowed him out of her sight until he went off to school. But by the
time he was sixteen the good blood descended to him from Jorge
and Elvira, the Colonel and old Jamie, had come to claim him; and
save for the fits of indigestion born of eating too often as a child at
the Crescent House and at farmhouses during political campaigns,
he was as tough and hardy as a Canadian thistle.

He was born of all that procession of ancestors which had begun long ago on the seacoast; of Englishmen like the Willingdon who had come as a soldier from Shropshire to Boston; of Jacobite Scotchmen, like the first MacDougal to come to Maryland; of Germans and Dutchmen like the van Essen who had come from the Palatinate to Pennsylvania after the Thirty Years' War. Like all of them, he was forever destined to be seeking one thing and running away from another. But these first ancestors were very distant and shadowy and, save for the impulses which had brought them out of an old country into a new, there were in him no characteristics which could be traced very definitely to sources so remote.

There were, however, other things which one could find only a little way off in the grandparents and great-grandparents, in the schoolmaster and clergyman, the farmer and the squire, the small shopkeeper, the amateur philosopher and mystic, the amateur musician. It was a curious mixture of qualities, diverse, contradictory, and sometimes colorful, in which one element was obviously lacking. There was no materialism in any of them. There was no talent for making money, and none of them, save Great-aunt Jane who married it and spent it all before she died and old Sapphira for whom there was no explanation, ever had much money. And there was another element which seemed common to all of them. This was curiosity—a curiosity about living, about heaven and hell, about new country, about trees and plants and rocks, about morals and books, and about people.

Johnny at sixteen, still in the vague mists of adolescence, was an odd composite of those who had gone before him. There was in him the love for the land which had been in the Colonel and old Jamie, but at the same time the awful restlessness which had tormented The Old Man. There was the stubborn willfulness of old Jamie, and in Johnny's big, rather loose mouth, one saw a heritage from Jorge van Essen and the emotional sensuality of the stormy Marianna. But there was, too, something of the awful coldness and detachment from life which had paralyzed Marianna's son, The Old Man. And there were stores of ungovernable vitality, so that no matter how weary he might grow of the battles which took place within himself, there was never for him to be the peace which comes of exhaustion; there would always be that powerful, almost malignant force which would keep him moving on and on, struggling when he was weary of struggle, in spite of everything. It was that force of old Jamie which never allowed anyone who possessed it to stop moving, which at times even demanded fierce physical effort in order to quell it, a force which never permitted anyone in its power to rest for a moment save in sleep. It was a gift which was at once a curse and a blessing. Driven by it one was never free from the awful conviction that the span of life was at least three hundred years too brief.

And whatever else, Johnny had also been made out of the world into which he had been born and lived up till then, a world changing so rapidly that within the lifetime of a man no older than old Jamie it had passed through four stages of civilization which elsewhere in the world had needed hundreds of years to ripen, to rot, and be transmuted into something else. For old Jamie had seen a pastoral world, still half wilderness and then a great agricultural democracy, and he had lived to see the world of the farmer decay and yield before a new autocracy of business men and industry. The world into which Johnny was born could be bewildering, and certainly it brought no peace to one whose inheritance was largely composed of energy and restlessness. In that world, nothing was allowed to grow old, because it was always being overtaken by change and progress. There was no room for old houses, for old customs, or for old habits of mind. One might cling, furiously, to the old, but one was only left behind, trampled, abandoned, and forgotten by the new. Yet out of all the confusion and change Johnny was aware, without knowing it, that he belonged to a family which somehow in all that hubbub of change had acquired a fixed tradition and a way of living—a formula which one day he would know clearly was as out of date as the Farm and Trefusis' Castle. It was a way of living which had come to belong to the Old and was futile and useless when one continued trying to live by it in the New Era. One might try, but it only ended in broken hearts like old Jamie's.

At sixteen Johnny did not know the reasons why there were times when he felt shy and resentful and sometimes even bitter. He did not understand why, although he had not the faintest thing in common with the dark people who lived in the Flats—neither by blood, nor manners, nor language, nor tradition—he should have a pugnacious sympathy for them, and at times experience a feeling bordering upon hatred for the Sherman Place and the people who lived in the battlemented houses nearby. It was wrong and puzzling, for outwardly, at least, the people in the ugly houses with plate-glass windows were *his* people. They were the people he saw and their houses were the houses to which he went. Yet he could never wholly escape from the feeling of resentment and a contempt, born perhaps out of the lack of material success which always afflicted his own family. There were times when, because they touched his life more closely than the dark people, they seemed to be more foreign than the people herded together in the distant Flats. I think that even then, before Johnny had ever thought of such things, he disliked the prosperous world of these battlemented houses because he was aware dimly that the people in them had betrayed something which was fine and destroyed something that would not soon come into the world again. And they had done it for money. Perhaps he did not think of them at all, one way or another. It may have been that his feeling toward them was something which had soaked into him without his being conscious of it, out of the black, dead scorn which The Old Man silently expressed for them and the resentment and contempt which old Jamie exhibited boldly. Something perhaps came to him also from the defeat of his father who would not play their game, and the baffled fury of his mother for something which she did not understand. The people in the Flats might be, as most of the Town believed, foreigners and enemies, but as such they were strangers, aloof and apart. They were not traitors within the gates.

By the time the Willingdons left the gray house Johnny was aware that the Town was not his home and had not been for a long time, and that, whatever happened, he would never return to it or be any part of its life. He might come to inhabit Abyssinia or Timbuctoo, but never would he return to the Town or any community like it, and because he was, after all, the child of the Colonel and Elvira, old Jamie and Ellen Willingdon, he had to have a dream in order to live, and so the Farm became the dream. It was as if he and old Jamie, his father and his mother and his brother, driven out, were withdrawing to the Farm, to live there, entrenched in the last remaining fragment of a world which scarcely existed any longer.

When they came to tear out the wall of the dark room to let in the light, they found there what was left of the Colonel's museum in cupboards and on shelves. There remained two or three arrowheads, hidden away where they had been safe from the pilferings of the grandchildren, two books filled with pressed specimens, turned black with age, of the wildflowers of the countryside, collected long ago when there had been forests nearly everywhere, and there were two old leather-bound books with a few torn pages of brown butcher paper covered with the Colonel's handwriting. Until then Johnny had not known that the books existed, for it was a family which continued its tradition not so much by possessions as by feeling and by word of mouth. Even his mother had forgotten their existence. But when Johnny opened them to read what life had been like when the Colonel had shared the dark room with Jed and Henry, he found there was very little left of that long record kept meticulously each day by his great-grandfather. Most of the pages had been torn out raggedly, any way at all, to start the fires in the stove of some tenant farmer's wife. She must have found her way into the dark room and morning after morning have torn out the precious sheets of paper. All that remained were a few pages at the beginning of the first volume and a little which had been written the year before the Colonel died. Here and there in the middle of each volume fragments of a few pages remained, torn jaggedly across. The tenant woman had not even been neat in her pilfering, but slovenly, as all tenant women were.

And on the shelf behind the two wrecked volumes lay a bundle of papers tied together with string. They were the letters written to the Colonel by his friend the Jesuit who had gone to New Mexico, leaving the new country to the Colonel and to Bentham, the peddler. The priest was dead now, buried somewhere in Mexico or perhaps in some village graveyard in France. It was too late to write in triumph to his friend the Colonel that in the end he had been a

sound prophet and that it was Bentham, the peddler, who had won
the battle in the new country.

The rest was dust.

⊷

The borders of the Farm touched four other farms. To the
north beyond the woods lay the farm of the old Quaker, Job
Finney, who had seen the battle of Brandywine from a distance as
a boy of nine and lived long enough to be a "conductor" on the
Underground Railroad. But by the time Johnny came to live at the
Farm, Job had been dead for fifty years and his place was no longer
a farm, but a kind of amusement park owned by a rubber manufacturer who poured into it many thousands of dollars a year. It
had not even the aspect of a farm, but looked rather more like a
factory in which the cows had become machines which never
browsed like normal cows but were fed upon artificial foods compounded according to the latest formula and year in and year out,
never left their stalls save when they went to the bull (a necessity
with which no machine was yet able to cope). Calves no longer
played and romped in pastures but were kept shut in corrals where
food was carried to them. The " manager" was a young man, fresh
from an agricultural college, who in summer wore suits of pongee
silk and had the air of a factory superintendent, even to his pince-
nez, which were always bright and shiny. And the farmhands were
factory hands who worked indifferently eight hours a day and went
to Town on Saturday nights on the interurban cars, dressed as
clerks on an outing. In the pastures there were no longer any trees,
since there was no need to provide shade for cows which never left
the stables, and trees cut down the productivity of every field.
There were no hedgerows, and the little brook along which Great-
aunt Martha had led the Negroes to freedom on the morning the
slave hunters came, no longer meandered here and there through
the fields. It had been straightened and made into a miniature
canal which followed its orderly course between banks from which
the willows and reeds had been shorn. The barnyard had a floor of
concrete and from the house to the gateway ran a ribbon of hard
cement.

The farm on which Job Finney had lived well and even with a
great Quaker elegance no longer existed. Its beauty, its charm, its

warmth, its character were all gone. Even the jungle of a thicket which Job had preserved as a refuge for birds and small animals had been uprooted and destroyed. One visited the place now, not for any pleasure or the hospitality which once had filled the old house with warmth, but simply to see the latest in farming machinery and rows of prize cattle which ate prepared food. It was the toy of a rich man. On it was everything "modern" which a farm could have, but all the modernity solved nothing. It did not help the farmer. It showed him no way out of the muddle. Each year it cost its owner thousands of dollars to run.

To the west, on a farm which the wilderness was claiming once more, lived old Mrs. Wilcox and her half-witted son. The house had not been painted for years and the garden about it was no longer a garden, but a disorderly jungle. The old lady was worn and withered and past eighty and her half-witted son was fifty-two. He was a big man with a falsetto voice. He had a vacant eye and a persistent giggle which were frightening, and a simple friendliness which led him to call far too often on his long-suffering neighbors. The old lady treated him as if he were a child and kept him very neat and clean despite all his idiotic tendencies toward untidiness. She was bent double with rheumatism and was blind in one eye, but she went on living simply on account of Tommy. She lived in terror of what would happen to him after she was gone. Twice already, when he had wandered into Town without her, he had gone through marriage ceremonies, and twice the bride had turned out to be a farmhand dressed in woman's clothes as a joke. Tommy had not been offended. He would himself tell the story of his weddings if anyone asked him, giggling while he told it. He had brothers and sisters, but long ago they had left the Wilcox place for the cities. They it was who sent money to support him and his mother. One of them was rich. The old woman could have gone to live in the Town in a house of her own, but she was afraid of what would happen to Tommy in a city, and, anyway, she did not want to leave the farm on which she had lived ever since she was married. So the two of them stayed on, forgotten. They kept a cow and a few chickens and an old roan horse, and they had abandoned long ago any attempt at cultivating their fields. Tommy's wits were not bright enough to do the work properly, and the old lady could not support the sight of strangers in the fields which had always been worked by her own men. So sorrel and goldenrod took possession of the meadows, and on the edge of the woods the sassafras and locust and hickory saplings pushed a little nearer to the house each year. Johnny never saw her except when now and then Tommy, giggling, came to ask him for a hand in loading some logs or to help him dose the cow. Then she would come out of the house, choked and hidden by trees and bushes, to stand by with an air of suspicion, as if she feared that Tommy might come to harm. Johnny always spoke to her, and sometimes she answered him and sometimes she said nothing at all. Her other children, the successful ones, never came to visit her.

Beyond the Wilcox place lived the Widow McDonald and her old-maid daughter, Cora. Sometimes they had a tenant and sometimes they let out their fields, but whichever way things worked, they never made any money and just managed each year to keep off the holders of the mortgage. Sometimes that was not a difficult thing to do, because the mortgage-holder would rather have had his dribble of interest than to have found himself in possession of a run-down farm which couldn't be gotten rid of. Old Mrs. Wilcox and Tommy were simply relics of a more prosperous time when any hard-working man could make a living on a farm. Wilcox himself had been an honest, dull man, and his children who were right in the head had been able to make their way well enough in the world, but about the Wilcoxes there had never been any flavor. Old Jamie had respected and liked them as honest citizens, but he had never found either pleasure or stimulation in their company. The Widow McDonald and her daughter Cora were a different kettle of fish. They had something superior about them, and when Cora was still a young girl there had been enough money to send her to college. When she returned there was no one for her to marry, since the eligible young men all left the farms before they were twenty. She could not marry a farmhand or any of the young immigrants who were her neighbors, so slowly she had withered into the forties, becoming each day a little more a faint imitation of her mother. Their house was well kept and was filled with early-Victorian furniture. Every chair and sofa had an antimacassar and on the parlor table there was an apparatus with stereopticon views of the scenic wonders of the world, and a Rogers group of Lincoln signing the Emancipation Proclamation. They had a phaeton and an old gray horse which drew them on their trips to Town and the social calls which became more and more rare as the community changed and there were fewer and fewer neighbors whom they considered worthy of being called upon by a McDonald.

They lived on the edge of destitution, but neither of them ever gave any sign of it. The widow herself was one of those women who invest whatever they wear with an air of smartness, and even in her worn old satins and taffetas she had a grand air when she set out to make one of her calls. The daughter was exactly the opposite. She was a plain woman, almost a caricature of the fine-featured widow, and whatever she put on at once assumed an air of dowdiness. To Johnny, watching them as they came up the lane in the phaeton behind the old horse, they always seemed what a duchess and her companion must be. The widow was not popular in the changing community because she was a Tory, and in the bitterness of her poverty she found a consolation in asserting the superiority of blood and tradition. She was never, like old Jamie, a democrat at heart who did his best even to understand the immigrant farmers. Like Dr. Trefusis she made no compromises and asked no quarter. So there were times when she found it impossible to arrange with her nearest neighbors an exchange of work at threshing-time and had to drive miles to call for help upon other seedy members of the old regime like herself.

When old Jamie and the Willingdons returned to the Farm she was delighted and became prouder than ever. She told everyone that the neighborhood was growing decent once more; but worst of all, she deluged old Jamie with a series of social calls, assuming an intimacy which had never existed even in the days now so remote, when they had both been prosperous. He had never liked her, always deeming her a fool and claiming privately that she had driven her husband into an early grave by her pretenses and extravagance. He liked her no better now when they were both old. She bored him with her trivial talk, but at the same time she was a stimulation to him, for despite the fact that she talked far too much to be a sensible woman, she always had a fund of news and gossip (the fruit of her social visits) and they could talk together of people who had long been dead. At sight of her coming up the lane he would swear violently, but he never hid himself during her calls and would not, I think, have missed any of them for worlds. She was the temptress of his old age, and his conscience always troubled him after social intercourse with her. He felt that he had been wasting his time with a foolish woman and was ashamed of the triviality of the conversation. Cora rarely said anything, but sat with her meek, black-gloved hands resting quietly in her virgin lap. It was always the belief of Johnny's mother that the Widow McDonald had maliciously spoiled whatever chances her daughter may have had to marry, in order to keep her always by her side as a companion. And Cora had, indeed, the air of one from whom all spirit and soul had long since been trampled out. Whenever she spoke it was only to utter pious or moral observations which always drew explosions from Johnny's mother as soon as the door had been closed behind her.

Because the two women were disliked, stories grew up about them and their eccentricities. They were, as Dr. Trefusis had been, accused of all sorts of crimes and aberrations, and if a farmhand stayed with them for more than six months, stories arose at once. When Johnny came to live at the Farm, a man called Harry Bogardus had been with them for more than two years, and it was always said that he had stayed so long for no good reason. He was a big ugly man of thirty-four or -five who looked much older, with deep lines in his face and hair that was gray at the temples; but there was a crude animal force about him, like the power of a bull in its prime, which the neighbors sensed and which encouraged them to believe any story which they invented. He was a queer, silent man, too, who never had any communication with outsiders save when necessity demanded it.

Across the turnpike on the land which had once belonged to the nephew of Great-uncle Jacob's friend, old Anne Condon, there lived a tenant called Ike Anson and his family. The father was a gaunt man of fifty who drank and beat his wife and children. His wife may have deserved it, for she was a slattern who did not even cook decent food for her husband and her rickety children. When you went to her house to exchange work at threshing-time the food was greasy and cold and covered with swarms of flies.

To the east below the pasture where Great-aunt Martha had been killed in her fall from Dr. Trefusis's colt, lived the Schintzes. Of all the neighbors, including the young man with the Palm Beach suit and shiny pince-nez who ran the rubber manufacturer's pleasure park, it was the Schintzes whom old Jamie respected most. There were many things about them of which he disapproved. It seemed to him barbaric that their women and children should work in the fields on Sundays and weekdays from daylight until it was too dark to see the rows of corn. It offended his old sense of the farmer's dignity that at butchering time they should keep such things as hog's liver and brains for themselves to eat while they sold the best of the meat. He was revolted by the spectacle of the Schintz boys driving into Town each day to collect a load of garbage on which to feed the hogs. His own hogs in seventy years had never known garbage and he could not believe that pork which had not been fed upon hard yellow corn and pumpkins and skim milk could be worth eating. It offended him that when his grandson Johnny went there at threshing-time to help, he should find a good solid meal, but none of that lavish array of food which the wives of old-time farmers had served with pride as if it were a pagan offering of thanksgiving. There were many things about the Schintzes which offended him, but there were as many things which he respected.

The Schintzes, he said, always knew what they wanted, and that was a great thing, in life. They had an integrity of purpose which in his own integrity he respected. They lived for only one thing, and that was a determination to restore to the worn tenant-haunted soil its old richness. They lived to make their land pay, and toward that end it did not matter how great or how numerous were the sacrifices they made. To them the contents of a privy was not something revolting and repulsive; it was a gift from God, beautiful and full of a magic which in the following year made the corn a richer green than any corn for miles around. The soft things of life were forever excluded, since even the smallest of luxuries diverted them from the absorbing goal of their whole existence. They had no interest in politics or in the experiments which farm stations made in order to produce panaceas for the troubles of the farmers. They *knew* the earth. It was the same in this despoiled new country as it had been on the borders of Poland. They had their way of sowing and impregnating the land, and it was as old as time. They *knew* that one could no more bring fertility to the earth by newfangled ideas than the young man with the shiny nose glasses could impregnate all his mechanical cows by means of machinery. They lived apart, having no time for visits and "setting." They *knew* that when one worked the earth the task was never ended. When one had finished with one piece of work there was always another. If one weed was uprooted there was always another springing up just beside it. So they sacrificed themselves to their land, living apart, intensely individualistic, asking only to be left in peace. It was a tradition which old Jamie, the good citizen, with his passion for improving the human race, could understand and respect, but in which he could never have lived. The Schintzes were peasants. Old Jamie respected them most of all for what they had done to their land. In earth which ten years earlier had been abandoned as useless they now grew the best crops in the county. They had fine cattle and fine hogs and their big horses were fat and sleek. No farm could have been run better. No farm could have produced more. Not a hedgerow was wasted, nor a ditch.

But old Jamie knew that they did not make money. He knew that out of all their work and devotion they made some years perhaps a few hundred dollars to apply to the mortgages. It seemed to him a bitter scheme of things, that one should live a life scarcely better than that of an animal for so small an economic reward. I think he was too old and people like the Schintzes were too new and too different for an understanding of them ever to come to him. He did not understand that they, too, like himself and the Colonel, had a dream and that, like their dreams, that of the Schintzes had nothing to do with money. With them it was not democracy and not a Utopia. They cared little what happened to other men so long as they were left in peace. The land was their dream, the good, warm, dark earth. In them lay the force of a thousand years' terrible desire for earth of their own, no matter what earth. Even a rocky hillside or a patch of desert would have sufficed for in a little time they would somehow have cleared away the thorns and pulverized the rocks until they became good dark earth. It was not for money or the idle pleasures which money could buy that they worked. They wanted money only because money meant more land. That was their dream. Old Jamie had never known a peasant, and the Schintzes puzzled him.

They were Silesians and the father, Herman, was a stolid square man who at sixty had the body and muscles of a man of forty. He had a big golden beard with no gray in it, and blue eyes, and sometimes on Sundays and in the evenings he smoked a great porcelain pipe on the bowl of which was painted the picture of a flaxenhaired German girl surrounded by sprigs of forget-me-nots. He never learned to speak English very well, and in the rare moments when his heavy, phlegmatic disposition yielded to excitement he fell into guttural Silesian German. When he talked to you he always stood with his feet apart, his thick muscular legs arched and braced, like an oak growing out of the soil. Somewhere, far back, there must have been Tartar in his blood, for his small eyes slanted and his cheek bones were high and flat. He gave an impression of immense calm and security. It was as if everything about him—the handsome golden beard, the square head, the tough muscular body, the big blue eyes—all said, "Cities and people may rise and be destroyed. Banks and factories may disappear. Civilization may rot. But I am eternal."

As was proper in a peasant, he had sons, four of them, and all of them shared his passion for the land. They were not gambling fly-by-nights who ran off to cities to become traveling salesmen or clerks in offices. They were all four stalwart and hard-headed, yet each had his own personality. The eldest, Carl, was a man of near-ly forty, bullet-headed and stubborn and a little mean. If old man Schintz had all the good qualities of the peasant, his son Carl had a good many of the bad ones. He was miserly and suspicious and his attitude toward any man not called Schintz was one of hostili-ty. He worked his wife and children to the limit of their endurance, and he was a tough, hard bargainer. But already at forty he had possession of the Bangs place with the horse pond and he lived in the small yellow house where old Mrs. Bangs had stood long ago when the Willingdons passed on their way to the Farm. Death had come to her at last and when she was gone the Bangs place was sold to Carl Schintz. It joined his father's place and the two farms were worked almost as one.

The second son, Hans, had never married. He was an unemo-tional fellow whose life ran like clockwork. Seven days a week he worked hard, but on Saturday night he never worked. Then he dressed himself in store clothes, hitched up one of the fat farm horses, and drove off to the city, where he made love as he ate his meals, stolidly, treating it as a necessity. He was a small man, but hard and tough, and the hardest worker Johnny ever encountered in all his life. He was handsome in a peasant way and his good looks, coupled with a perfectly cold and cynical directness of pur-pose, brought him a certain success with women who liked cold-blooded sensuality better than romance and tenderness. He preferred not to waste good money on love, but if there was none to be had free, he lit his pipe and went straight to Sally Peters' establishment, where everything was safe and sanitary. But he never took any part in the gaieties of the parlor with the mechanical piano and rarely stayed more than half an hour, for there were always a certain number of errands to be done for old Mrs. Schintz and he disliked going to bed late. Sometimes he talked of his love affairs, but never in the fashion of a sensualist or a Don Juan. He always spoke of them with a detached coldness which in a strange way was worse and more shocking than gloating or boasting of the impotent and the lady-killers. He talked of them with a complete detachment as if he were talking about the breeding of farm animals. He seemed to find satisfaction only in work. He bolted his food in order to return to the barn or the fields. I think the visits to Sally Peters' place were made only as a grim necessity to satisfy an appetite which otherwise would have distracted him. It was as if he were possessed and only work could bring him peace. There was an air of dedication about him, as if he were an instrument of God. Love was no more than a physical ailment for which it was necessary to take a purge on Saturday nights.

The third son was dark and handsome and finer boned than the others, as if there was something in him of different blood. He was married and in five years had had four children. It was he and his wife who took charge of the cows and the dairy and he was the one who drove the milk wagon each morning before daylight into Town to deliver the milk. The Schintzes had no liking for middlemen and sold, whenever possible, direct from the farm to the consumer. It was one of the reasons why at the end of the year they had a few hundred dollars to apply to the mortgages.

The fourth son was gentle and feminine and he it was who ran the house and took care of the poultry and the pigs, working in the fields as well when it was necessary. Like the second son, he had never married, but unlike Hans, he did not go off on Saturday nights to Sally Peters'. Indeed, he rarely left the farm from one year's end to another. One could always find him there, whitewashing the chickenhouse or mowing the lawn or hoeing or transplanting in the neat, pretty garden. Often enough he had to do the cooking as well, for old Mrs. Schintz had a tumor which made her frail and sometimes she was not strong enough to stand on her feet.

She was a thin, small woman who had never learned to speak English, for, since she never left the farm and had been called upon only once or twice by neighbors, there was no need for it. For most of her life, she never spoke to anyone save her husband and her sons. She too, like her husband and her sons, lived only for the land, the house, the barn, and the chickens, and now that she was worn out and old before her time, she could no longer scour and scrub and bake and churn herself. She had no daughter, so she took her youngest son for a daughter and together they kept the place beautifully clean and prosperous. The whole farm was like that. Even the fields and the woodlot, with all the underbrush cut and the fallen twigs and branches bundled into faggots neatly tied, were like the rooms of a proud housewife. The old woman was patient with her illness and her tumor which could not be taken out because operations cost too much money, and she had only one desire beyond her passion for order and cleanliness and that was an obsession with her. She wanted all the village from which they had come in Silesia to see how they had prospered. She wanted all the Silesian peasants they had left behind to look upon the farm with its neat house and the ordered rows of fat vegetables. She had written news of it all again and again, but she was not sure that in far-off Silesia they would believe what she had written. She wanted them to *see*. She wanted, I think, to transplant the whole farm with its fields and cattle to that village near the Polish frontier just for a day. Sometimes she would talk of it to Johnny in her thick dialect, and old Schintz, listening, would chuckle and pat her thin back and explain in his broken English what she was saying. She talked a great deal of a man she called "Onkle Peder," and old Schintz explained that she wanted her uncle Peter to see the farm, because he had tried to keep her from marrying him long ago when they were both young. Even in that far-off village there had been snobbery, and Uncle Peter and all Mrs. Schintz's family had said her people were too good to marry one of its daughters to a boy like *der Schintz* even if he was the strongest hard-working young peasant in the village. I think the two old people had been bound together through all the years of marriage by other things besides love. They had their common passion for land and they meant to *show* the villagers back in the old country.

For old Schintz there were no doubts over what was to become of his "land." He had his four stalwart sons and in none of them was there any nonsense about leaving the rich life of the land for the meager life of the city. They were all old enough to be settled now, and one by one they were acquiring land all about him, so that by the time he died they would have hundreds of acres. The third son, Franz, was already angling to buy the place where old Mrs. Wilcox and Tommy lived in the ancient house with the choked dooryard. In the end, before Johnny left the Farm, old Mrs. Wilcox died and the Wilcox place became the property of Franz and his wife, and within a year it too began to look a little like the other farms owned by the Schintzes. The dooryard was cleaned and the house painted, the fencerows cleared out, and the tons of manure left to rot for years in the barnyard were carted to the fields. To men like the drunken Ike Anson it seemed that the touch of the Schintzes had magic in it, but the only magic was hard work and a passion for the earth which was so profound that it became genius.

These were the neighbors which Johnny and his father had when they became farmers. These were the people they saw most and these were the men with whom Johnny worked at harvesting time and when they cut the fresh green corn to fill the silos. They were different from the neighbors of old Jamie—Job Finney and the men who had founded the Academy at Onara long ago and organized the Patrons of Husbandry and listened to Ralph Waldo Emerson and Oliver Wendell Holmes. It was Johnny who saw most of them, because his father was still occupied now and then with projects in the Town which he always hoped would end successfully and make a little money to pour into the Farm. It was Johnny who did most of the plowing and cut the hay and did the milking and spread the manure over the starved fields. Old Jamie saw them sometimes when he sat helpless and resentful in his wheeled chair at threshing-time and when the silo was being filled.

Sometimes Old Man Schintz would come in the long still evenings for a visit. Johnny always thought of him as Old Man Schintz although he was thirty years younger than old Jamie. In the hot summer darkness the two old men would sit under the big catalpa tree, sometimes silent, sometimes talking, one with the thick accent of Silesia and the other with the faint nostalgic Scottish burr which he had never lost. Between them there was only one thing in common and that was the tenderness for the land. They both knew that the thick hot nights were making the corn spring upward green and firm. It meant fine fodder and thick, well-filled ears. When they were together something grew up about them which made all the others seem outsiders. They both knew well enough that in James Willingdon there was not the feel of a real farmer. They knew, I think, that he was merely playing at being a farmer. In Johnny there was old Jamie's own blood, and Old Man Schintz in his thick German accent told old Jamie that the boy had the makings in him, but that really his heart was not in it. The boy, he said, had too many ideas. He was too restless.

Once or twice the visits of old Schintz and the Widow McDonald and her daughter fell on the same evening, and then there arose a sense of social strain with old Jamie sitting in his wheeled chair between the two of them, trying to make a go of it. The Widow McDonald would become impossibly trivial and refined, and old Schintz, who in his peasant's heart knew he was the one on solid ground, because the future belonged to him, would sit there smoking his porcelain pipe, occasionally saying something in his thick English, and chuckling now and then in the darkness. Cora, the pathetic relic, never spoke at all. And presently old Schintz would say good-night politely and make his way out the lych-gate and down the long lane on foot, leaving the air scented with the odor of the ancient porcelain pipe long after he had gone.

No one had dared to tell old Jamie that he would never walk again. All the family kept up the pretense that one day when the bone had knit he would be all right again, just as, when he had come to live in the gray house in the Town, everyone pretended that some day he would return to the Farm, although no one at the time had believed it. In the end he *had* come back to the Farm, and now perhaps he thought that in the end he would walk again. No one knew what he really believed or whether he knew all along that he was being deceived and was unwilling to put an end to the bitter comedy of which he was the center. The doctor came once a week to see him, and always reported that progress was being made. When he was able to leave his bed for a wheeled chair he was pushed out each morning in spring and summer to sit in the shade of the catalpa tree planted long ago by Maria. The Colonel had chosen well the site of his house, for now old Jamie could sit there and look out over half the Farm, all the way to the turnpike. He could watch the cows in the pasture and Johnny cutting hay or cultivating the corn. He could see the brook and what was left of Maria's flower garden and the old graveyard where the Colonel and Susan and the handful of settlers lay under the apple tree beneath the blanket of periwinkle. And slowly, I think, he came to live not in the reality of the moment, but in his memory. He saw the fields as they had been long ago, and himself striding about his work, and even Maria watering and cultivating the specimens in her garden. Sometimes he would sit there in a waking dream, unaware of your presence, and sometimes he would doze quietly. As long as he could find refuge in the past he was quiet and resigned and peaceful, but there were times, too, when the old spirit would rise to torment him, and, bitter at his helplessness, he would grow cantankerous and scold Johnny and his father for the way they were running the Farm. At such times he would be filled with a desire to make a tour of inspection, and Johnny or his brother, or Ellen Willingdon, if the boys had pressing work to do, would set out along the lanes, pushing the wheeled chair as gently as possible while the old man looked from one side to another, discovering broken pickets or branches which needed pruning or a clump of dread Canada thistle which had sprung up unnoticed in the grassy bank of the lane. The roadbed was full of ruts and sometimes the jolts must have caused him pain, but he never spoke of that.

But as he grew weaker the spells of cantankerousness grew more and more rare. He came to live more and more in the past and to spend long hours dozing in the dooryard or beside the iron stove, lost between consciousness and sleep. Toward the end, I think that he *knew* that the return to the Farm had been no more than an impossible dream, but by then he was so weak and old that the disillusionment no longer mattered to him. If he was troubled at all, in his moments of consciousness, it was by the fear that the dreams might collapse before he died and that his end would come in some strange place far away from the Farm.

Of all the Willingdons, Johnny's mother was the only one who *knew* life on the land. She, who had been against the return from the beginning, was the one who had all the practical knowledge. She it was who knew how to make butter and cottage cheese and how to treat a cow or a mare after a birthing. Johnny and his father and his brother had it all to learn, and of the three of them Johnny was the only one with the taste or the talent for learning. Johnny's younger brother was like old Jamie's sons. He hated the Farm and he only wanted to escape, waiting half-sullenly until he was old enough. With James Willingdon it became more and more clear that the Farm was for him simply a refuge from the disillusionments of life. His love of the Farm was sentimental and romantic. He liked roaming over the fields with the dogs, starting rabbits and the pheasants which he hatched under white Leghorn hens who took their broods into the fencerows and with them returned to the savage state. He liked walking among his cattle in the big pasture and he liked lying under the catalpa tree in the dooryard, watching the woodflies dance. But with the work and the reality it was different. He had no farmer's blood in him, and at fifty it was not easy to change all one's life and acquire new tastes. He had no heart in the work and so whatever task he undertook went against the grain. It gave him no delight to leave a field of corn with each furrow neatly cultivated and every weed buried. There was for him no keen pleasure in the sight of a field of thick dew-wet timothy falling beneath the knives of the mowing-machine. He found no real satisfaction in the smell of the earth stirred by the plow. Heaps of manure had not for him the aspect of piled-up treasure; if he did not regard it with indifference, he saw it only as a pile of filth. The sight of corn burnt by an early frost before it was ripened did not fill him suddenly with a sense of pain almost as sharp as at the sight of a friend dead, cut off before he had lived. These things he did not understand. They were simply not him. They are born in one person, and in another lacking. There was nothing to be done about it. If one lacks these reactions, they only seem over-poetic and perhaps idiotic, and one is inclined to mock at them. Yet they are real. They are what makes a true farmer, different from other men. Johnny had them, and his father had not, and because Johnny had them a kind of passion entered into whatever he did, forcing him to go on working after his strength was exhausted. Old Jamie had the feeling. Johnny's father would begin to plow or to cut hay in high spirits, moved perhaps by the beauty of the scene about him and the feel of the morning air and the sun, but after a little while he would grow bored and for the rest of the day the work was only drudgery which left him at sundown tired, baffled, and irritable. It was simply not in him. He was a "gentleman farmer" and not a real one. Like the Colonel, he loved the land, but that was quite different from the feeling of old Jamie and Johnny. Those two loved the earth.

Johnny's mother, for all her experience and practical knowledge, had no love for the earth. The Farm she loved sentimentally because she had spent nearly half her lifetime there and because it was filled with associations and memories of the great-aunts, of Anne Condon, of her mother and Dr. Trefusis and her brothers and sisters. She would have liked keeping it as a souvenir, a thing apart from herself and the lives of her children, but she refused to belong to it, and so in her struggle one side of her nature came to hate it. To her, with all her smoldering ambitions for her children, the sight of Johnny plowing or hauling manure was an indignity which she was determined to crush. Having failed by open attacks, she tried adopting Machiavellian tactics, but for these she had no talent whatever. Like old Jamie, her weapons would always be bludgeons rather than rapiers, and her carefully veiled hints and her best attempts at subtle propaganda were always painfully naked and apparent. Most of them were directed at Johnny, for she knew the younger son, who hated anything which had to do with farming, was in no danger. She talked of wealth (which would certainly never be the lot of a farmer), of travel in far-off places, of music and the theater (which she knew were vulnerable spots in Johnny). She spoke scornfully of the neighbors—people like the Widow McDonald and the Schintzes and the drunken Ike Anson, and the pipsqueak scientific farmer on the Job Finney place. Why, she would say, was a son of hers living among such people? She knew, as always with her infallible instinct, the vulnerable spots. If she smote the vulnerable spot with a bludgeon instead of striking with a rapier, it was not the less effective. Only one element in the character of Johnny did she fail to take into account, and that was his stubbornness. For he had not only the aggressive stubbornness of herself and old Jamie, but a good dose of the passive variety, infinitely more difficult to deal with, come down to him through his father and The Old Man from the Congregationalist who had stuck it out for sixty years without ever losing his temper as the husband of the impossible Marianna. She never understood, I think, the dedicated quality which lies in the stubbornness of quiet people.

But in the struggle she had great forces on her side, how many and how great she may never have known; because in Johnny there was not only herself and old Jamie, but all the others belonging to the strange, emotional, contradictory assortment of ancestors. Johnny himself had the will to make the venture a success. Conscientiously he meant to become a farmer, a good, prosperous farmer as old Jamie had been. He *knew* that it was a good life, but there were moments when he also *knew* that it was a good life only if one could stifle everything in one's nature but a passion for the earth. And presently, as the months passed, he began to understand that the denials and sacrifices and concessions he was forced to make in his generation were greater than those made by old Jamie in his day and infinitely greater than those of the Colonel. At seventeen there were moments when he had doubts, just as the Colonel had known doubts on the morning he embraced his friend the Jesuit, aware that he had turned his back upon so much that he loved for the sake of a dream which would never be realized. In a way the Colonel had had a rich life even after he had come into the wilderness, and old Jamie had had many things in life beyond the borders of the Farm. There had been politics and abolition and the lectures and the academy, long since fallen into ruin. He had had neighbors. He had had a rich life.

In rare moments when doubts assailed Johnny, he looked about him and found almost nothing. The farmer no longer mattered in politics, and even if old Jamie had been born again into the life of the county, vigorous and filled with his Calvinistic ideas for jerking his fellow citizens into decency, he would have been helpless, for the material was changed and disintegrated. What could one do with a few old men ready for the grave, a few hundred listless tenant farmers, and the rest tough, indifferent peasants? The life, the world which old Jamie had known no longer existed. One could read, although there was not much time left for reading if one was a real farmer; but one had need, too, of companionship and talk, and when Johnny looked about him the landscape was barren. To the north there was the young man with the shiny nose glasses who tried out every newfangled idea for a farm which showed no profits but cost thousands of dollars a year. To the west there was old Mrs. Wilcox and Tommy and the Widow McDonald and Cora and their taciturn hired man. Across the road drunken Ike Anson lived in squalor with his rickety family. For the rest there were the Schintzes whom Johnny liked and respected, but with the Schintzes all talk, all interest, began and ended with corn and hogs. That could be good talk, but in Johnny Ellen Willingdon had already begun her work, even before the Schintzes had come into the county, and in the end all the ideas, all the ambitions, all the curiosity which she had planted in him as a child were to win her battle for her.

She had, too, on her side all the forces of economics, forces which were, unlike her arguments, unemotional and cold. One encountered them every day, every week, every month, bitter, agonizing, and unescapable. What good was it to pack apples carefully wrapped in paper, to ship to the big markets of the East, when shipping and the middlemen left nothing for the farmers, and often enough the middlemen took precious dollars off the price because the apples arrived bruised and damaged, a charge which the farmer could never know was true? What good was it to raise wheat for a price which made it sounder economics to feed it to the hogs than to send it to market? Why have a fine dairy when it showed no profit at the end of the year and the men who owned the canned-milk plant grew rich and built fine houses? Why grow potatoes for a dubious profit of a few dollars a field? Why? Why? Why? The cold unescapable answer was always there. Either one must quit the land or live like the Schintzes, and even if one lived like the Schintzes, a life brutal in its sacrifices, one could put aside only a few hundred dollars a year.

Johnny fought stubbornly, even after his father knew that the whole venture had been a hopeless impractical dream, but there were moments when Johnny, working in the fields, knew, too, that nothing could come of it. But there were moments when he was seized by an insane restlessness and a desire to run away forever, leaving it all behind him. If he went away he knew it would be never to return. If he ran away it would be far beyond the borders of the Town and the county, even of the state, for outside the Farm he was aware that there was really no place for him in that world into which he had been born. It was not his fault, but the fault of his ancestors and a tradition. If he went away he would never want to see the Farm again, fallen into the hands of a tenant farmer or peasants like the Schintzes. And all the time he was aware that outside in the world things were happening—things which he wanted to see and in which he wanted to take part. The world was no longer all about the Farm, as it had been in old Jamie's time. It had withdrawn to a great distance.

So he came to understand the young people like the children of old Mrs. Bangs and old Mrs. Wilcox who had gone away never to return.

THE END

A ND THEN ONE DAY IN SPRING JUST AFTER THE SNOW HAD LEFT
the wheat fields, old Jamie died. It was the first warm day of
spring and he had insisted upon going out in his wheeled chair
over the muddy half-frozen lane all the way to the woods where
Johnny and his father were boiling down sugar sap. Johnny's
brother pushed him, as gently as possible, over the ruts and across
the carpet-thick damp leaves into the shed filled with the scent of
maple syrup. For three hours he sat there, himself moving the long
wooden ladle which kept the syrup from sticking to the long pan,
and as the sun disappeared and the warmth went out of the air
Johnny pushed him in the chair back to the farmhouse. He was
tired and asked to be left in a corner of the long living-room which
had once been part of the dark room. Then he fell asleep, and when
Johnny's mother went to fetch him to supper he did not wake.

He was not buried in the graveyard by the brook, but beside
Maria and two of his sons in the family burial plot in the Town. He
should have been buried beside the Colonel in the earth which he
had loved, but his place was beside Maria, and I think by that time
every one of the Willingdons, even Johnny, knew that the dream of
the Farm begun long ago by the Colonel was played out. There was
no use in leaving him behind buried in the earth which belonged
to strangers. No one spoke of that reason, but everyone knew it.

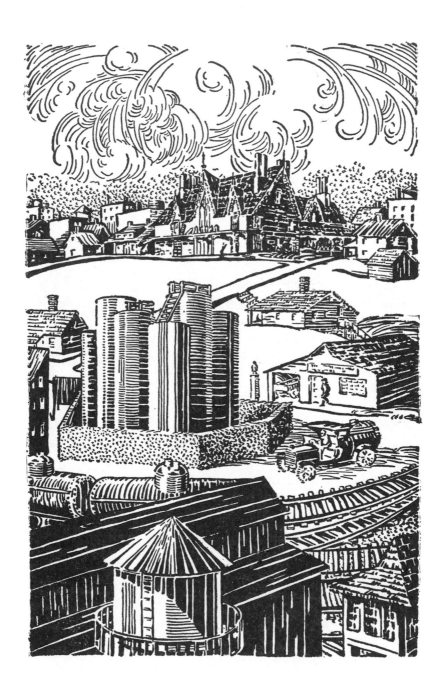

It was a funeral very different from that of The Old Man. There was a special service in the old brick Congregational church which young Jamie had regarded with wonder on the first day he arrived in the Town long ago. He was never a Congregationalist either by nature or by will, and he had never been inside any church since the day Maria, indignant at the Presbyterian preacher and his talk of original sin, had risen quietly and led him out of the old church on the square. But all his children had gone to the Congregational church and the old Scotch Presbyterian bond had long been broken, so it was fitting that he should have been buried from the church of his children. The place was filled by friends of his children, by some of the older good citizens of the Town who had known him in his power and vigor, and scattered here and there was a handful of old men and women who, like him, remembered the days of the Underground Railroad, the "bloody shirt," the academy, and the grange. The Congregational preacher made a long talk on his life, generously omitting the fact that the old man had never entered his church, and emphasizing the fact that it was deeds and not profession which made a man a Christian. In the Town papers there were photographs of him taken long ago in his prime, and long obituaries filled with the list of his accomplishments and virtues. It was the funeral of a patriarch and a good citizen and a man of action.

But over it all—the services, the sermon, the obituaries—there hung a curious aura of melancholy. It was as if the tribute of the Town which he had hated as an enemy came too late and had in it something of patronage. It was the tribute of a victor to the vanquished who was old and powerless, one who was less a potent enemy than a curiosity. One felt that he had lived too long, so long that he had come to acquire the interest of an antiquity left on from another day long vanished and grown strange and veiled in softening mists of the past. It was as if the Town was saying to its children, "See, that was what a pioneer was like." If there was gratefulness in the tribute of his ancient enemy, it was for the work he had done long ago with the men and women who had gone before him and the little handful of old people who had come to his funeral. They it was who had worked and built the foundation upon which all the new riches and the hysterical prosperity was founded. That new world saw no irony in the fact that in its essence it was something vastly different from the ideal for which these old citizens had worked, nor in the certainty that at the end the old man had hated everything it represented. Its victory was complete. It could afford to be generous to an enemy who did not matter very much.

Johnny, driving home from the cemetery, knew the same melancholy which overcame him at the funeral of Great-aunt Jane. With the death of his grandfather something went out of Johnny's world, just as with the death of Great-aunt Jane, the last traces of the eighteenth century had vanished. It was the end of something in which Johnny had believed, but he was not old enough to know what it was or why it had gone. He only knew that he was driving in a cab from Thomson's livery stable, smelling of ammonia, through the streets of a rather dreary industrial town and that he felt sad. Years after he had left the Town and the Farm forever he began to understand old Jamie and to think of him not so much as his grandfather but as a stalwart and a great man.

Old Jamie was dead, and with him the dream which had failed like the dream of the Colonel. The Colonel's dream had failed because, considering the state of man's development, it was romantic and impractical. In his heart perhaps the Colonel knew that it could never become a reality, for in his character and in his mind there always existed that faint, agreeable savor of cynicism which touched all the thought of his century. Old Jamie belonged to another day which was romantic and never had any doubts to give savor to its doctrines of righteousness. He belonged to a century of black and white, of self-conscious virtue or shameless rascality. There was no cynicism in old Jamie. He believed in his dream and until the evening he died in the dark room, built long before by Jed and Henry for the Colonel, he continued to fight for it. He had believed that honest democracy was practical and good, that virtuous, dignified government was not impossible, and that in a new country, with a fresh start, man could escape greed and dishonesty and enjoy a life which was at once both rich and simple.

But in the end the peddler had won. After old Jamie came to live in the gray house in Town and his active days were over, he had spent hundreds of hours among newspapers and books, trying to understand all that which had happened so quickly all about him, and out of these hours arose the only vindictiveness he ever knew in all his long life. It was directed toward the peddler, for he came to believe that it was New England which had corrupted the democracy, the New England which long ago talked of a king and worried over titles and precedence, the New England which swindled the Revolutionary veterans and whose clergy preached privilege from their pulpits and soiled their cloth with obscene abuse of Jefferson. I think he always understood the peculiar vulgarity of New England, which to him was the vulgarity of a peddler grown rich in ways which were none too scrupulous. He was no enemy of the Puritan for he was himself Calvinistic to the end of his days. Puritanism at its best made a strong people and a good life, but Puritanism at its worst was tainted by the ideals of the shopkeeper. For him New England was the home of Oakes Ames, Jim Fiske, Aldrich and Lodge and Hale. To him Aldrich was always the apprentice wholesale grocer who founded his fortune during the looting of New Orleans, and Lodge was a "spiteful tinpot Machiavelli" who sprinkled everything he wrote or spoke with the withered daisies of quotation, a dry relic of a stillborn culture. Aldrich had believed that the government should belong to business men and should serve them. Old Jamie did not live to see Lodge deliver his country to the corruption of the Harding gang. It is a pity, for I think it would have given him a bitter satisfaction. To him all these politicians had the ideals of petty shopkeepers struggling in fierce competition for a living. What, he used to ask, was a big-business man but a little shopkeeper magnified many thousands of times.

He held no belief that it was the Irish who were responsible for corruption. They were simply a race with a genius for politics who sometimes profited by the dishonesty of business men. What had the Irish to do with his own country or with the government in Washington? It was always New Englanders or descendants of New Englanders in the Middle West who were involved in the scandals and in those dubious dealings which should have been scandals. For old Jamie it was not Puritanism which had corrupted the Republic, but business, and the corruption had begun with the Essex Junto. For him Alexander Hamilton was a genius, but a genius without character, an *arriviste* and opportunist, a brilliant immigrant boy who had come from the Antilles on the make and who died none too soon for the sake of his reputation. With Hamilton all the trouble had begun. The roots of the corruption lay in his teachings—that the government should be, not in the hands of democrats or aristocrats, but of plutocrats. Out of the beliefs and teachings of Hamilton had come the decay he had seen slowly paralyzing the government during his lifetime. He had seen a republic, a democracy, come to be run as a business, an affair of shopkeepers and money-changers, who paid out money upon which they expected returns in laws and tariffs and land grants. He had come to see American citizens look upon such bargains calmly and without indignation, protest or complaint.

For him, that was the bitterest evidence of defeat—the fact that the citizen, the man in the street, so long as he was prosperous, no longer cherished a sense of duty, of honor, of decency. What puzzled him most were the men who somehow in the midst of unscrupulousness assumed a cloak of honor, men of character and wit and ability, who found virtue and credit in sharp dealing. It was not that they were hypocrites, but that, yielding, they came to believe that bargaining and compromise and bad faith were simply a part of the new system and the new political philosophy and must be accepted as such, for the general good, but most of all for the good of business. He could not understand that sly admiration which citizens had for men like Judge Wyck, a man known to be corrupt and criminal, because he had been clever enough to make a fortune and escape prison at the same time. He could not understand placing the holy affair of the government upon the level of business, nor could he understand those men who exalted material success as a God. For him, but for him almost alone, the crime of bribe-giving was no less evil than the crime of bribe-taking. How were public servants to be corrupted if there were not business men to corrupt them? And in his world it was never the Irish who were the corrupted or the corrupt, for in his small world there were no Irish. There were only Americans, most of them New Englanders.

In the end he came to believe, like most foreigners, that little mattered to Americans but money-making and prosperity. Why, he would ask, should American soldiers be sent to be killed protecting the interests of millionaires so that they might go on making money? Why should troops be sent out to quell the riots and disorders for which business men were responsible?

Long afterward, Johnny came to find his greatest pride in the integrity of old Jamie. Toward the end, when the old man was disillusioned and tired, his integrity became a little distorted into the fanaticism which long ago, he had detested in the Boston brand of abolitionist. In the end he had changed from a liberal, not into a Tory, but into a radical because it seemed to him that life in America had become insufferable. At ninety he was willing to adopt the methods of the Anarchist and the Wobblies.

In the beginning he had been a Republican because the Republican Party was against slavery; but the thievery and the brutal, shameless dishonesty of the party under Grant drove him from it. The theft of the election from Tilden and the machinations of "Burn these letters" Blaine, the Plumed Knight, and his little crowd, were too much for the honest Scotchman to swallow. He never forgot that Blaine, too, came from New England. And when the Republicans waved the bloody shirt to cover their own knaveries, he abandoned forever any idea of returning to the party. Once, long afterward, he was tempted when Roosevelt, after calculation, accepted the leadership of the Progressive Party, but he did not fall, for he was suspicious of the political tight-rope walking of the hero of San Juan. In all the hubbub, it was Beveridge whom he trusted and admired. Beveridge had integrity and that the old man understood. In spite of Beveridge's sympathy for business men and his attitude on tariffs, old Jamie admired and loved him. If Beveridge had been the head of the new party, the old man would have followed him anywhere. But Beveridge was not; and in the end old Jamie lived long enough to see that he had been right in his distrust. He always said that Roosevelt talked too much and said too little.

He lived long enough to see Woodrow Wilson as President, and in those moments when he no longer dozed and his mind did not wander among the shadows of the past—moments when his old vigor returned to him—he would talk for hours on end about Wilson. Here was a man, a strong man, full of integrity, who was fit to be a leader, a man who had not forgotten the ideals in which the founders had believed, a man who acted and who when he talked had something to say beyond hollow threats or veiled statements which might be interpreted in any convenient way later on. He knew every speech and message which Wilson made and every one of the long list of good laws for which he was responsible. That he was a poor politician only commended him the more highly in old Jamie's eyes. It was as if at the end of the old man's life a Messiah had come.

He did not live to see the return of what he always called the "shopkeeper, money-changer" party, and so never knew, in this world at least, the story of the Harding administration nor the "safeness" and indecision of the successors to the man who had come from the next county. Once, a few months before he died, he had burst out one evening in the old indignation, crying out to a renegade friend, "Wait! You will see where they will lead us, your bankers and business men! You will see they are not gods, but only men who want to make money! You will see where they lead you, that omnipotent crew with clay feet!"

In the end he grew bitter and his integrity became distorted, but he never admitted defeat, for he had faith in the ultimate wisdom of democracy and the inevitable dishonor of government by business men. If a whole people went astray it was because they had been corrupted by the leaders. The fault was not with the people themselves. When the time came, they would arise and overthrow those who had deceived them. If one had no faith in man, then there would be no reason for the world to go on.

He had lived all his life, fiercely, by those Spartan standards which he would have imposed upon every man in the county. In politics he always failed because he would never compromise. He had been without ambitions for himself, contenting himself with his own small corner in the world. In the end he died poor, in the

dark room where he and the Colonel had both seen their dreams fail. In the end he owned nothing. He went to the grave as poor as on the day he set off, weeping, down the lane of a Pennsylvania farm with a mule and eighteen dollars in the pocket of his home-spun pants; but in the end he died richer than most of those who lived in the battlemented houses west of the Sherman Place, for he had something which few of these ever had and which fewer still could ever understand or value. It was integrity. Once it had been an American quality, but it was a part of the dream which failed. It was the peddler who had won. In his Byzantine house on Maple Avenue and in his business on J Street, the grandson of Bentham no longer sold "silver buttons for your waistcoat. Fine silk for your neckerchief—just the thing for a gentleman like you," nor did he operate "Bentham's Great Bazaar. Household Goods, Hardware and Miscellany." He was in a bigger business. He traded votes and tariffs, labor laws and influence.

In the Town cemetery old Jamie had a simple granite headstone with the dates of his birth and death. There was no epitaph, but if there had been one it would have been brief and simple—"Here lies a good citizen." If there had been more like him, the history of the United States since the Civil War would have been different.

↭

With Old Jamie gone, something was gone from the Farm. For a long time he had been quietly fading, but even in weakness when his wits wandered, he had been there in his wheeled chair, a kind of symbol about which everything was centered. For Johnny he had existed always, like God, from that first day of memory when they carried Johnny in out of the snowstorm and put him into the Colonel's chair. When Johnny returned that day from the ceme-tery, it was as if a part of the universe was gone. In the months which followed there were times when Johnny's mind was occu-pied with other things, when old Jamie still lived, existing in the back of his consciousness, there among the rest of them at the Farm. He had to pinch himself to remember that the old man was dead. There were times when he entered the house and went as far as the dark room, filled half-consciously with the intent of saying good-evening to old Jamie and talking about picking the apples or husking the corn, and then suddenly he would remember that the wheeled chair was empty. In Johnny there was a good deal of The Old Man's quality of absent-minded dreaminess; when his mind was working, it excluded everything save that which occupied it.

Old Jamie was in his grave in the Town cemetery, yet he was there on the Farm, inexplicably, in every fence and hedgerow, in the apple trees and the stables, in the decaying fruit-house which once had been the wonder of the county. Uncles and aunts were there, too, and Maria, Johnny's grandmother. She existed in the thyme and the daffodils and grape hyacinths and the strange rich smell which had never left the kitchen and the dark buttery. The Colonel was there, too, only Johnny could not find him because he had never known him in life, and so he existed only as the marble tombstone under the old tree planted by Johnny Appleseed. Perhaps this was their immortality. When Johnny thought of them all, the old desire to carry on and to become himself a part of the procession possessed him once more. It was as if all of them were demanding it of him, but most of all the Colonel and old Jamie. That was what tradition was. That was what oldness meant. And presently Johnny understood what it was in other countries which kept generation after generation living upon the same land. And he understood, too, that such a continuity was impossible in the country in which he had been born.

The tree in the graveyard *was* Johnny Appleseed. It still lived on. Perhaps it was less than a hundred years old, but the vision of the half-mad old man who wandered over the Western Reserve with the Dauphin had come true. The New Country was the Promised Land. It was the richest spot on the earth.

With old Jamie gone, the adventure of the Farm lost its zest. It was as if while he lived, even while he drowsed in the sun, weak and old, there had been some will which had kept them all to their promise. And now slowly the force of the will grew weaker and weaker and the whole thing fell apart. It happened slowly, in a thousand small ways. The neighbors came to seem more and more small and lacking in significance. Either they were of the past, finished like Ike Anson and old Mrs. Wilcox, or they had dullness and limitations which, as in the peasant Schintzes, were almost animal.

There were times when Johnny was overcome by a sense of futility, as if in the work of each day he was going round and round on
a treadmill, sweating, to arrive nowhere. And the eternal uncompromising query of economics came to be a buzzing in his ears.
Why, the question would return again and again, should he lose so
much of life in a struggle which was solitary, to change what would
not be changed save by revolution, disaster, and bitter economic
necessity? "Someday," old Jamie had said, "there will come a reckoning and the country will discover that farmers are more necessary than traveling salesmen, that no nation can exist or have any
solidity which ignores the land. But it will cost the country dear.
There'll be hell to pay before they find it out." And always in the
background was Johnny's mother, filled with a determination not
only to drive him from the Farm, but from the Town and the county into the world. She gave him no peace and, fight against her as
he would, there was no answer to a single one of her arguments. It
was a struggle which was real, its roots in reality, as old Jamie's life
had always been. One had to choose—to quit and abandon the
Farm forever or to go on, fighting with waning faith a battle in
which it was impossible to win. There was no compromise. One
couldn't keep the Farm as a toy. For that kind of compromise one
needed money, and there wasn't any. Reality is a good thing, however bitter it may be, and long afterward Johnny came to understand its value, when he learned that inherited wealth may create a
strange paralysis which destroys the value of everything and cor-
rupts its possessor with a strange enchanted dullness.

The decision came at last, one morning in October, when
Johnny had gone to the woods to fetch a load of firewood. It came
to him in an instant, out of the air itself. It came in the moment
when he pulled up the team and the chocking and creaking of the
wagon suddenly ceased and in its place there was another sound
which seemed to fill the air. It was as if somewhere miles away in
one of those caverns which lay beneath the whole countryside
there was a giant at work hammering upon an anvil. It was a dull,
rhythmic, muffled sound, measured and monotonous, not sharp
and piercing and solitary, like the sound of a cannon. It possessed
the whole air. Standing quite still, he listened, puzzled and aston-

ished, and then slowly he knew what it was. It came from the new rolling mills which were pounding out shells to be shipped to France and the war. He felt a sudden sickness, and at the same time he knew that it was all over and that the Farm was finished. How could one any longer be a farmer with the sound of factories in your ears day and night forever? For a long time the smoke of the mills had been visible at the Farm by daylight, and at night one could see the clouds above the Town lighted by the glow of the flames from the blast furnaces. It had been so ever since Johnny could remember, and so it had never disturbed him as it had done old Jamie. The smoke and the glow for Johnny had been part of the landscape, as if, instead of a Town lying beneath the clouds there had been a volcano. But this new sound was different.

For a long time the mills and factories had been spreading, to the north and the east, over the fields and along the altered channels of Toby's Run, until on the north they had nearly reached the crest of that low hill where the Colonel embraced his friend the Jesuit for the last time and turned back to the settlement. Then the war came, the war which old Jamie declared fiercely had been made by business men—and the mills marched nearer and nearer. And now they had invaded the Farm itself. Old Jamie died a year after the war began, but he did not live long enough to hear the pounding of the mills gently shake the window panes of the rambling farmhouse.

Johnny loaded the wood into the wagon, and as he drove back down the lane into the wood-yard he saw Ellen Willingdon standing in the doorway of the kitchen. When he pulled up the team she was silent for a moment, and then said, "Listen." It was all she said, but she knew she had won.

⊷

The Farm was sold to a man who bought it as a speculation because now it was within the sound of the mills. The Town would come nearer and nearer until presently the great barn and perhaps the rambling house itself would be pulled down. Streets would be cut through it and hard ribbons of cement sidewalks laid down. The long double avenue of ancient locusts would disappear, and presently the whole Farm would cease to be.

It was over and Johnny went away, not into the Far West like his uncles and his cousins, but to Europe and to the war. Before he left there was a great battle with Ellen Willingdon which went on for days, because she was a primitive mother and never yielded to anything easily, least of all to his will to go to a war which was none of his business. There were moments when in the contest she approached the savage emotional magnificence of the stormy Marianna; but in the end Johnny won because he had not only the violent stubbornness of old Jamie but the passive stubbornness of The Old Man as well. Now, as so often in her violent life, Ellen Willingdon defeated herself because she planned and fought blindly without calculation. She it was who had made her children restless and curious and ambitious, and now she could no longer hold them, least of all Johnny. And in the end he repeated to her what old Jamie had said once, long ago, about the War of the Secession, "It is better to be killed than to miss the greatest experience of your generation." She yielded. Perhaps as she grew older she became a little softened and came to understand that nothing ever turned out quite as you planned it, and that no will, however violent, ever achieved exactly what it desired.

So in the end, in the fourth generation, something which was the Colonel did return to France out of what was left of his romantic wilderness. Twelve years after Johnny drove down the lane for the train to the East, he returned to the Farm for the last time. The great barn was falling into ruin and the fields were abandoned, but it had not yet been cut into town lots, for the Schintzes held the fort and would not sell their land which lay between the Town and the Farm. It was land which they had made themselves, and they clung to it, stubbornly, with the pigheadedness of the peasant which no real estate speculator could understand.

When Johnny knocked at the door of the farmhouse, it was opened by a flat-faced woman with a cotton handkerchief tied over her head. She only spoke Polish, but it did not matter whether or not she understood what he was saying. Johnny tried to tell her that he had come back to see the land which had always belonged to his people. She was new in the county and she was frightened of him, and in her heart she was still a peasant out of a world remote from that of the Colonel and old Jamie. The man who stood before her was prosperous and wore fine clothes and arrived in a shiny motor, and so she had no rights which he might not ignore. She never knew who he was or why he had come, and she made no effort to prevent him from doing as he pleased.

The visit did not last long. There was too much of desolation. He crossed the garden filled now with nettles and Spanish needles and beggar's-lice, to the little graveyard on the mound by the brook. The old apple tree was dead and lay prostrate across the graves, but from the base of the rotting trunk there sprang a few wiry shoots, still living. The gravestones of the first settlers were broken and chipped away, for they had been made of the soft red sandstone of the country which could not last out a hundred years. But the marble which marked the graves of the Colonel and the giddy Susan was still white and hard beneath the moss. The dates on the Colonel's gravestone—1763–1861—were only a little worn away. Johnny had come there thinking to move what remained of the Colonel and Susan to new graves in the Town cemetery where all their children and some of their grandchildren lay buried, but after a little while he saw that the Town graveyard would be earth which was more alien to them than this soil, unstirred since the beginning of time by any plow, where they lay. And after all, what was there to move? By now the Colonel and the giddy Susan were a part of the earth, like the arrowheads and the glacial boulders which long ago his great-grandchildren had scattered once more over the land from which they came.

Louis Bromfield and Edna Ferber on the Basque coast

"I have never encountered anyone with Louis Bromfield's capacity for enjoying life and his gift for communicating that enjoyment to others. Humor, amazing vitality, sympathy, a limitless zest for all are his."

—EDNA FERBER

Gertrude Stein, Louis Bromfield & Sheldon Whitehouse in Senlis France

"...Louis Bromfield the most brilliant and utterly master of his craft of all the younger generation ... I went out there to dinner one night and they had a lot of vin ordinaire and cats kept jumping on the table and running off with what little fish there was and then shitting on the floor."*

—ERNEST HEMINGWAY
in a letter to F. Scott Fitzgerald

*("*Though we loved animals and had lots of them, our house was never like that. Food and wine were well served and plentiful and dogs would never have allowed cats anywhere near any table."*)*
—Ellen Bromfield Geld

"The story rambles as freely as the many-winged farmhouse itself, and yet there is inherent in it a pattern, and one which serves Mr. Bromfield with a moral to adorn his tale. Mr. Bromfield's book has … sometimes too loving detail in its descriptive passages … [with] its wealth of incident, its rich store of characters, its pungent comment. THE FARM is an honest book, a deeply felt book and a valuable record for this generation and for those which are to come."

—*The New York Times Book Review*